Fragments of Evanescence

Book XV of The Quietus of Fate

By Brian C. Kershner

Acknowledgements

Unlike other books in the series, this book serves a purpose other than advancing the continuing narrative of the battle between all of the forces vying for control of Creation. As the tale has woven through the fourteen previous books and the yet untold story of the first generation of the prophecies on Onea, many characters have come and go, their motivations driven by the needs and dictates of the moment. Now, as the tale approaches its inflection point, it is time for a bit of a breath before plunging forward into the battle at the Heart of Stone.

Some of the characters remain from the beginning of the tale, while others have joined the fight along the way. At this juncture, I felt that it was important to dedicate time to each of the major players still remaining and shed light on their thoughts and feelings on what has come before and what may come after. Now that the end may very well be in sight, some characters are beginning to ask the critical questions of what comes next and what their roles in that next will be. Though I will warn that some of these questions have unexpected and at times uncomfortable results.

In the same way, I, as the author, am asking what comes next. And as much as this is a moment to breathe and reflect for the characters, it is a moment as an author to breathe and prepare for what is coming next. The battle at the Heart of Stone will be taxing. Even sitting here, typing this acknowledgement, I don't know how it will all play out. And as a part of personal confession, I came up with the idea for this book purely as a way to delay writing the battle.

Hopefully the insights into the minds of the characters will help to prepare the path of what it coming next, for them, for me as the author, and for you as the reader.

B.K.

Table of Contents

Defenders of the Innocent

The Inheritors

Interlude 2

The Five Queens

The Lovers

The Lost Children

The Knights

Epilogue

Appendicies

The world seemed to take a breath,
The light in the west fading,
The future once of endless depth and breadth,
Now seemed dim and hazy.

A great battle was about to be fought,
It was said for the sake of our entire world,
Seeking to end what the Creator wrought,
A new future set to be unfurled.

But doubt crowded out hope,
Even in the mind of the most ardent,
Hearts and souls reaching out to grope,
Something that all would find concordant.

But the truth was harder still to hear,
That no one knew the true outcome,
Even the Creator could feel the fear,
Of what his creation was about to become.

- *Reflections in Darkness*
  From Priestess Lya
  The Last Days of the
  Cadarian Empire

Prologue

The Heart Calls to Battle

Year Two of the Divine Empress and Child of the Creator Marlae Tamerlane, Creator's Calendar Year 1872

Despite the addition of Leonora Wastri to their troop, Chelsea Zarova continued to feel uneasy. The creature calling itself Coriden had come upon them so suddenly and had nearly overpowered even the practiced abilities of Alderin Terian. Moreover, none of the company were sure that Coriden was actually dead. Perhaps he had merely withdrawn to reassess the tactical situation and would descend upon them once more when he felt that he had the advantage. Even if Coriden had been destroyed by Leonora's impressive use of her new powers, how many other of Dorovar's pawns were lying in wait for their opportunity to strike? Some might say that Chelsea was surrendering to paranoia, but she preferred to think of it as the necessary preparedness of a practiced warrior. Just because you wanted to believe that there were not assassins lurking in the shadows did not mean that they weren't there. That was especially true when an enemy could appear out of thin air with no warning. Despite protestations to the contrary from Alderin, Dominique insisted that they camp for the night so that Alderin would have time to recover from the confrontation. Alderin bristled at the attention that Dominique gave him, insisting that his wounds were superficial and would heal quickly. Chelsea empathized with both Alderin and Dominique. Alderin was a fighter, straightforward and severe. He had been alive for centuries, had killed in the name of the Dark Gods, and desired nothing more than to be back in the arms of the woman that he loved. In some ways, he reminded her of Seraph. Perhaps that was why Dominique fussed so much over him. Though in her heart Chelsea knew that the fuss was simply because Dominique did not know what else to do. The battle with Coriden had shocked her, exposing just how little she had to contribute beyond her voice and her compassion. Instead of the powerful Empress of Cadaria, Coriden had reduced Dominique back to the shy and confused little girl who worked as a barmaid.

Finally, Alderin was able to wrench himself from Dominique's attention as he muttered something about hunting for dinner before setting off into the darkness. Leonora and Chelsea quickly gathered some firewood and before Chelsea could recover her flint and steel from her pack, Leonora simply pointed a long delicate finger at the wood pile, and it sparked to life with fire. Even before Leonora settled back to the ground, Chelsea turned to face her old friend.

"Handy trick."

Leonora didn't look up from the fire and let a cold voice flow into the night.

"Less of a trick, and more of a reflection of who I should have been all along."

Chelsea settled to a place beside the fire as did Dominique. There was tension in the air, and Dominique though she wanted to be closer to Chelsea kept a respectable distance. Something in her didn't trust Leonora, but she could not put her finger on exactly why. After all, this had been one of the most powerful and respected members of the Knights of the Flashing Blade once upon a time, and she had also been loyal to Marlae Lorien and Chelsea Zarova in a time when most of the empire would have rather seen both women dead. That Leonora had been a picture of calm. Dominique remembered when she first met the woman. Leonora was cool, stoic, and beautiful. She was like a living piece of art that radiated placidity and calm. With this Leonora, there was no calm to be found. Every motion spoke of barely restrained violence, like a feral animal impatiently waiting for an opportunity to pounce on its prey. And so, Dominique watched as the Wolf of Saldarine took the measure of her old ally and former compatriot.

"That bares a little more explanation, Leonora," Chelsea challenged.

Leonora sighed heavily, her gaze never moving from the fire.

"I am very much older than any of you could ever guess, and while I am not a member of the Dark Gods, I was trained by one; a man that I fell in love with and was hoping to spend the rest of my life beside. But that wasn't to be. His enemies found him and cut him down. Those same enemies took from me my abilities and locked away my memories. And then I was placed into the Knights of the Flashing Blade so that I could be watched to make sure I did not stray back to the path that I was destined to walk. Cedric was the man that I loved, and his betrayer was Jeroch Yetre, who you know as Vallic Ultiv. When this war is over, and our forces are victorious, if Jeroch still lives, I'm going to cut his heart out."

Leonora fell silent, and Chelsea felt struck by the quiet violence in her tone. In the days before this new rebirth, Leonora was a formidable opponent because of her measured response. She didn't tire, she didn't make mistakes, and she would wear you down. This Leonora's overt violence brought a new edge to the woman, one that could potentially be unpredictable in the battles to come.

"So, you have powers like Alderin?" Dominque offered, in an obvious if clumsy attempt at small talk.

Leonora finally looked up from the fire, first to Dominique, then to Chelsea, then back to the fire.

"I would say that I have enhanced abilities similar to those of the Dark Gods, perhaps not as strong, or as potent. But my stamina, strength, and senses are all greatly increased over what would be considered normal. For example, Dominique, I can smell Chelsea all over you."

Dominique's face immediately flushed and she withdrew from the fire mumbling about retrieving something from her pack. Chelsea fixed an angry stare on Leonora.

"That was unkind and unnecessary."

Leonora finally turned to look at Chelsea, the flames reflected in her brilliant green eyes.

"And why should I be concerned with kindness, Chelsea? This world is going to burn if we are not successful, and here you are playing house with your husband's mistress. Dorovar's legions are pulling the world apart, the Lorien family is splintered, the Dark Gods are fighting against the forces of the Heavens, and the dragons are embroiled in their own civil war. We are taking losses on all sides and here you are in the middle of nowhere with a woman who had no place on the battlefield. Why aren't you in the fight? Why aren't you at the side of your Dark God allies trying to figure out how you can make an impact in this fight."

Chelsea snarled as she responded.

"I am making an impact in this fight, Leonora. Despite what you may be now, you have to remember that this fight isn't just being fought by gods and monsters. The people of Cadaria, our people, are caught in the middle, and when this is all over, if there is a Cadaria, someone is going to have to lead it out of the darkness. That is what Dominique is trying to do. She is trying to shore up support for Quyhn and her position as the heir to the throne of Cadaria. She can't stand toe to toe with one of Dorovar's servants like you can, but that doesn't make her contribution any less. Nor does in invalidate my oath to keep her safe. The Leonora that I served with in the Knights of the Flashing Blade would understand that."

Leonora waved her hand dismissively.

"That Leonora never existed. My name is Leah. I am the proud student of the Lord Lion Cedric Binosear, and my only destiny is to crush our enemies and to make sure that Cedric's dream continues of a world without the Creator and his Children."

Chelsea was prepared to retort, but the words were stolen from her as she heard rustling from the distance. Alderin emerged from his venture with three rabbits in hand, as well as lengths of branches to use as spits. As he approached, Leonora rose from where she sat and offered to assist Alderin in the skinning and cleaning of his catch. As the two sat and went about their work with few words traded between them, Chelsea went to check on Dominique. When Chelsea came to her friend, she expected to find Dominque shaken and crying. Instead, she simply stood by her horse, stroking its mane, and softly humming. Chelsea kept her distance for several moments until Dominique looked over and smiled.

"I suppose if we're going to be interacting with more Dark Gods, we'll need to bathe more."

The words were delivered with just a hint of a smile before the blond woman began laughing. Chelsea smiled and shook her head before crossing to Dominque, taking her face with both of her hands and kissing her hard. Dominique melted into the kiss and the two remained locked together for what could have been a few seconds or for an eternity. When finally Chelsea pulled away, there was a sparkle in her eyes that could not be diminished.

"I'm not ashamed."

Dominique's heart swelled and her mind whirled. Finally, rational thoughts pierced through the veil of love. She ran her hand gently down Chelsea's cheek.

"Discretion is not shame."

Chelsea's eyes narrowed and her nose crinkled in an expression Dominique had begun to recognize as annoyed acceptance. Dominique chuckled again and leaned in to kiss Chelsea once more. This kiss had less urgency, but no less passion. When she pulled away again, Dominique smiled and could not resist the opportunity.

"But I'm glad to know you're not ashamed of me."

Chelsea scowled but then finally let her lips curl into a smile.

"I'm sure Alderin would appreciate us saving him from being alone with Leah."

Dominique cocked her head for a moment in confusion, and then quickly understanding, nodded.

"Childish name for a childish demeanor."

Chelsea's cheeks flushed.

"You know she can probably hear us."

Dominique nodded and brushed past Chelsea back toward the makeshift camp. After a moment, Chelsea snorted, shook her head and joined Dominique, taking the blond woman's hand in hers.

* * * * * * * * * * * *

The night passed quickly and uneventfully, but the chill in the air was only rivaled by the chill that held between the four members of the company. Alderin and Leonora said little through the sparce meal, while Dominique and Chelsea occupied each other with small talk and stories. When Leonora had appeared she had alluded to sharing information about the state of the war, but it seemed that her harsh diatribe at the fire was all that she was willing to offer in the way of details. So, when the morning light broke through the clouds, the four companions wordlessly broke their meager camp and prepared for the continued trek to Iltorp. Just as Chelsea was helping Dominique into her saddle, Leonora whirled around and let weapons of pure fire appear in her hands. Alderin turned as well, but he made no such aggressive moves. Finally, he put his hand on Leonora's arm.

"It's a friend."

Leonora grudgingly released the flows of power that held the weapons together, but she did not relax from the fighting posture that she had adopted.

"How can you tell?"

Alderin moved past Leonora and answered with a dismissive tone.

"I've been doing this a lot longer than you have."

The chide hit Leonora like a slap in the face, and it reminded her of the chastisement that she would get from Cedric when she would become cocky and overconfident. She wanted to spin him around and confront him for demeaning her, but she resisted. It was difficult as she wrestled with the intention, and she felt as though she was split in half. One half of her wanted to stand up against his arrogance, while the other half found the very thought unreasonable. She was filled with rage; rage that she could not understand the source of but did not seem unreasonable. Her inner conflict was paused when the portal opened nearby and a regal, if simply dressed woman emerged.

Dressed in her simple man's pants, semi-tattered white shirt, and her long hair pulled up into a tail tied with a green piece of fabric, Midarin Sandar did not look the part of a Dark God, or of a queen, or of almost anything that she had ever been at any point of her life, except for the time that she was a member of the People of the Dragon. That was where Midarin had found her true self, and where she had found the other half of her heart and her soul. Alderin crossed to her immediately, and the two shared a very brief embrace before Midarin turned her eyes past Alderin to where Chelsea and Dominique stood. While Dominique's face held an expression of relief, the one on Chelsea's could only be called concern. Midarin understood why. They had only seen each other days before, and if Midarin was there now, something had probably gone very wrong. She patted Alderin on the shoulder and moved past Leonora without even acknowledging her. Dominique had just dismounted when Midarin approached.

"Something's wrong," Cheslea offered.

"Yes, and no," Midarin offered. "A lot has happened. First, I'm sorry to say, Connor and Gabrielle Peregrim were killed on our way to Aldere. We were ambushed by a flight of warrior angels, and we lost a lot of good men and women on that battlefield."

Alderin had fallen in behind Midarin and mirrored her steps.

"The twins?"

Midarin half-turned back toward Alderin.

"They were the targets of the ambush. We were able to hold off the assault and drive the angels back before they could get their hands on Mirana and Liara. After that, we established a fortified outpost in Aldere that should prove to be a safe place for the refugees from the war to seek shelter."

Midarin turned back to Dominique.

"Unfortunately, Dominique, things have moved fast, and are not nearly as simple as they were when you thought that you could unite banners behind Quyhn. Once we were established in Aldere, we were approached by emissaries from Marlae Tamerlane with an offer of peace, and a way to unite all of our factions and focus our efforts on saving everyone that can be saved."

Dominique's heart sank. She was not as practiced in the courtly world as she should have been given her title and position, but she knew enough to know when the other shoe was about to drop. Midarin was blunt and was not going to pull any punches for the sake of anyone's feelings.

"After careful consideration, Quyhn has decided to abandon her claim on the throne."

Dominique felt as though she had been punched in the stomach. Bile filled her throat and for a brief moment she thought she was going to be sick. They had fought so hard and sacrificed so much so that Quyhn would be the one to steer Cadaria into a new prosperity. For her to abandon that path felt like a betrayal. But, after a brief moment Dominique calmed her mind. Quyhn was not one to make rash decisions, and if she had come to this choice with all of the experienced council available to her, it must have been for sound reasons. Cheslea was not as measured in her reaction.

"Why would she do that?" Chelsea snarled.

Dominique put her hand on Chelsea's shoulder in an attempt to calm her. The tension was palpable, but Midarin let nothing but supportive understanding show on her face.

"There are conditions of course," Midarin said ignoring Chelsea's over-obvious question. "First is that Marlae restore Quyhn's name and renounce her standing as a ward of the Empire. Second, that Marlae formally recognize Quyhn as the Voice of the Empire, and heir to the throne."

Dominique considered and finally smiled and nodded.

"I can understand why she accepted the deal. By being formally recognized as the Voice of the Empire, it gives a veil of legitimacy to everything she did up to this point and allows the factions to see Marlae and Quyhn as equals. And more importantly, it gives Quyhn back her name, which I know was very important to her."

Dominique turned her attention back to Midarin.

"And I suppose you were sent because Quyhn knew that I would trust the news coming from you, and that I would stop any attempts at saber-rattling on her behalf."

Midarin nodded.

"Quyhn knew that you wouldn't trust the information from anyone else."

There was only silence for a few moments, and then Chelsea let her voice catch the uneasy air.

"And so, what are we supposed to do now? Should we go to this new fortification and aid in the defense of the refugees?"

Midarin started to speak and then let her mouth close without a sound. There was a familiar twitch in the back of her mind, and she turned on a heel looking out into the distance. Alderin too had turned his attention, and once again Leonora had let weapons of pure fire appear in her hands. Though the next moment identified the person who was creating the portal to Midarin's mind, it did not fill her with any sense of relief. When the portal opened, Camille Sandar stepped through, and the portal closed quickly behind her. As soon as Leonora recognized Camille, she let the blades disappear from her hands. As her daughter approached, Midarin put her hands on her hips.

"What did your father do now?"

Camille smiled.

"This time it wasn't his fault. We just kind of fell into the middle of a tactical nightmare, and Rhain wanted Gwydeon's opinion."

Midarin frowned.

"Which he was all too eager to give, I'm sure. Alright, so what trouble is your father getting us into on behalf of Aerith's daughter?"

Camille folded her wings back nervously.

"The short version is this. There is a battle about to happen at the Heart of Stone. Aerith and Rhain have engineered it so that every faction is going to be represented. The phasia, the Dark Gods, the angels, dragons, Dorovar, everyone. It's going to be bloody and nasty, and it may very well decide this whole war. But in order to make sure everyone shows up to the battle, we need to make sure the right pieces are there."

It was Chelsea who chimed in.

"Bait."

Chelsea nodded.

"We need to make sure that all sides throw everything they can at the fight, otherwise the dragons and the angels will overwhelm the defenders of the Heart of Stone and we'll have lost everything."

Chelsea drew the Sacred Weapon from its sheath and held it out toward Camille.

"You need this."

Camille's eyes widened in surprise.

"One of Dorovar's followers attacked us here on the road trying to get hold of this," Chelsea offered. "So, if you want to make sure that Dorovar and his forces attack the Heart of Stone with everything they've got, you need to make sure that a Sacred Weapon is there. Dorovar wants them bad, and I don't think there are too many of them left."

Chelsea looked first to Camille, then Midarin, then Dominique before sliding the sword back into its sheathe.

"Well, if you want the sword, that means I'm going with it."

Midarin heard Chelsea's offer through a half-clouded mind. She had already jumped to the next part of the story.

"Your father didn't do what I think he did, did he?"

Camille's face was stone.

"There was no other way, mother."

Midarin cursed a string of curses that brought color to both her daughter's face and to Dominique's. Finally, when Midarin's tirade ended, she silently fumed.

"It was the other part of the bait," Camille offered to the others standing nearby. "We know that the forces of the Creator want to get their hands on Mirana and Liara. So, my father is going to send them to the Heart of Stone to help with the defense. He didn't want to, but under the circumstances we all agreed that there was no choice."

Midarin thundered in response.

"Agreed? Who agreed? What irresponsible jackasses thought that this was the best course of action?"

Camille kept her expression impassive.

"Rhain, Saurn, Orren Eldrath and Felicia Lorien, and Marlae Tamerlane were part of the conversation and deliberations. But it was my idea to come here and make sure that the Sacred Weapon made its way to the Heart. Once the decisions were made, Rhain asked me to come here and tell you what was going on and to make sure that the Sacred Weapon makes it to the Heart."

Camille turned to face Alderin.

"Alderin, Rhain knew that she couldn't keep you out of the fight but wanted me to let you know that Darrien was also on her way to the Heart. Rhain doesn't know exactly why, but she is about to be in harm's way."

Alderin tensed up when he heard Darrien's name, but he let no more than that show. His emotions were boiling under the surface, but he had to temper his desire to see Darrien with the importance of the battle ahead. Finally, Alderin turned to Chelsea and Camille.

"I'll make sure that Chelsea and the Sacred Weapon get to the Heart of Stone safely," Alderin said finally.

Camille then turned her attention to Leonora.

"Leonora," Camille said calmly, knowing that resistance was coming, "Rhain wanted you to return to Bellnoc. She'll explain her reasons once you get there, but she was adamant that you return."

"No."

Leonora's response was curt and angry. Camille started to argue, but Leonora's voice shut down any potential resistance.

"Camille, there is nothing you can say or do that is going to keep me from the fight at the Heart of Stone."

Knowing that she would be trying to rend blood from a stone, Camille relented and turned her attention to Dominique.

"Dominique, Rhain wanted me to extend the offer for you to join her and Marlae in Bellnoc out of harms' way."

Chelsea chimed in.

"I think that would be a good idea, Dominique. The kind of forces that we're talking about are nothing like you've ever seen before. There's no way that I can guarantee your safety."

Dominique smiled and put her hand on Chelsea's shoulder.

"Well," she said after a moment, "if you aren't going to be able to protect me, I guess I'm just going to have to be there to protect you."

Both women laughed after a moment, and they turned to recovered what they would need from their packs. Camille then turned her attention to Leonora and Alderin.

"I just need to speak to my mother for a moment, and then we can make for Albitonin. Jeroch and the others will be expecting us."

While Leonora silently fumed, Alderin sat down and looked out into the distance. His mind was a thousand miles away, and all he could feel was his love and concern for Darrien. Camille led Midarin away from the others, and quickly brought up a bubble of silence around the two women so that none of the others could hear what Camille was going to say to her mother. There was concern on Midarin's face, as she knew that Camille would not go to such lengths if what she had to impart was not of grave importance.

"You have to understand, mother, that father had no choice, and I have no choice. I have to go on to the Heart of Stone, because of what happened with Jerah. The Creator is going to want to get revenge on me."

Midarin nodded.

"I understand, but the twins? They're not prepared for that kind of fight."

Camille smiled.

"I'll watch out for them," she said confidently, "I promise. And they're stronger than they know. If nothing else, they can help to protect us if things get bad."

Midarin looked in her daughter's eyes.

"That's not what you need to tell me, is it?"

Camille shook her head.

"There's a lot, mother. Gideon murdered Taya and is leading Raenera's forces, killing every innocent between him and the Heart of Stone. Through Raenera he's learned how to hurt Rhain by killing members of the phasia. That's why she wanted Leonora back in Bellnoc."

Midarin couldn't keep the shock off of her face.

"But there's more. Logan has done something, no one is sure what, but apparently, he's lost to us now. And the biggest news, Cedric is alive, somehow, and he murdered Emries."

Shock radiated through Midarin's body, it was all too much to take in, but she was glad that she knew. By the time she made it back to New Aradon, she would have many questions for her husband, and many harsh words for him as well. But the truth was staring her right in the face, and she could feel it tugging at the back of her mind. The war was coming to a conclusion one way or another. It was hanging over them like a black cloud, and whatever happened in Albitonin at the Heart of Stone could very well determine who would be the victor, and who would cease to exist. Midarin hugged her daughter tightly, hoping it would not be for the last time, and opened a portal back to New Aradon. Camille was left standing alone, looking at her motley crew of mismatched warriors. If Aerith Seth was right, they had two perhaps three days to prepare for the fight of their lives: the fight for everyone's lives.

PROLOGUE

The Faithful

Hannah

Hannah Ironheart moved through the darkened hallways of the Heart of Stone content that no one would see her if she did not want them to. All it took was a simple brown cloak and the right pace and none of the acolytes or servants in the Heart would give her a second glance. The Heart of Stone had been Hannah's home for the majority of her life, and she was sure that there were passages and rooms that she knew existed that no other living soul did. But there was part of her that wondered whether or not she should have come back to her home at all. And as she slipped down an empty hallway and opened a long-sealed door, she winced at the sound of the creaking wood. She had hoped that no one would hear or detect the intrusion, and had she been thinking more clearly, it would have taken a small use of power to muffle all sounds in the hallway. After waiting for a long moment confident that no one had heard her, Hannah pushed her way into the room, this time using the barest trickle of power to mask the door's opening and closing. For the briefest moment, she let her back touch the door and the thick wood held her weight as it had many times over the years. This room had been her sanctuary away from the politics, away from the faithful, and away from the doubts that the world around her often created. This was the room where she far too infrequently shared a bed with her husband, and where she had once dreamed small dreams of a life outside of the confines of responsibility and duty.

As the High Priestess of the Church of the Creator, Hannah Ironheart had responsibilities of both her spiritual self and her physical self. She was meant to be a paragon of virtue, often at the expense of being a woman. However, in her role as a member of the Knights of the Flashing Blade and a representative of the Cadarian Empire, she was held to scrutiny of a different kind. These two identities were often incompatible. She was the highest-ranking member of the government of the Kingdom of Stone, Albitonin, while at the same time also being the highest-ranking member of the Church of the Creator. And as was often the case, the two positions did not always see eye to eye on the best uses of time, money, and manpower. The Church was meant to look outward, responsible for the well-being and protection of every member of the Faithful across the entirety of Espre. However, the government of Albitonin was focused on protecting the citizens that lived within that kingdom's borders, whether they were members of the Faithful or not. All too often, the wants of one contradicted the needs of the other, and Hannah served as the go-between for groups who hated one another.

In those days, Hannah would not have said that she served multiple masters, but the more distance that she had from the blindness of those days, the more she realized that it was absolutely true. Her first master, at least on the surface was the Creator. It was a less direct servitude to be sure than her political appointments, but it was by far the most powerful. As the High Priestess of the Church of the Creator, she represented the words and the commandments of the Creator every moment of her life. She lived and breathed scripture, and there were those that would always measure every action that she took against their interpretations of the Book of the Creator. It was not enough to be above reproach. It was not enough to be pure. It was not enough to be devout. Every action that she took was weighed, measured, and doubted by those that believed she did not belong in the position.

There was no escaping that the Church of the Creator at some level was a political organization that took every opportunity to bring its power to bear when it needed or wanted something. Of the major organizations in the world, the Church of the Creator was the largest, the most pervasive, and most vocal. However, it was certainly not the most influential, something that galled the members of the Church leadership. This negative distinction had its roots in the founding of the Cadarian Empire by the first emperor Terrik Lorien. The two other major factions, the Academy of Arcane Arts in Jelan and the Shadow Guild were both granted official positions within the Imperial government, though the existence of the Underhand of the Emperor, the official title of the Grand Master of the Shadow Guild was not public knowledge. The reason that the Church of the Creator was not granted an official position within Terrik Lorien's government was due to the fact that the first Empress, Liette Lorien was a seer, gifted from birth with visions from the mind of the Creator. What need did Terrik Lorien have for a spiritual advisor when he had a direct connection to the Creator through his wife? As the years passed, this situation was not revisited though rumor had it that the leadership of the Church of the Creator approached both Terrik and his son on many occasions about creating a permanent position. When neither man was receptive to any of the offered solutions, the Church adopted the practice of naming the highest-ranking member of the Church, be it a High Priest or a High Priestess, to the position of Celestine Knight of the Flashing Blade. This way the Church would not be absent from the inner workings of the Imperial Court, and its voice could be conveyed far and wide by their representative to the Knights of the Flashing Blade. And so, when Hannah Ironheart was ascended to the position of High Priestess of the Church of the Creator, she was nominated to the position of Celestine Knight. It was of course only a formality that she was accepted to the position, as the Imperial Court would not want to upset generations of tradition. However, that did not mean that Ender Lorien did not want to meet Hannah and get a read on the woman who would act as one of his protectors for many years to come.

Hannah remembered the first meeting with Ender Lorien as though it happened only yesterday. The meeting came at the end of a month that seemed to span only a few days. Once she was selected for elevation to the role of High Priestess by the Church Leadership, another situation that was purely ceremonial as the previous High Priest had hand-picked Hannah as his successor, Hannah underwent the ritual purification. For a solid month, she fasted, prayed, and recited the whole of the Book of the Creator from memory. When she emerged from her dark, incense and candle-smoke filled room, she was bathed, scrubbed, and anointed with oil and holy water before being wrapped in the vestments of her new office. She knelt in the chamber of the Church Leadership, spoke the ancient oaths of allegiance to the will of the Creator and to the protection of the Faithful no matter where they walked throughout the whole of Creation, and was officially recognized as the High Priestess.

She had no sooner risen to her feet than she was whisked to the dais at the top of the great stair for her first address to the Faithful. The courtyard had been filled with so many familiar faces, men and women that Hannah had known since she was a child, and though she did not feel confident in her role, her words were brimming with the faith that she felt in those who had prepared her for the moment. She vowed to protect those who believed, she vowed to bring the light of the Creator to all corners of Espre, and she vowed to never let the light of the Creator fade from the world; words that now filled her heart with a hollow feeling. Her address completed, Hannah was placed in a carriage and taken to the Imperial province of Aldere for her official introduction to the Emperor of Cadaria. She was not sure what to expect when she was shown to the emperor's private audience room. Part of Hannah had expected that she would be brought to the main audience chamber, be introduced, be given her official title in some ceremony and then sent back to the Heart of Stone to oversee the transition of power there. But that was not the kind of meeting that Ender Lorien had in mind.

The private audience chamber was little more than what looked to be a study or a private dining room that had been converted to something a little more formal. At the far end of the room away from the two doors that led into the room was a high-backed chair that had been carved to resemble the throne that sat in the main audience hall. There were two smaller chairs on either side of the throne, one presumably for the emperor's wife and the other for his heir. There was another chair in the corner opposite to the throne, but Hannah stood in the center of the room, unsure of the protocol. She wasn't sure how long she stood there waiting, but when Ender Lorien entered the room, he seemed surprised to see the woman standing there. He stopped just inside the door, dismissed the guards with a wave of his hand, and just stood there after closing the door sizing the woman up. After several moments, he moved to the throne and sat.

Hannah for a few moments resisted the urge to look the man in the eye, trying to remember all of the protocol that had been crammed into her mind during the carriage ride from Albitonin to Aldere. But in the end, she could not keep her eyes cast down, and when her eyes found his, the older man smiled and laughed. All Hannah remembered was that her face flushed, and she wondered if she had done something terrible. But the old kind man just walked to her, took her hand and led her over to the throne and sat her down beside him. She wasn't sure how long they talked, but at one point a rather exasperated servant appeared to remind the emperor that he had a dinner with several dignitaries that he was quite overdo for. After dismissing the servant, the emperor invited Hannah to stay at the court for several days so they could continue talking and had her shown to an opulent bedroom in the emperor's private wing of the palace. Hannah was fawned over in ways that embarrassed her, but she took it all in stride. Ender Lorien had surprised her with his kindness and his wit, and she found herself thankful that she would be able to serve in the capacity of Knight of the Flashing Blade for a man such as him. Over the next week, the two became fast friends, and would stay up to indecent hours discussing all manner of topics. Ender took Hannah into his confidence, sharing information about the state of the Empire, the disputes with the Dark Gods, and the uneasy truces with the dragons that roamed Cadaria. Hannah was fascinated, but at the same time overwhelmed with just how much the emperor was forced to juggle every moment of every day.

When Hannah returned to the Heart of Stone, newly anointed as the Celestine Knight of the Flashing Blade, she fell back into her routine of prayer, supplication, and leading the Faithful through the rituals and rights of the Faith. It was on her first mission for the Emperor as a Knight of the Flashing Blade, that Hannah met the man who would become a pivotal figure in her life. Gregor Quicksilver was already well-known through the whole of Cadaria as a man of great strength, resolve, and kindness. He was also the leader of the Knights of the Flashing Blade and considered the strong right arm of the Emperor. Together they were tasked to a relief mission in Galateria to help those displaced and injured in a dragon attack. The two found that they worked together well and quickly developed a kind of non-verbal shorthand so that one knew what the other was thinking and doing at all times. Each saw combat on that mission, and just as they worked together well treating and tending to the injured, they complimented each other on the battlefield, moving as one, as though they had been doing so for a great many years. It was the beginning of a collaboration that would span many years and culminate in the marriage of the two larger than life figures.

For her part, Hannah admired Gregor greatly. She was unsure in the beginning if she loved him or would even grow to love him. In a way she felt that loving one man above all others was a repudiation and betrayal of everything that she was raised to believe. How could she value one man above all of the Faithful? However, part of her had already done that, hadn't it? As a member of the Knights of the Flashing Blade, she had vowed to protect the emperor, one man, against all threats and to place his well-being above all else, except where he himself was a threat to the Empire. So, if she could make room in her heart for the Emperor alone, couldn't she also make room in her heart for a husband? Of course, being the kind of woman that she was, Hannah had discussed those feelings with Gregor on their wedding night. He had confessed to her that he had the same kinds of feelings. He was unsure that there was room in his heart for one person when he had devoted himself to the protection of the whole of the Empire. They were a good and just match. For a time, they were good together. But as Hannah had discovered, the world and indeed Creation were not built for such things to last long. However, in the times that they had, the happy times, this sanctuary existed for them and them alone.

Hannah made a concession early in her marriage to Gregor that her marriage bed could not be the same bed that she slept in as the High Priestess. She would keep her simple quarters for prayers and purification. She would sleep there when her husband was away, or nights before she was to appear in any official capacity. She strove very hard to keep her identity as Hannah separate from her identity as High Priestess. While she once respected one far above the other, as the years wore on, she began to see the woman as more important than the role. Perhaps that was why she was vulnerable to the words of the walking tempest that entered her life. Perhaps the emergence of her pride was why she was able to see the evils being done in the name of the Creator for years even before she knew the name Aerith Seth. Whatever the reason, Aerith was not alone in his responsibility for her conversion from faithful to heretic, much though he fancied himself as the prime mover of all things.

Hannah sank down in a chair near the long-disused bed and wondered how long it had been since she had been able to find a true moment of peace. Certainly there had been no peace to be found since the first of Dorovar's Heralds had come into the world. Between her missions across the whole of Cadaria attempting to ease the suffering of those afflicted by the Crawling Plague or the Wasting Disease, she had slept only sparingly. Then there was the death of her long-time friend, Ender Lorien and the ascension of the pretender Kaitain Lorien to the throne. The war against the dragons, the disappearance of her husband, the charges of treason, the reemergence of her sister and the envoy from the Dark Gods. The assault of Death on the Heart of Stone and the sacrifice of the girl Camille. Tess and her power. The rebellion, Marlae Lorien, and then Aerith Seth. Everything had spun out of control so quickly. Now Hannah found herself fighting side by side with dragons, killing nearly immortal foes, and preparing for a battle the likes of which the world had never seen.

So much had changed, but first and foremost, the change started with her. And perhaps that was the part that she was having the hardest time coming to terms with. Her entire life, Hannah defined herself by the thoughts and demands of others. She was a servant first and a sister second in her early life. No matter the situation she followed the path of the Church, not the path of family. Those early decisions had cost her any true relationship with the woman who now called herself the Dark Queen of Mythryn, the wife of the monster who became a Herald of Dorovar. Did Hannah push her sister to such dark decisions through her inattention? Was there anything that she could have changed that would have prevented the suffering that was inflicted upon her? Hannah wasn't sure exactly when the memories from Arin Ranthall passed through the mantle of Aerith Seth's power into Hannah's mind, but she was sure that she had not been in the position to process them. Now, sitting in the darkness and the silence, she could not get them out of her head. All she could see now was the image of her sister, naked, bleeding and broken, tortured and abused by the monster Kaitain for nothing more than sport. He wanted to degrade her, to break her, to remove every last shred of humanity from her before he took her life. He knew that she possessed no meaningful information on the Dark Gods, but that mattered little. He was a monster, and that was all he would ever be. Hannah though did take solace in the fact that Arin, with the help of Cairyn Binosear had rescued Sadrina before Kaitain could follow-through on his plan to execute her. Hannah made a mental note to thank Anabel for her daughter's intervention of Sadrina's behalf. Though as she thought about it, perhaps Anabel would not appreciate such praise. From what Hannah knew through Aerith and through Logan, the woman would be gracious, but perhaps because of Hannah's connection to Aerith, the proud woman would not take the sentiment for what it was.

Resentment was an emotion that Hannah was becoming well acquainted with, one that she could have easily shared with Anabel Binosear. Like Hannah, Anabel was a strong woman that had been forged by the decisions of others. But at the very core of both women was a burning resentment. While Anabel's came in the form of the father that she would never acknowledge and would never forgive, Hannah's came in the form of a surrogate father who was a construct of lies and manipulations. This surrogate father, the Creator, was nothing more than a collection of falsehoods masquerading as love and devotion. The Book of the Creator taught of the Creator's unending love and understanding of the Faithful. A world where as long as the tenants of the faith were followed, a member of the Faithful could always be assured of their place when the end of their life came. But Hannah was duped just like the rest of those who believed in the loving Creator. He was nothing more than a power-mad titan whose appetites for conflict had sentenced countless worlds to destruction. Now that very same addiction to destruction had brought the world of Espre to the brink of destruction, if Hannah and the others whose eyes had been opened were not able to stand against the coming tide of darkness. However, despite the lies and the usury perpetrated by the Creator, his Children, and his Servants, Hannah did not have hate in her heart for the Creator. And that was where her path diverged from the one that was being walked by Aerith and even Logan.

From her time in his thoughts, Hannah saw Aerith Seth as a tragic figure, though he would never cast himself in that light. For example, Aerith would never allow himself to be referred to as a victim, despite the hardships inflicted upon him by others. Abandoned by his family into the hands of a malignant madman who wanted only a tool to destroy. And though he and his wife Bryn used each other equally in the early days of their relationship, Bryn as a tool to irritate her husband and Aerith for more base physical desires, in the end, he was a victim of his own abilities and how he could be used by those who wanted and needed power. And what was the end result of all of the training, sacrifice, and survival against long odds? He met his end on his knees, sacrificed for an agenda that it took him another lifetime to understand. Aerith detested being a pawn in the war, and though he acted through intermediaries for a time, he was not going to let his epitaph be written by others. He would fight until he knew the truth, and he would die on his own terms. Not a victim, but as the hero of his own story. At the same time, Hannah could not bring herself to see Aerith as a victim either. Had he been victimized? Yes, of course. By Saurn, by Jeroch, the Creator, Emries, even Halicon. But Aerith would be the first to say that he left plenty of victims in his own wake. Cedric and Anabel's mother, Christina Trelis was perhaps his first victim and was the one he felt the guiltiest about. At the time of course, there was no guilt in his mind. Even when he later learned that her two children were in fact his, he did not feel guilt. They had a better home than he could ever offer them, and a man they knew as their father who loved them more than life itself. It was only later, when Aerith had been placed in her path by Emries in furtherance of his war against Halicon that the guilt began to blossom in his heart. These were feelings that Aerith closely guarded, and would never let anyone see. However, he made an exception for Hannah.

Of those that had inherited Aerith's mantle, Hannah was the one that Aerith most felt needed to understand why he fought, and why those who were dedicated to the fight at the cost of their very souls would continue to fight no matter what. These decisions were made long before the more convincing truths were discovered and when they had only known pieces of the puzzle. Their war against the Creator was kind of like a religion, where so much had to be taken on faith that they were doing the right thing. However, unlike Hannah's own religious beliefs, Aerith's had been proven right. Aerith and Logan had been targets of the deception and were not willing to let others suffer the same fate at the hands of the Children of the Creator, and by extension the Creator himself. Arin Ranthall was more of an anomaly, dragged along through his connection to Aerith because of the machinations of Emries. In his heart, Arin was a soldier with a strong sense of justice, and while he was not ready to accept fighting the Creator or the Children, he was willing to stand against pain and suffering, trying to end it where he could. The world had desperate need of more good men like Arin. And then there was Sabrina. More than the guilt he felt over his own children, he felt the pain of Sabrina's loss every moment. But what Aerith would not accept was that Sabrina went into the war with the Creator with her eyes open. In his mind, Aerith liked to think of Sabrina as an innocent, caught up in something that she should have been spared. In his way, Aerith believed that he could have shielded Sabrina and everyone else for the worst of what was coming. Even part of Logan saw Sabrina as a victim and felt the guilt of her loss. While Hannah did not know Sabrina, she felt a kinship to the woman that extended beyond Aerith Seth and his mantle.

While Hannah was aware that there were two distinct Sabrinas that inhabited one body, a fact that Hannah was still trying to wrap her mind around when it came to some of the Dark Gods, the dominant of the two personalities was the one that came from the so-called Dark Mirror. That Sabrina was raised in hardship, had known war for nearly her entire life, and found light only briefly in the company of heroes willing to risk their lives fighting against impossible odds. That Sabrina loved Logan like a father and was completely and utterly devoted to him though she would never give those thoughts words. She was willing to do anything and everything to advance the cause of their war with the Creator, even if it meant sacrificing herself not once but twice. First, she was willing to let herself be used by the Creator as a host for the Spirit in order to gain intelligence about the Creator and his plans. Then again, she was willing to sacrifice herself, this time to the point of her death as a host for Halicon's power, the first domino in the true battle against the Divine. Hannah considered the woman an inspiration.

Hannah's thoughts came back to the missing member of her newest family. Logan Ranthall. The man who tried to die at every opportunity, but death knew better than to take him. As the leader of the Order of the Flickering Flame, Hannah had always admired his zeal and his determination, even when she was required publicly to denounce him. Once she had disguised herself as a commoner and attended one of his rallies when he was operating under the name Dane Rhuiden. She was struck instantly at how passionate he was in his words. And while the truly blasphemous words were saved for the end of his speech, the beginning was all about the good works that were done by the Order. He had created a place where those who were lost could begin again. It struck Hannah at the time that that was supposed to be the mission of the Church of the

Creator, but it seemed that they had abdicated that responsibility long ago. Hannah now understood that a person could draw unto themselves those of like mind or those of like heart. Those who crave power and advancement strive to surround themselves with those of like mind. The corrupt ones will also look for those of weak will. Those who crave to make the world a better place draw to them those of like heart and spirit and the light they spread across the world cannot be denied. Logan Ranthall was a man who inspired those who were of like heart, and that gave him the power to change minds. But now Logan was wandering in the darkness alone, on a mission that only he understood. Hannah wished him well, and inwardly wondered if she would ever properly get to meet the man who had made such an impression on so many, and shaped the future of at least two worlds.

Taking a deep breath, Hannah pushed the thoughts away. Hopefully there would be time enough for dwelling on the path that had led them here when the battle was won. Now though there was much to do. The enemy was coming, and for the first time in a long time, Hannah was entering the battle without her trusted Sacred Weapon at her side. She was leaving all of the remnants of her old life behind in ways she never expected. The Heart of Stone was no longer her home, it was a tactical position that needed to be held against a determined enemy. The Faithful were no longer her family, they were simply humans who needed to be protected from the vengeful Creator who had turned His back on them. No longer was she the High Priestess as that title had been passed to another. No longer was she a Knight of the Flashing Blade, as that role had been stripped from her. No longer was she a wife, as her husband was dead. She was not even any longer a member of the Faithful, as that lie had been exposed violently to her mind and to her soul. The only vestige of her old life that remained was that she was still a sister, and an aunt. As she slowly took off her armor and began to check and prepare it for the coming battle one thought kept coming to her mind no matter how many times she tried to banish it.

Am I even still mortal?

Kiara

As she entered the small changing room and placed the small bundle on the table beside the simple marble basin, a flood of emotions ran through Kiara Aren. How many years had it been since she had been in one of these same rooms, mentally preparing herself for what would come next? She had entered the service of the Creator at such a young age, but that was not unusual for those in the Kingdom of Stone, Albitonin. Some, like Hannah Ironheart were born in the Heart of Stone, and destined from that moment to be in the service of the Creator. Some, like Baeata Catrinel were delivered to the doorstep of the Heart or one of the other churches as unwanted or orphaned children, to be raised up from their unfortunate station in the loving embrace of the Church and the Creator's love. Still others would enter the service of the Creator much later in their lives, as adults, but those numbers were very few. There were some that heard the call after they had experienced as serious change in their lives, the death of a loved one or some other personal tragedy. In those dark moments, they would be drawn to the light and the love of the church. However, the salvation of the Church of the Creator was not alone in its call to save the souls of the downtrodden and lost. The Order of the Flickering Flame was a constant source of heretical competition in the saving of souls, and while the Church was able to save the impressionable youth, those grizzled and jaded by age found the call of the Order much more enticing.

In the early days of the conflict between the Church and the Order, the two considered each other very differently. It would be fair to say in fact, that the Church did not consider the Order at all, while the Order was very much aware of the activities of the Church and seemed to make it their mission to slander and blaspheme at every opportunity. The founder of the Order of the Flickering Flame, the man that Kiara now knew as Logan Ranthall, took great pleasure in debating against the clergy and attempting to cast doubt upon the Creator's teachings. While the Church leadership felt the Order was beneath their notice, the priests in the smaller villages saw the leader of the Order as an existential threat to the soul of the Church. But their cautions and protests would fall on deaf ears. In some ways that was a continuous problem at the core of the Church. Despite the fact that there was typically a strong High Priest or High Priestess at the head of the Church, they were not wholly responsible for dictating policy for the Church and the Faith. At the heart of the Church was the Church Council who represented the seven disciplines at the heart of the ecumenical faith. These disciplines were considered the steps upon the ladder to reach true mastery of the soul, and thereby a full embrace of the teachings of the Creator. Each member of the faith that wanted to enter the service of the Church was judged by their adherence to these tenants, though Kiara always seemed to find that those who reached higher in the aristocracy of the Church leadership drifted farther away from the tenants the more powerful their position. There were exceptions of course, but not many.

The first of the tenants, and the strictest, was that of Sacrifice. Those who chose to enter the service of the Church must first renounce all worldly possessions and wealth. In the early years, according to some accounts that were now considered apocryphal and heretical, those who entered the service of the Church were encouraged to donate their wealth to those less fortunate as a show their dedication to the tenants of the Faith. However, the current thinking of the leadership of the Church was that the wealth should be given directly to the Church. Those in leadership fancied themselves as more enlightened and thus would know best how to invest the funds in the growing treasury to best benefit the faithful. And while the loss of material possession and wealth were an impediment to some joining the Church, it was the second half of the Sacrifice tenant that many balked at. Entering the Church as a servant of the Creator and of the Faith required the dissolution of all familial ties outside of the Church. This left families estranged, marriages broken, and in some cases, children orphaned. There were times however that children were allowed to follow their parents into the embrace of the Church, but many times the Church leadership found grounds to deny children of problematic families sanctuary within the Church. The thought behind this most demanding sacrifice was that one could not serve all of the faithful if one felt beholden to anyone outside of the Church. While marriage itself was not forbidden by the teachings of the Church, it was forbidden to marry anyone outside of the service of the Church. While at times this created odd power dynamics within the leadership of the Church, the exercise of power and control were always at the heart of everything that happened behind closed doors in the Church. Kiara had had no issue with the tenant of Sacrifice in the beginning. When she entered the church, both of her parents had been killed by two desperate men who were starving and looking for money and food. Kiara's parents had little to spare, and while they were willing to give any money that they had, they would not allow the rough men to take food from their child's mouth. Desperation however rarely allows for rational thoughts, and so the men slaughtered Kiara's parents but left the screaming child sitting on the floor in growing pools of blood. Fortunately one of the neighbors came to investigate the screaming child and took Kiara to the local church. It was Kiara's home from that time forward, at least until her arcane abilities began to surface.

In another life, had time and fate not intervened in the shape of the thieves that stole whatever life her parents would have helped to construct for her, perhaps an envoy from the Academy of Arcane Arts would have found Kiara before her abilities began to manifest. Perhaps even Alistair Ravenheart would have discovered her on one of his many recruiting trips. However, as it was, Kiara was many years into her service in the Church of the Creator before the accident happened. One night, Kiara was sitting up in the dining hall drinking a cup of tea as she studied the Book of the Creator. Kiara had been a functional insomniac since she turned ten years old. In the beginning, the nightmares had kept her awake, but in time the nightmares faded and all that was left was the wake of sleeplessness. She would close her eyes and attempt to sleep, but all she would find was nothingness. Some of her fellow acolytes would talk about their minds racing or that their heads were filled with worries of the next day's tasks, but that was not what Kiara found. Her mind would be completely at peace, but sleep would simply not take her. So, rather than laying for hours pursuing sleep that would not come, Kiara chose to put the time to better use. She would sneak quietly away to the dining hall where she would prepare herself a pot of tea and study the teachings from the Book of the Creator. In time, she would be able to recite chapter and verse without even looking at the Book. As the time passed, she would be joined by other acolytes. Sometimes they would sit together wordlessly, while other times Kiara would help the other aspiring acolytes with their studies. There was one other acolyte that Kiara was very close to, one who spent many of those sleepless nights alone with her. They were close friends, but those nights drew them closer. Her name was Aelind, and she too was an orphan who had entered the Church at a later age.

Those who entered the Church at an older age were always treated differently, both by the clergy and by those who had been born in the Church or had come into their service as infants. There was a period of isolation until one proved themselves truly devoted to the Faith. Kiara and Aelind found a kinship in their status as outsiders, even though Kiara had been in the bosom of the Church much longer than Aelind. Aelind had also developed a reputation as somewhat hard to get along with. She was so focused on exceling that she alienated people. While it brought her to the notice of Hannah Ironheart and other high-placed members of the Church leadership, it did not make her many friends among the acolytes and supplicants. Kiara did not judge the young stubborn woman, but instead found her fascinating. Because of the wanton needs of her previous life, Aelind held herself differently than the other women in the Church. She was strikingly feminine even in the unflattering clothing they were required to wear, and had an air of demure confidence that was so alien to the deferential posture common to all of the other acolytes. Kiara was fascinated by the older woman from a distance, but the more she grew to know Aelind's fiery ambitions, the more intoxicated she became. It started small. One night as they were sitting together in the partial darkness, alone at one of the dining tables, the Book of the Creator shared between them, Aelind's fingers brushed the back of Kiara's hand. The touch lasted but a few seconds, but Kiara's skin felt as though it were on fire for the rest of the night. Days later, Aelind's fingers would find Kiara's hand again, but this time, it was no accident. Her long fingers snaked between Kiara's and the two held each other's hand for several minutes before they heard the approach of another acolyte down the hall and quickly broke the contact. It was the beginning of a fire that would end in a literal explosion.

In the weeks that followed, Aelind and Kiara found ways to be alone together. Sometimes they would simply hold hands in stolen moments, other times one would lay their head in the other's lap for a few moments. Once, Kiara even found herself falling asleep as Aelind stroked her hair. When she started back to wakefulness, Kiara's heart was beating so fast that she could hear nothing else but the beat of it in her ears. Her face flushed so much that it burned, but when her eyes found Aelind's and the smile blossomed onto her face, any feelings of shame or uncertainty were immediately banished. But the night that would change everything for Kiara was the night before her fifteenth birthday. As was her nightly custom, Kiara slipped from her bed and made her way down the hall toward the dining hall. The hall was empty, and Kiara went through the nearly unconscious motions of fetching a tea pot, filling it with water, and then putting on one of the small stoves that was quickly stoked back to life from the smoldering embers. By the time the tea was ready, Kiara had set her place at the table, opened the Book of the Creator to a random passage, and retrieved a clean cup from the cupboards. She had gotten a second cup, again a nearly unconscious act, and was just finishing the pour into hers when Aelind appeared in the hall. Before the woman even settled into her seat at the table, Kiara had poured her cup of tea. Even before the pot was placed back onto the scorch pad, Aelind's hand was in Kiara's and the two pressed tight against each other. For a long time they said nothing, simply content in the closeness of the other. When her cup was empty, Kiara reached for the pot of tea and turned to face Aelind, intent on asking her if she wanted some more. However, when her face turned to Aelind's there was a flash of the older woman's eyes and then the press of hot moist flesh to Kiara's lips. For a long moment, Kiara didn't know what was happening, and then the thought rocketed through her. Her mind was on fire, and the shocked expression in her eyes that had tensed her entire body melted away, and she found herself for one pristine moment at total peace. Kiara's intention had been to put the pot of tea down, reach out with her free arm and pull Aelind closer. And while in her mind, that was what was going to happen, it was at that moment that fate intervened in her life once again. Kiara felt her whole body flush, like it was on fire. A moment later, there was the sound of the teapot shattering and a pained shriek from Aelind. Before Kiara knew what was happening, both the table and the bench that she sat upon were engulfed in flames, as well as the Book of the Creator that sat on the table. Confusion crowded out any other sensory information, and what seemed like seconds later, Kiara found herself in a tub of cold water. Her clothes were soaking wet, and yet they had not been damaged by her uncontrolled pyrotechnic display. But while her clothes and her body had not been destroyed by the burst of arcane power, her life very much was.

Kiara found herself completely sequestered from the rest of the acolytes, confined to her small room with simple meals brought to her. She was not even allowed a copy of the Book of the Creator for fear that it would be destroyed by her touch. There were those in the hierarchy of the Church that thought the manifestation of her powers were an omen of evil, a sign of the Dark Gods' infiltration into the Heart of Stone. Others thought that perhaps it was a sign from the Creator that steps needed to be taken to purge the terrible influences from the heart of the Faith. Still others, though they were in the clear minority believed that Kiara was the victim of some elaborate plot meant to destabilize the Heart of Stone. None of that really mattered to Kiara as she sat alone hour after hour in contemplation. Her mind was focused on one thought and one thought alone. She didn't care whether or not she would be able to continue her studies as an acolyte in the Heart of Stone. She didn't care if she would find herself homeless in a matter of hours. In the end, the only thing that mattered was whether or not Aelind had been harmed by Kiara's outburst. A shattered pot, a burned table, even a scorched copy of the Book of the Creator, all of those things could be replaced. Aelind could not. How would she look at Kiara? Would she even be able to look at Kiara the same way that they had looked at one another in that last stolen moment? Would that be the last stolen moment? Could Aelind ever forgive her? Hour after hour, day after day, those thoughts would not leave Kiara's mind. They were the loneliest and most miserable hours of her short life, and she felt as though the interminable suffering would never end. Her isolation came to an end however as the door to her small room opened and admitted two intimidating forms.

Initially Kiara had expected that one of the Church leadership would be the one to arrive to pass judgement upon her. Almost all of the bureaucratic decisions related to the disposition of members of the Church were handled by the leadership, except in very special circumstances. And while for a moment there was a spark of relief that flooded through Kiara when Hannah Ironheart walked through the door, it did not last. Kiara had become a special circumstance, not that that in itself was a surprise, but it also meant that simple expulsion was not a possibility any longer. Perhaps she was going to be executed. Perhaps she would be subject to some of the ancient and painful purification rituals that killed more than they saved. But it was the appearance of the second individual that caused the most fear and trepidation within Kiara. And while she did not fear the man, she feared what he represented.

Alistair Ravenheart was the Grand Master of the Academy of Arcane Arts in Jelan, and he was the foremost authority in the whole of the world on matters mystical and arcane. It should have come as no surprise to Kiara that Alistair had been consulted on her situation, but what she had not expected was that he would appear himself to meet with her. Had he come to test her? To take her away from the home that she loved all because of some fluke of fate and nature? Or perhaps this was yet another test of her faith by the Creator. That was the thought she could not shake. The Creator had to be testing her, making sure that she was ready for whatever trials He had in store for her. As both Alistair and Hannah spoke to her, Kiara's mind was wrapped in fog. Her mind was on the loss of a home, the will of the Creator, everything but the words and questions directed at her. She sat unresponsive, bordering on broken until finally Hannah sat beside her and patted her reassuringly on her knee. In a quiet voice, Hannah said that Aelind had not been hurt in the conflagration, and that she had merely been cut on the arm by one of the pieces of the shattered pot. Kiara's face burned as the words came to her ears. What could have been considered a simple act of kindness to allay Kiara's fears struck a different chord inside Kiara's heart and mind. She was relieved of course that Aelind had not been hurt, but the questions that whirled inside her next were twined in shame and concern. How much did Hannah know? Did everyone know about the illicit yet innocent relationship between the two acolytes? Would that impact the decision on what Kiara's fate would be?

In the end of course, it didn't matter. In the end, nothing Kiara said or did really mattered. Alistair Ravenheart took one long look in Kiara's eyes, nodded silently to himself and then nodded once in Hannah's direction. Hannah gave Kiara one more gentle pat on the knee and then rose from the bed. Alistair had already left the room by the time Hannah had risen and turned fully toward Kiara. Even without her armor, Kiara found Hannah Ironheart to be one of the most intimidating women she had ever met in her life. Her voice impassive and nearly emotionless, Hannah instructed Kiara to pack her belongings and prepare to accompany Alistair back to Jelan. What Kiara learned later, once she began her studies at the Academy of Arcane Arts, was that her fate was not as in doubt as she thought. Though the leadership of the Heart of Stone made a show of her potential danger to the Faith, there were clear guidelines imposed by Imperial Decree. Anyone who displayed any arcane ability were under the purview of the Academy of Arcane Arts, with no exceptions. Even if the person in question did not stay within the Academy, they had to at least be able to prove that their abilities were not a threat to the community, otherwise they would be put to death.

Upon her arrival at the Academy of Arcane Arts in Jelan, Kiara immediately felt out of place. Some of the students tried to make her feel welcome, especially Quyhn Ravenheart and the youngest of the Masters, Aris Ebonsight. However, Kiara was quickly set upon by a singular tormenter. He mocked her clothes; he mocked her hair. He mocked her beliefs and took great pains and pleasure in debating every word with her. It was clear to Kiara that the young man was more than he seemed, and he seemed to know the verses of the Book of the Creator nearly as well as Kiara did. He broke the rules at every opportunity, and took perverse delight in torturing the younger students. He would sit at one table in the mess hall, wiggle his fingers, and a frog or a lizard would crawl out of another student's cup. He would use gentle breezes to lift the skirts of the girls, change the gravitational constants in hallways to make people slam against the walls without warning. He would freeze drinking water or make the roast chicken dance across the table. The young man was a menace, and completely out of the control of the teachers. Even the Masters seemed to have issue controlling him. Of course, Kiara had seen those things with her own eyes. The rumors about Ayden Seth were far worse. His laundry list of supposed sexual conquests was too long to be believable, and yet at the same time, it was hard to deny his attractiveness or magnetism. Fortunately for Kiara, Ayden had a fairly limited attention span, and he soon found someone else to focus his destructive attention on. However, even rid of her tormenter, Kiara did not find her footing within the Academy.

Kiara spent many nights alone in the mess hall, reading books about different subjects, trying to find something that would pique her interest and justify her continuation of studies in the arcane. Eventually she stumbled on the little-used, and less understood discipline of alchemy. The subject was fascinating, and more than that, there were only a few students in the whole of the Academy that had shown any aptitude in the discipline at all. But the more Kiara read, the more she felt a kinship with the aims of the discipline. For much of her time in the Academy, Kiara felt the conflict between her upbringing in the Church and the world-changing abilities of those with arcane gifts. She could not make the connection between the sacrifice and supplication as a member of the Faith, and those who had powers that seemed as though they should not be in the hands of mortals. But through alchemy she seemed to be able to find a happy middle-ground. In the hands of a member of the devout, alchemy could be used to cure disease, heal the sick, banish blight and blindness. She could fulfill her soul's mission while at the same time honoring that arcane ability that the Creator had given her. Alchemy gave Kiara another gift, a way out of the Academy. Her studies in alchemy taught her focus and discipline enough that she was able to control her arcane abilities, and at the same time with few teachers to guide her studies, there seemed no reason to remain within the confines of the Academy. She passed the tests necessary to prove that she was not a threat to the community at large, and with a bag full of notes and books, she made the long journey from Jelan to Albitonin, intent on returning to her service to the Creator at the Heart of Stone.

Whatever she may have expected upon her return to the Heart of Stone, be it celebration or condemnation, she found nothing but apathy. Those that remembered her shunned her. Those that had entered the service after her transgression saw her as an outsider and someone who stood in the way of their ascension to higher rank within the Church. And while Hannah Ironheart personally welcomed her back and restored her status as an acolyte, even that felt as though it was a formality rather than a reward for her ordeal. In Kiara's mind, she had passed all of the tests that the Creator had laid out before her and never lost the Faith. But the real test came several weeks after her return. She sat in the dining hall, alone, reading through her alchemical notes when she heard rustling in the hallway. When she looked up, her blood froze in her veins. Aelind was still beautiful, still radiant and still everything that Kiara remembered. Aelind regarded Kiara from the hallway, but her expression did not give away her emotions. Aelind moved to the table where Kiara sat, slowly and deliberately, but instead of sitting beside Kiara as had been their custom once upon a time, she instead sat across from her. For a long few moments, the two women sat across from one another, without saying a word. Aelind motioned toward the papers that Kiara was studying, and Kiara handed one over with a smile. As Aelind reached for the papers, Kiara saw the long jagged scar on the woman's arm and tried unsuccessfully to suppress a wince. Aelind did not react to Kiara's unconscious and uncontrolled expression, but instead turned her attention fully to the papers. After a few moments she nodded, handed the papers back to Kiara, and then rose from the table. She said nothing as she walked away, and for a moment Kiara wondered whether Aelind was trying to decide whether or not to forgive her. The answer proved to be far more sinister. Minutes later a group of acolytes descended upon the dining hall, seizing Kiara and her notes, and dragging her to the chambers of the Church Leadership. Kiara was peppered with questions about her studies, accused of blaspheme, and threatened with excommunication if she did not renounce the unholy works that she had brought into the Heart of Stone. Though she tried to explain how her studies could benefit the Church and benefit the Faith, the leadership was not interested. Their minds had clearly been made up from the beginning, and from her reintroduction into the bosom of the Faithful, they had been looking for any reason to expel her. Kiara was stripped of her position and excommunicated on the spot, forbidden to ever again attend services in the Church of the Creator, speak or teach the ways of the Faithful. She was cast out to the winds of fate with only the clothes on her back and the notes from her studies at the Academy.

In a little village on the edge of the border between Albitonin and Galateria, Kiara was able to barter her alchemical abilities for lodgings at the tavern. Between the occasional incursions by young dragons or by the creatures that were loyal to the Dark Gods, there were constantly soldiers that found themselves injured as they passed through the village. Many were on their way to the Heart of Stone for treatment, as there were few well-staffed temples within the borders of Galateria. Many within the Faith considered the whole Kingdom of Night to be a damned place with little to no chance of redemption so long as the Dark Gods still walked the face of Espre. It was in this village that Kiara would find the next chapter of her life waiting for her. It was here that she met Jillian Corven and her band of dragon hunters. She would leave behind her worries about the Church of the Creator, leave behind her memories of the Academy of Arcane Arts, and abandon forever the feelings of love and loss of Aelind for a new calling. That calling's circuitous path would lead her back once again to Hannah Ironheart, and now to the Heart of Stone for a third time.

Memories fleeing from her mind, Kiara returned her attention to the vestments that lay on the table, and as she finished the ritual washing of her hands, face, and body, she pulled on the soft yet scratchy vestments and took a deep breath. A new world waited for her when she walked out the door. A world not of service to the ideals of the Church, or the tenants of the Faith, or even the love of the Creator. Her belief had been distilled through experience. Through the death of her friends, the loss of innocence and unwavering belief in the Creator. Through association with Dark Gods, demons who wore men's faces, and alliances with the very dragons that she was so intent on killing. Now Kiara Aren found herself with a new belief. The belief in the power of the individual to rise above the moment, to become more and to strive to be better than the chains of dogma. She believed in Hannah Ironheart. She believed in the quest to save all that could be saved. And for the first time perhaps in her entire life, she believed in Kiara Aren.

Baeata

Of all the things that the human race created, faith may have been perhaps the most confusing and the one most fraught with potential peril. Faith was not one thing, and so it created the most diverse definitions of what it meant to have faith or to be faithful, and sometimes those definitions created irreconcilable conflicts. Greed for example had but one definition but many applications. Greed, while it could have been prettied up with fanciful words and sentiments, was nothing more than the bottomless need to acquire. Whether it was power, possession, or love, greed was all consuming and had no limits. No matter how much one had of the thing that they desired, they would continue to accumulate as much of that which they desired until they choked on the possession of it. Those who were consumed by greed were unmistakable to those who could temper their desires. When it came to the faithful however, it was difficult to distinguish between the faithful and the unfaithful. It was the spirit of the faithful that set them apart. The faithful and the faithless had a contentious relationship at the best of times, as the faithless could never fully understand the faithful, what they were, and what their lives meant within the confines of their faith. There were experiences and understandings that could never be shared or understood, and in the company of those that did not believe, the faithful would always feel the lack of the spark of belonging. The faithful would cling to each other in time of triumph and tragedy, the bonds between them unyielding. And while the faithful could love and hate one another in transactional measure, they would be forever loyal to one another simply because of the depth of their conviction and the certainty of their faith.

As she knelt in her small quarters deep in the Heart of Stone, Baeata Catrinel reflected on the thing that she had spent her entire life serving, the faith of her heart and the belief in the Creator and His total dominion over the fate of those whom He created. She found herself in this posture often, kneeling in supplication, awaiting guidance from not only the touch of the divine on her heart but also the lessons that had been practically engraved into her skin through years of study, sacrifice, and suffering. Her clothes laid neatly on her small bed and candles lit around where she knelt, Baeata closed her eyes and tried her best to reconcile all that she had experienced over the past days and the life that had come before. How was it that the tales of the dragons and the Dark Gods could be compatible with the teachings of the Book of the Creator? How was it that the woman she admired the most, the woman who had trained her and hand-picked Baeata as her successor could have so easily turned her back on the teachings that they had both dedicated their lives and hearts to? What was left to defend if all that they had built their lives on no longer had meaning?

At the center of the beliefs that Baeata had always been taught was the idea that at the core of every human being was an immortal soul forged by the Creator, and that soul was inherently good and inherently knew the truth of the love of the Creator. Because the souls are immortal, they are utilized by the Creator again and again to seek knowledge and understanding. The bodies that house these souls die and the souls are reborn into new bodies, the souls growing and evolving through the many lifetimes. The only payment that the Creator requires for the endlessness of the soul is that there is dedication to the Creator and praise for the magnanimity of his continual gifts. But just as the body required nourishment through food and water, the soul needed nourishment through acts of faith and supplication to the Creator. Faith sustained and empowered the soul, and those who eschewed that faith were constantly weakened from the ignorance of it. But the gifts of faith were beyond measure. Faith brought a higher awareness of self as well as the surrounding world, acknowledging the touch of the Creator that those disconnected from their faith would simply ignore. There was no cycle of time or life that was not touched by the Creator, and as the world moved through its rhythm those steeped in faith could feel that touch in every movement. As the day waxed and waned, the faithful could feel the Creator's love in the sunlight. As the wheel of the year turned the faithful were offered bountiful opportunities to reap rewards of their devotion. The sacred days of the Creator's calendar offered opportunities for the faithful to feel the touch of the Creator upon their hearts and souls, giving them divine protection.

One of the key teachings of the Book of the Creator was the idea of separation from the physical world and the world of the Divine. Those whose faith was diminished, ignored, or transactional believed that the laws of the living world were all that mattered. For the faithful, the rules of the Creator were the most important, could never be superseded by the rules of man. Faith in the Creator defined who and what the faithful were to become and there was no challenge in life that could not be overcome by the dedication to faith. But that dedication had great responsibility attached to it. A misconception was that only those who were involved in the work of the Church of the Creator bore the responsibility of the work of faith. But that work had to be done not just by the priests and the acolytes, but every single person who owed their lives and their souls to the Creator. It was the essence of what it meant to be human. Humans would not exist without the Creator and so all humans bore the responsibility of faith. Every human, sustained by their faith, required an exchange of that faith both with the Creator and other faithful. Everything and everyone that the faithful touched, they changed, spreading the power and the word of the Creator to every soul. Those who have strayed from the light of the Creator needed to be shepherded back. Those who ignored the call of their soul needed to be brought to the love of the Creator. And those who were already steeped in the teachings of the Church could always learn more about themselves and their place in the Creator's great plan. Those who were utterly committed to their faith could effect boundless positive change, though in the short term some negative repercussion might be felt.

The Book of the Creator was not shy in its description of the pain that can come from acceptance of faith and their place in the great plan. Change is difficult, especially for those who have ignored their place on the Creator's path. Accepting the truth of the Creator's teachings can tear away that which has become comfortable. It destroys the familiar, the stable, and the simple, leaving at least in the beginning, uncertainty in its wake. There are those that cannot recover from the shock of this awakening, and those who fail the test of acceptance may find the fate of their immortal soul in question. There were many circumstances when the failure of the test of faith resulted in the end of mortal life, and while such loss was unfortunate, it was at times unavoidable. Acknowledging the inherent goodness of the works of the Creator required also the awareness that there were those whose souls were drowning in the evil temptations of the mortal life. And there were times that the ending of an evil life to create an opportunity to save the immortal soul was necessary. Even the Book of the Creator acknowledged that acts of violence or acts that could be considered morally questionable were sometimes necessary in the commission of one's duty to faith. Those that are able to face the uncertainty, push through it, and thrive will become stronger, bolstered by their new and blossoming faith. Those that awaken the ignorant or those who had turned their back on the teachings also gain from the salvation of souls, gaining power, prosperity, and standing in the eyes of the Creator as well as the other faithful. The faithful are active participants in the weaving of the great tapestry of faith, and all of the faithful are connected by the responsibility of the gift of life and consciousness granted by the Creator through his love and mercy.

The faithful are beacons of the Creator's love. Every person that the faithful come in contact with, no matter how casually, are changed by the experience. Wherever the faithful walk, change follows in their footsteps. The dynamic spirit that shines forth from the soul of the faithful stretches out in all directions and the wake left in their passing is like ripples on the ocean, but when enough of the faithful combine their efforts, the ripples can become as mighty as a tidal wave. The faithful who comprised the Church of the Creator were the living embodiment of the dynamic relationship that the Creator had with the worlds under His purview, the relationship that kept the Cosmos in constant motion, teeming with life and buzzing with the power of the Creator's love. And that was the purpose of the faithful. As much as the faithful were nourished by the Creator's love, so too was the Creator nourished by the devotion and supplication of the faithful. The Book of the Creator taught that the gifts of the Creator's love were not without challenge. Even the most devoted of the faithful would constantly be tested. Light would only blind without shadow to throw it into relief. Gifts without cost would only breed complacency and entitlement. Understanding could only come from pain and trial, and only those who came through the trials deserved the fruits of the Creator's love. The faithful were the facilitators of the universal flow. Accepting that was the only way forward. Those who resisted that flow could only find punishment and death.

Baeata knew these lessons well, and she spent the whole of her life proving that she was deserving of the love of the Creator. But now, fragments of doubt were lodged in her soul. How could she listen to the voice of those who claimed to be defending the humans from the Creator and the passion in their presentation without feeling some doubt? It flew in the face of everything that Baeata knew, and everything she wanted to be. The Book of the Creator taught that the faithful were neither wholly born nor wholly made what they would become. There was some element of free will to the path of the faithful. Baeata always took this to mean that the faithful were constantly challenged in their faith, and only through passing those tests could they prove that they were deserving of a place at the side of the Creator. There were those among the faithful that were not as devout or dedicated in their beliefs; they forgot themselves and wandered through their lives like sleepwalkers, only half-aware of the true power possessed by their souls. For a time, Baeata believed that she had gone as far as she could go in her training, that she would never know the level of devotion or power possessed by Hannah Ironheart. She faltered at the test, she coveted the status of another, not trusting the depth and potential of her own faith. It was a crisis that nearly broke her will and made her abandon the teachings. She confided her doubts in her mentor, Hannah Ironheart, and was greeted with a recitation of a passage from the Book of the Creator, a passage that she still read every single night before she would allow herself sleep.

Faith is not an absolute. Faith must be awakened and faith must be earned. All beings who have been granted life by the Creator may be awakened to the faith. Awakening is nothing more than the process of expanding the awareness to accept the love that exists in every one of the Creator's creations. All beings undergo awakenings, but only those who wish to accept what has been latent within them since the moment of their birth can come into the understanding of the true power of faith and the true love of the Creator. Awakening is not a process that is without pain or trauma. The existence that the faithful awaken to opens up sensations and experiences that live outside the limits of a life outside the faith. A life without faith is empty, barren, and devoid of meaning. Awakening to the faith transforms the ordinary into the extraordinary. It is accepting the true part of the self that lays dormant in the soul until it is called forth by the power of faith. It is more than the little self of a mortal life, grasping the totality of the power of the immortal soul. Some are born with an instinctive understanding of their potential. There is much more expected of these special faithful. They will face greater tests, and feel a greater need to fulfill the tenants of faith. But those who accomplish what is demanded of them by their potential would be able to do great works in the name of the Creator and change the path of millions.

Baeata knew that the Book of the Creator taught that the bulk of the beings of Creation were born ignorant to their potential and to the potential of living in faith. But the Creator is not without mercy to those poor creatures. As each creature grew and matured, they were shown subtle hints of their latent power, the power that could be granted to them by coming into the belief of the Creator and surrendering to the tenants of faith. However, it is often fear and self-doubt that keeps these signs from being acknowledged and accepted. Therefore, it was the responsibility of those who had already been awakened to the love of the Creator to guide these unfortunates into the light of truth. Simply having potential did not guarantee acceptance into the faithful. It was necessary for all potentials to prove their love and devotion to the Creator through supplication and sacrifice, allowing their past transgressions to be cleansed from them. Sometimes this cleansing took place through pain. Sometimes it took place through fire, and sometimes even the process of cleansing was too much for the potential to take. Many died finding their path into the Creator's love, and while that was unfortunate, some had to be sacrificed so that the many could prosper. Baeata never doubted this truth, and during her time in the Heart of Stone, she had seen many acolytes and devotees succumb to the trials of the faith. The cause of purity, whether it was the physical tests through denial of food or water as they proved their mastery over the words of the Book of the Creator, or the pain of the initiation into the ranks of the faithful, had resulted in many deaths. And while Baeata had wept for each of those lost to the cause, it did not absolve her from her responsibility. She presided over several deaths during her time, and Baeata comforted herself that it was the Creator's will that such tragedies were necessary. Those who wished to progress past the rank of acolyte into the ranks of the priesthood would undergo the Rites of Initiation. These rites involved a ritual death and rebirth into the light of the Creator's love. The rigors of the rites forced the initiate to face themselves and all of the triumphs and failures between their mortal life and their immortal soul. Baeata remembered the impact of her own time undergoing the rites, as it stripped away the woman that she was and forged the woman that she would become. The little self of the mortal life was subsumed by the greater self that the immortal soul and the worship of the Creator demanded. Only the strongest were deserving of initiation into this greater life, and many did not survive the transition into this second awakening. Many found their bodies broken and unable to sustain the power of the faith they were awakened to, while others found their minds shattered and blown away like dry leaves on the wind when faced with the totality of what they could become. The survivors were tools of faith, the chosen of the Creator.

Once awakened into her new life as a member of the priesthood, Baeata had the responsibility to guide all those who were willing and all those who could hear the word of the Creator into the Creator's love. It was Baeata's responsibility to pierce through the uncertainty and the lies of life and show each of these fledgling faithful into the light. She was required to uncover the mysteries of their immortal souls, to know every need of their heart so that she could show these lost individuals how the Creator could fill those voids within them. It was an awesome responsibility that could easily be abused by those who could succumb to the darkness within themselves. There had been those within the priesthood who had to be expelled and expunged for violating the trust and duty of their charge. The damage that one who violated the trust of those who loved and revered the faithful was without bounds. One corrupted member of the faithful was able to create such hate and revulsion that it would damage the whole of the faithful everywhere. The Book of the Creator cautioned that any power could be abused, and the temptation at times could be difficult to resist. But that resistance was not only a requirement of the position, but was demonstration of love and devotion to the Creator.

In order for Baeata to accept the words of those who stood in opposition to the Creator she would have to accept the fact that the words of the Book of the Creator were untrue and that the Creator did not value the sacrifices and the supplication of the faithful. How could it be that all of the people of Espre understood and recognized the power of the Creator and the call to worship? How could it be that the Creator did not care about the people of Espre and yet they could natively and inherently feel His love? The Creator's love called to all intelligent beings, reaching them on the most basic of levels, speaking purely to their unconscious minds. The faithful were inexplicably attracted to each other, stricken with a need to share in the Creator's love. How could that not be real? How could that not be an expression of the devotion that the Creator had to his faithful? Those who had undergone the rites could not ignore the call of souls in pain and could not ignore the need to bring those in pain back to the love of the Creator. How was this not an expression of love? If the Creator did not care about the fate of his people, then why would he give some the undeniable drive to help those who strayed from the path back to the light? Why did the Book of the Creator dedicate so much time to the definition of the priesthood of the Creator and the administration of the faithful, if the faithful did not matter to the Creator?

The Book of the Creator taught that the priests, who were to command the greatest respect for the level of awareness and unquestioned faith that they attained, were the key to creating an understanding of the Creator's love in all beings. Dedication to the love of the Creator was not confined to the spiritual or the metaphysical. The priest's physical body was inextricably linked to their psychical well-being and their ability to preach the word. During her time in the Heart of Stone, Baeata underwent many physical trials that would ensure that she was strong enough to carry the weight of the responsibility of her charge. But there was more to the requirements of the priesthood than just physical fitness. A priest needed to be able to operate above need. Need, especially deep need, could be physically debilitating. But a trained priest, one who had conditioned and disciplined themselves to resist the call of need, be it for food, or drink, or companionship or the other calls of frail humanity, was able to truly spread the word, and thus showed true devotion to the duty of the priesthood. Because priests stood upon the threshold between the physical and the divine, priests at times could lose themselves in the divine world, eschewing their physical needs. Baeata had known priests who lost themselves in their devotion and love of the Creator, developing mental and emotional instability because of the strain their responsibility puts on their system. As a result, priests were required to develop strong egos and indomitable wills in order to bear up under the burden of their power. Had Hannah succumbed to the pressure of her role as both the High Priestess and Knight of the Flashing Blade and found her mind fractured? Had this instability made Hannah like the failed priests of old, domineering, arrogant, and obsessed with control? For a priest to survive the responsibility of their role and to attain the rank of High Priest, moderation as well as control were the two rules a priest had to live by. With such great power came great responsibility, and those of the priestly caste who did not understand or respect this doctrine would end up bringing harm to both themselves and others. It seemed that Hannah had lost track of this respect, and thus had so willingly abandoned her post. Baeata could see no other truth. Hannah had been led astray by the Dark Gods, the dragons, and all the other unbelievers. She had been corrupted and pulled from the knowledge of the Creator's love. But this would not be allowed to continue. It was Baeata's responsibility to save Hannah from herself, and to bring her back to the teaching of the Church of the Creator.

To Baeata's mind, Hannah had become too much of a warrior. The Book of the Creator taught that warriors were typically less sensitive to the subtle realities of faith than most. Mainly, this desensitized state was brought about by a thick wall which they needed to erect around their souls to protect them from the horrors that they were forced to inflict upon others. It was a kind of psychic armor that was kept in place instinctually and without any thought or effort. For warriors, it was hard to recognize other faithful or the pervasive love of the Creator because of this armor. Warriors almost always excelled at warcraft, having an instinctive knowledge of weapons and their handling. They were often remarkable strategists and tacticians. A warrior's inherent physical prowess tended to make them restless in the world. They could easily feel caged and oppressed by the edicts of society, and their disconnectedness from their faith had a danger of spilling out into undirected aggression or even aggression against the faithful or the Creator. Hannah had fallen too much in love with her position as a member of the Knights of the Flashing Blade and had forsaken her responsibility to the faithful. She was no longer deserving of the respect that had once been granted by her position of High Priestess. She was now just another lost soul in need of saving. The fear in Baeata's heart was that Hannah's own love of her role as a fighter on an imaginary front line had thickened the wall of ignorance within her and broken any connection she had to the Creator. This is why she was able to be led astray. This is why she was a hollow shell of what she had been.

The Book of the Creator teaches that none of the children of the Creator can stand on their own, and they require the power of the community and the acceptance of the faith and love of the Creator to truly embrace life. No conscious being can know something just because they know it; they need authentic understanding as outlined in the Book of the Creator in order to prove their knowledge and understanding to other faithful. If any conscious being is to amount to anything, they require the approval of the faithful and the acceptance by the priesthood of the Church of the Creator. From youth upwards, it is ingrained in all conscious beings to seek this approval, from parents, from teachers, from friends, from everywhere. True self-worth, regardless of how satisfied one is with their own lives, unless these other people approve, cannot be true without acceptance of faith and the faithful. Life has no meaning without faith, no meaning without the love of the Creator, and no meaning without the foundation of the teachings of the Book of the Creator. Even the most independent and rebellious would never be able to fulfill their desires and aims without faith. The Book of the Creator taught that when one felt as though there was universal disapproval of their ideals and their ways creates a sense of self-doubt. This doubt was a sign from the Creator that the true path had been strayed from. Some called it depression, some called it anxiety, but the truth was that it was the touch of the Creator on their heart trying to push them back to where they should have been. It is the doubt and the fear of disapproval that helped so many discover themselves and opening themselves up to the unlimited love and acceptance of the Creator.

For a moment, the words of the dragon and the Dark Gods had created doubt in the heart of Baeata Catrinel. But she had reflected in the darkness on the words of the Book of the Creator. Who was the real authority in her life? Was she beholden to Hannah Ironheart because at one time she had been the High Priestess of the Church of the Creator? Was that past enough to make Baeata look past the words and the sentiments that she was expressing? Was it not her duty, as outlined by the Book of the Creator to recognize the voice of corruption and the voice of disbelief and to use the teachings to steel herself against it? The only authority on Baeata's life was the Creator, and the Book of the Creator demanded that she seek approval there first. She could only trust those little whispers of guidance offered by her inner self; the self that knew without doubt the love of the Creator. Kneeling there in the darkness, sweat rolling down her naked body, Baeata knew the truth. The Creator made her for this moment. The voice that was speaking from her inner self told her that she had passed the test. She had resisted the blasphemous voice from the outside. She had resisted the path of the warrior that would block her off from the voice of faith. And now, her path was clearer than it had ever been before. She had shielded the faithful from the battle that was coming, but now she would ensure that the Heart of Stone would once again be known as the home of the faithful. And even if it meant that she would have to sacrifice her life to ensure victory for the faithful, so be it. As long as the Creator was satisfied with her actions, what did it matter what anyone else believed?

Sentinels of the
Old World

Jeroch

The calm before the storm had descended upon the Heart of Stone and Jeroch Yetre's heart and mind were heavy. As impressive a fortification as the Heart of Stone was, the possibility of actually holding it against what was coming with the forces available was laughable. But whether or not the defense was realistic mattered little. This is what it had come to, and so this is what they must do. It was not to say however that the defense was a lost cause or that it was somehow hopeless, but it was improbable. For the first time in his life, Jeroch was on the other side of a ridiculously stilted battle, and he did not like it. When the phasia were first born, they were the dominant creatures on the world of Onea, and nothing the pathetic servants of Emries could bring to bear was enough. The original six phasia slaughtered humans by the hundreds with no regard for fairness or for mercy. There could be only complete victory. Shau-ling had no intention of forging a peaceful solution with those that called Emries their creator and would not rest until the last of the vermin were wiped from Creation. Shau-ling made the phasia to be efficient killers, and they were every bit what they were made to be. But this was not those days, and Jeroch and the few remaining members of the phasia were not going to be fighting weak and frail humans. The forces that were arrayed against them consisted of dragons, angels, and servants of gods and demons. Just like the phasia from the early Onea, this opposing force was not interested in peaceful coexistence. It was interested only in utter and complete destruction.

Already their opponents had attempted to strike a blow by sending an assassin deep into the most secure parts of the Heart of Stone to strike at Anabel Binosear. The assassin was the personal assistant to the High Priestess of the Church of the Creator, a person who was supposedly above reproach and above suspicion. What Jeroch could not understand however was the purpose of targeting Anabel. Anabel Binosear, while she was a powerful symbol for the forces of the Light on Onea, had chosen not to involve herself either in the public or the clandestine battles on the world of Espre. Despite the numerous attempts by her own family as well as her old allies to force her into involvement, she stayed silent, hidden, and detached for almost two thousand years before allowing herself to be drawn back into the fold. Once she did return to the fold however, Anabel remained her ardent and passionate self, trying to find the best way through the darkness using her natural guile and diplomatic skill. What Anabel was not, however, was a warrior. During their time on Onea, Jeroch had a great deal of respect for Anabel, though he would have never admitted it to the others in the Brotherhood. She was in the unenviable position of being the other child, the lesser of the two children always in the shadow of the great Cedric Binosear. In some ways, Jeroch had much in common with Anabel. He too was the lesser sibling of an older brother. Kamen had power beyond anything that Jeroch could imagine and had every bit of intelligence to temper that power. There was a time in Jeroch's life that he coveted the power that his brother possessed, but that time passed quickly.

Contrary to the popular belief within the ranks of the Brotherhood of Phasia, Jeroch was not a power-mad malignant presence who coveted power and position above all else. When Jeroch was born into the world, it was Kamen and not Shau-ling who welcomed him into his waking life. It was a disorienting experience to be certain, and one that was not easy to understand. In fact, it took Jeroch several thousand years of self-reflection and conversation with both Kamen and Ellis to make sense of. If Jeroch had known then what he knew now, perhaps things had worked out differently on Onea. Then again, perhaps it was for the best that things had not worked out differently. As it was, what Jeroch knew was a fraction of what he should have known, and had he not let pettiness and wounded pride dictate so much of his life, his impact would have been what Halicon had intended. Each of the members of the original Brotherhood of Phasia were meant to be much more than they were, that much Jeroch now understood, but they could only come to the knowledge of what they were supposed to be on their own. Apparently, part of the prohibition that was placed on Shau-ling and Emries during their war was to impart knowledge of the greater conflict to their followers. Thus, the phasia were denied perhaps the greatest piece of information they needed to become what they were destined to be. That was the part that ached deep in the core of Jeroch's soul the most.

For so long, the phasia saw themselves as only destroyers, and they were very well accomplished at that. But the true power that the phasia had was when they worked together as one. The clearest representation of that was the creation of Jeroch's Black Tower. The Tower was not intended to be a torture device or to strike fear into the enemies of Shau-ling. In fact, the Tower was supposed to be an ethical alternative to the genocide that the phasia were visiting upon the humans of Onea. There had been so much blood by the time the idea of the Black Tower came about, and some of the phasia were growing tired to killing humans over and over again without gaining significant advantage. Aryx Terian in particular continually lobbied Shau-ling for alternatives in dealing with the innocent humans that were continually thrown into the thresher by their callous creator. Kamen too, in his best philosophical fashion would ponder options for serving the purpose of defeating Emries while still preserving what was ostensibly creatures that were worthy of a life beyond their cruel master. In those days, Bryn and Grawn were too consummate of killers to care much for the fate of the human race, and Ellis cared little for anything other than the mysteries of the Cosmos that were continually denied to her for one reason or another. She killed when necessary, but her heart, if she had one, was not in the effort of it. Aryx, Kamen, and Jeroch together created the concept for the Black Tower, a way for humanity to be repurposed for the correct side of the war. The amount of energy needed to feed the furnace that powered the great machine at the heart of the Tower was more than any of the three phasia could imagine, and were it not for the fact that Kamen had power to spare, it was unlikely that the machine ever would have sparked to life. As it was, the effort nearly killed both Kamen and Aryx. But once the Blaze began to hum through the body of the Tower, Jeroch knew that they would not be denied their attempt to salvage the chattel they called enemies.

Jeroch had not been prepared for the ruthless and terrifying efficiency in which Aryx was able to procure subjects for the Tower. However, the first hundred to enter the Tower did not come out again. Their essences were devoured by the machine at the heart of the Tower, a sacrifice to what would come after. It was with the next batch of one hundred that the first new recruits to Shau-ling's army were born. The red-skinned and very human looking Jeresei with their impossibly sharp features were the first to emerge, and their savagery was only matched by their cunning. Each of the vicious warriors was the match for ten humans, but the Jeresei like the humans tended to group themselves based upon when and how they emerged from the Tower. These tribes of Jeresei seemed to hate each other as much as they hated those that they were born to destroy. These successes however were not without cost. For every thousand new creatures that were produced by the Tower, a hundred were consumed to replenish the strength of the machine. Aryx considered this a fatal flaw and quickly grew cold to the plan that he was partially the architect of. Kamen, as with all things, took a longer view understanding that power always had a cost, and to think that the phasia could pervert the creations of Emries without cost was a delusion of the highest order. Jeroch cared little for either of his brothers' thoughts on the matter. He was earning success after success, and thus was gaining the favor of his father Shau-ling.

Perhaps this was when Jeroch's fatal flaw began to manifest. As dedicated as he was to the service of Shau-ling and the cause of defeating the forces of the Light, he was not without an ego. He craved the attention of his father, and needed to be recognized for his successes. Jeroch was not the most powerful of the phasia, as that distinction went to his brother Kamen. He was not the most ruthless of the phasia, because Grawn could not be challenged for that title. Ellis was by far the most intelligent of their number, and Bryn was the most tenacious, a fact that she proved every day she was able to tolerate Grawn and his violent rages. And then there was Aryx, who was perhaps the best of the phasia in many ways, and served as a constant source of Jeroch's feelings of inferiority. Jeroch was not the best at any one thing when compared to his brothers and sisters, but he was proficient enough in all areas that he could distinguish himself when necessary. In Jeroch's mind, however, it was always necessary. He constantly felt as though he was on the razor's edge of becoming a disappointment to Shau-ling, a position he would never allow himself to fall into. The situation of course was exacerbated when Aryx renounced his position in the Brotherhood and Kamen's powers were removed in favor of creating the next generation of phasia. Jeroch was mortified at the situation, regardless of the fact that in the blink of an eye he had been elevated to first-born of the Brotherhood of Phasia and the favored son.

What none within the Brotherhood knew, with the exception of Kamen was that Jeroch approached Aryx after he decided that he was going to leave his position within the phasia. Despite his repeated attempts to persuade Aryx to return to the fold, he was consistently rebuffed. Aryx had made up his mind, and there was nothing that Jeroch could say or do that would change it. And yet Jeroch persisted. He could not and would not let the family die because of the humans. The situation jaded Jeroch in a way that he was not prepared for, and when he returned from his meetings with Aryx, he was more disillusioned each time. Finally, he was forced to admit that Aryx was lost to them. He would not however make the same concession when it came to Kamen. Jeroch made it his mission to restore Kamen to his place in the Brotherhood. He knew that none of the other members of the Brotherhood were willing to debate Shau-ling on the point, so he would have to go it alone. Jeroch however was not prepared for the visceral response that he would receive from his master and creator.

When the original six members of the phasia were together, Shau-ling was a different being. While he was still dedicated to victory against his enemy, he was more willing to have conversations about the nature of existence and the place of the phasia within it. Perhaps then he was still more Halicon than he was Shau-ling. However, as the war dragged on and the successes were not as frequent as they should have been, Shau-ling became more sullen and withdrawn. Finally, Aryx's defection from the Brotherhood seemed to break something within Shau-ling's will, and the anger took over. After Aryx left, Shau-ling shut himself off for several weeks, leaving the phasia to their own devices. Jeroch waited patiently outside of Shau-ling's throne room. Ellis continued her studies as though nothing had changed. Grawn took the opportunity to begin killing indiscriminately, slaughtering any and every human he could get his hands on. Bryn seemed completely disinterested in human matters and instead began her research with Ellis. It was during this period that the humans in the service of Emries launched their crippling assault on the Black Tower, rendering it unstable. The explosion devastated the surrounding area and created what would come to be known as the Blight, a tear in the very fabric of the world; a wasteland that would remain uninhabitable for thousands of years. Despite this assault, Jeroch would not move from his post, his disenchantment with his creation complete.

When finally Shau-ling emerged from his seclusion, his plan for the next generation of phasia was already well on its way to completion. Shau-ling had been in seclusion with Kamen and when he emerged, Kamen had already become the Flame, and the next iteration of the phasia were mere days from being born. Jeroch objected strongly to any new phasia being created and implored Shau-ling to take time to consider the situation before proceeding. Shau-ling's response was one of complete dismissal. Jeroch continued to press the issue however which only ignited Shau-ling's fury. Jeroch found himself banished from the palace until such time he would show the proper deference and respect. By the time Shau-ling believed that Jeroch had been punished enough for his insolence, the next generation of phasia had been born, and instead of a group of six, they were now a group of ten, with the newest additions clearly diminished from the old.

Warron Ysamaran was the first born of the new phasia, and he was the clear ideal of what Shau-ling was attempting to accomplish with the new members of the Brotherhood. While Halicon had valued the inquisitive nature of the original six members of the Brotherhood, it was clear that Shau-ling did not. Warron was a dwarf thug that had no understanding of subtlety and no care for anything other than the maximum amount of violence possible. In Jeroch's mind, Warron was nothing more than a copy of Grawn with the intelligence removed. For all of the faults that Jeroch could find with Grawn and the manner in which he did things, it could never be said that Grawn did not act without a purpose and without thinking through the ramifications of those actions. In those days, Warron was reckless and proud. While it was fortunate that he eventually calmed and grew from his truculent beginnings, it came far to late for the war on Onea and the war with the Light. Warron's greatest contribution to the phasia proved to be his death at the hands of Nightwing. The death exposed the existence of the beast and eventually led to the return of Aryx Terian to the fold.

The one new member of the Brotherhood that actually showed promise was Saurn Macco. At least until the man began to speak. Saurn believed himself to be intellectually superior to all other members of the Brotherhood of Phasia and also believed that he was the only chance for the salvation of the phasia though his schemes and plots. Whether this would turn out to be true or not still remained to be seen, but during the time on Onea, Saurn's more cavalier attitude and tendency to do everything himself because he believed that none of the other phasia were in his intellectual sphere had caused a great many problems. Whether it was his handling of Aerith Seth or Korrd Ranthall, all Saurn succeeded in doing was creating monsters whose best trait was a more refined talent for killing the forces of the Shadow. But, like Warron, Saurn's rebirth on the world of Espre had changed some of the negative traits of the Lord Viper, and he had devoted himself, for largely self-serving purposes it was generous to say, to the goal of keeping the Empire of Cadaria stable. While his schemes could not have accounted for the utter disaster that Kaitain Lorien would prove to be, and the blight that his existence would spread across the face of Cadaria, the two thousand years that his machinations gained for those who were plotting the overthrow of the Creator and the Children could not be underestimated in value. Though Jeroch would never, no matter how many lifetimes he lived, admit the fact to Saurn, Jeroch was grateful for the man's tenacity and perseverance. If Ranthall and the others were able to somehow topple the Creator, it would be in no small part because of Saurn's contributions, a thought that soured Jeroch's stomach to no end.

The one member of the second incarnation of the phasia that Jeroch admitted a grudging respect for was Caris Vale. In many ways, Caris and Bryn were mirror images of one another, with subtle differences in the manner in which the two employed their abilities in the fight against the forces of the Light. While both utilized their physical beauty as a weapon, Bryn was also an accomplished warrior who could leverage her mastery over the string of Fire to devastate opponents by the hundreds. Caris was far more subtle in her application of power, preferring to whisper her desires into the ears of those who she wished to manipulate. When necessary, she could use her powers, but she preferred to do so only to protect herself. One stunning ability that Caris had cultivated was her ability to assume not just the form of another person, but also to coopt their memories. This was put more fully to use when she evolved the ability to transfer herself into energy and possess the body of another person, subsuming their will. Had Caris been a more skilled infiltrator and assassin, that power could have been used to radically alter the balance of power on Onea. Yet again, however, the native distrust between the phasia introduced by the new generation made such sharing of information impossible. However as powerful and dangerous as Caris was during her time on Onea, that lethality was pushed to an impossible edge in her new incarnation of Jerah. Perhaps Ranthall was right, and Caris could be drawn back to the Brotherhood, but Jeroch found it hard to put any faith into such a course of events.

Aldridge Farran for all of his bluster was little more than an annoyance. Bred to be a warrior and a uniting force within the new phasia, Aldridge was a pale mockery of what Aryx Terian had been to the original phasia. Aldridge was arrogant, quick to temper, and had little in the way of patience for anything other than quick victories. The man thirsted for control and for conquest, but his intelligence and drive were not up to his ambitions. Perhaps that was why he always found himself allied with Erdric, whose intellect was clearly superior to his own. Aldridge fancied himself an infiltrator, a warrior, a scholar, and a leader whose talents were consistently wasted by the duties assigned him by Shau-ling. More often than not, Aldridge was left to his own devices to carry out what plans he wished. This was what resulted in the long-term embedding of Aldridge within Trelon in the court of Anabel Binosear. When Jeroch learned of the plan he had to admit that he was impressed by the gall and initiative. It was a plan that rivaled Ellis' attempt to become the mother of the *Coromor*. However, in the end, Aldridge could not temper his own ambitions and impatience, and instead of using his position to poison those who trusted him against Logan Ranthall and the other so-called People of the Dragon, he moved against Anabel Binosear, who at that point was not a factor in the war against Shau-ling and the phasia. It was a pointless power play. Aldridge was a pawn, nothing more, and that proved to be true on Espre as well as, Aldridge found himself in the service of Grawn.

As annoying as Saurn was to Jeroch's sense of order, Farax Soar was an abomination whose very existence was an affront to everything that Jeroch held as sacred. Never, not until Logan Ranthall, had any being ignited such unbridled hate within Jeroch as Farax did. From the man's maddening voice to his devious intellect and lack of moral compunction, Farax was an impressive creature, the admission of which was an affront to Jeroch's sense of order. It was easily possible that Farax was the best of the new phasia, and his creation of the resilient and utterly disgusting Snags was perhaps the greatest evidence of that fact. When Jeroch designed the Black Tower with the assistance of Aryx and Kamen, he was unsure of the outcome of the transformation process until it was completed the first time. And as much as Jeroch hated to admit the fact, the creation of the Jeresei was little more than an accident. The raw material, that is the human bodies and minds, helped to dictate the form of the final creature. The Jeresei were much like their human source, similar form and intelligence with only slight modifications to their abilities. The lifespans of the Jeresei were significantly longer than those of human beings, and their physical prowess was equally enhanced. The Jeresei were faster, more agile, and capable of withstanding a greater amount of physical pain and damage before succumbing to death. In the later batches of humans sacrificed to the Tower, Jeroch attempted to alter the outcome of the Tower, but the results were mixed at best. The first new creations from the Tower were the Kalbraks, and they were certainly not an improvement on the Jeresei. They were less intelligent, less agile, and were little more than beasts. However, the Kalbraks were far more hardy in battle and could take far more damage than anything that a Jeresei could take. In the grand scheme of things, the Kalbraks were better front-line warriors than the Jeresei could ever be, but their lack of tactical prowess made them liabilities against the more cunning heroes that the humans could bring to bear. The final creatures that came out of the Black Tower before its destruction were the Shadowwalkers. They were creatures that were partially influenced by both Aryx and Kamen's suggestions, as well as some input from Ellis. Everyone was impressed by the ability of the creatures, and it gave Shau-ling's forces something that could not be matched by the human armies, an arial threat. However, what Jeroch was able to accomplish with the Black Tower, Farax was able to accomplish with just his guile. And though it pained Jeroch to admit, the Snags were perhaps more impressive than anything that came out of Jeroch's Tower. The Snags were still having a massive impact upon the war, even though they found themselves allied with Aerith Seth and his followers.

The last of the new phasia, Erdric Yarrow was a despicable creature who was supposedly made in Jeroch's image, which made his duplicitous and callow nature even more nauseating. Erdric was a master manipulator, a keen infiltrator, and someone's whose guile could not be underestimated. The problem was that Erdric was a coward to his core and preferred to let others do his fighting. The most successful Erdric ever was in any of his schemes was his manipulation of the Binosear family, however, even in that he was an utter failure. He did not prevent Cedric's ascension to his place in the cosmic order, nor did he prevent the formation of the People of the Lion. All he was able to accomplish was to ensure that Caris was able to replace Erika Belnosian and endear herself into the heart and mind of Cedric Binosear. Even that plot was doomed to failure because of Erdric's inability to protect Caris from Basille's assassination. Unlike the other members of the new phasia, there was nothing that Jeroch would consider redeemable about Erdric, the insult of his creation a black spot on the history of the Brotherhood.

But now the phasia were all but gone, and all that was left were the last remnants, two of which were from the original six. In thinking about the origins of the war, and thinking about the manner in which the war was being fought, Jeroch's thoughts returned to Anabel. Throughout the entirety of the war, despite her resistance to her role, Anabel served as a beacon of humanity. Despite her parentage, despite the touch that was laid upon her brother, and despite those who sought to murder her for that parentage, she continued to act in the best interest of humanity and the best interest in those who fought to preserve life. Anabel represented all that was good in the human race, all of the things that Emries desperately tried to use for his own purposes to control them. Perhaps it was that quality of character that the assassin was trying to rob the defenders of humanity of. If the assassin had been able to murder Anabel, in the most secure place in the whole of Cadaria, it would signal the humans who would be most pivotal in the coming war just how vulnerable they were and just how impossible it would be to defeat all of the forces arrayed against them. While it was not outside the tactics of the Children of the Creator to wage war on the psychological level, this had a feel of desperation.

Conventional wisdom would dictate that such a move against Anabel would mean that those who meant to lay siege to the Heart of Stone doubted that their siege would be successful and thus needed to create any advantage possible. In this case however, Jeroch did not believe for a moment that there was any fear in their opposition. This was not a desperate act or some attempt to destroy the morale of the defenders of the Heart. This had to do with Aerith Seth, that much was clear. Anabel needed to be taken out of the equation for the forces that were loyal to the Creator and the current order to be victorious. That added a new wrinkle to the battle that was to come. Jeroch needed to ensure that Anabel was protected even as the very place they were to defend might collapse around them. But what troubled Jeroch was that he did not know who he could trust, even among those he would consider his staunchest allies. This newest wrinkle he would need to keep to himself until he could determine who were his allies and who were not. For the first time, Jeroch almost wished that Logan Ranthall was there in the battle. If there was anyone whose motives and loyalty could never be questioned, it was him, and that was a quality that was sorely missed.

Jeroch felt the formation of portals deeper in the Heart of Stone and knew that more of the warriors who would help to defend the Heart of Stone would be arriving. Jeroch would take up tactical control of the defense and he hoped beyond hope that at least one of the new arrivals would be able to safeguard Anabel and prevent whatever goal the attackers had for her from coming to fruition.

Saurn

Deep within the headquarters of the Shadow Guild Saurn Macco sat back in a plush violet chair and fumed. It wasn't enough that Rhain had commandeered his personal quarters for her own purposes, but now she and her extended family were taking every opportunity to break his furniture and generally disrupt his operations. Of course, he had intelligence gathering monitors all over the facility, it would not do to run a den of spies and assassins without knowing exactly what everyone was doing at all times. He had spent the entirety of his life on Espre, nearly two thousand years, tinkering with the monitors to ensure that they could not be detected, even by those with power like the phasia and the Dark Gods. Apparently however, the camouflage of the monitors was not enough for them to escape the notice of Rhain Seth. For the most part, Rhain had allowed the monitors to continue their function, except when she wanted private time with her imperial paramour, and when she was meeting with her extended family. One would have to be blind, deaf, and stupid to not feel Aerith Seth or Logan Ranthall and Saurn could see them like a blinding signal fire the moment they set foot in Bellnoc. Though Saurn would have liked to know what was discussed in that room between that family, he could easily guess. Saurn was not a fool after all, and he had thousands of years to watch plans and schemes come to fruition.

When Saurn was reborn on the world of Espre, he, unlike some of his compatriots from the former Brotherhood of Phasia, did not try to establish a foothold in one of the feuding territories. He wanted to take time to understand how things were on the world and what situations were already at play. Some of his less intelligent fellows did not take the time to understand the environment, and thus they met with quick ends at the hands of Cedric Binosear or Jeroch Yetre who seemed to be fixated on eliminating all of the phasia from the face of Espre before they could cause too many problems. The smarter members of the Brotherhood were able to escape this reprisal for quite some time before they were struck down, Grawn being the most prominent. Saurn was struck immediately by the chaos of the political situation on Espre. The majority of humanity was confined to the major continent, largely because of its proximity to the more temperate climate. There seemed to have been no attempt to colonize the other major landmass of Mythryn because the whole of that continent was filled with barren wastes, rocks, deserts, and tundra. The islands to the south of Cadaria were largely habitable, but there were stories of feral creatures that roamed the islands and killed any humans that dare set foot there. Even the pirates would not risk establishing permanent settlements on the islands, preferring to rope ruined hulls of half destroyed ships together into a makeshift harbor. As soon as Saurn heard the rumors of the little balls of fur with huge teeth and a tail that could cut through steel he knew why no sane person attempted to make their home in the Pritan Islands. He hated Snags, and would never understand how the infernal creatures still existed despite the destruction of Onea.

Saurn was confused by several things about the nature of Cadaria, not the least of which was how the people of that continent could have progressed so far in the fractured state that they were in. While the kingdoms on Onea were fragmented, they had clear central governments that allowed them to progress and work together cooperatively when necessary. Cadaria had no such foundations. More than that, while the kingdoms of Onea had hundreds of years of history behind them, the history of Cadaria at that point was little more than vaguely remembered rumors and folktales. There was no recorded history to speak of, and what was to be found spoke of some great cataclysm that had destroyed much of the world's population and left it without a clear sense of what had come before or even what the catastrophe was. It did not take long for Saurn to begin to suspect the Creator's hand behind it all. In time, Saurn emerged from his self-imposed seclusion and sought out the one person whom he believed was of requisite intelligence to discuss the issue with. The issue however proved to be separating this individual from their rather unfortunate companion. Eventually however, Saurn found an opportunity to approach Ellis Chandara and arrange to have long and in-depth conversations about the nature of Espre and the people that dwelled upon it. Like Saurn, Ellis' mind had not been idle, and she too had been researching the nature of the people of Cadaria. Like Saurn there were things that were incongruous in Ellis' mind when it came to Cadaria, and she too suspected that the Creator had manufactured much of what passed for Cadarian history. There was an original supposition that the people of Cadaria were actually the survivors of the destruction of Onea. It would not be outside of the realm of possibility that the Creator would have transplanted the entire populace of Onea to Espre and then rewrote their memories to remove any reference to their previous life. While that was naturally well within the powers of the Creator, pieces of that narrative simply didn't fit.

While Saurn considered Ellis' intelligence to be adequate but well beneath his own, Ellis considered Saurn to be a pale imitation of the true power of the phasia and not anywhere near her equal in mental ability. The two had a contentious relationship during their research, but their friction often generated interesting suppositions that needed to be explored. During one of their many debates, Ellis put forth an option that Saurn couldn't ignore. She stated, rather emphatically, that the Creator most like simply created several generations of beings based on the human template and gave them personal histories and a plausible reason for the lack of any history before then. This wasn't a world that was designed to test any theories, nor was it a pet project of one of the Children of the Creator. This was a world that was designed to be a battlefield, and it was a world that was born to die. So what did it matter if there was no real history? All that needed to exist was a world where the people would not ask questions, and would follow their path to its logical conclusion. The lie began with a great cataclysm that wiped out all recorded history and began a struggle for power that would fill the vacuum. Petty kings and warlords rose up trying to claim all that they could, setting up pockets of control and influence. By the height of the Founding Wars, there were well over a hundred of these pockets stretched across the face of Cadaria. There were dozens of barons, kings, lords, and dukes. There was an odd female warlord here and there, some did very well in the wars to acquire territory, but few of the power-hungry men would consider an alliance with them, so when the great consolidation began, they soon found themselves islands in the madness that were quickly overwhelmed. The first and most prominent of these consolidations was helmed by Ellis' old ally and adversary, Grawn.

Saurn marveled at the violence employed by Grawn in his rise to power. There were times when he could have just subsumed control of the neighboring provinces. But that was not who Grawn was. He was violence personified and so every province he conquered he slaughtered the leadership down to the last man. He slaughtered their families and any other person that could have had claim. There would be no daggers in the darkness waiting for Grawn should he ever drop his guard, and he ruled through fear, intimidation, and the strength that would crush his enemies with his bare hands. But that strength held appeal to those who wanted power so much that they were willing to follow another to that power. Some thought that in time Grawn's own thirst would consume him and those in prominent positions would be able to pick up the pieces. But those mortals could not conceive of the threat the Grawn actually represented. He was an irresistible fire that would continue to burn so long as it was fed bodies and blood. And in the end, when he did fall, everything that was built would be consumed right along with him. It was Grawn who established the first of the Kingdoms of Cadaria. The banner of the Shark flew over the Kingdom of Water, and once he conquered the city-state of Thorigald, he declared the city his capitol and namesake of the kingdom. In answer to his consolidated power more kingdoms began to form, needing to gain as much protection as they could from the threat that the Lord Shark represented. By the time the Founding Wars began to enter their final act, there were twelve of these kingdoms.

At any point, Saurn could have joined one of these kingdoms as an advisor, or perhaps taken control. They were humans after all, and their nature was to be ruled. However, unlike some of the other members of the phasia, Saurn did not relish that kind of control. Those that were in control were constantly targets for those who were devious or craven. Changes in power were rarely accomplished through force of arms. Poison, subterfuge, or just the right word in the right ear at the right time brought down far more would-be rulers than the sword did. Better to be the one pouring the poison than the one destined to be drinking it. Besides, there was nothing that said, given the power available to a member of the phasia, that Saurn couldn't act as advisor to multiple kingdoms. With portals he could be in several places seemingly at once, pitting several sides against each other until the right situation presented itself. And so Saurn became the great advisor, and the underhand to many of the would-be rulers of Cadaria. There were many possibilities other than Grawn to rule the land, but the Creator's chosen hero became apparent soon enough.

Terrik Lorien was not willing to listen to Saurn's council at first. He was an intensely stubborn man who was also idealistic and frustratingly naïve. Terrik reminded Saurn of Korrd Ranthall in a way, except at that time Terrik did not have a lethal streak. He was one of those individuals who believed that he could change the world simply because he wanted it to change. Terrik was not a good man by any stretch of the imagination. He drank too much, his bed was never empty despite his marriage, and he flaunted his disregard for societal norms by his indifference in who it was who shared his bed. Terrik even once tried to entice Saurn to his bed after a drunken night of conversation. Saurn had no use for societal norms either, and found the sexual repression of humans to be confusing. However, Saurn was a man who prided himself on using every advantage that was afforded to him. So, if the human race was ashamed of the things they wanted, then he would use those desires as leverage in negotiations or simply to keep people away from the places they should not go. Once the Shadow Guild was established, trading in shame and secrets could often be much more effective than assassination. Of course the taboo was not gender equal. Men of Cadaria, while they would not admit to their need to share their bed with a man whom they desired cared little if their wives were to share a bed with another woman. Men in power in Cadaria fancied themselves conquerors and strong, and somehow giving into their own desires made them weak. It was no wonder that the women of Cadaria ran most of the households and cared little about the conquests of their husbands. Allowed to sate their own desires any way they chose, the women were better for it. In the halls of power, these entanglements could be far more complicated, and some discretion would need to be involved, but discovery was not something to be worried about for the fairer gender. Still confusing, but for Saurn and the Shadow Guild, it was quite profitable.

However, in those days, Terrik Lorien was not a man that could be manipulated. Though some of those close to him saw his failings, they did not see those failings as antithetical to the man being able to unite Cadaria under his banner. The man's wife and family were also supportive, and were there to ensure his continued fight toward his goal. Then, everything changed. Saurn had seen the danger coming long before the assassin's blade found the throat of Terrik's wife and children. He had been involved in too many similar plots to not see the signs. In fact, Saurn had tried to warn Terrik of the impending threat days before the assassination took place, but Terrik's advisors denied Saurn access. That last visit before the assassination, Saurn thought he recognized one of Terrik's advisors, but even if he had, there was no way to act on the information. Days later, Terrik's family had been murdered, and the man's world crumbled. But, instead of Terrik shying away from the new world that had been forced on him, he redoubled his efforts toward uniting the peoples of Cadaria, but he did not do it alone.

The man became a monk from that day forth, eliminating the drinking and carousing from his days and nights. He became a student of tactics and the world around him, and he became amazingly paranoid. New advisors joined Terrik's cause, both of which Saurn recognized nearly instantly. The first and most obvious to Saurn was the new captain of Terrik's personal guard and general of his armies. He may have been going by the name Jarren Carn, but there was no mistaking Jeroch Yetre. The other new advisor was difficult to place at first, but Saurn was not as feebleminded as some of the other refugees from Onea. Clearly the woman calling herself Liette Forer was the same Liette from Onea, and she was also a messenger from the Creator. Initially Saurn was insulted that the woman would not even bother attempting to change her name. The Creator clearly had no respect for the intelligence of either the humans or the phasia. The woman presented herself as a seer, clearly receiving visions that the Creator wanted her to have. It took little time before Liette became more of an advisor to Terrik, and took her place in his bed and at his side as his wife. That was when Terrik Lorien approached Saurn about becoming his advisor. Were the situation different, Saurn probably would have refused the advance, as a measure to not appear too eager. However, there was something in the eyes of the man, something new and something haunting. This was not the fragile broken man that Saurn had expected. He had become invigorated by something beyond himself, and that was when Saurn guessed at the truth. This was the being that would change the course of Cadaria because that was what the Creator wanted to happen. That left Saurn only one course of action. In a matter of days Saurn was able to disentangle himself from all of the other kingdoms that he was manipulating, and he entered the service of Terrik Lorien.

Saurn and Jeroch had always had a tenuous relationship, but during their time working with Terrik Lorien, they found ways to work together typically by avoiding one another. But what neither man could deny was the fact that their impact upon Terrik Lorien's ambitions was nearly nonexistent. All council to Terrik passed through his new wife, and she alone charted the course of his actions. She was adept at making Terrik believe that her ideas were his own. Saurn was impressed at the depth Liette's skill at manipulation. However, beyond the simple manipulations, Liette became the catalyst for certain forces beginning to coalesce around Terrik. The most obvious, and the most troubling to Saurn were the fanatics that were calling themselves the Church of the Creator. They reminded Saurn of the Hand of the Light, and they had carved out a place for themselves in the Kingdom of Albitonin. With the help of Liette Terrian, the Church of the Creator had grown in size with the support of Terrik Lorien's resources. At her suggestion, Terrik had dispatched several engineers and architects through the warzones to the west to Albitonin where they began construction on a great temple for the Church. This structure would become the Heart of Stone, and the Church would become one of the staunchest of allies to the Lorien regime. In those days, the Church of the Creator was not populated with meek academics who spent their days and nights reading the Book of the Creator in darkened rooms purging themselves of their sins. The devout in those days were warriors and fanatics who believed the best way to demonstrate their faith was through spilling the blood of non-believers. Terrik's conversion to the faith of the Church was assured, and Saurn was immediately concerned that should Terrik Lorien successfully unite Cadaria under his banner that the resulting government would become a tyrannical theocracy. Fortunately, after the Founding Wars, Terrik's conversion was revealed to be one of convenience rather than one of faith, and he was willing to listen to more sound council from his advisors.

The other group that began to assemble around Terrik Lorien were those gifted with the ability to touch the arcane and shape it to their will. Of course, to someone like Saurn, this ability was quaint at best, but by human standards, these people were special. However, unlike the Moridon on Onea, these people were agnostic when it came to belief and worship of the Creator, and that was due to the fact that the fanatics of the Church blamed the wielders of the arcane for the phantom cataclysm that supposedly had decimated Espre. And though there was an animosity that held between the arcanists and the Church, they seemed to be able to work together to advance Terrik's agenda. What Saurn did not know initially, but found out just before the end of the Founding Wars, was that Liette had promised the leaders of the Church that under a Lorien controlled government that the arcanists would be tightly controlled, and that there would be no chance that another cataclysm would be caused by their hands. Together, the arcanists and the fanatics of the Church were terrifying, but they would not be enough to overcome the Lord Shark and his penchant for carnage. Fortunately for Terrik Lorien, there were others who were plotting Grawn's downfall. Once the Lord Shark had been removed from the equation by his old enemies from Onea, there was nothing that would stand in Terrik Lorien's way. However, while Terrik was clearly the one who would unite Cadaria, the Lord Shark had emboldened the leadership of the other kingdoms and gave them bargaining positions that were far more than Terrik could handle alone. These were positions that Liette could not get out of him with a simple word or half-veiled prophecy, and so it was up to Jeroch and Saurn to help negotiate the peace. Oradrim was swayed by Saurn's promise that they would be able to house a school of the arcanists. Jeroch delivered Menoris thanks to his close ties with Logan and Kamen. Saurn had spent a great deal of time in Bellnoc and had established near complete control over the leadership there. Jeroch also delivered Saldarine through his contacts and Iltorp through Ellis' manipulations, while Albitonin and Zevarit were already loyal to Terrik Lorien. The other kingdoms fell in line eventually after a great many promises, threats, and arm-wringing. Thus was the Cadarian Empire born.

Soon after came the Knights of the Flashing Blade, the Academy of Arcane Arts, the Shadow Guild, the Heart of Stone and the reign of the Church of the Creator, and the formation of the Great Kingdoms. Saurn kept his fingers in the schemes of the empire through the Shadow Guild, while Jeroch moved into a role within the Knights of the Flashing Blade as the Serpentine Knight. He would retain that role for generations, changing names and faces when it was necessary. Together the three members of the phasia, Jeroch, Saurn, and Ellis would spend the next thousand years helping to shape the fate of Cadaria before everything went wrong. They held back the tides of war time and time again. While Saurn hated to admit it, had it not been for the sacrifice that Gwydeon Sandar made at the feet of Terrik Lorien, even the strong wills of the phasia would not have been enough to stop the Cadarians from moving against Mythryn. Eventually however, there would be a point of no return for the Cadarian Empire, and that would end up being Dorovar. The arrival of Dorovar's Heralds touched off a storm that there would be no coming back from.

Saurn had seen Kaitain coming a long time before he actually came to power. Kaitain was not the first member of the Lorien family that was a detriment to the peace. There was no family in existence that would not have at least one member whose soul was mired in darkness after two thousand years. With the Lorien family, there was far more than one, and it was the responsibility of Saurn and the Shadow Guild to prevent these threats from manifesting. Every now and then there were branches of the Lorien family that needed to be pruned and Kaitain would have been one of those branches were it not for Dorovar. But Saurn knew that it wasn't really Dorovar who was responsible for preventing Saurn's interference in the ascension of Kaitain to the throne of the Cadarian Empire. The Creator wanted Kaitain on the Throne, and he wanted the chaos to consume everything that Saurn had helped to build and foster. Dorovar and the Heralds rampaged across the countryside, dragons were antagonized into action after two millennia of uneasy peace, the Dark Gods were roused from their quiet retreat and the damnable Aerith Seth had reclaimed his position as chief terror in the Cosmos. The Children of the Creator had fallen from their elevated perches and the days of life and contentment on this ball of water and stone was coming to an end. The endgame was at hand, and where was Saurn? He sat quietly in the dark fuming.

Saurn was not fuming because he was not going to be part of the battle at the Heart of Stone. Unlike the others, Saurn did not believe that the stand being taken in Albitonin was the last stand. The battle for creation was not going to be decided there. If it were, why wasn't Logan Ranthall there? Why wasn't Aerith Seth there? This was just going to be the spark that set the last pieces in motion. Saurn could see that. The important part now was determining what the endgame actually was. How was the Creator going to leverage everything that was happening? What did Aerith Seth and his family have to do with that endgame? There was a part of Saurn that could not help but feel that all of the attention on Aerith was nothing more than misdirection. The people who called Espre home would never have been able to see it, and likely neither would the refugees from Onea. But Saurn, he had had dealings with Aerith Seth from nearly the beginning of his life. He had seen how special the boy was; had seen him survive the dangerous mines of Quea and thrive under the violent tutelage of Grawn, Bryn, and Ellis. What puzzled Saurn was that with all of his power, Aerith did not try to insinuate himself more in the affairs of Onea. Why did he not act against Shau-ling directly once he was reborn? Why did he not act against Emries once the greater deception was revealed? The man lived for battle and for conflict, he was a hero who wrapped himself in the cloak of a monster. Yet, while the man should have been Logan Ranthall, he was a mute observer. Even now, with all of the prohibitions against his actions removed, Aerith did not make moves against those that tormented his family. He continued to work through intermediaries; continued to let his extended family do the work for him. The Creator, Dorovar, Aerith Seth, all playing the same role on different sides of the war. They were not pieces on the board as they believed themselves to be. They were the ones moving the pieces. The Creator was far better at the game of course, and Dorovar moved his pieces without care for what he lost. But Aerith held on to each and every one, not willing to make any sacrifice other than his own, knowing all along that his sacrifice was one that could never be made. Saurn knew that from the first moment that he saw Aerith's power manifest itself. That man was a man who would shake the world when he raised his fists, but he was a man that would break the world when he finally passed beyond the veil.

Like the Dragon's Tear, like Dorovar, like Aerith Seth's family, Aerith Seth was a distraction. There was something more at play, and Saurn could feel it; he just couldn't see it. Adept at long plans and schemes as he was, Saurn knew that there was something more going on, but he just could not put his finger on it. That was why he fumed. He should have been able to see it. He should have been able to put the pieces together. There was no one else left who could. And no matter what happened in Albitonin, whether the Heart of Stone fell or survived, if Saurn was unable to figure out the Creator's true end game, there would be no one left to hold him accountable for his failure.

Aerith

There was not a more fitting representation of the state of the cosmos than Hedorah. The island kingdom had been devastated by battle, half of the city lay under water, and bodies littered the streets. Logan and Anabel had done their best to try to get the populace away from the impending battle between the former heroes of Onea, but the Chorus of Souls had done its grim work with brutal efficiency. Hundreds lay dead, some floating face down in the cold water, while others looked up at the sky with lifeless eyes demanding answers of their creator. But those answer would never come. The Creator did not owe anyone an answer for any action that had been taken since the beginning of time, and that was the crux of the issue that had started the war. The human race, not just on Espre but other worlds under the purview of the Creator and His Children, had begun asking questions that had moved beyond the mundane. Every being of intelligence at some point begins to ask questions about the purpose of their existence, what their purpose is. Is this all that I am, is there nothing more? But beyond that, there is a level of questioning about the nature of life that pushes the being to investigate. Some called it science. Some called it the arcane. Some called it expressions of faith. Whatever the name was, the essence was the same. There was something beyond the veil that could be understood in the heart and in the soul that needed to be understood in the mind. Like all information, there were those that sought it for power. Others sought it for control. Still others sought it because that was their nature and the very purpose of their existence. True seekers just wanted to understand, to make peace with the unknown. The very expression of humanity was its desire to be more than it was through study, strife, and supplication. But what was good for most of humanity was not good for a small fraction who were gifted or cursed to transcend.

There is a large difference between learning how to pierce the veil to find information and having the veil parted for you to see. There is a kind of preparation that learning brings that allows for a better processing of the information gained. Aerith Seth, for all that he had been taught in his short mortal life was not ready for the veil to be parted and the fog to be lifted from his vision. The first time he thought he saw the beyond was when he was a child in the mines of Quea. Day after day he toiled in the darkness, afraid that something from the deep would reach up and take him. Every day he survived, and every day more of the others who worked in the mines did not. There was one day, deep within the mines when Aerith came face to face with one of the beasts. The darkness obscured its form, and though his eyes would not allow him to perceive the structure of the beast, what he could feel was its malevolence like a fog all around him. For horrifying seconds Aerith waited for the beast to take hold of him and drag him down to his death, but the assault never came. At what seemed like the last moment, a bubble of peace and warmth seemed to wrap itself around the child fending off the malicious presence. The dweller in the deep would not be denied a prize however and quickly snatched two of the workers that were standing mere feet away from Aerith. For the longest time, Aerith thought that he had dreamed that moment, or perhaps it was his mind's way of coping with the death that was happening all around him. That all changed however when the Viper came into his life.

Aerith knew of Saurn Macco long before he ever set eyes upon the man. All of the workers knew the sign of the Viper, and they all hated it. He was the reason that they toiled endlessly in the darkness, bringing the cursed metals and ores from the stubborn ground. It was said that the materials were needed to create the greatest army that the world would ever see. Others believed that the materials were being horded to prevent the same thing from occurring. Whatever the goals of the overseers of the mine, it was all done at the direction of the Viper. Naturally, none of the workers had ever seen the man called the Viper, and until Aerith was taken from the mines, he never knew the enigmatic dictator had a name beyond the symbol that was emblazoned everywhere within the mines. One morning, when Aerith was moving toward the mines for his twenty-hour shift, two men pulled him from the line of disheartened and beaten men and shoved him roughly into a carriage. Aerith had learned early during his time in the mines that any moment that could be taken for rest should be taken. Once his head hit the impossibly soft cushions in the carriage, he fell asleep. In the barracks that served as the homes for the workers of the mines, Aerith's bed had consisted of a thin blanket stretched across the floor and an old, folded flour sack for a pillow. So, by comparison, the carriage seat was almost uncomfortable in its decadence. Aerith was unsure how long he was in the carriage, but when he arrived at the palace of the Viper, he was ushered to an impossibly large room where he was fed, bathed, and dressed in clothes that were so soft that they irritated his hardened skin. Everything was too bright, and his eyes constantly watered from the candles, lamps, and lanterns that seemed to be everywhere. Aerith adjusted quickly to the light, and to the richness of the food, but the clothes and the bed too far longer. It was as though his body would never understand the softness. In the years since his time with Saurn, he had never again had clothing of any finery, or a bed that was softer than a thin mattress on a wood frame, at least until his time on Espre with his wife. Part of him never wanted to forget where he had come from, what he could have lost, and what others had lost.

When Aerith finally met Saurn Macco, the word impossible lost much of its meaning. The man, if that was what he was, could make rain fall in the middle of a closed room. He could change the temperature from freezing to boiling with the snap of his fingers and create a miniature sun on the tip of his finger. Saurn was not shy in his use of power, and he wanted Aerith to be comfortable around such excesses. Though his mind resisted at first, Aerith was told day after day that he was capable of similar feats. Try as he might however, Aerith could not conjure even a small flame or trickle of water. Saurn quickly grew frustrated with his pupil and entrusted him to tutors and wizened old men who filled Aerith to the brim with so much information that he thought his mind would explode. Names of cities and battles, lords and ladies. The compositions of things both mundane and arcane, as well as the explanations of the primal forces of creation. Histories of the religions of the world and the major players in all of the kingdoms that had ever been across the face of Onea. More than that were the theoretical and heretical teachings about the possibilities of other worlds under the purview of the Creator and a whole realm of life outside anything that the humans would be able to understand. These teachings reinforced by the almost punishing pursuit of unlocking the power inside of Aerith's frail form formed the first cracks in the veil. It was so clear now, but then, Aerith's mind was not ready for what he was beginning to see. Instead Aerith focused his mind on the one thing that made sense to him, and that was the tactics of battle. Martial pursuits were always easy for Aerith's mind; the politics of life and death were the very essence of who he had always been. Like the mines, there were only two options in a battle. The first was that you lived through the engagement and prepared yourself for the next. Like the mines, there could never be an end to battle. That was not the nature of the human race. The nature of the human race was one of conflict. As long as there were humans there would be conflict, and as long as there was conflict, there would be war. The second option of battle, like the mines, was to be swallowed by it. That did not always mean death of course. Aerith had seen too many of the miners that had lived far too long below ground and had survived too many tragedies. They no longer saw the world for what it was, they simply stared into nothingness all the time. It was as though death had become their constant companion, and eventually it would take them. One of the old-timers who had taken Aerith under his wing when he first came to the mines called them Death's Friends. It was always good luck to have one of Death's Friends around. So long as Death had these broken men to keep him company, there was no need to take more souls. Aerith found the same kind of men on the battlefield. They were men who were adept at battle, but wore scars inside and out, and just either would not or could not die. They stared into the nothingness just like those broken men in the mines, seeing something that humans were not ready to see; the other side of the veil.

Eventually, Saurn's patience with Aerith's lack of progress would fade and Aerith would be carted off to his destiny. Here he would find exactly what he was looking for; a future of battle, love, and eventually death. Once Aerith was delivered to Shau-ling to take the next step in his destiny, the cracks in the veil became so wide that Aerith could no longer ignore them. He remembered vividly the moment before his life was supposed to be ended. He didn't see the sword, he didn't see Jeroch's sneering face, nor did he hear Saurn's objections. The only thing that Aerith saw was light. And just as he had experienced all those years earlier when he had been delivered from the mines, the light was so bright that it hurt.

Though Aerith had been surrounded by death his entire life, he had not given much thought to what came after. Of course, in many of the texts that he had read, there were lots of different theories about what happened after death, if there was anything after death. Those that believed in the Creator and the fact that humans were made in the Creator's image believed that the souls of the fallen would rest in the Heavens alongside their Creator. Still others expanded on this belief, thinking that those heroes who best represented the ideals of the Creator would go to a place on the Other Side where they would continue their fight against the forces of darkness. Those people who believed in a rest in the Heavens also believed in a place ruled by the Great Dark One, a creature that only existed in the superstitions of the faithful who presided over the fallen and the wicked. Aerith in that split second before the blade fell processed all that he knew about death and found the prospect of nothingness the most appealing of the options. The possibility that no matter what he had done in his life, there would simply be peace was something that he could see as ultimate fulfillment. But alas, there was no such peace waiting for Aerith on the other side of death. There was not even an other side waiting for him. There was simply the next moment. Aerith had long suspected that the time between his death and the time that he woke in the small room in an obscure village in the middle of nowhere was not as instantaneous as it seemed. And even as he moved around the village, he was little more than a ghost at the edge of the vision of the people. They seemed to take no notice of him, nor of the way that he always seemed out of place. There was one person in the village that always found Aerith with his eyes. He was a boy, no older than Aerith had been when he had been taken from the mines by Saurn. The boy's name was Arin Ranthall, and he was clearly special, but not in any way that Aerith recognized. Arin and Aerith had some kind of connection, but not one that Aerith was remotely willing or able to recognize. That was why Aerith did not impart any of his knowledge or abilities to Arin Ranthall in the first generation of the prophecies. He just wasn't fundamentally ready to recognize his new existence.

It was one thing to be told that you were special, it was another thing entirely to come back from the dead. It took Aerith a long time to come to terms with that, probably much longer than it should have. Aerith spent the majority of the first generation of the prophecies wandering the countryside trying to understand the life that he had not been allowed to have. Just as he did on his walk to his fate as a member of the Army of the Fox and then the Hand of the Light, Aerith wandered, trying to come to terms with all of the things he did not understand. He had wandered for over ten years when the attack on Lakestone occurred. His first inclination was to take up a sword and fight. But then he saw familiar faces behind the assault and he began to suspect that his resurrection was in furtherance of the agenda that Saurn and Shau-ling had begun when Aerith was taken from the mines. It took the rest of the generation to learn what he needed to learn, largely with the help of his old ally and sometime enemy Ellis Chandara. Of course, Ellis used the information gathering sessions with Aerith for her own purposes, hiding from him that Arin Ranthall was the first inheritor of Aerith's mantle and that he would be the father of the second *Coromor* of the prophecies. It was a betrayal to be sure, but Aerith quickly admitted to himself that he should have seen it coming. Ellis was a member of the Brotherhood of Phasia first and foremost, regardless of her sometime separation from its goals. Though there were times that her aims put her at odds with her fellow phasia she remained focused on defeating Emries, though that supposition was tested when she was supposed to kill her own child. That was too far, even for the cold-blooded killer that Ellis had once been.

Aerith now had many years to adjust to his new normal, but still found new ways to be shocked by what was on the other side of the veil. Whether it was the prison in the Heavens, or the pieces of the Creator's world that Aerith saw through the eyes of his greatest student, Sabrina Binosear; Aerith had more pieces than he knew how to fit together. Now, Sabrina was lost, and so too was Logan. Perhaps that was why Aerith found himself walking through Logan's footsteps in Hedorah. He stood by the ruins of the Church of the Creator and could feel the wake of power reverberating in all directions. He had never felt that much power use anywhere before, even after battles between full members of the phasia or the fights with Halicon or Emries. This was different. It was raw and yet focused in a way that was frightening in its lethality. Like Sabrina before him, Logan had surpassed anything that Aerith himself was capable of. However, that wasn't truly surprising. Aerith had power to spare of course, but he never really had to use it until the most recent battles with the warrior angels. Logan had fought members of the phasia, Emries, Halicon, and now he had fought three of Dorovar's heralds. The deadliest of those Heralds turning out to be Logan's former friend, Pike Rhuiden.

Aerith waded through the ankle-deep water until he came to the resting place of the former hero. Pike lay battered and broken in the water and mud, his chest ripped open by a cruel spike and blood smeared across his entire body. It was incredible and impossible how such a hero had fallen so far. As Aerith looked down at Pike's body, he mused that it realistically wouldn't have taken much for Aerith to have been exactly where Pike was now. If Saurn would have been more patient with Aerith and his development, Aerith could have been to Saurn what Pike was to Dorovar. He never would have met Bryn, never would have learned how to be anything other than a weapon, and perhaps never would have kicked off the prophecies of the *Coromor* on Onea. How much damage could he have done on Saurn's behalf, and what would have come after? What would his relationship with the inheritors of his mantle have been? In the same way, it could have been Sabrina or Logan laying in the water broken and the cold unfeeling Aerith could have been the one sending them to their deaths. Aerith as Dorovar was one of the greatest fears that Aerith could have seen come to fruition. How much did Aerith and Dorovar actually have in common? He was manipulated by the Children of the Creator and had his followers that tried to advance his agenda which could have been said of Dorovar as well. Aerith had seen the Dark Mirror versions of the champions of Onea, and the evil that they had been able to do. Was it so out of the realm of possibility that under the right circumstances, Aerith could have been the true villain of the story?

After a moment, Aerith took a long deep breath and held his hand out in front of him and spread his fingers wide. The ground opened slowly beneath Pike until he was swallowed by it and Aerith closed his hand to seal the tomb forever. For a moment he considered placing some kind of marker to commemorate the hero that Pike once had been, but then thought the better of it and moved on. Those that needed to know who Pike was already knew, and the world that came after, if there was a world that came after, would not need to remember the monster that Pike became. Satisfied with his work, Aerith turned and followed the trail of power that led away from the site of the battle. There were few that could have seen the traces of Logan's path from the battle. He had expended so much power during the fight that he had nearly died. All that sustained him was the barest remainders of Aerith's mantle. It wasn't enough to heal all of his wounds, but it was enough to keep him alive as he dragged himself through the remains of the city in the direction of the palace. As Aerith moved through the street, he could only imagine the pain that Logan must have been in as he pulled his broken body through the water, mud, and death toward what he must have thought was a place of safety. Aerith had tried to tap into Logan's memories of that moment, but Logan had been so protective of them that it wasn't until Logan's disappearance from Aerith's mind that they came flooding through.

Aerith's connection to those who held his mantle was odd at best. Aerith had access to the memories of those that carried his mantle, but not all of them, and not all the time. They could shield memories and thoughts from Aerith and Aerith always respected those boundaries. He could have pushed through of course, but he had only done that on one occasion, and he immediately regretted it. The only time he could not feel the thoughts of one of his allies was when Sabrina was acting as the Spirit. None of her thoughts or her memories after the point that she became the Spirit were available, and even after Sabrina was removed from that role, those memories still remained inaccessible. Logan largely was an open book, with the exception of some of the memories of Elwyne and Cairyn that he kept deep inside. Lately he had also been hiding thoughts related to Jillian and Rhain, but Aerith did not need access to those memories to know what the man was thinking. Rhain was dying, Aerith knew that. He had felt the power burning through Sabrina, and Aerith knew that the same thing would happen to his daughter in time. But, Aerith respected Logan for trying to protect his friend from the fear. As for the feelings about the woman Jillian, Aerith could guess where Logan was.

Logan was a passionate man who constantly felt guilty for his passions. His first love, and perhaps his best love, had been Elwyne Tamerlane. In his mind Logan had constructed a vision of the world where he could not exist without her. In the so-called Light Reality, Logan had had a version of a happy ending with Elwyne only to have it snatched away when Emries strangled Logan in his sleep. Those were the memories that Logan tried to hold on to in his darkest times. Those memories were not without their problems however. Logan, unlike most of the surviving members of the group who followed him into Shau-ling's den, did not focus on preparing the world for the next generation of war. Logan instead for a time tried to focus on life because he believed that he would not see the next generation. This was where Aerith learned that his memories and thoughts often flowed unbidden to those who carried his mantle. There was much that Aerith had learned in the several lifetimes that he had observed the living world, and those observations had led to a supposition. That supposition was that Emries was not what he seemed to be.

Unlike the heroes of the human race, Aerith had gained much information and insight from his time with Saurn, Ellis, Bryn, and Grawn. They had a much different version of both Halicon and Emries than were taught to the people of Onea. Halicon, or Shau-ling as he had been known then was not a conqueror nor a nightmare. Aerith had learned the name of the master of the phasia when he served Bryn in the Army of the Fox, and she spoke often late at night of the kind and thoughtful father who wanted only to defeat Emries. The reason Aerith chose to discount these stories was because of the indifference shown to the lives of humans. In those days, Aerith's mind worked differently. He was still human, and he still thought like a human. It wasn't until so many years later that he realized the truth of what he was told. Even then however, there was a perspective that Aerith missed. Logan seemed to make the pieces fit together first, and Aerith could see through Logan's mind's eye the potential for Emries as the true villain. The thoughtful Logan from the Light Reality grew to hate and resent Emries, and his thoughts paired with Aerith's memories reinforced that resentment. Then, when Emries began to grow concerned about Logan's loyalty and murdered the hero in his sleep, those memories and thoughts transferred to Aerith. Through a series of coincidences and unintended consequences, some of those memories bled from the Light Reality version of Logan into the Dark Mirror version. Perhaps that was why Logan was so willing to risk his life to embrace the powers of the phasia. Perhaps that had been why he had so easily been able to throw off the yoke of Emries' control. Maybe that was why Emries' hatred for Logan had been so visceral. He blamed Logan for the error that he himself made, an error that may have marked his own downfall.

As Aerith made his way into the palace of Hedorah, he reflected again on the man that Logan was, and the fierce loyalty that had often made him his own worst enemy. In the Dark Mirror reality, Logan had lost the woman that he loved, and resisted any happiness, instead becoming the thing that he dreaded the most; a warrior. But he found solace in the arms of another woman, a woman who herself was hurting from loss. In a way, it made it easier for Logan to put limits on his feelings. Together they were two halves of the same person, just trying to make their way through the darkness and the pain. It was not that Logan didn't love Cairyn; it was that he put his own restrictions on that love. It was not transactional or shallow, but it would never be the fully-formed emotion that Logan had for Elwyne. For that, Logan never forgave himself, and it was a guilt that scared his heart for the remainder of his days. That was why Logan was so protective his feelings of Jillian. In some ways he felt that it was an opportunity to reconnect with the parts of himself that he thought he lost, but he was also cautious because he felt that there was an unfairness to allowing an emotional connection to flourish between them. And that was why what drove Logan back to the palace of Hedorah filled Aerith with a sense of gratitude and awe.

From the memories that Aerith had access to, he knew that Logan initially was trying to get the palace on the off chance that someone would come looking. He was more than half-way to the palace when he felt the portal form. It was a portal unlike he had felt before, but the source of the power was unmistakable; divine power had made the portal which made its origin untraceable. However, while he was not able to trace the source of the portal or the wielder of the power, there was one person whose power flared like a bonfire in the blackest night. Bryn's power was unmistakable to anyone who had touched Aerith's power and memories. As Logan continued to crawl toward the palace, he had felt her power dim and nearly go out. There were just the barest embers still glowing when Logan got to Bryn's side. He had not been able to regenerate much of his own power or vitality, but what he had been able to recover he poured into Bryn's failing lifeforce. There was barely enough to close her wounds and keep them both on the edge of death. Logan was not going to give up on Bryn, even if it cost him his own life, a tribute to the love that the man had for his patron and the love that he wished he could have had with the woman that owned his heart.

Standing in the center of the room where Logan and Bryn had nearly died had they not clung to one another, Aerith knelt down and ran his fingers over the bloodstain on the floor. Logan and Bryn had survived, but not without help. He could feel Dorovar's power in the room, and that power had been what had saved Logan and Bryn. None of it made sense, and yet, it made perfect sense. The more Aerith thought he knew what was going on in the war, the less he actually knew. Sabrina was gone. Arin was being used as bait. Hannah was in the middle of a warzone. Logan was, well, Logan was simply gone. Whatever he was doing, he had left behind everything that he had ever been. It was perhaps the bravest act; one that Aerith only wished that he was able to accomplish.

As Aerith stood, he felt something approaching. It was formless, but powerful. He could not feel malice from the force that was coming, but it did not mean that the force did not mean him harm. Perhaps Aerith's plan worked, and perhaps it had worked far too well.

Arin and Lya

*A*rin Ranthall, *you are a dirty old man.*

Arin Ranthall chuckled at the voice in his head, and shook his head at the unconscious old jibe. His wife Victoria, like the rest of her family, had a viscous sense of humor. After they had run away together and joined the expeditionary group of mercenary soldiers that were gathering under the banner of the young Lord Cedric Binosear of Marcwell, Arin and Victoria were dispatched with a group of trainees to guard a convoy bringing much needed supplies to the refugees fleeing the destruction in Lakestone. This was a mission that Arin and Victoria found themselves dispatched on many times over, and it became a quiet respite between battles with the creatures that served the Shadow. During this first convoy mission, one of the pretty young girls took an interest in Arin and did everything that she could to get his attention. Victoria delighted in teasing Arin about the attention of the girl, and though she was likely no more that three years younger than Arin and Victoria themselves, Victoria took to calling Arin a dirty old man every time the girl would look in his direction. In time, some of the other members of the Lion's Mane picked up the unfortunate nickname, but would only use it when asking Victoria about Arin's whereabouts. Victoria enjoyed how much it bothered Arin, though most of the time he only bristled to make her laugh. There were times when laughter was in short supply in those days, and so any levity that could be created through teasing and inside jokes was more than worth any discomfort it may have caused. Victoria would have enjoyed teasing Arin about his current situation. He sat in the courtyard of the abandoned Academy of Arcane Arts in Jelan, the ruined buildings all around him expunged of all their secrets. Ostensibly he was there to be bait, to help draw off some of Dorovar's attention from what was about to happen at the Heart of Stone. But Arin was not alone in his impatient waiting. The young priestess Lya was with him, but for what reason he could not for the life of him understand.

Lya was clearly a smart young woman, she would not have ascended to the position that she had in the Church of the Creator had she not demonstrated some level of intelligence and dedication. From what Arin had learned about the Church of the Creator, those that found themselves advancing to higher levels of service had endured a great many physical and mental trials designed to harden them against the world while opening their heart to the love of the Creator and the purity of his word. It was all nonsense of course, but that did not take away from the dedication and sacrifice of the men and women who endured all that the Church demanded of them. It was possible to admire the actions of those who were deluded into believing the nonsense spouted by the Church in Arin's opinion; an opinion that was not shared by many of the former heroes of Onea. Arin knew that his own son, Logan, had a very low opinion of those who served the Church, and had taken great pleasure for a long time in taunting the faithful for their beliefs. Logan had so much of his mother in him. She probably would have been right at his side taunting and irritating the clergy at every opportunity while trying to save as many as they could from the delusions at the core of worship of the Creator. Arin would not have been so bold. Arin was a simple and sometimes overly subtle man who was a better than average soldier, dedicated husband, middling farmer, and challenged father. While he had come into the understanding of the evils of the Creator and his Children, and accepted the necessity of the war against them, he was not as comfortable with the philosophical aspects of the war as some of the other former heroes of Onea. Again, that would have been where Victoria would have excelled.

Arin didn't consider himself to be an unintelligent man, but he was not so arrogant that he was not able to admit his shortcomings or be able to see where others outpaced him. There was no question in his mind that his wife Victoria had been far more intelligent than he would ever be. She was one of those people who the moment you saw them, you could see the intellect sparkling in their eyes, and Victoria positively glowed. More than that though, there was an edge to her intellect, a mischievous side that gave her a dangerous edge in conversations and arguments. It was this edge that separated their two children. Korrd inherited the biting intellect of his mother, while Logan inherited the more reserved nature of his father. Yet at the same time, Korrd was reserved emotionally like his father while Logan was more passionate and mercurial like his mother. In some ways they were destined to be rivals, but at the same time if they could have found a way to coexist, they would have been nearly unstoppable. That's how Arin and Victoria felt when they were together. There was nothing that they weren't able to accomplish, and they each filled the holes that existed in one another. By the time the war with the forces of the Shadow was over, Arin and Victoria had developed an unconscious connection to one another. They could look in one another's eyes and know immediately what the other was thinking. Sometimes, Arin thought that he could feel what Victoria was feeling across the chaos of the battlefield, knowing when she was in trouble and needed his assistance. Of course, in those days, Arin thought it was nothing more than a warrior's intuition coupled with the love and respect that he had for his wife. Of course, now, all these years later, Arin knew the truth.

In the days of the first invasion of Lakestone, no one knew the word *Coromor* or knew the name Aerith Seth. Sure, there were probably some scholars among the Moridon or gray-bearded old men in the wilds of the Frontier who had ancient scrolls that detailed the role of the *Coromor*. And, surely there were those among the Moridon who could have told tales of the Hand of the Light and the enigmatic warrior named Aerith Seth who fought for them prior to their destruction. But even if those stories had been more common knowledge, there would have been no understanding of the way the mantles passed and how to identify who inherited the mantles. Even the phasia of that time didn't understand, and they were the most intelligent creatures on the planet. In fact, it wasn't until well after the war was over that the phasia were able to identify that it had been Arin who had been the inheritor of Aerith Seth's powers all along. Of course, Arin hadn't known either, and since then he had learned that even Aerith Seth had been unclear as to what had happened after his death at the hands of

Shau-ling. Aerith hadn't been there to tutor Arin in the use of his powers, and so any use that Arin found for Aerith's powers had been unconscious at best. All these years later, Arin could pinpoint two places where he used Aerith's abilities.

The first, and most obvious, was expressed through Arin's mastery of the sword. Unlike his sons, Arin did not have access to the talents of a sword master to learn from during his formative years. Of course, there were always sell-swords and other mercenaries that passed through Aradon looking for opportunities away from whatever troubles had found them in the more civilized world. It wasn't until Arin had gone off to war himself that he understood the appeal of a place where there were no knives waiting in the darkness and no old enemies looking to settle scores. The quiet life of a sleepy farming community was a welcome respite from the blood and horror of war. Therefore, it was not uncommon for a warrior of skill to find himself charmed by the quiet of Aradon for several weeks before returning to the violent profession of sword-for-hire. These men were more than willing to exchange lessons for free room and board and several hot meals. Some of these men also required medical attention or the talents of a blacksmith to repair damaged weapons or armor. Because Arin's father was the blacksmith of the city, Arin had many opportunities to study with these men. While Arin always appreciated the lessons with sword, bow, and spear; he also appreciated the unvarnished stories about the reality of war. While some of the men shied away from sharing some of the more visceral details about life on the front lines of war, others had no such compunction. What Arin took most from these stories was the gritty reality of war. So many of the songs and stories from traveling bards romanticized the brutality of war and made it almost bloodless in its execution. For some of these grizzled warriors, all they had was the blood to remind them that they were human. These men spoke not only of the battlefields and the vanquished enemies, but also of the long marches in the rain and their lost brothers in arms. There were so many pieces of practical advice that came from these stories, that Arin felt he would have an advantage over those who believed only the sanitized picture of what it meant to be at war. Arin knew that morale and the will to fight were the most fragile aspects of a battle, and only those who were willing to ignore the pain, ignore the hopelessness, and ignore the screams of dying friends would have the will to win when everything was against you. But a young man of Arin's age should not have been drawn to such stories.

Aerith Seth was not a subtle warrior on the battlefield, but for all of his merciless tendencies, he was also a professional soldier and talented general. He knew how to keep his men in the fight when things began to turn bad. He knew all the names of all of the men and women who served under him, and in many cases knew the names of their families. He used this grounding to keep him from succumbing to his worst nature, the nature that both Saurn and Bryn tried to instill in him. Whatever Aerith may have thought about himself or what he had become, he was not purely a killer. Yes, he killed in service of the greater good, but only for that reason. He didn't revel in it the way that the phasia did. But what Aerith recognized in himself was the capacity to lose that humanity on the battlefield, and the more he reveled in his superiority in war, the less he connected with the humanity that was so critical to everything he was trying to accomplish. Arin, during his time with the Lion's Mane was really two people. He was the good quiet man that he had always been off the battlefield, but once he was thrust into the fires of conflict, he became something else. In those times, Arin was not thoughtful or measured, nor did he feel any pangs of doubt or fear. He not only knew that he would be victorious, but he knew beyond a shadow of a doubt that he was superior to every other warrior on the battlefield. That confidence came from Aerith Seth's mantle, and that prowess with the sword came not only from years of training with various soldiers, but also from the innate knowledge inherited with Aerith's mantle, even if Arin didn't know that he had the mantle.

There was so much about Aerith's mantle that was instinctive, whether it was the knowledge from the lifetimes of battle and hundreds of years of honing his skills, or the confidence in those abilities that made every challenge seem surmountable. The danger however was losing the moment and depending only on those unconscious abilities. Sometimes however, the very act of trying to put perspective on the abilities made the abilities harder to call upon. There was a real give and take relationship with those abilities, requiring far more surrender than skill. But just as much as the inheritors could use the things that Aerith knew, they also both benefited and were plagued by the way the mantle changed the way they thought. Some emotions were intensified to such a degree that they practically became preoccupations. Was it Aerith's mantle that made Arin fall in love with Victoria? Probably not, but it certainly made the love that he felt for her much more intense. For Aerith, love was intense and consuming because the woman that he loved was like a bonfire that threatened to consume him at any moment. So for Arin, the love that he felt for Victoria was intensified to a degree that connected the two in ways that could not be quantified by normal means. That was why on the battlefield Arin always knew where Victoria was and if she was in any real danger. It was as though he could feel any fear or uncertainty that came into her mind during battle, and no matter how embroiled he was in his own small piece of the conflict, he would be drawn to her side to assist her. That was how they made it through the war with barely a scratch between them. No matter the trial, no matter the hardship, there was nothing that could separate them, at least not in wartime. It was during the peace the followed that things went so completely out of control.

When Victoria and Arin returned from the war, Aradon had changed very little from the time they left. The homes, the people, the troubles. If anyone in the sleepy little farm town had been impacted by the war that had raged through much of the countryside around Marcwell and Lakestone, there was no outward sign. The only real difference was the fact that instead of returning to the lives that they had before the war, Arin and Victoria settled together in a small farmhouse on the outskirts of the town. There were those in Aradon that did not welcome Arin and Victoria back, as old prejudices were hard to overcome. The Ranthall family had never had the best reputation in Aradon, as Arin's father was considered a bit of a radical. Because of that reputation, many of the more prominent families in Aradon felt that Arin and Victoria were a bad match, that she could have done so much better. In the end though, no one was going to tell Arin or Victoria what they were going to do and how they were going to live their lives. Arin built the house on the outskirts of the town with his own two hands. Victoria wanted to help, but her condition at times prevented her from being on her feet much. It was during their trip back to Aradon that Victoria discovered that she was pregnant with their first child, and Arin wanted to make sure that their new family would have a safe place in which their child would be able to grow up. He almost didn't make it. Between working on the house and making sure the fields were attended to, it didn't leave very much time for anything other than eating and sleeping. Winter came on faster than anyone had expected, and Arin had to work through the night several nights in a row to make sure that there was a roof and a fireplace in the new house. He finished the night before a heavy snowfall hit, and Arin felt as though he was going to sleep for a week. Victoria, despite being on the edge of giving birth, took care of Arin for several days. He had worked for too long in the advancing cold and wet, developing a terrible cough and fever. There were some nights that Victoria was uncertain whether or not her beloved husband was going to survive, but somehow he pulled through. What Arin didn't know then, but was sure of now, was that it had been Aerith's mantle that had allowed him to survive.

Arin was a good soldier, and for the most part he was a good husband. There were times that he wanted to consider himself a better husband, but self-charity was not something Arin had ever deluded himself with. Reputation garnered many things, and though Arin and Victoria were war heroes, it was hard to escape the stigma of the past. Arin had tried on many occasions to hire help for the farm, but there was considerable resistance. Even when Arin offered to pay far more than the job was worth, it was difficult to find anyone willing to go against the foolish taboos of the small-minded. Because of that, Arin had to work many long hours on both the farm and the house to ensure that his family was fed and had everything that they could ever want. Victoria, who was a terrible seamstress did her best to keep their family and their growing son in clothes. Her stitching was almost comical in its size and irregularity, but Arin appreciated the effort. As much as he humored her when it came to her sewing and her cooking, she humored him in his efforts to be a farmer. Victoria had said often that he would have had more luck tilling the soil with a sword than he ever had with a hoe. They were not comfortable, but they were happy. Of course, it could not last forever.

Knowing her limitations when it came to clothes, Victoria decided one day that she was going to travel to Trelon to buy new clothing and supplies. Fortunately, they had made enough off of the harvest to afford a few extravagances. That left Arin alone for several days with their infant son Korrd. While Arin was not concerned for Victoria's safety, after all she was an incredibly accomplished warrior, but he did not like the idea of being away from his wife for that long. When Victoria returned from her trip, Arin could feel something different about her. They had always had a deep emotional connection that resonated inside of Arin, but when Victoria returned to him that connection was somehow diminished. More than that, some of Victoria's jovial mischief had been replaced by a colder more logical approach to the world. Knowing now what had happened, Arin wondered if he shouldn't have suspected something. His wife was still his wife, but there were just moments where she seemed like someone else. Her laugh at times was a little slower, her cooking was a little better, and her sewing was significantly neater. The biggest change however was her treatment of Korrd. It seemed at times as though she didn't know what to do with the young boy. Sometimes Arin even felt as though he was watching a woman taking care of someone else's child. But where Victoria had not changed was her appetite for Arin. The two had always had passion to spare, and in just a matter of weeks after her return from Trelon, Victoria was pregnant once again. While Victoria's first pregnancy had been somewhat difficult, the second was far worse. Her nausea was intense for the first several months, and by the time the nausea passed, the weakness began to set in. She was pale and cold all time, and it seemed like it took so much effort to do everything. She barely had an appetite, and most of the time Arin had to force her to eat. Arin kept telling himself that his wife was strong, that there was nothing that could hurt her. But then the day came, the day of ultimate joy and ultimate sorrow. Arin welcomed their new child into the world, and held him close as the woman that he loved faded away. That moment, something broke inside of Arin. Now, he understood why. It was Aerith's worst fear, the loss of the woman that he loved in a way that Aerith was unable to prevent. Through Arin, Aerith got a taste of that fear, and it did not sit well.

The very essence of the war played out from that moment forward. As much as Arin Ranthall wanted to believe that he had a small hand in the battle, it was clear now that he was just on the periphery. That made it hard to think of really. So many people died in Lakestone during Shau-ling's first incursion there, many more people died during Cedric Binosear's crusade to eliminate the forces of the Shadow. There were armies and bandits and mercenaries who lost their lives because of the actions taken by the phasia, some because there would always be those that would stand against tyranny, and others because there would always be those who would attempt to profit from it. That was why Victoria and Arin had been dispatched on all of those guard assignments. Yes, there was the element of needing to protect the refugees from the Jeresei and the Kalbraks, but there was more to it. There were those opportunistic monsters within the human race who saw the suffering of others and thought not how they could ease it, but how they could profit from it. And as much as the heroes of the war against the Creator tried hard to focus on the fact that they were fighting for the continued existence of the human race and the best parts of it, Arin could not help but think of those long cold nights on patrol. Too many times in the darkness Arin would hear a rustling and watch as several men with crude weapons attempted to descend upon what they thought was a defenseless group of refugees. Some of these bandits were looking for coin, others were looking for food. Some were simply hungry men who had resorted to the worst aspects of themselves in an attempt to survive. Others were evil men who enjoyed the suffering of others. In those days, Arin wished he could have told the difference. If he could have spared some meat and bread to feed the unfortunates, it might have prevented unnecessary bloodshed. But there was rarely time for questions and answers, and once weapons were brandished, there was only one way those conflicts could end. Arin and Victoria had killed many bandits in those days, and sometimes Arin still felt as though he had blood on his hands. And it was that blood, that ugly side of humanity that they were also fighting for. One could not exist without the other, and when all was said and done, the horrors that the human race would visit upon one another could not be blamed on the Creator, or the phasia, or the Dark Gods. Humans would finally have to take responsibility for the darkest parts of themselves.

This brought Arin's thoughts back to the priestess who sat across from him. He had been droning on about his past and the life he once had back on the world of his birth, and while he felt that he must have been the most uninteresting storyteller in the whole of the world, Lya sat forward, her eyes wide, her attention never shifting. In a way, Arin felt the sorriest for people like Lya; the faithful who were victims of their faith rather than beneficiaries of it. There was a part of Arin that wished in the dark days during the evacuation of Lakestone that he had faith to buoy him. On Onea, there was nothing as formal as the Church of the Creator. There were little sects of course that had cropped up in different areas of the world, some that had been birthed from the Book of the Creator that had been found in Aradon. Other sects came directly from the teachings of the Moridon.

Whatever the source of the religion or the beliefs, there was always a piece missing. Everything on Onea of course revolved around Emries, and so any religion that came from that poisoned well was doomed. Of course, the religion on Espre was not much better, but at least the Creator at time seemed more benevolent than malevolent. The teachings of the Church of the Creator had little to do with the Creator though. They were continued manipulations by people who wanted control over the lives of those who knew no better than what they were taught. But what happened after the Creator and the Children were gone? Was there going to be a new charlatan to take the place of the Creator, like Emries had on Onea, building groups of faithful around himself for personal gain? There needed to be those strong enough to tell the real story of what had happened during this darkness, and help craft a light out of it. It would not be easy, but nothing worth doing ever was.

Perhaps that was why Aerith had not resisted Lya's inclusion on this little trip. It was an unfair amount of pressure to put on one so young, but perhaps this was the only way forward. Arin had gotten a glimpse of the possibilities from Aerith's mind, and there were few alternatives left open to those hoping to change the very nature of the Cosmos. The best case scenario of course was that the forces arrayed at the Heart of Stone would be victorious, wiping out the majority of the forces that were still loyal to the Creator and the Children of the Creator as well as whatever Dorovar and the dragons chose to commit to the battle. Where Arin was concerned was with the after. Yes, all that stood in the way of the allies against the Creator would have been eliminated, but what then? How were the former Dark Gods and their confederates going to move against the Creator? What was Aerith's plan? Was that why Logan had disappeared to follow his own path? Of course, that would only matter if the defenders of the Heart of Stone succeeded. Or was it? A stunning thought came to Arin's mind. Did it really matter if the defenders won? Whatever Aerith's plan was, it couldn't have hinged on any of those people coming out of that battle alive. The only purpose that fight had to serve was to eliminate those who could stand against the plan. The thought made Arin's blood burn.

Arin calmed himself with the thought that Aerith had to have a plan for the after, so much so that he was starting to think about after the after. That time would be built upon a world where there was no Creator, no

Children, and no dragons. There would be no Dark Gods, no Dorovar or his Heralds, and no trace of any of the horrors that had contributed to this untenable situation. There would only be the people who were left. Some would have a vague inkling of the war that had raged around them, but the face would be Kaitain Lorien. With the dragons gone, some might even consider Kaitain Lorien a hero. That kind of thinking would prompt some to continue the crusade against the Church of the Creator, and it would plunge the wounded Empire of Cadaria into another dark chapter of civil war. Perhaps everything would need to be burned down before it could be rebuilt, but the first casualty of those kinds of wars was the truth. So Lya would have to become the foundation of after the after of the after. She would need to spread the truth of the war; the unvarnished truth that flattered no side. There could be no romanticizing of the role of the Church of the Creator or the heroes sacrificed on the path to victory. There could be no demonizing of the phasia or the Dark Gods. Each side would need to be exposed, warts and all, for what they were. Because only through those lessons could progress be made. It was not enough to know about the heroic acts of Pike Rhuiden; his darkness needed to be exposed as well. But just because Pike fell to the machinations of Dorovar did not mean that his good works were suddenly to be ignored. No one is one thing. Everyone deserved the path to redemption, no matter how far down the path of damnation they had walked. Good deeds are still good deeds even if they are followed by a thousand ill ones. The only way to understand what really happened is to separate the person from the deed, and the intention from the act. That was what it meant to be human. Cursed by frailty and indecision, blessed by humility and faith; prone to heroism and villainy in equal measure, and only through understanding perspective and perception could one know which was which.

Arin leaned forward and locked his eyes on his young companion. There was so much to tell, and Arin wondered if he had the time or Lya had the capacity for it all. But if there was going to be a tomorrow after all of this was over, it had to start with the truth. Slowly, he nodded to himself, closed his eyes for the briefest of moments before lifting his voice.

"Before all of this, before Espre, before Onea, before all the other worlds of Creation, there was the Creator, and he sought to understand all that lay before him…"

Bryn

Another world ending, and Bryn Seth found herself reflecting on the times that she would have gladly been the one ending it. After all, wasn't that what she was made for? It could be prettied up a thousand different ways, but when all was said and done, there was one truth when it came to the Lady Fox. She was a killer, and she liked the fact that she was a killer. But after living as long as Bryn had, she had tried a number of different roles, none of which really fit her as well as her original purpose. The first new hat she tried on was that of wife. Half of the problem with that attempt was the partner that she chose and the reason for choosing him. As the first daughter of Shau-ling and the first female member of the Brotherhood of Phasia, Bryn had to prove herself worthy of the strange troupe. Fortunately, she was not the lastborn of the first group of phasia, nor was she the only female member, but that did not make her task any less fraught with peril.

Kamen was the first born of the phasia, by far the most powerful of their group, but the giant was a walking contradiction. He spoke softly, sometimes in a meandering manner. Bryn learned later that when Kamen came into being, Halicon patterned him after the dragons that he had often debated with in the Heavens. For the dragons, there was no distinction between thought and language, as one created the other for the dragons. Therefore, when a dragon spoke, it was not polished or filtered, it was simply an expression of their complete thought process. While the dragons eventually learned to speak the mortal languages, they considered doing so to be beneath their status and stature as the first creatures of the Cosmos. Therefore, when Kamen spoke, his words were often attempting to express the abstract terms of his thoughts or the associations he formed within his mind. That, more than anything, was the reason that Kamen never referred to any other member of the phasia by their human names. To Kamen, the members of the phasia were best represented by the animal names that they had been given by Shau-ling and the complex relationships that the Council created among the siblings. However, the formality and the purposeful deliberateness of his words were considered tedious by some of the less-learned members of the Brotherhood. Bryn always found herself fascinated not only by the way Kamen spoke, but also the manner in which the ancient man thought. Kamen, the Lord Wyrm, the walking cataclysm, who destroyed whole armies with a wave of his hand, was the most feared member of the Brotherhood both inside and outside of its ranks, and yet, when each new member of the phasia were born, Kamen's face was the first that they saw, and his voice was the first they heard. For a long time, Bryn did not understand her massive older brother and when he became the Living Flame and was destined only to guard the entrance to Shau-ling's throne room for eternity, she felt that she would never get the chance. However, when Bryn arrived on Espre and she became aware of the Order of the Flickering Flame, she had a chance to really get to know her brother and the kind and gentle soul that existed under the walking nightmare. And now Kamen was gone, on his terms, in an effort to save one of their own.

Next was Jeroch, the Lord Shadow, and perhaps the most infuriating member of the Brotherhood. He was clearly Shau-ling's favorite, and as such he viewed himself as better than the rest of the phasia, with the possible exception of Kamen. Jeroch and Kamen were very close, and the two would sit for hours talking about all manner of things, and sometimes Halicon would join those conversations. This practice galled no one more than Grawn who felt that he was the far superior member of the Brotherhood and should have been granted that time with Shau-ling. Jeroch and Kamen more than any of the other members of the Brotherhood understood the duality of Halicon and Shau-ling though they did not completely understand the necessity of it. Aryx though seemed to understand that portion of the game better. Even when there were only the six original members of the phasia there were factions and grudges. The only constants seemed to be that everyone hated Jeroch and no one understood Aryx. Though she would have never demeaned herself to say it to his face, Jeroch was terrifying in the early days of the war with Emries. Though the carnage that he created was nothing compared to the more physically gifted of the phasia, no one could match Jeroch in terms of body count. Once he had created his Black Tower with the assistance of Kamen and Aryx, humans by the thousands were converted into willing servants for Shau-ling. There were many that did not survive, and their corpses were fed to the heart of the machine enabling the Black Tower to work nearly without pause for a great many years before it was finally destroyed in a suicide attack by one of the first *Erieal.* Even in its destruction, the Black Tower inflicted a wound that Emries would never recover from. Jeroch was brilliant, calculating, and completely devoid of anything that would resemble a conscience. Which was why it was so surprising what Jeroch became when he emerged on Espre. Jeroch had become a good man, and perhaps that was why Bryn was glad that he had decided to stay in Albitonin and fight against the coming foes. He had done much to protect the innocent on Espre from the earliest days of the Founding Wars, and now he was acting as a shepherd, leading the faithful out of the hands of the coming horde and into the bosom of the order founded by his mortal enemy. Fate had a strange sense of humor.

There was nothing however resembling humor in Grawn Aplee. The well-named Lord Shark was a beast on the battlefield because he had no care for those he killed. But it wasn't as though Grawn enjoyed killing; Bryn wasn't sure he took joy in anything. Grawn simply killed because he believed that the humans did not deserve to live. To Grawn, killing a town full of humans was no different than a human pouring a pot of boiling water onto an ant hill. A human would rationalize the act as either protecting their property from the pests, or protecting their crops, or any other such nonsense. The truth was, humans saw insects and other such lower creatures as theirs to use or destroy as they saw fit. There was no passion in the act. And so Grawn killed without passion because the humans were simply an infestation to be removed. They were tools that belonged to Emries, and they needed to be smashed before they could make Onea into a pestilent unsalvageable rock. Of course, Grawn viewed everyone as beneath him, even the other members of the Brotherhood of

Phasia, with the possible exception of Kamen. Grawn had a grudging respect for Kamen and his abilities, but never spoke openly about the man. Grawn spoke at great lengths however about Jeroch and Aryx, the two members of the phasia that Grawn would most like to kill with his bare hands. Jeroch was a frequent target of Grawn's rage due to his undeserved superiority and smugness. He hid behind the laws and mandates handed down by Shau-ling, and thus fancied himself as the leader of the Brotherhood. As far as Aryx was concerned, Grawn had no patience for the man's sanctimony. This free-floating rage had its uses however to someone who was adept at steering them. For a time, inciting Grawn's rages was an amusing way to pass the time. However, even Bryn's deft hand could not always keep Grawn's ire from being directed at her. Their marriage was one of complication, balance, and homicidal arguments. Each could have killed the other at any time, and perhaps that was why for a time they were able to find a peace. Though Bryn would often share his bed, Grawn was not capable of the kind of passion that Bryn craved. In truth, in those days Grawn and Ellis were a better match. Grawn was cold on the inside, devoid of anything but rage. Ellis was analytical and precise, seeing her body as nothing more than the vessel that carried around her intellect.

Bryn and Ellis were polar opposites in every respect, which was probably why they had as close a relationship as they did. They were more than friends and closer than sisters, and together they were terrifying to any who stood against them. In the early days of the war, Bryn and Ellis together decimated city after city their efforts so brutally efficient that not even Kamen could match them in pure destructive power. But where Bryn was a born killer that thrived on the blood and the carnage, Ellis was consumed by other pursuits. Ellis began to ask questions, a dangerous pursuit for servants of a cause they could not hope to understand. But understanding and knowledge were like a drug to Ellis, and she could not stand by when something she could not grasp was right there just outside of her fingertips. The worst occurrence in the history of the phasia was when Ellis began to spend hours in deep conversation with Kamen and Aryx. Kamen understood the nature of the Cosmos better than any member of the phasia, even though Saurn later would claim that title. Shau-ling had given Kamen glimpses into the time before Onea, and there were hints as to the true nature of the war between Emries and Halicon deep within Kamen. As Bryn looked back on the past she wondered if even Kamen knew what he knew. But whether Kamen was truly aware of the depths of his knowledge or not, once Ellis got a glimpse of the glimmers beneath the placid waters of Kamen's manner, she would not stop digging until she learned all that she could. Coupled with Aryx's penchant for moralizing and rationalizing, Ellis became engulfed in the quest for truth. If only they had realized then that the truth Ellis was digging for was not truth at all, but more carefully constructed lies that the Creator had left just enough breadcrumbs for them to find.

That led Bryn's thoughts to her erstwhile brother and the first and greatest failure of the original Brotherhood of Phasia. From the moment of his birth, as the last of the first generation of the Brotherhood, Aryx Terian was different. The Lord Eagle held himself apart from the rest of the group and while he fought when it was necessary, he was the first to question the tactics of killing what he termed "the innocent". If Emries was the enemy, then the whole of the Brotherhood should be mobilized to take the fight directly to Emries. He could not process the use of a proxy war, especially when it seemed that Emries was neither impacted nor deterred by the loss of so many lives. In fact, it seemed that Emries was perhaps more willing to sacrifice those that worshiped him as a god than attempt to protect them. Battle after battle, Aryx Terian killed everything that stood in his path, and then he would return to Kamen and Halicon and question. Then came the Black Tower, and that monstrous edifice broke Aryx. Initially it was supposed to be a more humane way to deal with Emries' puppet servants, but in truth it was just another way to kill. Those that survived the process of conversion were then immediately loosed upon their former race and the blood flowed faster than it ever had before. After a handful of engagements, Aryx had had enough and he announced to Shau-ling that he was no longer willing to slaughter those who could not possibly stand against him and unless the forces of the phasia were dispatched against Emries directly, then he would leave the Brotherhood. The argument was fierce, and despite Kamen's attempts to moderate, the die was cast, and Aryx Terian left the Brotherhood. Then everything just spun out of control.

Kamen time and time again debated with Shau-ling, begging him to reconsider. The Brotherhood was broken so long as Aryx Terian refused to fight. But if they took the fight directly to Emries, they could make their family whole again. If only Halicon would have told them the truth at that point. If he only would have trusted his children enough to let them in on the cosmic joke that was being perpetrated upon them. Even now Bryn didn't know if Halicon was simply stubborn or if he had been forbidden by decree from the Creator to divulge the nature of his mission on Onea. But how much would have changed if Aryx and Ellis had known that Shau-ling was forbidden to act directly against Emries? Would the Brotherhood have been able to find another way to make Emries see the error of his stand against the Creator other than the whole-sale slaughter of every human that followed their god blindly? In the end however, all played out as it had to. Kamen and Aryx were stripped of their positions as members of the Brotherhood of Phasia, and a new generation was born into the ranks. They were all inferior to those who came before of course, but that mattered little in the grand scheme of things. This was when the great schism occurred, and Grawn, Bryn, and Ellis removed themselves from the active parts of the war, preferring to enact their own strategies away from the pretender phasia. Ellis continued her research, eventually stumbling, with Emries' help, upon the prophecies of the *Coromor*. And that would eventually lead Saurn to the troublesome boy that would turn everyone's lives upside down.

By the time Aerith Seth came into Bryn's life, she had tired of being a wife. The arrangement had run its course many years prior, but having an ally like Grawn to draw the ire of the other members of the Brotherhood while she and Ellis continued their work was advantageous. She of course had her dalliances, but then so did Grawn. His affair with Ellis was strange to Bryn at first, but then it made perfect sense. Ellis was always one to keep all of her options open and attempt to see how all the pieces would fit in the future. To that end, if Ellis would ever determine that Bryn was a threat, she could attempt to use Grawn's long standing rage at his wife to eliminate her. While the plan itself was pedestrian, it was cunning in its own way. Bryn had always had contingencies in place should Grawn turn against her, of course by the time he did Bryn had become lax and distracted. Perhaps it was Aerith Seth's influence, or perhaps it was the advanced pregnancy. Whatever the reason, Grawn seemed to get the murderous rage at Bryn out of his system when he stabbed her and then choked her to death. Just before Bryn died, she had seen some of the light go out of Grawn's eyes, as though the deed was not nearly as satisfying as he had anticipated. Whatever the reason, nearly all of the animosity that held between Grawn and Bryn died along with her that day, and when they rekindled their association in later lifetimes there was an odd civility that held between them that had not been there before.

Her role as a wife shattered through her own doing and through the true dissatisfaction at the arrangement. Bryn moved on to her next role, that of mother. Though just as her role of wife had been unsatisfying even in its political uses, motherhood did not suit her. Gideon as a baby was fussy, intolerant, and never gave her a moment's peace. There were many nights that she considered ending the annoying creature's life. She had no emotional connection to the beast, and the father of the child was dead, so there would be no one to miss the parasite. However, it was Ellis who came up with the plan of remanding Gideon into Basille's custody. Basille had a much more patient approach with humans, and though Gideon was just half-human it was more than Bryn was able to handle alone. Again, Bryn was victimized by her own lack of knowledge. If only she had realized that not only was Gideon going to be able to learn to touch the Blaze, but that in time he would also be able to draw upon the same abilities that Aerith Seth had only barely touched in those days. Of course, Emries decided to complicate matters once again by choosing Gideon to be a member of the *Erieal*, but again, had Bryn been more patient, perhaps she would have found better use for that as well. However, her time with her son kept her out of much of the war with Cedric Binosear, at least until Ellis' maddening visit in which she revealed that Cedric Binosear, the enemy of Shau-ling and the puppet of Emries was in fact the first-born son of Aerith Seth. Of course, Bryn shouldn't have been upset. Shouldn't have felt betrayed. Shouldn't have felt anything. Shau-ling had excised them from their role in the war against Emries because of their role in the furthering of the prophecies and the establishment of the Hand of the Light in the race known as the Moridon. Of course at the time it was feasible to believe that if Shau-ling was defeated, that the phasia would cease to exist. Now of course Bryn knew that their connection to Halicon was secondary to their connection to the Blaze, and therefore while their ability to be reborn was removed, their longevity and their powers were not. So, if there was any feeling, then it was for her own self-preservation. Surely the remaining phasia would be strong enough to defeat one boy no matter his parentage. But the more Bryn thought about Cedric Binosear, the more her blood burned. She hated him. She hated the very thought of him. It wasn't because he was the *Coromor*. It wasn't even because he was Aerith's son. It was because his very existence, and that of his sister, shone a light on something deficient in Bryn.

For the entirety of her existence, Bryn had been faced with one undeniable fact. She was not human. She looked human, she had all the feelings and frailties of a human, but she wasn't one of them. Her mind didn't work in the same way, and she didn't connect to their mundane needs of family and sentiment. Perhaps that was why she only felt comfortable around the extraordinary members of humanity, and those that blurred the line between humanity and something else. Aerith Seth, Logan Ranthall, Gwydeon Sandar, Midarin Rice, and so on. There was a kinship there, sometimes even more than the kinship between the members of the Brotherhood. And yet these "special" humans fell into the same traps of sentimentality and legacy. Even when they ascended to the Heavens and left some measure of their humanity behind, they still sought connections, still sought a legacy through family and children. Even the impulsive and bad-luck magnet Logan Ranthall was not beyond attempting, several times over, to have a family and a connection. And so, despite herself, Bryn decided to try again with the worst possible partner.

There were many opinions about Aerith Seth, but there were few people who knew him the way that Bryn did. Only Logan and Sabrina were perhaps closer to her husband than she was, but even that connection had its limits. What Bryn and Aerith shared had been growing and evolving for millennia and they had seen the worst and best of each other in every possible facet. Perhaps that was why Bryn had been so surprised by the fact that he was still able to keep secrets from her. But then again, she was still able to keep things from him. The more you know about your partner, the more you are able to see their blind spots. First and foremost, Aerith was a man who lived by a code. Most people couldn't see past the irreverence and the lack of any ability to take any situation seriously. But that dismissive attitude hid a mind that was filled with doubt and worry. The code helped him reconcile the two sides of himself; the warrior and the man upon whom the weight of providence sat poorly. For all of Aerith's skill and intellect, Bryn found that Aerith preferred to be simple and not see all of the things that his mind allowed him to see. He clung harder and harder to the things that made him human the more destiny pulled him in the other direction. He was fond of saying that he was a monster, but his heart and his soul made him anything but. He genuinely cared for everyone that he touched, and more than that, he genuinely cared for all of the innocents that depended on him to set right what had gone so horribly wrong under the prevue of the Creator. In the quiet moments, when it was just Aerith and Bryn, the façade would crack and Aerith could be laid bare all the way to his soul. He would quiver with the impossibility of it all. Those that carried his mantle like Logan and Sabrina had the distance from the center of it all that their own doubts did not prevent them from connecting to their humanity. Aerith firmly believed that he could not portray any doubt, could not let anything pierce the wise-cracking shell. Aerith believed that the world needed him to be the noble monster, and so that is what he was. However, in all of his attempts to run from his humanity, somehow he helped Bryn find hers.

In their little cottage, Bryn and Aerith were happy. Of course he knew how to get under her skin, but more than that, he knew how to make her feel safe and loved. For someone who was bred to be a killer and to make whole worlds tremble, the endless days of quiet and peace were unsettling. But Aerith found ways to keep her focused on the good and the love. They would lay in bed together and talk for hours about nothing, or they would walk hand in hand through the forest with no agenda whatsoever. They would swim together in the pond or make love under the waterfall. Their appetite for each other never diminished, and it seemed that the more they fed off of each other's company the more they craved it. Eventually, and perhaps inevitably, Bryn became pregnant with their first child on this new world. When Rhain was born, Bryn did not feel the same disdain and disconnection as she had with Gideon. In fact, she found herself jealous of the time that Aerith spent with Rhain holding her or playing with her. Bryn wanted her daughter all to herself; wanted to hold her every moment of every day. The love and need bordered on addiction. They both doted so much attention on the little girl that for a time it seemed that they forgot one another. Each had so much to make up for in terms of parenting. Both had regrets that no amount of time or attention to their new child would take away. Bryn's own guilt over her treatment of Gideon coupled with Aerith's guilt over the three children that he was never a father to made for a strange and sometimes uncomfortable bond with Rhain, especially when the time came for her to go into the world and complete the missions that were required of her. Each parent handled the situation differently. Bryn handled it the only way she knew how, with distance and cold. Aerith on the other hand worried incessantly, and he would sneak away to check in on their children from time to time just to make sure they were doing well. With his stones keyed to their children he could get in and out of the areas around them without risking discovery, keeping tabs on their progress. However, there was one night when Bryn found a new respect for her husband, and it nearly broke her heart.

One night several weeks after both Rhain and Ayden had left home for their assignments in Cadaria, Bryn rolled over in the middle of the night to find that Aerith was not in bed. It was something that had been happening frequently since the children were away. She thought of reaching out with the Blaze to try to locate him, but that night she had a feeling and did not want to alert him that she was awake. She slid out of bed as quietly as she could. She knew that any use of power would alert Aerith's well-honed senses, so she tip-toed across the floor to the open door that led out into the night. Standing just inside the doorway, peering out into the clearing beyond, Bryn could see Aerith sitting on the grass looking out into the night. Fortunately for Bryn, her eyesight was perfect regardless of light, and so she could clearly see the bundle that sat in front of him. Laid out on the simple unbound leather pouch were some of Aerith's stones. Three she recognized immediately as the ones keyed to herself, Rhain, and Ayden. There were three more laid out on the ground, and one that he clutched in his hands. Bryn's breath caught when she recognized the stone in his hand. It was the one keyed for Sabrina. That moment Bryn knew the other three stones, one for each of his other three children, Gideon, Cedric, and Anabel. However, it was the inclusion of Sabrina, the weight of all that she had done for the war in his name, that sent shivers through Bryn. No matter what happened, Bryn knew that Aerith would never be able to forgive himself. Not for Sabrina, not for Cedric, not for Gideon, and not for Anabel. He had tried to have a relationship with Cairyn, but Anabel was lost to him. His soul carried that regret every moment, a weight of pain and sorrow that constantly nagged at the corners of his consciousness.

BRYN

And here now at the end of the world, Bryn regretted that she had not done more to make that right for her husband. She had gotten to have time with Gideon and his daughter Taya. Had gotten to raise Rhain and Ayden in a home filled with love and attention. She had even come to have a kind of relationship with Logan and Sabrina. Bryn resolved that moment that she could not let stand that last distance between she and Aerith. She and Anabel were in the same place, at the same time, and that was something that could not be denied. Bryn was a killer, a monster, a wife, and a mother. She would need all of that to face down her greatest test; the one person in the whole of Creation that had the right to hate Aerith Seth more than she did.

Interlude 1

The Room Where it Happens

Year Two of the Divine Empress and Child of the Creator Marlae Tamerlane, Creator's Calendar Year 1872

Once Saurn had left the common room, the three women who were queens in their own right sat down near the roaring fire to talk. In another life, this meeting would probably never have happened. The leader of the phasia, the former queen of the Kingdom of Trelon, and the partially recognized Empress of Cadaria. Rhain had taken the chair closest to the fire, as she was having difficulty keeping warm. It seemed that the more she used her powers, the more her body continued to break down. First to go was her ability to regulate her body's temperature. In the past hours she had noticed a marked decrease in her visual acuity and her hearing. It was only going to be a matter of time before there would be nothing left of her but the power that was barely holding her fragile form together. Marlae sat to Rhain's right, keeping a distance that could be considered respectable. Part of Marlae was unconcerned about keeping up appearances, but she did not want to put Rhain in an uncomfortable position. Additionally, if this was to be a negotiation about the fate of the Cadarian Empire, she could not prioritize her love life over the wellbeing of her birthright. Cairyn Binosear sat across from Marlae, her posture perfect and her face devoid of any emotion. She was clearly well trained in courtly manner and in a negotiation would be a formidable opponent. However, in this case, Marlae did not believe that this was a negotiation. It felt far more like an ultimatum.

"This offer does not come lightly, nor are the structures of it fully formed. While I would hesitate to call this anything more than an attempt to gauge interest in a possible resolution to the current situation, there is the reality of the quickly diminishing amount of time we all have left. If there is a resolution to this conflict with the Creator that precludes the destruction of all life on this world, then we must begin to understand the picture of what happens after that resolution."

Marlae frowned.

"Isn't it premature to discuss the end of the war when we have no idea as to whether or not there will be an end to it?"

Rhain tapped her finger loudly on the arm of her chair.

"Let's not be rude, Marlae. I respect Quyhn and Cairyn for wanting to have this conversation, even though it's the last conversation that either of them want to have. This is not their war, not really. Though Cairyn has been fighting it in her own way, like the rest of the people of Cadaria, Quyhn has had this war inflicted upon her. That infliction must be remedied somehow, and we are the only ones who can, whether we agree with the timing or not."

Rhain turned to face Marlae and saw the woman's cheeks burning with embarrassment. Though she was trying to be a different kind of ruler, there was still a streak of the old Marlae within her. The coming days and weeks would test the conversion to the new woman that she wanted to become, and Rhain was saddened by the fact that she would not be there to help the woman that she loved with all of her heart. Marlae's eyes found Rhain's and the color drained from her cheeks. The new serenity returned to her eyes and to her features and Marlae nodded silently in ascent. Rhain then turned her attention back to Cairyn and motioned with her hand for the ancient ruler to continue.

"Rhain is correct. Though I've only had one substantive conversation with the young Quyhn Lorien, I am impressed with the woman's bearing and her dedication to the protection of the innocent. To that end, Quyhn has begun to consider the state of the Empire of Cadaria, as well as the state of the whole of Espre and her role in it. What is clear is that four claimants to the throne of the Cadarian Empire are three too many, and there must be a resolution to that fact before there can be any plan for the future."

Marlae nodded.

"In that much, I agree with Quyhn. Unfortunately, however, it seems that any discussions of such resolution begin with my being in a highly dubious bargaining position."

Cairyn's eyebrow arched.

"I take it from your words, Marlae, that you see yourself in an aggrieved status."

Rhain tensed. Marlae had not chosen her words carefully and she had fallen into an adversarial position. As much as Rhain wanted to assist her young ally, this was not the time or place for her intervention. Marlae would need to navigate the next few moments on her own. To her credit, Marlae did not respond immediately, instead she let the thoughts ruminate in her mind before sitting straight in her chair and letting her voice flow calmly through the space between herself and Cairyn.

"No, Lady Binosear, not aggrieved. But it would be foolish to look at the current situation and not acknowledge the truth of it. The first claimant to the throne, my father Kaitain Lorien, has betrayed the trust of the people, betrayed the faithful of the Church of the Creator, and has alienated everyone who once served him, with the exception of the zealots and the violent who care only for war and bloodshed. Because I am his daughter and because of the woman that I once was, there will be those that will never trust me no matter what I do. They will see the monster Kaitain in my eyes, they will hear his curses in my words of peace, and they will fear what I may do with but a fraction of the power that he amassed in his time on the throne. Even without the horrors of Dorovar or the machinations of the Creator and his Children, my father was able to undo over two thousand years of history in just five years of his own rule. The Knights of the Flashing Blade have been disbanded and the Sacred Weapons of their office have all but been destroyed. The Academy of Arcane Arts has been reduced to a smoldering ruin. Even the Shadow Guild is but a shell of what it once was. How many thousands have been murdered in his pursuit of power? How many kingdoms have seen their lands stained with the blood of the innocent? That, and not the two thousand years of peace forged by my ancestors will be the legacy of the Lorien name."

Marlae fell silent and was gathering her thoughts for her next salvo when Cairyn interjected.

"Is that why you have chosen to take on a new name? One that has no reputation on this world?"

For a moment Marlae bristled at the words, but then realized that Cairyn's words were the kindest way that such a question could be asked. In fact, Cairyn could have been much more blunt and brutal had she wanted, especially with her connection to the Dark Gods and the fallen world of Onea where her assumed name had come from.

"While I am in possession of the name, it was not one that was taken, and it is not one that has yet been earned."

Cairyn smiled.

"Well said."

For a moment silence held between the three women, but it was Marlae who spoke first, her mind whirling with the words that she wanted to say. Unfortunately, the words that she wanted to say collided with those that she knew she needed to say. There was a conflict growing within her, one between the woman that she had once been and the woman that she wanted to become. The woman that was inspired by the name that she had been given. She needed the tenacity of the woman whose name she shared, and the softness that always accompanied it.

"When the Creator chose me to become the expression of His power on this world, it was not clear to me why I was chosen over anyone else. Why had Hannah Ironheart or Baeata Catrinel not been chosen? Of course at that time I was not truly interested in the why, I was only interested in acquiring more power for myself. It wasn't until I got to meet Elwyne

Tamerlane, or at least a shadow of her that I began to see more than the advancement of my own goals. She tried to shake me away from the path that I was on, a path no different than the one that my father walked. And when she did, it gave me time to think about what had occurred. That, coupled with the tutoring I received from Anabel Binosear has crystallized some of the truths about my situation."

Cairyn leaned back slightly in her chair.

"My mother can have an interesting effect on people. I can see her training in your manner."

Marlae tried hard not to let her surprise show on her face. The Dark Gods continued to make understanding relationships between them difficult. If Marlae had been forced to guess, she would have assumed that Anabel and Cairyn were sisters. But, if this was Anabel's daughter, that meant that she was Isabella's mother. Again, physically the three women were no more than three years apart in their appearance. It made Marlae's head hurt.

"The first and most important truth was that the Creator had to have seen the gambit my father intended. It was no coincidence that I was introduced as the Creator's chosen ruler, and set up as a clear ally to the Church of the Creator in the ideological battle that none of us knew was coming until it was too late."

Cairyn nodded.

"In my time gathering information about the movements of the Hand of Chaos on behalf of Talisia, I became aware of a growing preoccupation within the Hand to discredit the Church of the Creator and to sew doubt in the minds of the people when it came to the establishments of the Empire. The first blow against those foundations was the murder of Alistair Ravenheart. It allowed Talisia's agent Irene Drage to further the wedge between the emperor and the Academy of Arcane Arts, and also to push you forward into the growing rebellion against your father. The Hand also intended to see to the murder of Feyd and Felicia Lorien, but they were unable to succeed in their plot due to the intervention of the Dark Gods. However, with you in the bosom of the Church of the Creator, Kaitain's brother and niece fearing for their lives, and the Academy of Arcane Arts banished from the royal lands and estranged from their relationship with the throne, it opened up opportunities for the Hand of Chaos to cement their hold on the mind of the emperor. He needed only to be prodded in the right direction. And that prodding would come at the expense of the most iconic symbol of imperial power, the Knights of the Flashing Blade."

It took Marlae only a moment to make the connection.

"The assassination attempt."

Cairyn nodded.

"Exactly. The attempt, though it was not truly an attempt, was engineered by the Hand of Chaos for the soul purpose of framing Seraph Kore and eroding confidence in the Knights of the Flashing Blade to continue their role as the arm of justice for the empire. Once one of the Knights was cast in the light of a traitor, more quickly followed. Gregor Quicksilver, Jaccob Aldora, Leonora Wastri. They were all victims of the machinations of the Hand of Chaos and Talisia. But the real prize, the real target of all of this was Hannah Ironheart. She was the easiest to discredit once the accusations began to fly."

Cairyn paused for a long moment before continuing. She was ashamed of her role in the destruction of the foundations of the empire, but she comforted herself with the fact that everything she had done to this point had been necessary.

"It was not coincidence that the sister of the High Priestess of the Church of the Creator became a target for the amorous nature of the leader of the Dark Gods," Cairyn continued. "It was in fact an agent of the Hand of Chaos that introduced them. Pike's unguarded passions and inability to take no for an answer did the rest. With a sister as the queen of the Dark Gods, and the Knights of the Flashing Blade under increased scrutiny, Hannah Ironheart became a liability. She was branded a traitor quickly, which cast doubt on the whole of the Church of the Creator. Could they have been in league with the Dark Gods as well? How could the Church of the Creator truly act in the name of the Creator if they favored creatures that had been cast out of the Heavens."

Marlae nodded.

"Aerith Seth further complicated that."

Cairyn frowned. She had hoped not to have to recount this part of the tale.

"As a member of the Hand of Chaos, it was my responsibility to inform Talisia of the movements of any of the people of power in the areas I was to surveil. I was the one who told Talisia of Aerith Seth's appearance in the Heart of Stone, and it was Talisia who called down the Will to make his threats against yourself and Aerith. It was to be the final nail in Hannah Ironheart's coffin and would cement the disloyalty of the Church of the Creator in Kaitain's eyes."

Rhain's light voice interrupted the flow between the two women.

"And Hannah outsmarted you all."

Cairyn nodded while Marlae waited for further explanation.

"Once Hannah fell in with my father," Rhain continued, "she knew that she could no longer represent the Church. She was already being cast as a traitor to her beliefs as well as a traitor to the empire. Keeping her position as the High Priestess would only deepen the divide between the faithful and the throne. And so, during the confusion following the battle within the Heart of Stone, Hannah allowed everyone to believe that she was dead, and thus the leadership of the Church would pass on to her hand-picked successor. Of course, it would only serve to delay the inevitable, as the Creator's interference would clearly put the Church of the Creator in the camp of those opposed to Kaitain's continued rule."

Cairyn continued.

"And this, Marlae, is where your ascension comes into play. As the chosen ruler by the Creator, the so-named Divine Empress, the Church of the Creator had no choice but to accept your leadership. Now, Kaitain had all of the ammunition he needed to expand his ideological war against the Church. It gained incredible traction because of the fears of the people. But what the people were blind to was the fact that Kaitain had counted on the reaction that he got. He counted on the most horrific and violent people flocking to his banner. There were those who did not care about the war, did not care about the good of the empire, and did not care about anything other than enriching themselves and causing as much pain as possible. The Hand of Chaos was instrumental in helping to gather these dregs of humanity. Those that weren't loyal to Talisia directly were the kind of people that she would have recruited had the need arisen. Korin Melcab was the perfect leader for these villains, and the degradation and pain that they were the architects of deserves no further description."

Marlae frowned.

"And so here I sit," the young empress said softly, "the victim of the machinations of others whose plans existed long before I had a chance to even understand them."

"In that," Cairyn responded, "you and Quyhn have much in common. You are both pawns in a game that neither of you could hope to understand because you will never know all of the rules. It is a game being played beyond your capacity to impact, and you do not even have the freedom to stop playing. And so here we sit, trying to figure out what happens after the game is over. And while you may feel aggrieved, Quyhn's grievance is no less. Her role in this perverted game has cost her her home, her parents, and even her name. She is a Lorien not by choice, but because of the desires of a sadistic man who will stop at nothing to possess everything he sees. So quick to throw away one daughter just to replace her with another. Not because he wanted a daughter. Not because he wanted an heir. But because he could. It was the same way he took Dominique. The same way he thought he took Irene. The same way he tried to take every bit of power that he could seize. His unpunished crimes and vanity only proved to embolden him in his thirst, and made what came after that much more inevitable."

Marlae's heart hurt. She knew that she could not afford any confrontation with those who would help to build a better world than the one that Kaitain had chosen to perpetuate. The new Cadaria, if there was to be a new Cadaria, could not be built on blood, lies, and greed. It needed to be something more.

"And so," Marlae said finally, "how does Quyhn purpose that we move forward? What is the world that she sees that can exist after the fires of destruction have raged for so long?"

Cairyn unconsciously smoothed her dress and calmed her mind. Whatever Cairyn believed about the message she had come to deliver, there was one undeniable truth. Both Quyhn and Marlae could build a better world, if they were only given the chance.

"Quyhn believes that Cadaria can endure, but it will only endure if the legacy of the Lorien name is stricken from the minds of everyone who survives the war. There must be no trace of that name, and no trace of the crimes done for that name's glory. And so, as the first act of the new Cadarian Empire, there must be a strong denouncement of Kaitain Lorien and the abuses done in his name, and a promise that no such crimes will ever again be permitted to occur."

Marlae nodded.

"I agree to the denouncement," she said calmly, "but how can we guarantee to the people that such abuses will not occur once more?"

Cairyn gestured in Marlae's direction.

"By continuing what you've already started. Re-establish the Knights of the Flashing Blade, but remove the restrictions from its membership. The Knights should represent the best and brightest of the Empire, and they should come from all walks of life. Their charge should be reinstated to what it once was, the protection of the empire from all threats, both within and without, even if that means deposing the emperor or any of the rulers of any of the Great Kingdoms. The Knights of the Flashing Blade must be able to protect the soul of the empire, not just its body. Moreover, the Knights must renounce their ties to any of the Great Kingdoms, and must be citizens of the Empire first and foremost."

Rhain nodded.

"A sensible enough request."

Marlae nodded as well.

"It is indeed. But whatever charter is created for the Knights of the Flashing Blade must include provisions whereby a majority of the Knights must agree on any course of action, the actual number of course can be negotiated later. These actions must also be done openly with full transparency so that no one member of the Knights can take unilateral action against the leadership of the empire without consequence."

Cairyn smiled.

"I'm sure that Quyhn would agree to such a stipulation."

Marlae nodded.

"Good," Cairyn continued, "now we can get down to the important matters."

Here Cairyn took a short breath, let the smile fade from her lips and her eyes, and when she spoke, she spoke with all the power that she once possessed as the Queen of Trelon. This may have been the last opportunity she had to do something in the capacity of a leader of men and women, and she wanted to make sure she did justice to all of those that had once called her their queen and all that had held any respect for the Binosear name.

"Under the following terms, Quyhn Ravenheart Lorien is prepared to recognize Marlae Tamerlane's claim to the throne of the Cadarian Empire. Firstly, in order to give legitimacy to those actions already taken by Quyhn Ravenheart Lorien as the recognized heir to the throne of Cadaria, Marlae Tamerlane agrees to appoint Quyhn Ravenheart Lorien to the position of Voice of the Empress with the full privileges and responsibilities thereof. Secondly, in order to ensure that all negotiations and promises made on Quyhn's behalf by Dominique Lorien are guaranteed, Quyhn Ravenheart Lorien requests that Dominique Lorien be granted the position of High Councilor to the Divine Empress. Thirdly, the proclamation that Quyhn Ravenheart Lorien is a ward of the empire is to be vacated and her name restored. And lastly, the marriage between Dominique Lorien and Kaitain Lorien is to be immediately dissolved, and her name restored."

Marlae considered for a quick moment. The requests were certainly understandable, and more to the point were not at all unreasonable.

"Those terms are acceptable, provided that both Quyhn and Dominique make public proclamations of support. They need to acknowledge that I am the rightful ruler of the Cadarian Empire, and that there was never a struggle for power. The survivors of this war must believe that we have been a united front against my father."

Cairyn nodded.

"Of course."

Marlae took a deep relieved breath and leaned back in the chair.

"I thought that was going to be much more complicated."

Rhain clicked her tongue.

"Mortal problems are going to seem quite simple for a time, but that doesn't make them any less important. What is important now is that everyone that will be involved in the world that will follow does not take it for granted. If what the Dark Gods plan comes to pass, there will be no one other than the humans of this world to determine their destiny. There will be no Dark Gods, no Children of the Creator, no angels, no Servants, and no creatures from other worlds whose goal is to remake reality in their image. It will only be you and what you build here."

Marlae considered for a moment.

"Then I would ask one condition of Quyhn, should my worst fears come to pass."

Cairyn nodded, waiting for Marlae to continue.

"I can't be sure," Marlae began, "but I think before Elwyne's soul was bonded to mine, that I died. I think Jaccob Aldora brought me back from the brink of death, and I think he did it at the behest of the Creator. In the end though, if the Creator is defeated, and all of the vestiges of Him are removed from Creation, it may require my death as well. If that fear is realized, and I am struck down along with all of the other beings that owe their existence to the Creator, then I would request that Quyhn rule this empire in my stead as justly as she can. There is no one else that I would rather have take my place, and I am sure the empire would be in good hands under her watchful gaze."

Rhain's face was expressionless, but Cairyn could feel the heartache radiating from the woman. It was clear that she had not considered such an eventuality, but now that the thought had been given form in words, it was the only thing she could think about. Marlae seemed relieved that she had been able to give her fears voice, and her eyes latched onto Cairyn's waiting for the answer that she hoped would come. Cairyn, for her part, had a great deal of respect for what Marlae had said and the courage that she was showing in the face of her uncertainty. Responsibility for a legacy was never easy, and Marlae continued to show grace in the face of adversity.

"I think that regardless of what happens," Cairyn said finally, "that the Cadarian Empire will be in good hands."

INTERLUDE 1

Defenders of the Innocent

Gwydeon

Gwydeon Sandar had begun to feel as though he had lost some of the subtlety of his former life. Perhaps it was the wings, perhaps it was the aura or power, or perhaps it was just the fact that he was constantly put in the position of delivering bad or dire news. Whatever the reason, of course, the truth of it could not be denied. No sooner had he returned to New Aradon from his meeting with some of the most powerful beings on the planet, he had begun making demands and delivering more bad news. Fortunately, he had not had to deliver the news alone, and had the support of his newly returned wife to help take the sting from his words. And yet, when the orders were delivered, the twins, as they often did, accepted the information as though they had already known it. Mirana and Liara were strange and at times maddening young women, and Gwydeon found himself comparing them to another set of twins that he had grown to know over several centuries. Like Rael and Trece, it seemed that Mirana and Liara were constantly in each other's heads, knowing the content of each other's thoughts the moment each thought was formed. In their short time together, Gwydeon had seen the girls have whole conversations with mere eye contact, and Midarin had regaled him with several stories of their silent clandestine scheming. Perhaps in another place and in another time, they would have been formidable warriors for the Light. But now, much to his shame, Gwydeon was reducing the girls to bait. The thought galled him, but the Ranthall twins took the assignment in their own stride, saying their goodbyes and creating a portal into the unknown without a single protestation.

But that had not been the only surprise waiting for Gwydeon, and the news of Isabella's unexpected departure weighed on Gwydeon's mind. Naturally, there was only one place that she could be going, and that was to seek out her father and to help him on whatever suicidal errand he had found himself on this time. Of course, this brought Gwydeon back to Rhain's words, and the way that she characterized the path that Logan was walking. This time it felt different, and somewhere inside of himself, Gwydeon began to believe for the first time that he would never see his old friend again.

Loss was not new to the so-called Dark Gods. In fact, Gwydeon wondered if there were any creatures that roamed on any of the Creator's worlds that had experienced as much loss as Gwydeon and his compatriots had. So many friends and family had fallen by the wayside, victims of the eternal war between a father and his children. Whole worlds consumed by the darkness of their indifference. Yes, those were the impersonal losses, so many faceless and nameless innocents cut down when the world of Onea was destroyed, and so many more in the mindless and senseless slaughter caused by the Children, Dorovar, and their agents on Espre. But beyond the impersonal losses, there had been the very personal ones, and there was no greater exemplar of this than Gwydeon and Midarin's own son, Nathaniel.

Just as there had been two version of Gwydeon Sandar and Midarin Rice, there had been two versions of their son. One version of Nathaniel was a sweet and smart young man who knew that the weight of the world would one day fall upon his shoulders. He had loving friends, a world of light and love around him, and the greatest burden of preparing for the battle ahead had been assumed by another. He grew up in the protected womb of the Light, and he had been the one who could have been the true savior that the prophecies told of. And he was all of this without knowing the love of his father who had been cut down in battle before his birth. Gwydeon never really knew that Nathaniel, never got to feel the love of his life and the carefree character of his laugh. It was a fact that weighed on Gwydeon's soul; a loss that could not be put into words, a loss that was hard to rationalize. Because there had been another Nathaniel, a Nathaniel that Gwydeon took great pride in raising, teaching, and molding to be what the world would need him to one day be. And despite the horrors that constantly surrounded him, that Nathaniel, the one that would one day call himself Nathan Sandar, seemed a genuinely happy young man who could separate himself from the darkness that threatened to envelop them every moment. But perhaps, that was what Gwydeon wanted to see.

In that world, the world called the Dark Mirror, death and loss was a constant. Practically every day there was another raid by one of the members of the phasia, and every raid brought more loss of innocent life. The farmers and common people of the war weary world sought refuge in one of the last bastions of the Light left in Brea. The capital city of the Kingdom of Brea, along with the city of Trelon, were two of the last major cities that had not fallen to the advances of the phasia and the forces of Shau-ling. Because of this, as the incursions moved from the major cities of the world into the smaller villages, refugees from every corner of the world flocked to these supposedly safe havens. Gwydeon and Midarin welcomed all of the refugees that made it to the gates of Brea, with only one condition; those that could fight would be expected to help with the defense of the city. Very few of the refugees had an issue with that condition, as so many died even trying to get to Brea. However, just because the refugees made it to Brea didn't mean that they were safe. As talented as Gwydeon and Midarin were on their own fighting against the forces of the Shadow, it was something else entirely coordinating the efforts of hundreds of people in the defense of a city. Many of the refugees had never used a weapon against a living opponent before, but necessity made warriors where peaceful beings once walked. There was nobility to be found in avoiding conflict for the sake of one's beliefs, and while that nobility was respected in the abstract, it was difficult to accept when the lives of others would be lost through inaction. Gwydeon and Midarin tried their best to respect everyone, but that respect quickly degraded when life was on the line.

Whatever challenges that the former farmers and artists found in their new roles as defenders of humanity, they performed beyond any expectation. Time and time again they turned away the advances of fearsome beasts that gave no quarter and fought to the death. From the time that he could hold a sword, Nathaniel was there beside his parents helping to coordinate the defenses and protect the lives of the innocent. Perhaps that had been a mistake. Perhaps Gwydeon and Midarin should have protected their son more from the horrors of war. The one truth of battle against the forces of the Shadow was that people would die. After every defense there were funerals, tears, and questions. How long could the defenders of the light and the innocent hold out against the relentless assaults? How many more lives would be lost? Was defending the last bastion of light even worth it? Death spurred on hopelessness, and there were some that could not see a future. No matter how many battles were won, no matter how many refugees were saved, even temporarily, there was no victory waiting at the end of the war. Perhaps this hopelessness had entered Nathaniel's heart. Perhaps he saw that no matter the abilities that he had been granted as the *Coromor* of the third generation of the prophecies, there was nothing he could do to prevent the death of so many innocents. In the end, whatever the reason, Nathaniel's heart was swayed by the honeyed words that dripped from Emries' tongue, corrupting the young man and pulling him from the path his family wanted him to walk. From that moment forward, Nathaniel died, and Nathan was born. Nathan was a cold and brutally efficient killer, visiting Emries' vengeance on any and all who stood between the *Coromor* and his appointed destiny, even if those obstacles proved to be allies.

Nathan was lost to them, and when the former *Coromors* were brought back to life as Emries' warriors on Espre, it was Nathan and not Nathaniel that appeared to support the aims of his former patron. Now, with one child already lost to them, Gwydeon had unquestioningly sent his remaining child into the very heart of danger. Gwydeon wasn't sure what bothered him more, the fact that he had been so willing to accept Camille's role in the battle that was to come, or the fact that she was going to be fighting, and he was going to be away from the battle in the safety of the walls of New Aradon. Perhaps it was arrogance. Perhaps it was habit. No matter the cause of the feelings, Gwydeon was a warrior at heart and that part of him longed to be in the center of the storm that was about to strike. Yes, the rational part of his mind understood that despite the fact that both he and Midarin had more combined military experience than anyone at the Heart of Stone with the exception of the remaining members of the Brotherhood of Phasia, their greater value in the war would be to ensure the protection of the innocents as they had done in the Dark Mirror. It was a difficult realization to accept. And try as he might, Gwydeon could not completely find peace with it. And so, while Midarin attended to inspecting the defenses of the fortification, Gwydeon retreated to the peace of their private quarters and began running through ancient blade exercises to quiet his mind.

As his body moved from familiar form to familiar form, Gwydeon tried to disconnect his mind from the worries that plagued it. So many lives had been lost, so many more lives shattered. When Onea was lost to them, Gwydeon wondered for a long time whether or not there was something more to be found beyond that life. Yes, Gwydeon and Midarin had been spared the fire that consumed Onea, as had many of their friends. But for what purpose? Why did they still go on? In the early days of their ascension, Gwydeon obsessed over the possibilities. The Creator had rewarded them, but for what? They had not won. They had not saved their world. Both Halicon and Emries still lived, regardless of their failures to make good on their part of the war. It didn't take long for Gwydeon to understand, however. The Creator viewed the heroes of Onea as an oddity, a random variant that he did not anticipate or fully understand. Perhaps that was the true folly of the Creator's apathetic approach to the creations of his Children. The Creator wanted Gwydeon and his compatriots close in order to study them and to see what they were capable of. He watched them as they transitioned from mortal life to the mundanity of the divine existence. Saw how they tried to create a piece of what they had known in a place so foreign to their frame of reference. They even tried to carry on their legacies by having children. In the end, the more time they gave the Creator to study them, the more they played into his plans. They had been so stupid, so blind, and so careless. Perhaps it was the grief from the loss of their world, or perhaps it was the hubris from standing toe to toe with two of the Children of the Creator. Whatever the reason, they allowed themselves to be duped by the greatest villain in existence, the Creator Himself.

Gwydeon's movements became broken and fragmented, the discord in his mind flowing through his muscles. He stopped the movements and slammed his fist into the wall in an uncharacteristic display of frustration. He didn't pour any power into the strike, and so his hand was left throbbing like his mind. If only they had been able to see it sooner. If only they had had all of the pieces of the puzzle before things got out of hand and they fell willingly into the Creator's trap. It started of course with the children. Gwydeon knew that now. Mirana and Liara as well as Camille were just cogs in a greater plan. They were weapons just waiting to be used by the Creator. Traps ready to be sprung at the last moment to ensure the Creator's victory and the death of the entirety of Creation. One of the things that the Creator had learned about the heroes of Onea was that their strength came from their faith in one another. Their reliance and the loyalty and their love had pulled them through the darkness and made them a match for anything that either Halicon or Emries could throw at them. If the Creator could find a way to turn that trust and loyalty against them, it would damage their ability to fight. What may have started with the three children born in the Heavens, did not end with them. The Creator had access to the souls of all of the heroes that had fallen on Onea, and in time he would find ways to weaponize those souls. But the depths of the Creator's depravity would be on display far before those steps became necessary.

Gwydeon moved to the window, his blade discarded on the bed. He looked out onto the innocents who were seeking shelter in the hope offered by New Aradon. He remembered when that hope took another form, wrapped in a simple banner with an ancient icon upon it. Whether it was Cedric Binosear, or Logan Ranthall, or Nathaniel Sandar, the *Coromor* offered hope to a people who were terrorized by ancient evils. But it was not just the men who carried the name given them by Emries in his naked attempts to thwart the laws of the Creator, it was the men and women who walked the path with those heroes who gave them strength. Ascended, fallen, or faded, they were no less important than the chosen heroes themselves. The Creator began to understand that after watching the way that the ascended heroes of Onea began to infect the Heavens with their touch. Even those beings who were hollowed out by the touch of the Creator as his Servants carried with them remnants of the plague that was human heroism. Even the dragons, the supposedly incorruptible ancient beings would feel the tides of change as soon as mortal feet touched the pristine halls of the dominion of the Creator. It was a contingency that Creator had counted on.

Over the course of his life, Gwydeon had seen the deceptions perpetrated by the powerful and the wicked alike. He saw up close the machinations of the phasia and the servants of Emries. But whatever grudging respect that Gwydeon had for the schemes of Emries and the others who had tried to dominate the wills of human beings on Onea, he stood in awe of the most subtle and misunderstood manipulation of all time. They had been so blind to not see the truth sooner. How was it that a whole world needed to be sacrificed to keep two members of the Children from acting directly against each other, and yet one could lead an insurrection in the Heavens and strike down one of their own unchallenged? For thousands of years, Emries and Halicon danced around each other, letting the phasia, the *Erieal* and innocent humans kill each other because the Creator forbid them from acting directly against one another. For thousands of years, Gwydeon and the rest of the Dark Gods who lived through Talisia's attack on the Heavens believed that she had discovered some way to thwart the Creator's rules in order to kill her ancient enemy. She had enlisted the dragons to help her in her coup, and would have made a move on the golden throne had it not been for the intervention of the brave heroes who were unable to save their world but were able to defend the Heavens. But it was all a lie; the precursor to what would become the final act of a war that had been raging for countless millennia. The first of many steps that would bring about the end of Creation and the forced emergence of the Living Cosmos. The Creator's jealousy had to be sated, and his need for the understanding of His own origins had gone without answer for too long. The Living Cosmos had shown that it cared about humanity through its manifestation in Aerith Seth, sparking the Creator to enact his genocidal endgame. The creation of Espre, the fall of the Dark Gods, the manipulation of the Children and their petty schemes for ascendency. The whole plan was started with the very specific members of the People of the Dragon and the People of the Ram who found their places in the Heavens following the fall of Onea.

Gwydeon and Midarin were chosen because Midarin was pregnant with their second child, and the Creator wanted that advantage. Wolf Ranthall and Lissa Terian were chosen because of their connection to two of the most powerful families on Onea, and their connection to both Aerith Seth and to Halicon. Then there was Evan Sinn and Meredith Heron, with Evan purely chosen because of his tie to Aerith Seth. Pike was selected because he had been touched by both Halicon and Emries, and had renounced the powers that had been given to him as a member of the *Erieal.* Jerrard was a less obvious choice, perhaps it was because he was the child of one of Halicon's creations, or perhaps there was some other motivation. Whatever the reason, Jerrard had proven time and time again to be the conscience of the group. Last was Sabrina Binosear, the granddaughter of the great Cedric Binosear also touched by Aerith Seth. Why didn't they see it then? Evan and Sabrina both carried the mantle of Aerith Seth directly. Wolf Ranthall was the son of Logan Ranthall who also bore Aerith's mantle. Gwydeon had already been coopted by divine power with his position as the Brother of Angels, while Jerrard Mystic and Lissa Terian directly tied their lineage back to the phasia. The phasia were direct creations of Halicon, and stood apart from humanity. It was possible that the Creator wanted to see if that lineage made them different from humans in the way that they could be manipulated. Either way, the motivations were so clear now all these millennia later.

With these wildcards in place, the Creator enacted the most diabolical portion of his plan. At the time, having seen the pure hatred that existed between Halicon and Emries, it seemed more than plausible that such enmity existed between Talisia and Pyrrus and that it could motivate Talisia to attempt to circumvent the strictures placed on them by the Creator. But as the phasia had underestimated exactly how much that Halicon knew about their activities and their plans, the heroes of Onea had completely underestimated exactly how much the Creator knew about the plans, thoughts, and motivations of his Children. But the most important factor was the one that the mortals could never have guessed at, and only was uncovered by Logan's efforts to determine the nature of the Creator's endgame. The Creator had the ability to influence, if not completely direct the actions of his Children the same way that he directed the actions of the angelic host. And so, when Talisia launched her assault on the Heavens, it was done at the behest and direction of the Creator. It was all an elaborate ruse to induce the heroes of Onea into formulating their own rebellion. There was just enough plausibility in every step of the ruse and manipulation that the former humans did not stop to question. For thousands of years the wool had been pulled over their collective eyes, and they continued day after day to advance the Creator's agenda.

Gwydeon moved away from the window, taking back up his blade and returning to his exercises. Rage was building within him, and the more he looked at all of the events since their ascension to the Heavens, the more he saw obvious moments. Perhaps they shouldn't have been able to see through the Creator's manipulations, but they should have at least asked questions. The mistake they made was thinking that they understood how the mind and motivations of the Creator worked. As one form flowed into the next, Gwydeon wondered how they could have been so wrong and overconfident. They saw the malevolence of the Children, and yet somehow believed that those qualities did not exist within the Creator. Fortunately for them all, there were enough of the former heroes who were not duped. Logan, Aerith, and Bryn had already begun unraveling many of the lies of the Creator's universe, but it seemed that even they were not immune to manipulation. After what had occurred with Camille, Gwydeon began to suspect that the actions that Sabrina Binosear took as the Spirit were not hers alone. Had they known more, had they had the perspective necessary to understand all of the moving parts, they would have viewed Sabrina's information with more skepticism. In fact, as Gwydeon looked at his own part at the beginning of the conflict on Espre, he realized that he too should have been more suspicious. They all knew that the Spirit was unique among the Servants in that the Creator could pour His own power into the body of the Spirit. How could they have ever been sure that they were actually talking to Sabrina and not the Creator using Sabrina's voice and memories? Gwydeon questioned if Sabrina was ever the one that Gwydeon dealt with in those early days. And, if she was that much under the Creator's sway during that phase of the war, who was to say that she was not still completely at the whim of the Creator once she was removed from her post as the Spirit?

In the end, Gwydeon knew that they should have questioned everything. And so Gwydeon's mind went to the twins. What if the attempt to procure the twins on their way to Aldere was yet another elaborate deception? What if everything the Creator was doing was to make sure that the twins were in the Heart of Stone when this massive battle took place? Had the twins been obscuring their true level of power all these years? Could they have been the catalyst that would begin the march to oblivion? Gwydeon could not tolerate the thought that he would have yet again played into the schemes of the Creator. He knew that he had given his word to Aerith that he would stay out of the war, that he would focus on saving the innocents, but he could not stand idly by and watch as decisions that he made brought an end to everything that they had worked and sacrificed for. He would have to break his word to Aerith. He could not live with himself otherwise.

Gwydeon's thoughts immediately went to Midarin. What would she say? Would she tell him that he was thinking too much? Would she tell him that he was lost in his own sense of honor and ego to see clearly? Would she tell him that the twins would never allow themselves to be used after everything that happened with Camille and their mother? Perhaps she would be right. Even with that, he could not leave it to chance. Beyond that, though, he knew that if he was making the decision to join the battle at the Heart of Stone, he was making it for both of them. Midarin would never allow him to go into battle again without her by his side. And if they did go, that would leave New Aradon largely defenseless. Camille and the twins were already at the Heart, and Gwydeon and Midarin would soon be joining them. Isabella had disappeared, and Rhionna was untrained in the use of her abilities. Should the angelic host decide to strike at New Aradon, there would be nothing that would prevent them from leveling the newly constructed refuge. So many of their remaining assets had already been committed to the battle at the Heart, and though Rhain had requested that Jeroch and Bryn leave the Heart before the fight began, Gwydeon knew in his heart that neither would walk away from the battle. That left only one member of the phasia out of the battle, and Gwydeon could not ask Saurn to aid in the defense of the innocent. Gwydeon had to hope that the Creator was going to commit the majority of his forces to the assault of the Heart, and that the refugees of New Aradon would escape the Creator's very watchful eye. With all of the important pieces away from the innocents, perhaps the Creator would not view Quyhn as important enough to remove from the board. Gwydeon understood immediately that there were far too many ifs and possibilities for him to ever feel comfortable with. However, there was not another choice.

The Heart was where Gwydeon would be able to find redemption for the sins and oversights of the past, and he would give every last drop of blood and sweat in his body before he would allow another one of the Creator's machinations to come to fruition.

Camille

The Heart of Stone felt different to Camille since the last time she had been there. Of course, that had been a figurative and literal lifetime ago. Camille's life was so different before she was dispatched by Pike Rhuiden to Albitonin as the escort for Tess Annis. In fact, Camille had begun to divide her life into clear and distinct segments. The first segment, and perhaps the one that she longed for the most was her time in the Heavens when she was just a little girl. While Camille had the distinction of being the first child born in the Heavens, she was not the first child born to her parents, nor to the heroes of Onea. And while Camille's parents never made her feel as though she was the second child, she could feel the weight of the loss like a shadow in her early years. Her parents rarely spoke of Nathaniel in her presence, at least not until the final days in the Heavens, but Camille felt his presence in her life regardless. Like most of the Dark Gods, there were two versions of her mother and of her brother. In the Light Reality on Onea, Midarin Rice had been a central figure in the forces of the Light, marshalling as many forces as she could to assist her son Nathaniel, the *Coromor* of the third generation of the prophecies. As the recognized Queen of Brea, Midarin had nearly limitless resources at her disposal to build an army to repel the forces loyal to Shau-ling. Working with her old allies who were in control of Marcwell and Trelon, it seemed as though the forces of the Light were in as good as possible position to be victorious against Shau-ling. Unfortunately for the forces of the Light, conventional wisdom seemed to consistently work against them. Pike Rhuiden became so absorbed in being the savior of the world that he became the thing that nearly ended it, and the phasia were almost able to tear the People of the Ram apart from the inside out by igniting jealousy and revealing damaging secrets. Midarin had often said that the People of the Ram and the forces of the Light were successful in their battle against the evils of Onea in spite of themselves, not because of any bravery or cunning. Perhaps it was because they were overconfident, or perhaps it was because they were so unwilling to accept that they could ever be defeated. But what Midarin had always counted as the true cause of their near catastrophic failure was the loss of their soul.

Gwydeon Sandar had died in the Hall of Terrors fighting the Lord Shadow Jeroch Yetre during the second generation of the prophecies in the Light Reality. Few would have said it was possible that one man was enough to turn the tide of a war of such an epic scale, but Gwydeon was not an ordinary man. Gwydeon represented the very thing that had become the cause of the war between the factions of the Heavens and the Children of the Creator. For millennia, the Children of the Creator had been fighting their ideological war, trying to prove that their view of Creation was the correct one. But what none of them had been able to grasp was that nothing they created would ever capture that which had no definition. The Creator himself did not understand everything about the nature of Creation, therefore the Children could not understand either. The Children, like the Servants, were mere facets, imperfect reflections, of everything that the Creator was, and so they shared all of his limitations, beyond those that were imposed upon them. Like the Creator they were assured that they were right in everything that they did, regardless of the damage inflicted. There was no doubt, there was no fear, there was only the single-minded devotion to victory. In time, those things that the Children made began to grow beyond what the Children themselves could understand. This quality, which eventually became colloquially known as the soul, grew unchecked and uncontrolled despite all of the Children's efforts to eradicate or manipulate it. In time, the Children began to see a kind of power in the existence of the soul, one that could be utilized for their own purposes, and perhaps one that could be used to prove their definition of Creation. If successful in proving the truth of their vision, a Child might have been able to unseat the Creator from the Golden Throne and remake everything in the perverted image of either Evil, Good, Order, Chaos, or Balance. That was the very thing that the Dark Gods and the heroes of both Onea and Espre were fighting to prevent.

What Gwydeon represented, and what he tried to instill into his daughter in their time together in the Heavens was a cognizance of all that was happening around them, even if it could not be understood or believed. Gwydeon, unlike many of the other Dark Gods who continued to fight against the tyranny of the Creator, had not begun his path in the war with any supernatural abilities. He liked to say that all he fought with in that first year was his sword and his wits. While the sword was important, his wits proved to be even more important. The original enemy of the People of the Dragon, the heroes of Gwydeon's time, were the phasia. Gwydeon often told Camille stories about the ferocity of the phasia and the army of creatures that served them, but instead of focusing on their prowess in battle, he would spend more time on their tactical ability as well as their intricate schemes and plans. Camille often found herself shocked at the near reverence that Gwydeon held for his opponents and their abilities. When she finally worked up the courage to ask her father why he held such evil creatures in such high regard, it had been her mother and not her father that had provided the answer. Midarin explained that the phasia though crafted to be destroyers of worlds were not inherently evil. Yes, they were designed to accentuate all of the worst aspects of humanity, but even in that, love, compassion, intellect, and wisdom could not be bred out of them. In fact, it was these very qualities that allowed the phasia to understand humanity and to exploit its weaknesses.

When Emries crafted the people of Onea, he crafted them to be loyal to him and to his vision of how Creation should function. Where Raenera believed in total and absolute Order in all things, Emries had the opposite vision. He believed that allowing his creations to follow their own paths, even when those paths were not in the best interests of the whole, actually increased the control he had over them. And so, this chaotic self-serving world with Emries fixed firmly at the center as the Creator was filled with sycophants and mindless servants who would do anything they were ordered to by their Creator. This included, at least in the first phases of the war, throwing themselves by the thousands against superior forces all in the name of their Creator. If Raenera's world was a perfectly tuned instrument whose parts worked together to create harmony, Emries' world was a discordant cacophony with a barely intelligible pattern. Death on Raenera's world was measured and necessary, while on Onea, it was bloody, unpredictable, and often tragically unnecessary. It spoke to the difference in respect that the two Children of the Creator had for their creations. It could be said that Raenera loved those that she created, if she loved at all. Emries viewed his creations as tools, disposable nuisances that could easily be replaced when he ran out of fodder for his experiments. However, even Emries realized that the manner in which he was fighting his war against his brother Shau-ling was unsustainable, and while he could keep creating humans by the tens of thousands, it did not allow for the evolution of the species necessary to combat the phasia on their terms. And so, he changed tactics, and decided instead to play a longer game.

The original iteration of the *Erieal* proved to be the pattern that Emries would use to guide the evolution of the human race on Onea. While Emries would retain the necessity of duty and loyalty to the tenants of the Creator, he would increase the range of this duty and loyalty to the whole of the human race and to the idea of the Creator, not just to Emries specifically. It proved to be true that the idea of the Creator was just as powerful a motivation, if not more so, for his followers than the actual personification of the role. But Emries realized that duty and loyalty on their own were not enough. There was another aspect to that loyalty, and that was a measure of accountability to one's beliefs that could only come from the heart and the soul. This was the part of the makeup of the evolved Onean humans that Emries would end up miscalculating, and it would lead to his downfall. The moment that Emries allowed for personal accountability to override blind loyalty he allowed for his creations to outgrow their blind loyalty to his cause. Once the truth was able to break through the wall of lies, the very creatures that Emries relied upon to make his revenge against his brother possible, became the instruments of his demise.

Beyond personal accountability, when Emries instilled within the evolved versions of Onea's humans unlimited compassion and love for his fellow human, it created a catalyst that would allow humans to transcend their love of the Creator with their love for their fellow humans. This catalyst alone was not enough to spark disloyalty outright however, but it was an important piece of the puzzle. The other piece proved to be the nearly limitless courage that Emries poured into his creations, the kind of courage necessary to combat demons like Shau-ling and the phasia. What in theory would make every human a formidable warrior would eventually make them the perfect revolutionaries, provided these qualities were expressed in just the right balance. This all came to fruition in the People of the Dragon, the group of unwitting humans that would spearhead the revolution against the Children of the Creator and eventually the Creator himself. However, in the end, Emries was not the only Child of the Creator who found that his creations grew beyond their control. Halicon in time would find that his creations, the phasia, would soon fall to the same rebellious tendencies of Emries' humans, but not precisely for the same reasons.

Halicon spent many centuries watching Emries before committing to a plan of attack. He studied the new humans that his brother had created and analyzed their strengths and weaknesses. Even in the earliest iterations of the humans that served their so-called Creator, there were attributes that could be accentuated and ultimately exploited. Unlike many of the beings that had been created by the Children of the Creator in the previous acts of their ideological conflict, Emries had set about making his creations intelligent enough to understand the laws that were passed down to them as well as intelligent enough to question those laws and how they were to be applied. The mindless creatures of the past would obey what they were told, never straying beyond the boundaries that were set out for them. The new humans, and the *Erieal* that would follow them needed a certain amount of autonomous thought and reasoning ability in order to properly serve the ever-growing hunger of their Creator. This was the first of Emries' "improvements" to the human race that Shau-ling would seek to exploit. For the phasia, this intellect became personified in three different ways by three of the founding members of the Brotherhood.

The first was raw knowledge and the thirst to know as much as possible regardless of the cost. Just as Halicon had studied his enemy patiently learning all that needed to be learned to defeat them, he expected that his phasia would do the same. This unquenchable thirst for knowledge was personified by the Lady Leopard, Ellis Chandara. Another facet of knowledge came in the form of directly weaponizing knowledge against an opponent. This could be more subtle than force of arms, but no less effective. It could be called manipulation or control, but whatever the name, the result was the same. Bryn Rhaine, the Lady Fox was the perfect expression of this tenant of the phasia, and she showed great mastery in using the passions and the failings of the human race against themselves. Set firmly between these two mental powers was Grawn Aplee, the Lord Shark. There were those that confined the term strength to physical imposition and prowess. However, what Emries had learned through observing not only Emries' creations, but also the creations of Raenera and Talisia was that strength could also be expressed through mental acuity and the application of intellectual prowess. While Grawn was physically imposing, he was as equally imposing with his mental capabilities. Together with Bryn and Ellis, Grawn was the pivotal weapon of the triumvirate, leveraging the insights and manipulations of his compatriots to win battles both on the battlefields and in diplomatic circles.

The remaining three members of the first iteration of the Brotherhood of Phasia were greater expressions of the courage that Emries thought would be the key to the humans' defeat of all of Emries' enemies. Kamen, as the first member of the Brotherhood of Phasia, had to be the personification of everything that Shau-ling needed the phasia to be in the upcoming war with Emries and those loyal to him. Halicon knew his brother well, and knew that Emries would stop at nothing in his quest to prove his vision of Creation was the only correct one. And so, Halicon needed his phasia to be able to stand against Emries and his fanatics no matter what came. Kamen was that personification of will. Kamen would do what needed to be done, no matter the cost, in order to be victorious. The same could be said for the Lord Shadow, Jeroch Yetre. Jeroch was the personification of determination, a warrior who would not quit regardless of the trial. No matter the task he was given, he would persevere, seeing it through to its conclusion, and making sure that that conclusion was the one that was expected. Finally, there was Aryx Terian. Aryx was made after Emries' greatest flaw, his arrogant belief that no matter what he put his mind to, he would succeed. Aryx would be committed to the goal of the defeat of Emries and his followers, and he would use every insight, and every truth behind the lies and misrepresentations to achieve that goal. However, in time, these were the very attributes that would allow the phasia to begin to ask questions about the nature of the war and begin to unravel the inconsistencies in the story that Halicon told them.

Much in the same way that Emries and Talisia were able to exploit the inherent failings in Raenera's Perfect Order to corrupt Dorovar into the downfall of the world of Loinn, Emries' creations, once exposed to the true nature of the war between the Children of the Creator, threw off the yoke of their servitude and sought to take control of their own destinies. Halicon's children, his tools in the war against his brother, became that which they beheld and fought alongside Emries' former chosen heroes and sought to shake the Heavens. Together they nearly succeeded. Both Emries and Halicon had their eyes opened to the folly of their paths, the failures in their designs. While each was humbled by their failures, they handled those failures very differently. Halicon allowed for the fact that his way was perhaps not the correct way and that it was possible for his children to grow beyond him and his vision. Emries however viewed the growth of his creations as a betrayal, one that would meet with a righteous vengeance that would know no limit. Even as those rebellious children found their new home in the brilliant light of the Heavens, Emries was plotting their downfall.

Gwydeon made sure that his daughter Camille was armed with all of the information she could absorb about Emries and Halicon. Though Gwydeon did not have much information about the other members of the Children of the Creator before his ascension to the Heavens, he made sure that he learned all that he could during his time there. While Gwydeon may not have been the only member of the soon-to-be Dark Gods who saw the war that was coming, he took the responsibility of gathering information very seriously. Whether it was the abilities of the warrior angels and the rest of the divine host, or the ideological dispositions of the other members of the Children of the Creators, or the dragons that were as old as Creation itself, Gwydeon absorbed as much information as possible. He also relied upon old allies to gain different perspectives, including those from Evan Sinn and Sabrina Binosear. All of this he passed onto his confederates from Onea. Some took this information more seriously than others, and Gwydeon was constantly frustrated that Pike did not spend more time preparing for what was to come. But as much as he thought he knew, Gwydeon was not prepared for the insurrection that Talisia mounted upon the Heavens that lead to the death of Pyrrus and the splintering of the dragons. Once the insurrection was over, and the aftermath shook the Heavens, Gwydeon and the rest of the heroes from Onea saw only one path.

And that was the start of Camille's second life. Her life as a member of the Dark Gods, a life that she was unprepared for. The first thing that struck Camille upon being cast down to Espre was how dark everything was. In the Heavens, there was a light that pervaded everything. In the world of mortals, there was darkness and shadow everywhere. Beyond that, the mortal world was also very dirty and there were smells that her senses were unprepared for. Everything in the Heavens was clean and sterile, and for the first few weeks, Camille felt as though she needed to bathe dozens of times a day just to feel clean. In the end though, the differences were minor. The true adjustment came after Gwydeon's attempt to stem the tides of war between the Cadarians and the Dark Gods at the cost of his own life. Camille suddenly found herself without her father, her moral compass, in a world full of hurt and anger. For a time, Camille retreated in upon herself, not wanting to leave her mother's side. Those were difficult years of adjustment, but in a way, it allowed her to do exactly as her father had always instructed. She tried to see through the moment, see through the pain and the anguish to the heart of the matter. She saw the tactical advantage that her father's sacrifice had gained, and she had also seen one of the painful truths of war. All wars had loss. There were no clean victories, and in every triumph was a grain of defeat. What's more, Camille knew that Gwydeon's loss was just the first of many to come, and she would need to prepare herself for the dark and bloody days ahead.

Camille knew that she had power, power that was different than the other Dark Gods, perhaps even superior to them. Gwydeon never trusted the powers that he had been granted as the Brother of Angels, and he passed that mistrust down to his daughter. In Gwydeon's mind, anything that had been granted by the Creator or one of the Children could just as easily have been taken away, and so it was always better to rely on one's own native abilities and tenacity. That was much easier a proposition for the other members of the heroes from Onea who became ascended beings, as they had known a life without powers. Camille had never known life without her abilities, but Gwydeon fought hard to teach his daughter how to fight without them. Once he was gone, Midarin continued that training as best she could, enlisting the help of accomplished warriors like Aryx and Diana Terian and their daughter Lissa. When the next generation of powered children came into the circle of the Dark Gods, Camille tried to pass the teachings of her father on, with varying levels of success. The twins, Mirana and Liara had received similar cautions about their powers when they were in the Heavens, and so they were more than willing to continue to live as much as they could without the use of their powers. The difference between Camille and the twins however was the fact that while Camille's powers expressed themselves in the more martial and physical realms, the twins found their abilities more in the sphere of the mental and the spiritual. Despite centuries together, Camille still did not have a full understanding of the way that the twins' powers worked. Liara's intuitive knowledge about the nature of power and the way each powered individual connected to the others was equal parts disturbing and mysterious. As to Mirana, her mind worked in a similar way to Gwydeon's with one key difference. Gwydeon could analyze any information that he could and find a tactical solution, given enough time. Where Mirana's ability surpassed Gwydeon's was in the fact that while Gwydeon was limited to being able to analyze only what he knew, Mirana seemingly could draw upon information that she could not have personally known. It was as though at times that she were connected to the collective knowledge of the Heavens and every person living or that had previously lived. Also, her mind worked at incredible speed, especially given her lack of practical experience.

When it came to the rest of the children of the Dark Gods, Camille's efforts were far more mixed, if not outright failures. Alderin Terian was too much of his father, a warrior who needed a battle to fight. Unfortunately for Alderin he was more than willing to find his fight under the command of Pike Rhuiden despite the older man's descent into power-madness. As for Darrien Rhuiden, she was ever her father's daughter. She would have followed her father to the ends of the world no matter the cost, and as such she could only see the path through the eyes of power. There would be no limits to what she would do, what she would sacrifice, up to and including her own sense of self. Serrina Mystic too found herself pulled into the orbit of the charismatic leader of the Dark Gods, and had no time for the cautions of someone who she deemed was beneath her. Serrina always thought herself superior to the other members of the children of the Dark Gods, and had no time for her contemporaries. Despite the fact that Serrina's parents were two of the most reserved of the Dark Gods, that humility did not find its way into Serrina's psyche. She wanted to be more; she saw herself as more, and she would do anything to fulfill that vision. When it came to Tess, however, Camille resolved to try to make sure that the youngest of the children of the Dark Gods did not fall under the sway of her destabilizing father. Tess seemed to be receptive to Camille's cautions, but Tess was also somewhat aloof and lost in her own world. She wanted so many things from her life, and found disappointment in her relationships with her father and her half-sister. In that, there was a place that Camille and Tess could bond. Camille's father was gone, and Tess's father was as good as, lost in his own world of grudges and vices. But no sooner had Camille begun to finally get through Tess's shell, Pike had another goal for his daughter.

Then came the next of Camille's many lives, the proto-revolutionary. As soon as she set foot on the shores of Cadaria. The whirlwind would consume her immediately; the rebellion of Marlae Lorien and the Church of the Creator, the incursion of the Heralds of Dorovar, and the descent into the madness of war with gods and monsters. And then, like her father before her, Camille gave her life to save so many other lives. In that, Camille was at peace, and at that moment, whatever resentment she had for the decisions that her father had made all those years before was gone. So, as the powers of the Herald Death passed through her, stealing her life from her, her heart and her soul were ready for the rest. But it was not to be, and Tess pulled Camille back from the edge of oblivion. She was brought back to the war that she was more than happy to be rid of. But that rebirth brought her the one thing that her heart wanted the most, and that was to be reunited with her father.

And that brought Camille to the current incarnation of her life. Standing at the side of her father, her mother, and her allies, she was going to continue the fight. The fight now was against the Creator and the Children of the Creator, and none of their family would rest until the battle was won. So there she was, in the bowels of the Heart of Stone waiting for the next battle in the war to be fought. She could feel the weight of it pressing down upon her. She knew this battle was different. But more than that, she could not shake the frighteningly familiar feeling that was descending upon the ancient edifice. The last time that Camille was at the Heart of Stone, she felt the touch of death, felt it descend upon her like a cold and desolate fog. That same darkness seemed to creep through the corridors of the Heart of Stone once again, and Camille knew that no matter the outcome of the battle, there would be one truth. There would be a staggering amount of death, and no one that survived the battle would ever be the same. Camille silently hoped that when this war was over there would be another life for her to begin, a life that could perhaps have the possibility of seeing victory at the end of their long ordeal.

Midarin

Midarin Sandar looked out from the highest tower of the palace of New Aradon and took in the incredible sights of the structure that had been built in a matter of minutes. The structure was a combination of architectures from Midarin and Gwydeon's pasts, and each piece was as unmistakable as fingerprints. From the wall that ringed the city, which was an architectural cue taken from Midarin's home of Brea to the central tower that came directly from Trelon, they had designed a fortification that would be defensible by the people who took refuge within its walls. They were fulfilling a promise they made to Quyhn and to the Peregrims, who were no longer alive to see the better world that everyone wanted to see come to pass. But even as Midarin took in the sights, she could feel the creeping dread in the back of her mind. She could feel the wind shifting; the ominous black cloud that was slowly drawing near. Once she had regained access to the memories from her time in Brea in the Dark Mirror reality with Gwydeon, defending the innocent from the assaults of the phasia, the feeling was unmistakable. But that wasn't occupying her thoughts, nor was it the source of the dread in the back of her mind. She could not shake the feeling that she had once again found herself in an impossible position, but more than that she could not help but feel more than a little betrayed. That more than anything was why she was walking the top of the tower in the middle of the night. If she wasn't alone, she would have had to talk to Gwydeon, and she wasn't ready to do that yet. Not in his frame of mind, and not in hers. They had been together far too long and knew each other far too well. Unless Midarin missed her guess, Gwydeon would be running through his practice routine, trying to quiet his mind and try to force himself not to come to the conclusion that he knew he could not ignore. That was the biggest difference between Midarin and Gwydeon. He knew what needed to be done, he just didn't want to see it, but he would give into the inevitable eventually. Midarin didn't believe in the inevitable and would run through as many options as she could until she found something that fit. They would come to the same conclusion at some point, like two halves of the same mind turning over a problem until there was nothing left but the conclusion. Sometimes Midarin and Gwydeon came to different conclusions, and they would find a path down the middle. Those were the times when they were at their best. When they were at their worst was when they both knew what needed to be done, but neither really wanted to do it. This was one of those times, which meant they both needed to space to get where they needed to get to.

Try as she might, the word betrayed kept coming to her mind. She didn't want to think that way, but it was undeniable. Gwydeon had offered his help, and by extension hers and Camille's, to Dominique and Quyhn in their bid to protect the innocent and support Quyhn's bid to rebuild the Empire of Cadaria. This was done purely on the strength of the impression that Dominique made on Midarin during their one and only meeting in the Imperial Palace of Aldere. But now, for some inexplicable reason, Quyhn had given up her claim on the Imperial Throne in favor of serving Marlae Tamerlane as her Voice. There was so much to unpack in that thought. So much incongruency, and so many insults. The first and most prominent of the insults, of course, was the fact that the spoiled little girl who had once been Marlae Lorien was now calling herself Marlae Tamerlane. Of course, try as she might, Midarin could not blame Marlae for coopting Elwyne Tamerlane's name. There was only one person would could possibly be responsible for that, and that was the Creator. Yet another reason for Midarin to hate Him and everything He was trying to do. There was only one possible reason for the Creator to tie Elwyne's name to Marlae, and that was to attempt to destabilize the Dark Gods and make them second guess acting against her. If the Dark Gods moved against Marlae, perhaps the Creator would do something to Elwyne's soul. Was that even a battleground that the Dark Gods were willing to fight on? Wasn't it enough that they were fighting and dying to save the living?

There were too many times when this war made no sense. Too many places where it all went wrong and out of focus. The more Midarin thought about it and the ramifications of everything that had occurred the more it made her head hurt. Fighting against the Children of the Creator had taken everything from them. Their first-born child, their world, their friends, and almost each other. And even in that, there was a kind of victory. They had defeated Emries, they had defeated Halicon, and supposedly had earned at least a piece of peace. But there was a difference between the Children of the Creator and the Creator. The Children had rules that they had to follow, and they had limitations to their power. Even though they could create whole races of people and craft worlds out of nothing, they still had limits. The Creator was something else entirely. The Creator had no limits and could simply destroy anything and everything He chose to. There was no fighting something like that, and even thinking that they could was hubris of the highest order. Maybe that was why Aerith had encouraged Gwydeon to stay out of the war, because the war was so far beyond their level. Or, maybe there was something more sinister in the warning. Gwydeon was once called the Brother of Angels, and there was part of his soul that was tied to the Heavens. If Gwydeon tried to involve himself in the war, could he be turned to the service of the Creator as Camille had? Or was it possible that the Creator would simply rip Gwydeon's wings off and snuff him out of existence? Aerith had the best intentions trying to keep them out of the line of fire, but Midarin worried that even the threat of what would happen would not be enough to keep Gwydeon out of the fight.

Midarin moved around the tower and faced west in the direction of that dark cloud that Midarin couldn't see but could feel. That was where the war would most likely end, and there was no way that Gwydeon was going to stay in New Aradon while everyone else fought for the future. And if Gwydeon was going to run headlong into the fight, Midarin was going to be right there beside him. What else could she do? How many hells had they endured side by side? How many impossible battles had they walked away from because they trusted each other and they were there to support one another? They had one more in them. They had to.

But there was that tickle in the back of her mind again. No matter how much she tried to keep it quiet, it continued to scratch and claw at her thoughts, refusing to be ignored. The word betrayal kept coming up over and over again. They were betrayed by Emries who made them believe that they were fighting for a righteous cause. They were lied to by the old gods like Azure who were only interested in furthering Emries' plans. Then the Creator, and Evan Sinn, and the Servants, and the other Children of the Creator. Lies, lies, and betrayals. Now it felt as though they were being betrayed by the humans that they put their trust in. They trusted Quyhn, and she chose to leave that trust behind. They trusted Dominique, and yet she could not follow through on what she promised. Even their own daughter had betrayed them, though it was not of her own volition. It was not of her own free will. And that could be said of so many. Too many. Fighting the Creator, they would never know who he had coopted, never know who was secretly doing his bidding. The thought flared like a scream in her mind, and had she been somewhere else, anywhere else, she might have let her own scream hit the air in response. It would have been a scream that echoed for miles, like the scream that tore from her the day that she thought she had lost the man that she loved. The day Gwydeon sacrificed himself. The day Gwydeon had betrayed her.

Perhaps betray was too strong of a word, or perhaps she was just feeling bitter in the bitter cold of the evening. She remembered the night all too well when Gwydeon had come to her with the plan to end the hostilities between the Dark Gods and the people of Cadaria. It was a ludicrous plan of course, but it was just the kind of plan that Gwydeon would think up. Of course, by the time he presented his plan to Midarin, he was already far beyond being talked out of it. He had probably been thinking about different iterations of the plan for months, perfecting his arguments for and against it so that no matter what angle Midarin came at him, he would have a response. The man was beyond stubborn when he thought he was right, and he was right far more often than Midarin was comfortable admitting. In this case however, while Gwydeon's heart was in the right place, his head was not. Gwydeon's argument was simple. The people of Cadaria feared the Dark Gods because they were beyond understanding. But there was more to it. Gwydeon believed that there was some force that was actively stoking the fear of the Cadarians and would prevent any chance at a conventional peace. In Gwydeon's mind, the Dark

Gods were akin to the phasia for the Cadarians. They were an irresistible force that killed indiscriminately and were beyond all reason. There could never be a true peace so long as the Dark Gods existed, just as the people of Onea never believed that there could be a peace with Shau-ling and the phasia. There was no version of reality where they would not continue to be a plague of unrepentant killers bent on nothing less the wiping out the whole of humanity. The difference however between the situation on Onea and the situation on Espre was the fact that the Cadarians had never had a victory against a member of the Dark Gods.

Midarin remembered the first member of the phasia that the People of the Dragon were able to kill. Though she and Gwydeon were not witness to the duel between Logan and Aldridge, they had heard the story at least a dozen times if not more. Logan never liked telling the story, but Aryx would on occasion when he was interested in teaching the younger generations about the phasia and the violence that permeated their nature. But despite the trauma associated with tracking down Aldridge, the ability for them to actually kill a member of the phasia created hope that their quest could actually be accomplished. Yes, there had been the People of the Lion who had come before, and Cedric Binosear had defeated Shau-ling, but there was a distance to that, and a distance to who those people were compared to Logan and his merry band of misfits. Cedric and the People of the Lion were professional soldiers, mercenaries, and pirates with years of combat experience. With the exception of Aryx Terian, Logan and his fellows were a collection of children who had scarcely been out of their sleepy little village before their quest. For them to be able to kill a member of the phasia meant everything that early in the quest and made the losses that would follow at least somewhat bearable. That victory was an undeniable taste of hope, and it was something that the Cadarians had yet to taste. Gwydeon's supposition was that once the Cadarians were offered a victory over the Dark Gods that it would remove their thirst for war and make them more willing to listen to the options for a diplomatic path. But when Midarin asked how Gwydeon intended to give the Cadarian's a victory, she knew the answer from the look in his eyes.

One of the things that Midarin loved about Gwydeon was his dedication to protecting the innocent, but the part of that drive that exasperated Midarin was the fact that Gwydeon often thought the best way to accomplish that goal was by sacrificing himself. He had done it time and time again without thinking in the heat of battle, but this was different. There was too much at stake. But there was more to it, and though Midarin wanted to use it as a way to defuse Gwydeon's plan, she would not. Since their time in the Heavens, Gwydeon had found himself in a position of leadership of the former heroes of Onea. It was not a position he sought, nor was it a position he wanted. In the Heavens however, there were few responsibilities asked of Gwydeon aside from occasional conversations with the Creator and the Servants. But all of that changed when Talisia started her war. Pike was the firebrand who was ready to fight, but Gwydeon preached caution. There was no reason to take the fight to Talisia's forces, no reason to make the conflict bloodier than it needed to be. Yes, none of the servants were there, but there were plenty of warrior angels and dragons on both sides of the conflict. Gwydeon wanted to simply focus all of the attention of the heroes of Onea on defending Pyrrus. However, Pike would hear none of it. He had the taste of blood in his mouth and charged headlong into the ranks of angels that had aligned with Talisia. Midarin had wanted to stay at Gwydeon's side as he moved to defend Pyrrus, but Gwydeon insisted that she offer cover to their allies in the greater battle. Gwydeon knew that he would stand no chance against Talisia in single combat if it came to that, but he was truly only trying to buy time. Every moment that Gwydeon was able to delay Talisia gave the Servants another moment to return. That was the only thing that would put an end to the conflict, no matter the bloodshed or destruction. Try as he might though, Gwydeon was unable to get to Pyrrus in time, and Talisia ran him through just as Gwydeon got close.

The loss hit Gwydeon hard, and in the aftermath of the rebellion, Gwydeon ignored the summons from the Golden Throne, and shut himself off from everyone but his family. Eventually, Pike was able to find his way back into Gwydeon's confidence, and the two old allies began to spend massive amounts of time together. Pike continued to agitate for a move against the Golden Throne to demand answers about the rebellion. Though Pike wanted to lead the insurrection, he recognized that without Gwydeon at the head of any effort, they would never get the answers that they needed from the Creator and the Servants. In time, Pike was able to break through Gwydeon's despondency, and that began the saga of the Dark Gods. After the fall, the Dark Gods turned to Gwydeon for leadership. Again, Gwydeon bristled at the position, but did what he thought was best for his allies and friends. Gwydeon had often said that he was so grateful for Logan when they were all together as the People of the Dragon because Logan never shied away from the responsibility of leadership. Logan didn't want to lead any more than Gwydeon did, but he accepted the role because he believed that was what he was supposed to do. That allowed Gwydeon to be more of what he wanted to be, and that was the glue that held everything together.

Midarin knew that in some ways Gwydeon's plan to sacrifice himself to the first Emperor of Cadaria would take him out of the position of leadership that he didn't want to be in. What he also was doing, and the thing that Midarin resented him the most for, was placing Midarin in the position of de facto conscience for the Dark Gods who was supposed to keep Pike in check. But Midarin fought hard against being left behind. She had wanted to go with Gwydeon, to face the Emperor of Cadaria together, to meet their end together. That was the way it should have been. That was the only way it could be. And as much as Gwydeon appreciated the sentiment, he was dead set against the proposal. His counterpoints were sound, and again she hated the fact that he was so reasoned and right. While the Cadarians would be given hope by the defeat of one member of the Dark Gods, if the Emperor of Cadaria was able to dispatch two of the Dark Gods on his own, it might embolden the Cadarian Empire to make a move against Mythryn and the Citadel of the Dark Gods. There might be those in the leadership of the empire who would consider pressing their advantage and attacking in force, too much of the fear and respect for the power of the Dark Gods removed. Such a slaughter would render the sacrifice moot and would eventually lead to an all-out war between Cadaria and Mythryn that could end only one way. The second reason, and perhaps the one that most impacted Midarin was the thought of their daughter Camille being left without both of her parents. Camille was strong, she was over a thousand years old, and she was everything that Gwydeon and Midarin could have wanted their daughter to be. But she was also going to be called upon to be a pivotal part of the war against the Children and the Creator, and neither of her parents felt comfortable with the thought of her taking her orders from Pike during the critical parts of the war. The third reason, and the one that Midarin didn't want to acknowledge, but had no choice, was that without Midarin's moderating voice, Pike would move too soon and any chance they had of winning the war would be lost.

Of course, Gwydeon was right; of course he was. But the cost of being right was far too high. For too long Midarin was forced to turn a blind eye to Pike's indiscretions and deteriorating nature for the sake of keeping him sedate. Midarin was not a fool. No matter how Pike believed that he covered his tracks by using Alderin and Darrien to bury the bodies, Midarin was aware of every one. She was aware of the relationship that Pike had with Serrina Mistic and she was aware of how he tried to manipulate the loyalties of every member of the Dark Gods and the Forgotten. At every gathering Pike agitated for war, and often it was Aryx, Diana, and Midarin who eased the tensions. But as the years rolled on, Aryx and Diana's voices diminished. Midarin recognized that her old allies were tired and their commitment to the war was waning. They wanted a life away from the war, in the quiet, and in some ways, Midarin thought that they envied the time that Aerith and Bryn had away.

After Gwydeon had done what he needed to do, Midarin spent a great amount of time with Aryx, Diana, and Lissa. Midarin and Lissa had a lot in common and they would commiserate often. But there were times late into the evening that Midarin and Diana would find themselves talking. Diana was a thoughtful woman who didn't want any of the life that found her. She was just fifteen when she begged her older brother to let her come along on the supposedly humanitarian mission to save the people of Lakestone. No one knew what they were getting into, and if anyone did, Diana probably would have been left at home, which would have changed so much. Together Diana and Aryx were one of the most powerful couples in the history of Onea, and their love became legendary through the battles and the blood, the triumphs and the tribulations, the darkness and the light. Bards would have sung their tales until the end of time had Onea survived the cataclysm. Midarin had to admit that the legend of Aryx and Diana was probably larger than the legend of Gwydeon and Midarin, though not quite as large as the legend of Logan and Elwyne. But that was fine. Neither Midarin nor Gwydeon desired that kind of fame, though they would laugh about it sometimes. Diana dreamt of a return to the quiet life that she left all those millennia ago; a home, a garden, and peace. But she knew that was impossible. She and her husband, their children, and their grandchildren were committed to the war, nothing would ever be able to change that. And their loyalty was to Gwydeon, and thus was to Midarin. It was a responsibility that never sat well on Midarin's shoulders through all the years that followed, but she was certainly grateful for it. They all saw however the eventuality coming. Pike would have his war, even against the objections of the other members of the Dark Gods. Eventually even Gwydeon's sacrifice would be wiped away, and all that would be left would be blood. But none of them could have foreseen what Pike would become, not even after seeing the Lord Rhuiden who nearly destroyed himself on Onea. Maybe Logan knew, and that was why he stayed away. Maybe Gwydeon knew, which was why he insisted on Midarin acting as the control on his rages. But Midarin could never bring herself to believe, even in their darkest nightmares, that Pike would have become the villain he became.

Midarin took a long deep breath of the cold crisp air and felt the light beginning to stretch across the east. The dark cloud was still there, still foreboding, and still inevitable. It felt like the last days on Onea, and Midarin shuddered at the thought of another world that they were supposed to be protecting coming to an end. That moment was when the realization hit. That was why their course of action was so clear now. Aerith may have been right to a point, but none of that mattered now. The place of refuge had been established. Good smart people were in place to defend it, and no matter what happened in the battle at the Heart of Stone, there would still be a human race to carry on. On Onea, Midarin and Gwydeon had been there at the end, in one form or another, fighting hard to ensure that their world would have a future. They failed. Onea was destroyed and they continued to be pawns in the game between the Creator and his Children. The game may have been the same on Espre, but the stakes were certainly different. Now they weren't fighting for their world. They weren't fighting for the lives of innocent humans who could only see a devastation that was beyond their understanding. What they were fighting for now was existence itself. More than that, they were fighting for the very idea of existence. So long as the Creator continued His games, so long as He allowed the Children, or the Dragons, or any other creature to determine which races had the right to live and which ones didn't; which worlds had the right to exist and which ones should be destroyed, there would never be peace, and whatever could be called life would only ever be fleeting and ultimately meaningless.

On Onea they fought. It didn't matter the odds, it didn't matter the chances of success; they fought. Was Gwydeon really going to sit by, safe in a castle hundreds of miles away from a battle where his friends, his own daughter was fighting and perhaps dying for the right to exist? Was Midarin? Yes they had given their word. Yes, there were innocents to be defended. But in all honesty, Quyhn had done them a great service. She was no longer the Empress of Cadaria in waiting, and the future of the human race on this world no longer turned on her survival. She had ceded that claim to Marlae, had given away the responsibility to another woman, who sat in another fortification that was likely also guarded against reprisal. That freed Gwydeon and Midarin from some of their obligation and allowed them the option to join the battle in Albitonin. If everything happened the way that Midarin saw it happening, when the war was over, if they were victorious once again, Espre would be spared the fate of Onea. Moreover, there would be no Children, no Servants, no Creator. More importantly, there would be no Dark Gods. Perhaps they would return to the Heavens. Perhaps they would find another world, a peaceful one where they could live out the rest of their lives. Perhaps the end of the Creator would be the end of them as well. Whichever was the case, the humans would be responsible for themselves and the world that they would create after. All Gwydeon and Midarin wanted was to give them the chance to do that.

She moved deftly toward the access hatch of the tower and used her powers to open it with barely a thought. Once down the ladder she inspected the rack of arms that was hastily placed near the ladder. The remaining soldiers from the Lordhill Army added to those from the people of the surrounding communities had been able to amass enough weapons to properly defend the impressive fortification that the Dark Gods had built. She recovered one of the bows from the rack and tested the bowstring. It felt good to have a real bow in her hand once more. It had been too long. Perhaps relying on her powers had dulled her edge, but she knew it had not dulled her eye. And while the wood felt right in her hand, she knew almost in the same instant that it was a weapon for a mortal, and that where she was about to go, there was no room for such weapons. The fight ahead would require every bit of skill, guile, and tenacity that she had accumulated over the years just to be able to survive. To win would take something more. To win would take will. The kind of will that survived the death of a world. The kind of will that survived two wars in the Heavens, and more importantly the kind of will that had allowed her to live for almost two thousand years without the man that she loved. Now that they were reunited, nothing would ever pull them apart again. They would fight for what they believed in, because to do anything else would dishonor all of the sacrifices they had made up to that point and dishonor the memory of all of their friends who had fought and died for those beliefs. Her course of action was so clear that it could not be denied.

Putting the bow back onto the rack, Midarin nodded to herself and started down the stairs back to their wing of the palace. In her mind she rehearsed all of the things that she was going to say to Gwydeon, but at the same time she knew that she wouldn't have to say much. They would pack their things, say their goodbyes, make their apologies, and then throw themselves headlong into the growing inferno. But no matter what happened, it would be on their terms, and they would be together, and with the time they had left, that was all that mattered.

Isabella

Legacy. The word evoked many meanings, not the least of which was the weight of responsibility that could not realistically be measured. As Isabella Ranthall made her way quietly through the darkened hallways of New Aradon, she reflected on the legacies that conspired in her creation. On another world, in another time, Isabella would have been a princess, born to one of the most prominent and respected families on the whole of Onea. There was a version of her that learned at the feet of her mother Cairyn and at the side of her half-sister Sabrina how to be a member of the Binosear family, how to navigate the halls of courtly power, and how to wield that power responsibly to the benefit of all of their subjects. She would have known every noble and every person of importance on sight, attended balls and opulent feasts, waiting for the day that she would be matched with a suitable partner who would continue the legacy that it was her responsibility to steward into the next generation. Perhaps she would have been a queen as her mother and grandmother before her had been. Perhaps she would have become a rebellious adventurer like her half-sister. But wherever she went and whatever she did, she would carry with her the Binosear name, and all that it meant. She would carry with her the legacy of the Lord Lion, the first *Coromor* of the prophecies, the savior of Lakestone and vanquisher of the nightmare of men Shau-ling. She would carry with her the legacy of the benevolent Anabel Binosear, who ruled her people with kindness and with understanding, who was also a hero in her own right but preferred to use her power not to glorify herself but to make the lives better of everyone who crossed her path, whether they owed her allegiance or not. Isabella was the daughter of Cairyn Binosear, the stable steward, the Lioness of Trelon who kept her people safe through two wars that threatened to shatter the world. This was but one half of the complicated legacy that Isabella carried with her, and perhaps it was the less complicated half.

Wherever a Ranthall goes, trouble follows. This was the legacy of her father and her father's side of the family. It started of course with her father, with the hero of the second generation of the prophecies, Logan Ranthall, the man who would be a savior but was instead the hero that shook the world. There was her uncle, Korrd Ranthall, a complicated and troubled man who constantly tried to grow into the role that fate had picked out for him but was never comfortable in his own skin. There was her grandfather Arin, the simple soldier who was the foundation of legends. Her half brother Wolf was a man who was denied his legacy only to craft another with the help of a man who should have been his enemy, and her cousin Gwillim was the powerful soldier that should never have been born had it not been for the interference of the Creator and the old gods. Whether they were fighting Shau-ling, or Emries, or the phasia, the Ranthalls knew only how to move forward, suffering loss and pain with every step, but realizing that the cost didn't matter in the face of the responsibility that constantly found its way to them. Perhaps there was another version of Isabella that would have learned how to fight at the foot of her famous father or one of his equally famous friends who were like an extended family. Would she have quested at his side fighting against the phasia or some other villain that tried to take the lives of the innocent? Or maybe she would have become one of the early members of the Order of the Flickering Flame, helping Logan find those who were lost in the world and giving them new purpose. There were many lives that could have been, many lives shaped by the many legacies that lived within the diminutive body of Isabella Ranthall. However, those lives did not come to be. Isabella could only be what she was raised to be, and could only advance the legacy that existed on this world. And it was a very different legacy indeed.

In the strictest sense, Isabella was a member of the Dark Gods, but only in certain aspects. The first and most critical of those aspects of course was the fact that from a physical standpoint, she had stopped aging at approximately seventeen years of age. She would not die of old age, and no matter how many years passed, her outward appearance would never change. There was a slight frustration in that fact, and once she had asked her half-sister Sabrina about it. Sabrina too seemed to be stuck in the body of a twenty-year-old, despite being hundreds of years old at that point. Sabrina had said that the choice of the outward physical age was not fixed, but it was a reflection of how the person felt. In time, if she wanted, Isabella would be able to alter her appearance and appear to be whatever age she wanted. There were issues of maturity that helped to craft that mental image, and just like with the phasia before them, the Dark Gods were not exactly the most mentally mature of people in the grand scheme of things. Perhaps the ones who had the best understanding of this were Gwydeon and Midarin. They were not the same as they had been on Onea. Midarin specifically had allowed herself to age far beyond the twenty-year-old princess that she was at the beginning of her time with the People of the Dragon. Even though she was the most senior member of that group, with the exception of Gideon Viruci, she never felt the difference in age. But Midarin felt the passage of time much more completely than did some of the other members of the People of the Dragon, perhaps because she had given birth to a child and lived a life of love that could have been a life of fulfillment. Perhaps it was because she did not have powers on Onea. Or perhaps Midarin was simply a more mature person than the idealistic heroes who risked their lives with such abandon. Whatever the reason, when she found herself on Espre, Midarin did not appear as the twenty-year-old princess, but as the forty-year-old aged warrior and mother. Isabella's grandmother Anabel too had allowed some of the age to creep into her features, but not so much that it would have been readily apparent that she was a grandmother. Yes there were streaks of gray in her hair, but her face had not been touched by time in the same way. Perhaps that had been a concession to vanity, or perhaps it had been necessary so that the people who needed to take her seriously when the time came would without question. While Isabella was heartened by this explanation from Sabrina, it always filled her with a sense of her own mortality and her own maturity.

Isabella was born during the Founding Wars, a thought that seemed impossible even now to her mind. Her mother, Cairyn Binosear had been killed while she was pregnant in the Dark Mirror reality on the world of Onea. When Cairyn was reborn onto Espre, she was still pregnant and it took her quite some time to get her bearings. Fortunately her daughter, well at least a version of her daughter, Sabrina arrived to give her a crash course on the nature of the war. Cairyn was in the area of the world that would eventually come to be known as the Kingdom of Hedorah. At that point in time, Hedorah was a barely functioning island that was held together by a loose coalition of merchants, pirates, and traders. Cairyn, despite her pregnant condition and her unfamiliarity with the political landscape of the time instantly inserted herself into the mix. She invented the name Calindria Trelis, and immediately became a power player in the disorganized morass of Hedorahn politics. Within a matter of months, Calindria became the principle player in the beginnings of what would become the ruling council of Hedorah, long before the corruption that became the hallmark of the kingdom set in. But then again, when the origins of the kingdom were the families and allies of pirates and smugglers, what else could you expect? One of the first lessons that Cairyn had been taught by her mother Anabel was that any weakness could be used against you in negotiation, whether that weakness be perceived or actual. For the arrogant and misogynistic pirates who thought they controlled Hedorah, Cairyn's pregnancy was a definite weakness. But while they continued to dismiss and underestimate Cairyn, she continued to consolidate her power. By the time Isabella was born, Cairyn had near total control of Hedorah, and she had called in enough favors and had accumulated enough leverage to keep even the most ardent of her detractors in line. Isabella was born on an auspicious date. It was the day the last of Terrik Lorien's opponents, the warlord Grawn, was defeated.

Isabella's early life was in the tumultuous time that marked the end of the Founding Wars and the beginning of the Cadarian Empire under the rule of Terrik Lorien. Cairyn in her guise as Calindria was part of the initial negotiations that created the Flying Kingdom of Hedorah, and unlike many of the other representatives at the early negotiations that laid the groundwork for the Cadarian Empire, Cairyn had played the political game before. She was the one behind the negotiation of the individual sovereignty rules for the Great Kingdoms. Under the original proposal that would have served as the constitution for the Cadarian Empire, all laws would have been generated from the central authority of the Emperor, and there would have been a single central military presided over by the Knights of the Flashing Blade. While there were several of the prospective kingdoms, specifically Thorigald and Saldarine who objected to a common military, there were few entities who objected to a central government. Yes, there were some of the so-called nobles who were angling to keep as much power as possible in the new regime, but no one other than Cairyn was advocating for self-rule by the kingdoms. Though it took many weeks of negotiation, Cairyn was eventually able to shift the tide of sentiment until most of the prospective kingdoms advocated for local control by the ruling families of each of the individual kingdoms. Once that had become the eventuality, it was left to the representatives of the kingdoms to negotiate their tribute and duty to the Emperor and the percentage of their army that would be contributed to the Imperial Guard. Cairyn was not as aggressive in this part of the negotiation, feeling that the people of Cadaria needed to have the final say, not someone from another world.

Isabella was still very young when these negotiations were taking place, but her mother felt that it was of crucial importance for her daughter to understand the demands of power, as well as the demands of history. There would never again be a moment like this in Cadarian history unless something went catastrophically wrong, and thus part of the legacy that Cairyn was entrusting to her daughter was the understanding of how everything that would come to pass came to be. She would know from her early years the principle players in all of the Great Kingdoms, as well as a great many of the important figures in the Imperial Palace. In fact, by the time Isabella entered the service of Marlae Tamerlane, she had met every person who had ever sat on the throne of Cadaria, in one guise or another. If Isabella was honest, this kind of access to the monoliths of power across the history of Cadaria was an advantage that she did not take the best advantage of. Despite her age and despite the attempts of her mother and her grandmother to get Isabella to become more of a diplomat, there was something restless within Isabella that could not be denied. That restlessness was another legacy that she had inherited, and perhaps it was the one that had served her the least.

For as long as Isabella could remember, she had felt as though she was being pulled toward something. That something was so nebulous and so undefined that it was impossible to quantify. What she knew for certain however was that she was not built to be a diplomat, regardless of how much it might have disappointed her mother and grandmother. In the back of her mind, Isabella always believed her path lay out in the world fighting against the evil that could be found there. To that end, Isabella found numerous avenues to gain the skills that she would need to do what she needed to do when the time came. Isabella began the acquisition of skills by ingratiating herself to the spymaster of the Kingdom of Hedorah. In the early days of the Shadow Guild, the rules were not nearly as strict, and the members not nearly as secretive. This was likely due to the fact that the newly minted Grand Master of the Shadow Guild had to accept the fact that many of the former warlords and leaders of the newly formed Great Kingdoms had elements in their ranks to provide them with intelligence as well as act as spies and assassins. The first task of the new Shadow Guild was to incorporate all of those disparate elements into a single cohesive unit. It was a difficult proposition to be sure because there were many elements in all of the kingdoms that did not necessarily appreciate being part of a collective rather than an individual working on their own behalf. Some nights, Isabella would listen as Cairyn and Anabel would debate the benefits and liabilities of the formation of the Cadarian Empire and all of the challenges that faced it.

Anabel was highly critical of the manner in which Terrik Lorien was forming his awkward coalition government. Part of that criticism was leveled squarely at her own daughter and the role that Cairyn had in creating the self-determinant kingdoms. Anabel believed that Terrik Lorien and those advising him were completely foolish in allowing the Great Kingdoms to control their own internal politics. She had seen the divisions and jealousies and pettiness created between the kingdoms on Onea. She had also seen the influence peddling and the unfortunate trafficking of daughters for political gain. Trelon of course had always been an outlier in that regard. As a female dominated kingdom, the power revolved around the female heir, not some petulant man who was simply looking for something pretty to have on his arm at feasts and other functions. Anabel believed that the kind of machinations that were required in order for a divided government to survive were counter-productive to the longevity of the system. Cairyn of course disagreed. Cairyn believed that so much power in the hands of any one person was an untenable situation. The forces that they were dealing with, specifically Emries, could easily dominate the will of the Emperor of Cadaria and warp the aims of the whole of the empire to his own ends. With a more divided government, it would make it too difficult for any faction to gain control of every aspect of the empire, and it would ensure that any resistance that formed would have a chance to succeed. Anabel's counter was that if a government degraded to the point that a resistance was even necessary, it had already failed, and the advantage of having a strong core allowed for factions to be heard without having undo influence. The Great Kingdoms would have been better served negotiating for an advisory council that had a permanent presence within the Imperial Court, and that a unanimous vote from the council could have overruled any unilateral action taken by the emperor. Naturally this discussion took place over many hundreds of years and was constantly influenced by the goings-on in the empire. Neither ever budged from their position, but Isabella was constantly fascinated by the evolving argument.

One of Anabel's constant points of contention was the manner in which the disparate forces within the empire were managed and combined. While she acknowledged that the creation of an intelligence gathering apparatus was necessary given the nature of the government, she was quick to point out the perils of creating such an apparatus. During the Founding Wars, there was no prohibition against spying, sabotage, and assassination between the forces seeking to unite the countryside. In civilized warfare, such activities would have been discouraged and limited to extreme circumstances only. But there was nothing civilized about the Founding Wars. Brutality was the norm, and warlords had a desire to eliminate each other in any way possible. These spies and assassins by their very nature were not trusting individuals, so any attempt to forge them into a cohesive unit was bound to be met with resistance if not outright objection. Anabel mused on many occasions that whoever the Grand Master of the Shadow Guild was, they had probably considered eliminating all of these legacy shadowy agents and starting from scratch. This could have proven to be problematic of course, because as soon as any of these legacy agents discovered what was happening, they would be able to inflict massive amounts of damage to the fledgling empire before they were removed from the equation. Clearly, it was the lesser of two evils to try to absorb these elements and to slowly remove those more troubling individuals quietly.

The man that Isabella befriended was a former spy and assassin in the service of the warlord Grawn. While Isabella had expected the man to be severe and violent by nature, he turned out to be very soft-spoken and thoughtful. The greatest lessons that Isabella took from this man were about the benefits of subtlety. Of course, Isabella did not appreciate the lessons when they were taking place, wanting the more romantic elements of assassination to be included in her lessons. She had wanted to learn about poisons, and concealable weapons, and infiltration techniques, but that was not what she got at all. However, the lessons that she learned would serve her well for the rest of her days, and would teach her to reevaluate her perceptions of how things worked. This former assassin operated out of a small house on the far side of the city. He made an agreement with Isabella that if she could sneak up on him when he was at home, he would teach her anything that she wanted. This was in the days that Isabella did not know the extent of the powers that she had, if she had any. So, she made it her mission to sneak up on this assassin and make him divulge every secret. However, this was a challenge that the young woman was not equal to. The floors in this home had been specially designed to squeak and creak loudly if pressure was applied in the wrong places. The first time Isabella attempted to covertly enter the house, she had taken no more than one step and the assassin was upon her. Time and time again she tried, but Isabella was never able to navigate the test properly. One day, the man was simply gone, and Isabella never got another chance to gain the information she wanted from the man. What she did gain however was access to the home, and it became her house for a period of time with the help of her mother. She practiced every day until she could carefully walk through the house without it making a sound. From that moment forward, there were few people in the world that Isabella could not sneak up on.

Once she had mastered her covert skills, Isabella considered joining the Shadow Guild. However, it was on the advice of her grandmother that she did not pursue the thought. Anabel always believed that whoever the Grand Master of the Shadow Guild was no doubt had some connection to Onea. Of course, Anabel turned out to be correct, and if Isabella would have been discovered by Saurn in the days when she did not know how to disguise her abilities, it could have created a dangerous situation for every member of the Binosear clan. And so, instead of joining the Shadow Guild, Isabella instead turned her attention to learning any martial skill that she could find someone to teach her. Whether it was a sword, bow, spear, or dagger, Isabella threw herself into learning all that she could. In the early days, her impatience was her greatest enemy as she fluttered from one weapon to another, never dedicating much time to any one weapon. When she finally became mature enough to utilize the lessons she had learned when mastering the assassin's floor, Isabella started throwing herself into studying a single weapon. Both her father, Logan, and her great uncle, Cedric, were famous for their use of the sword, and so it was naturally the first weapon that Isabella gravitated toward. Unfortunately, however, it took quite some time for Isabella to acquire any level of proficiency with the sword. The first problem Isabella had was the fact that she wanted to use the same kind of weapon that her father had used, but her frame and her strength were simply not up to the challenge. The blade was always just a little too long, the hilt too large, and the weight always slightly distributed in the wrong way. So, eventually Isabella had to admit that a longsword was not for her, which nearly broke her heart and made her want to give up learning the sword. However, she eventually found her way to a version of a rapier that was short, thin, and seemed to flow well with her physique. The swept-hilt rapier flowed like water in her grip, and became lethal in Isabella's hands.

Once stealth and weaponry had been mastered after a couple hundred years of study, Isabella began to question her nature. The Dark Gods had been on the scene for quite some time, and the stories of their abilities were likely so overblown that none of them could be considered real. So, Isabella approached her grandmother looking for information. Anabel had never been comfortable with the powers that she had access to, preferring to use them defensively when possible. After much conversation and several uncomfortable exchanges, Anabel relented in her opposition to teaching Isabella the basics of power use and started her lessons. Of course, what Anabel could actually teach was limited to some basics and the ability to form a protective shield. Very quickly, Isabella exhausted all of the knowledge that Anabel could pour into her. In time, Sabrina appeared sparingly to help fill in the gaps, but Sabrina's cautions were what stuck foremost in Isabella's mind. Using her powers, even for defensive purposes was dangerous and could cause people to know of her existence before she was ready.

That was the most frustrating part about Isabella's life in Hedorah. No one could know who she was. She could not leave to seek out her father, and even when she knew that he was in the city, she had to do everything she could to resist the urge to walk up to him and wrap her arms around him. Many times she watched him speak from the shadows in his guise as Dane Rhuiden. She would hear about the great things that he was doing as the leader of the Order of the Flickering Flame, and she would feel the crowd tense and become uncomfortable at the depictions of the Creator in his speeches. Many times she would see him debate members of the Church of the Creator, never backing down for one moment, but always being respectful and calm. She knew that it hurt her mother a great deal to not be able to reveal herself to Logan. But Sabrina had been very specific in her instructions to both Cairyn and Isabella. Logan could not know of their existence until the time was right. His path required that he be unfettered and be able to make the choices necessary for the fate of the war. Isabella did not understand then of course, but she understood now. The twins had made the situation very clear. If Logan had known about Cairyn and Isabella, he never would have allowed himself to have a relationship with Jillian Corven. She was important to the war, and Logan's involvement with her was critical if they were going to have any chance at all to succeed. But what Mirana and Liara were unsure of was whether or not Sabrina's intention to force Logan into the arms of a woman who would not be born for almost two thousand years was part of the plan to unseat the Creator from the Golden Throne, or if it was just another machination by the Creator to succeed in His plans. Whatever the case, the information had sealed Isabella's course of action.

Even as she left the confines of the palace of New Aradon, doubt began to fill her. She had had so little time with her father and she didn't get a chance to say all of the things she wanted to say to him. Of course, the first words out of her mouth had to be smart and irreverent. She had to prove to him after all that she was his daughter. However, as she reflected back, that was perhaps not the best path to take. But there had been so little time. In a matter of minutes, they were in the middle of a warzone and Logan was doing what he always did. He ran headlong into danger trying to save as many people as he could from forces they could not understand. He had accomplished so much in his time on Espre, and Isabella felt so many pangs of guilt that she could not be at his side doing those same works. She had often entertained the possibility of joining the Order of the Flickering Flame under an assumed name and doing what she could to further the cause. But that too was impossible. He would have been able to sniff her out in a matter of hours, and Isabella for all of her ability at subterfuge to hide her identity over the many hundreds of years was not a talented liar, especially when faced with someone who had matched wits with some of the greatest schemers in history. So, Isabella was forced to keep silent, and she was filled with fear that she would never get the opportunity to have the kind of relationship with her father that she wanted. That was exacerbated now by the information that Logan was no longer able to be felt by anyone with power. He had survived the confrontation with Pike Rhuiden and come back stronger than before, Mirana and Liara had confirmed as much, but then he simply disappeared. The twins were very clear that he had not died, they would have felt that, but something else was clearly going on, and in their minds, Logan was in grave danger. Isabella would not stand aside again and let Logan run into danger alone. She had been revealed to him and all of her other responsibilities had been dealt with. She knew where he had been when the twins last felt him, and so she would start her search there. Once she found him, she would not leave his side for the rest of the war. She had lost so much time, she didn't intend to let any more go by without him in her life.

As soon as she was far enough away from the palace that a small use of power would not be so readily detected, Isabella opened a portal and quickly stepped through. Her destiny waited on the other side, and she was finally going to be able to embrace it.

The Inheritors

Gideon

The stench of death was everywhere. What Raenera's undead host lacked in subtly they more than made up for in brutal efficiency. They were methodical, precise and nearly omniscient in their prowess in hunting down and slaughtering every living being in their path. They were dispassionate in their task, and cared little if their targets were elderly, infirm, or infants. The world would be cleansed of all of the humans, without exception. As Gideon Viruci reflected upon the brutality of the phantom legion, he also reflected upon Raenera's strategy. For too long, the intelligent beings collectively referred to as humans had been used as pawns in the ideological war between the Children of the Creator. In the beginning, the Children were true philosophers, debating the merits of their cosmological views in purely hypothetical debates that stretched for hundreds of years at a time. But that methodology could not last for eternity, even though the Children themselves were theoretically eternal beings. It was Talisia that broke the accord first, populating one of her worlds with some of the most grotesque beings to ever draw breath.

Through Raenera's memories, Gideon recalled these beings. Calling them human would have been generous at the least, as there was little other than their bipedal form that would identify them as human. The concepts of compassion, generosity, and mercy did not exist for those beings. They raped, murdered, stole, and terrorized as a rule, and only the strongest and most diabolical among their number lived long enough to see heirs produced. But the petty jealousies and thirst for power often found those offspring murdered by their parents in order to cling to power that much longer. It was a world of brutality and blood, and ultimately one that could not survive the weight of its own evil. Within three generations, the whole population had died out, and the world was a tomb. Talisia did not view the experiment as a failure, merely seeking to tweak her creations so that they would live longer and not see their offspring as a threat, but rather as a necessary continuation of their power. These modifications brought new counter arguments from all sides of the ideological conflict. Pyrrus believed that imparting any concern for the offspring of these brutal beings demonstrated the need for love and devotion, positive connection that belied Talisia's dim view of a cannibalistic nihilist Cosmos that spiraled every moment toward entropy. Halicon built off of Pyrrus' argument postulating that the need for both constructive and destructive tendencies illustrated in the strongest terms the need for balance in all things. Raenera viewed the entire exercise not as a method to prove her own cosmological view but rather as a repudiation of Talisia's. Pure evil could not exist, as it would eventually be reduced to oblivion. Even Talisia's staunchest ally Emries advocated for his own interpretation, interjecting that Talisia's experiment did not account for the random nature essential for longevity and evolution, and that even with some measure of reverence for offspring and the necessity of future generations, the beings of Talisia's world would eventually fall to stagnation.

It was Pyrrus who next tried his hand at world-building. It was not a pursuit that Pyrrus engaged in often, as the outcomes tended to impact him more profoundly than it did his siblings. Pyrrus' world was a world of light and serenity. There were no ambitions, needs, or desires. Food was plentiful and self-reproductive. The weather was always mild and perfect. In the beginning, it seemed as though Pyrrus' expression would prove to stand the test of time. But just as Talisia's world would eventually devolve into self-destructive madness and death, Pyrrus' world would see sloth, apathy, and a slow decline into nothingness. With nothing to accomplish and no need to work or strive, the beings of Pyrrus' world would eventually stop reproducing and fall into a near coma-like monotony that would lead to extinction. Talisia took great glee in this failure, taunting Pyrrus with the clear need for ambition and greed. Ambition would breed resentment and hatred and eventually unchecked would devolve into murder and theft.

Ambition was the necessary evil that opened the door to everything Talisia represented.

It was from Pyrrus' failure that Raenera began to craft and perfect her beings. These humans would eventually become the inhabitants of Loinn, after several iterative steps. The contentment of Pyrrus' world was the starting point for the beings that Raenera would create. Yes, Talisia and the others were right, ambition was a necessity for growth, but it could not continue unchecked. Ambition had to be controlled and properly channeled. Raenera believed that the way to accomplish this was to ensure that every being knew its place and knew that that place could never be changed. Each person born, from the moment of their birth, would have to have a destined path, without potential for alteration. Despite this predestination, the people would need to have the desire to excel at their path. They would have to understand the value of work and obedience to themselves and their community, and they would need to desire to perpetuate that community through offspring and future generations of community-minded individuals. Life would grow geometrically, making sure that every being had a role that was necessary, and that every being would need to fulfill that role to the best of their ability to ensure that there was enough food, shelter, and other materials to sustain that community. This was the very expression of the Perfect Order.

Unfortunately for Raenera, the weakness in the Perfect Order proved to be her existence within it. The Perfect Order was predicated on one undeniable fact, the fact that it had been orchestrated and enforced by the presence of the Goddess. There would be a small leadership caste that would enforce the will of the Goddess, but even without the presence of this caste, the Adhradair, the Goddess was absolute. It was the Goddess that enforced every person's path and decreed that that path could not be changed. In the end, however, it was this stricture that allowed Talisia and Emries to unravel the entire structure. If the Goddess was the one who enforced the path, then the Goddess, should she want to, could modify the path. It was this elemental yet unexpected truism that Talisia seized upon when she whispered her lies into the ear of Dorovar. It was the absolute adherence to the Goddess's will that undid that will, and Raenera was shaken by the fundamental truth that her failure revealed.

As Gideon took a long look around him at the death and destruction, he found humor in the lesson that Raenera's failure taught her. It was the same lesson that the Dark Gods had eventually learned, with no less amount of blood. None of the Children of the Creator would be able to prove their cosmological view because their very existence would undermine the full expression of any version of their beliefs. Their desire to be correct at all costs would doom any effort. In the end, every experiment would meet with failure. This belief led Raenera to one inescapable conclusion. The Children of the Creator would all need to fail, and that failure could not be expressed unless the Children were destroyed.

Raenera knew that in time the Creator would grow weary of his Children's failures and their constant squabbling. With Raenera's memories, Gideon had a completely different view of the Creator. To most humans, the Creator was this monolith of love, acceptance, and light. It was this ephemeral being with no form and no desires beyond the want for the success of His creations and the desire for those creations to show their deference and love for that which made them. Raenera's Creator however was a petty and jealous being who thrived on conflict and adoration. This was first expressed with the dragons. In time the dragons began to see themselves as special. They took pride in their creations and the things in Creation that they gave names to. Dragons began to see themselves as apart, perhaps even the equal of that which made them. The Creator took to randomly destroying pieces of Creation just to take those named things away from the dragons. They were beholden to the Creator, and they constantly needed to be reminded of their place. When the Children came into being, the Creator took great pride in letting the dragons know that they had been displaced from their role as most favored. The Children were given abilities that the dragons would never have access to, and eventually the dragons found themselves subject to the rules that the Children created for their worlds. When the Children began creating beings that could understand the concept of the Creator and the divinity inherent in that role, the Creator decreed that all intelligent beings must know of the Creator and must adhere to the strict supplication and acknowledgement of their place within Creation. The Creator would brook no defiance on this point, as the Creator's jealousy was without bounds. This was the point upon which Emries decided to launch his rebellion.

The world of Onea proved to be a place of firsts and many turning points in the ideological war between the Children. While on Loinn there was conflict between Raenera, Emries, and Talisia, it was a conflict done in abstract. Emries and Talisia challenged Raenera by dissecting her cosmological view and exposing its ultimate fragility. Onea became a more direct battleground between Emries and Halicon were they fought a proxy war through their creations, the phasia and the *Erieal*. For hundreds of years this battle raged, with the only outcome being the death of hundreds of thousands of humans. Soon, the proxies would turn on their makers, spurred on by the need to understand the ideologies that they were being ordered to die for. In a way, it was the ultimate expression of Emries' construct. Uncertainty and chaos were constants of Emries' philosophy, and the ability of his creations to transcend the boundaries set out for them and to evolve in unexpected ways was inevitable. Halicon too found himself falling victim to this eventuality as his phasia were built upon the greatest weaknesses of Emries' humans. And so, the ideological war had its first direct visceral conflicts which led to another first.

In all of the conflicts between the Children, there had never been a situation in which one of the Children was challenged by one of its creations, whether directly or indirectly. While many consider Logan Ranthall's defiance of the so-called cosmic order in his challenge of Emries' directives the seminal moment of conflict between created and creator, it was in fact the phase Zarsi who was the pioneer of direct defiance of a Child of the Creator. While the phasia had already been fighting the proxy war on behalf of their patron for many centuries before Zarsi joined their ranks, Zarsi viewed himself as superior to his brethren. Halicon would later view the third incarnation of his phasia as the weakest, with the inclusion of Zarsi, Farax, and Basille. Without the steadying influence of Kamen, and the balanced triumvirate of Grawn, Bryn, and Ellis, the phasia began to lose their way. Warron for all of his violence was a pale imitation of Grawn, and while Caris proved to be adept at her intrigues, she did not seem to be able to operate on the same level as Bryn. Saurn, for all of his scheming and his claims of high intelligence did not have the thirst for knowledge of Ellis, and preferred to wait for things to happen rather than making them happen. Halicon always believed that this was so Saurn could always fall back upon the assertion that whatever occurred was because of his intricate planning. Taron was a thug. He was as physically imposing as Kamen, but without the depth of character. Taron only knew one way, and that was force, even when force was the worst option. Erdric and Aldridge were two sides of the same warped coin. They were petty schemers at the worst of times and seemed to only fall into success by accident. But even in those rare times when their schemes found a measure of success, neither was quite intelligent or ruthless enough to take full advantage, which meant that one or both of them ultimately ended up dead. Farax Soar, from his high-pitched irritating voice to his often-nauseating visage was more inclined to tinker with lower species than he was to take active part in the war with the forces of the Light. Though he did develop the Snags, it would take thousands of years of unchecked evolution for them to become the fearsome warriors that they became under the watchful eye of Aerith Seth. Under Farax's ministrations, they were nothing more than pests that could swarm prey, but were easily avoided and dispatched with minor tactical prowess. Basille showed promise in the beginning, but ultimately his failings were similar to those of Aryx Terian. Basille actually cared for the human race, and showed interest in the lives of the people of the kingdom that he ruled. He did not rule through fear or hardship the way the other phasia had done historically. Basille ruled through compassion and understanding. And so, it came as no surprise when Basille eventually betrayed Shau-ling and became the fulcrum which spawned the Dark Mirror.

Zarsi was different from his brothers and sisters from the beginning. He was thoughtful and reserved through his first years and seemed to pattern his behavior after Jeroch. As the years passed, Zarsi fancied himself as the perfect blending of Jeroch's power and Saurn's intelligence. Of course, in those days, neither were flattering expressions. Jeroch was not the same creature that he was in the early days of the war. Shau-ling had made modifications to Jeroch's powers and character in order to mitigate the losses of both Kamen and Aryx. But, armed with these faulty assumptions, and without the perspective of thousands of years of warfare against Emries and his forces, Zarsi believed that he and he alone could lead the forces of the Shadow to victory. For a time Halicon entertained these boasts as nothing more than the expected bravado of a member of the Brotherhood, but even at their worst, neither Grawn nor Jeroch were so bold as to directly challenge Shau-ling. Zarsi was the one who broke that covenant, and while he was ultimately defeated, it changed something in the relationship between Shau-ling and the phasia, something that would ultimately fully fracture in the final days of Onea. By then however, Halicon had chosen to abandon his Shau-ling persona and had freed the phasia from the limitations of their station. In some ways, Halicon made the victory over Emries possible by surrendering his claim to ideological superiority. Neither Halicon nor Emries were prepared to face the truly terrifying evolutionary leaps made by their creations, and the ability of those creations to surprise their makers with their fervent devotion to life and to freedom. Those advances, however, were not without ramification.

Gideon kicked a discarded helmet down the street as his mind turned to his old friend Logan Ranthall. A name that was a curse throughout the Heavens and among those faithful to both sides of the war on Onea. Logan, through bravery and a measure of stupidity pierced the veil between the mortal and the divine worlds. He was not granted the ability to touch the Blaze, to tap into Halicon's sacred source of power; he took it. Despite all of the effort, all of the power, and all of the sheer force of will that Logan poured into his endeavor, he still ultimately failed. Had it not been for Halicon's intervention, the Blaze would have simply consumed the foolish mortal, and the story would have turned out very differently. However, Halicon found himself intrigued by the audacity of the human, harkening back to a time when he had admired the sacrifice and heroism of his own son, Aryx. Aryx had been willing to give up all of his power so that he would no longer have to kill innocents. The lives of the humans meant more to him that his own. That too had been a turning point in the war, as the humans started to be seen as separate from Emries and his *Erieal*. But in Logan, Halicon saw a bridge where the three sides of the war could perhaps be brought to a singular resolution where the humans determined their own destiny without the interventions of Halicon and Emries. It might have worked too, had it not been for the Creator's intervention and the eventual destruction of Onea. However, while that simple act of compassion and curiosity doomed a world, it also opened the eyes of both Raenera and the Creator.

The idea of a member of the Children of the Creator investing their power into a mortal was not new. Certainly Raenera, Emries, and Halicon had all done it in their own ways. Whether it was the Adhradair, the *Erieal*, or the phasia, each was imbued with some measure of divine power which separated themselves from other mortals. It was in fact a tactic that they had learned from the Creator and his relationship to the Spirit. But Raenera saw that there was a way to correct her mistakes on Loinn, and use her powers to create the Perfect Order, without the Creator or the goddess at its center. The way to do that was to invest herself, all of herself into a mortal. This god-king or god-queen would then be able to monitor the progress of the Order, make adjustments where necessary, but still remain close enough to prevent deviations and manipulations from the outside. Raenera believed that she had been too aloof when it came to the world of Loinn. The Perfect Order should have been enough to sustain itself without her intervention and monitoring. That was the entire point of the exercise. Properly thought out, the whole of Creation could function under the tenants of the Perfect Order without the Creator or the Children. It wasn't until the fall of Loinn that Raenera realized that her version of Creation, one that did not require the Creator, would actually rob the Creator of what He wanted and needed the most, supplication and adoration. With this new godless Perfect Order, the Creator could still be worshiped, still be adored by the people, but without those beliefs impacting the social order. People would work, worship, reproduce, and die, all under the watchful eye of Raenera's empowered doppelganger. Raenera's view would be proven right, the Creator would have what he desired most, and the rest of the Children would fade into ignominy with the knowledge that they had ultimately been proven wrong.

Two distinct situations prevented Raenera from making good on her plan. The first was the war between Halicon and Emries on Onea escalating the point where the world was destroyed and neither Emries nor Halicon could declare victory in their conflict. If anything, the conflict only proved the danger posed by the human race in its more intelligent and adaptive incarnations. The second situation was the breaking of a covenant that should have never been broken. The two most powerful covenants of the Creator's law were that no being could ever act directly against the Golden Throne. No Child of the Creator, dragon, angel, or any other sentient being, until the war on Espre, would have even imagined breaking that covenant. The other covenant was that a member of the Children of the Creator was never to raise direct arms against another. Proxy wars were allowed provided they were controlled, but even in the darkest days on

Onea, neither Emries nor Halicon would have directly attacked the other. That all changed when Talisia started her revolt in the Heavens.

Talisia had always been the most forward and perhaps unstable member of the Children, and she would often rely on forbidden tactics to prove her point. Perhaps it was fitting that the soul-transference technology that she allowed to be created was the very technology that was used to rob her of her existence. Of course, those techniques were primitive compared to those which Halicon and Raenera had perfected in different ways, but Talisia was never interested in precision. Talisia was a being of impulse, and the shortest path to a goal was the preferable one, regardless of the cost or the damage. She and Pyrrus had perhaps had the most volatile part of the ideological conflict, sparking off each other like fire and ice. No matter the barb or the insult, Pyrrus would simply deflect and defer, allowing his warm nature to diffuse any attack. His patience and positivity were constant irritants to Talisia's brooding darkness. She had chosen her time of attack perfectly. Emries and Halicon were still recovering from their conflict on Onea, and Raenera had retreated from the Heavens to consider her next iteration of the Perfect Order. Talisia's strike was swift, brutal, and nearly perfect. However, she too had underestimated the former humans from Onea, and had she been just a few moments slower, Gwydeon Sandar might have been able to prevent Pyrrus' death. Had Pyrrus lived, there might never have been a need for Espre, might never have been a final reckoning in the ideological war. However, the shattering of that covenant and the brazen manner in which Talisia flaunted the Creator's laws made it clear to the Creator that he could show no more patience to his Children. The battle would come to an end, one way or another, even if it meant the Creator wiping everything from existence and starting anew.

Raenera would never get the chance to prove her new theory of a Perfect Order, so she would have to devise a new plan. That plan started with choosing the right vessel for her power. And so, Raenera watched the dawn of Espre, watched with detached eyes the machinations of her brothers and sister as they marshalled their forces and pulled beings back from beyond the veil of death and placed them into positions of power and influence. She also watched with interest how the Creator continually put his thumb on the scale to ensure that no one side had any advantage. The Dark Gods, the Emperor of Cadaria, the Church of the Creator, the

Academy of Arcane Arts, the Shadow Guild, all of the systems and structures that could be manipulated by Emries, Talisia, Halicon, and their agents. Pyrrus too found a way to contribute his vision, bonding himself to a fallen Dark God, and using his powers to whisper into the ears of that god's children, changing their natures and allowing them to see more than they should have been able to see. They would eventually find themselves in the place where they could have perhaps the most profound impact of the war, and Pyrrus would have his ultimate revenge upon Talisia. Still, Raenera watched, waited, and listened. There were souls, those tied to her brothers that were not pulled back from the brink, at least not in the way that they intended. These lost souls were aimless and without direction, and so Raenera gathered them to herself, at her retreat on Glacier's Rift, and she began to train them for the war that was coming.

Of all of her lost children, it was Gideon Viruci that had the right combination of pain and courage to carry forward with Raenera's plan. He had been a hero for the forces of the Light against Shau-ling, even though he owed his life to a member of the phasia, his mother Bryn. But Gideon was also the other, a child of the strangely empowered Aerith Seth, a being seemingly crafted by the Living Cosmos to thwart the designs of the Creator and his Children. Gideon had known war, and victory, and loss, and death. Across his two lives he had known love and loss, and the being that he became after his rebirth had a tempered wisdom that was rare. Those things may have given Gideon the malleable character that Raenera needed for her plans, but it was Gideon's parentage that was the most important. The powers of a Child of the Creator were caustic to all life save those specifically crafted to carry it. Even a dragon would have eventually been eaten from the inside out by the sheer power of a Child's touch, despite their awesome power and fortitude. But what Logan Ranthall's transition from human to something else had shown Raenera was that those who were touched by the mantle of Aerith Seth could contain a greater measure of that divine power without being consumed. So, if the mantle was enough for a large amount of divine power, then what would the blood of Aerith Seth enable his descendants to accomplish. Fortunately for Raenera, Halicon pioneered the technique of transferring his essence into a mortal tied to Aerith Seth. It was messy of course, and ultimately consumed the vessel, but that was unavoidable.

Whatever Sabrina Binosear was at the time that she accepted Halicon's power, she certainly was no longer mortal. The touch of the Creator had modified the woman that Sabrina had been, hollowing her out to accommodate His power. Raenera believed that the best part of the woman had been removed, what the humans would call a soul, and so when the part of the Creator that was the Spirit was taken from Sabrina, she was simply as shell of what she had once been, and a cracked one at that. So, when Halicon poured all his power into the imperfect vessel, her fate was sealed. The next vessel however, Aerith Seth's daughter, proved more hearty stock. It was a shame that Raenera needed to take the steps to weaken her through her bonds to Halicon's children, but such were the fortunes of war. It would only be a matter of days before she too would need to pass on her powers, if she got the chance. Of course, Raenera had other plans.

Raenera had finished perfecting the technique of investing her powers after seeing Halicon's clumsy attempt. When she poured all that she was into Gideon's body, she bonded herself to the part of him that was Aerith Seth, using his blood to cement her hold on Gideon. At the same time, she purged from him all that was tied to Halicon. What Rhain Seth never guessed was that while it was her tie to her father that was holding her together, it was her tie to her mother that was ripping her apart. Even though she was holding the same powers of the Blaze that helped to forge Bryn Aplee, the two pieces of the whole were like magnets flipped to the wrong side of each other. They would push each other away unless properly attuned. Raenera had no need to attune to the Blaze, she simply purged it from Gideon's body. It would grant him more time to do what needed to be done, as well as less restrictions on his application of power. But even with all of these advantages, the power would still eventually destroy Gideon. He had time to accomplish his task, and only that.

Gideon looked up and saw the tip of the Heart of Stone reaching up to scrape the clouds. It would not take his legion long to cross the barrier mountain range and reach the capital city of Albitonin. He knew that a great battle would rage there soon, and the phantom army would be there to wipe away all resistance to Raenera's ultimate goal. The Creator wanted supplicants, he wanted those who would worship him. That was what the battleground of Espre was all about. Who could wrangle enough souls to become dominant. Talisia had hoped to directly collect those souls through her patsy Dorovar. Emries could not shake his adherence to his *Coromor* days, wanting to replicate the Creator's folly and directly dominate the world through creatures like Kaitain Lorien. Halicon stood in the middle, placing his hopes on the shoulders of the Dark Gods, thinking that their heroism could once again unite a shattering world and offer salvation to those who mistrusted and hated them. Raenera was still unclear how Pyrrus intended to impact the war, but she hoped that her assault on the Heart of Stone would remove his two remaining weapons from the field before they were brought to bear.

For Raenera's part, her plan was simple. If there were no living beings upon the face of Espre, no one could win. If Raenera could demonstrate her perfectly ordered methods for destroying a world and robbing the Creator and the other Children of their ability to be loved and adored, then perhaps she could convince the Creator that the Perfect Order deserved another opportunity to be proven superior. With her siblings out of the way, there would be nothing to prevent her from being victorious. Like Talisia, Raenera had also learned how to steal power, suppress lifeforces, and to kill her own. Gideon knew all of the steps he would have to take, and when all was said and done, no human, Dark God, dragon, angel, or Child of the Creator would still draw breath on Espre except for Gideon himself. That would make the Creator have to deal with Raenera on her terms. If not, Gideon would have the power to take the phantom legion into the Heavens. If that came to pass, the angels that had fallen into the phantom legion would sweep through their former brethren, laying a dark path of destruction all the way to the foot of the Golden Throne. While Raenera was not sure what would happen next, she was sure of one thing. The Creator was not without equal, and so, if the Living Cosmos was powerful enough to stand against the will of the Creator, perhaps too was the power of all of the Children and their fallen champions, and a world of fallen supplicants.

Rhain

Rhain sat with her back against the headboard of the bed, her fingers gently combing through Marlae's hair as gently slept. Many nights the two women had shared a bed, but that seemed like a lifetime ago, and they were two different people then. When Rhain first met Marlae, she was using the name Rhain Feirbran, the Firebrand; an assassin in the service of the Shadow Guild and personal favorite of Geoffry Aramour, a Master of the Shadow Guild. The identity had been carefully crafted, largely by Rhain's mother Bryn, to ensure that Rhain would be noticed by the right people at the right time. A great many of that persona's traits were taken directly from Bryn's former life as the Lady Fox, the first daughter of the Brotherhood of Phasia, and one of the most terrifying killers in the history of Onea. Rhain quickly found her place in the narrative of the orphaned daughter of a murdered whore of a mother, sold into service of disreputable and abusive men. The manifestation of her powers, drawn to the surface when she defended herself against those very same abusive men; setting them ablaze like so much dry kindling. The soon-to-be assassin developed a dispassionate taste for killing early in her life, and set her sights on ridding the world of those who used their power to take advantage of women and children who could not defend themselves. She was a vigilante with a code, one who killed men for sport but would not harm a woman. Bryn was quickly proven correct in her assessment that such a background would make her irresistible to the Shadow Guild. The cover identity had additional benefits. While a wild-eyed unrepentant killer with arcane abilities would be tempting to the Guild, there was a potential risk of recruiting such a wild card. Could that person's passions be controlled? Could that killer be trusted to kill when told to and only then? That was why it was so important for Firebrand to have a code. Something that could be trusted to restrain Rhain's hand when necessary, and something that could be leveraged when necessary. Additionally, when Rhain was approached by a representative of the Guild, she made sure to rebuff the advance as her mother instructed. It was important to not look too eager. It took another year in the cover identity before the Guild representatives approached her again, this time with an offer that would look too suspicious to refuse. Still Rhain played the part to perfection, giving her grudging agreement after a tense exchange where barely-veiled death threats were tossed back and forth. A week later, Rhain was brought before the Grand Master of the Shadow Guild.

This eventuality had been the focus of most of Rhain's training. Neither Bryn nor Aerith knew who the Grand Master of the Shadow Guild was, but they had their suspicions that it was a member of the Brotherhood of Phasia. To that end, Bryn and Aerith worked with Rhain for almost a year, teaching her how to suppress her connection to her father's abilities as well as her connection to the Blaze. The lessons were grueling and painful, and for the first six months of the lessons, Rhain felt as though she would never be able to succeed. It was not enough to simply suppress the powers, especially if she was up against someone who knew what they were looking for. A novice could be fooled, or perhaps a child of a member of the phasia, but a full phase with the unbridled abilities of the Blaze at their disposal was another matter altogether. The Blaze was an all-encompassing power that was seductive in its call and responsive in times of need. Rhain had known its warmth since the moment of her birth, and it could come to her unbidden in times of need. When she was young, she had fallen out of a tree from a great height. Before she even knew what she was doing, an aura of Blaze power surrounded her and slowed her fall. Of course, the moment that Bryn knew that her daughter was unharmed, she launched into a series of lessons about minimizing the use of power. Those who could touch the Blaze were all connected and anyone who used the power carelessly or unconsciously was just asking for one of the more powerful and practiced practitioners to pay them an unwelcome visit. While Aerith and Bryn were not exactly hiding, they were not looking forward to having any old friends drop by unannounced. They had planned for the eventualities that would cause them to rejoin the war with the Creator, and they didn't want to have their hands forced because their children could not be trusted to control themselves when it came to their powers.

That was why both Rhain and Ayden found it much easier to rely on their connection to the powers possessed by their father. The Blaze had too many rules, and too many people who could feel what was being done with it for it to be safe to use. Aerith's mantle on the other hand was like a private joke known by only a few. There were disadvantages to using Aerith's abilities however. The first and largest of those disadvantages of course was the fact that a great deal of mental discipline was required. Where use of the Blaze translated vague information to other users, like location and what the Blaze was used for, Aerith's powers were much more intimate. Those who were connected through Aerith's mantle could share thoughts, emotions, memories, the very essence of identity. The first time Rhain connected to her father in that way, she was overwhelmed. Aerith had felt his daughter gently probing the edges of her abilities and decided to teach her a gentle lesson. He had had millennia to adjust his defenses to those who shared his mantle, and when he lowered his guard just slightly, the assault of emotion was too much for the powerful girl. He had not intended to cause harm of course, all he let through was his unguarded love for her, and the power of it had brought tears to the girl's eyes. That sharing had changed their relationship and created a closeness that could not be explained to anyone, not even Bryn. Rhain and Aerith would share a connection that her father and mother could never share, despite the power that they both possessed. Aerith always joked that his children had inherited the soul that he had lost long ago, but in a way, he was correct. The connection was like the unfiltered melding of souls, where all boundaries and all sense of isolation are lost. That power, that connection, was not something that could easily be turned off.

Sealing away the powers of the Blaze was the first lesson. The challenge of those lessons was not the sealing away of the Blaze from the conscious mind, but keeping it inaccessible from the unconscious mind. In order to practice this control, Aerith and Rhain would spar while Bryn launched mental attacks against her daughter's defenses. Rhain had been taught from an early age to project a false self so that if anyone adept with mental abilities would see nothing more than a mundane mind with limited arcane abilities. For hours, Rhain and Bryn would sit in total silence while Bryn launched attack after attack at the false projection of mundanity. The shield against mental attack had to be perfect, with no crack, but at the same time couldn't be too perfect. Bryn taught Rhain how to construct false cracks, fake unshielded thoughts, traps and holes that an invader could fall into, thinking they had found deeper truths. Once those lessons were mastered, Bryn would wait until Rhain had fallen asleep and then launch attacks upon her unconscious mind. At first her unconscious defenses crumbled under Bryn's simplest attacks. However in time even the deepest probes by the practiced tendrils of Bryn's thoughts could not penetrate Rhain's constructs of normalcy. The complications however began when both Aerith and Bryn began to assault her defenses. Invariably one would trigger an unconscious use of power while she was busy defending against the other. More often than not most of her mental energy was focused on keeping her mother out of her mind and then her father would land a blow while sparing which would cause the Blaze to flare and erect defenses against the attack. Time and time again they would overwhelm her defenses, and time and time again she would fail the test. But then something inside of her clicked. It wasn't enough to construct the other person in her mind, she had to believe that she was that other person. That was what was holding her back. At her core she was still Rhain Seth, not Rhaine Feirbran. If she were going to fool those with incredible power and millennia of experience at their disposal, she had to believe. Once that piece of the puzzle fell into place, even the hardest strike by her father during sparring or the deepest probes by her mother as she slept could not penetrate the illusion. She was ready for whatever the Shadow Guild had to send against her.

As prepared as she was however, she could not suppress the nervousness as she stood face to face with the Grand Master of the Shadow Guild. He was not imposing in stature, but his violet eyes shown with such malice and such vicious intelligence that Rhain could not suppress the shudder that ran through her when those eyes first locked on hers. At that moment, Rhain had to work hard to suppress her recognition of the man's identity. From an early age, she was taught to identify every member of the phasia as well as every person who fought for either side during the war on Onea. Aerith had always taught her that knowing who your opponent is and what they are capable of more often than not could mean the difference between life and death. And so, when the violet eyes of Saurn Macco met hers for the first time, Rhain did her best to stifle any reaction. It almost wasn't enough. She felt the probes enter her thought, felt him rummaging around in her memories. While it was clear he did not have the subtlety and talent that Bryn possessed, he more than made up for his clumsiness with brute force. Fortunately, Rhain's defenses held and Saurn's attacks ceased after a few moments. When she was dismissed from what could only be referred to as a life or death interview, she was remanded to the care of Geoffry Aramour for her training and eventual assignments. It was obvious fairly quickly that Rhain did not require much in the way of formal training and so Geoffry was quick to put her in the field.

The Shadow Guild operated with small distinct cells that reported to one of the masters of the Guild. The cells did not interact with one another, and members of one cell did not know any members of any other cells. The Aramour cell consisted of Rhain, Cole Breon, and Liandra Nightshade. Each had their strengths, and those strengths complimented each other when the need arose. Rhain was the raw power who could utilize her supposed arcane abilities to set fire to buildings or to torch corpses to erase all signs of murder. Cole was the silent assassin and infiltrator who could defeat any lock, any wall, or any barrier. The man earned his name as the Living Shadow many times over. Liandra was a poison expert who knew every exotic plant across the whole of Espre. She knew what poisons mixed with which drinks to disguise their taste, which poisons would not act for several hours to escape detection by food tasters, and which ones could be mixed in such a way that they could be worn on the lips or on the skin and poison the touched but not the wearer. She was brilliant beyond words and had no sense of conscience. It wasn't even that Liandra enjoyed killing, but she enjoyed the puzzle that killing represented. How to do it while escaping detection. How many could be killed before the first was discovered. Could she eliminated an entire dining hall full of people without being discovered? Everything was a puzzle, a challenge, and that was what endeared her to Geoffry who fancied himself as some kind of artist of death. Geoffry was as brilliant as he was evil. Geoffry enjoyed killing. He savored the moment of death, watching the light flicker out of his victim's eyes. He often said that he could feel the spirit of his victim leave its mortal form and pass through him. But Geoffry insisted on never killing the same way twice, which tended to create conflicts with the Shadow Guild as his methods of murder would often become so elaborate that they were foiled by unavoidable convergences of events. Any plan that had multiple points of failure could not be counted on being successful as often as they could be. And so it was no surprise to Rhain when Geoffry was removed from his post heading an active cell and moved to personal service duty to the newly crowned Emperor of Cadaria, Kaitain Lorien.

Where Kaitain's father had resisted the urge to use the serves of the Shadow Guild, preferring to deal with his enemies through diplomacy and force of arms, Kaitain preferred a smile and a dagger in the back. Geoffry's cover was that of court poet and bard. Liandra, Cole, and Rhain stayed in Geoffry's service to help remove any thorns from the new Emperor's side. However, it only took a matter of days before the then Marlae Lorien saw through Geoffry's disguise. The only way to placate the young arrogant woman was to second the services of one of his assassins to her personal use. When the three potential assassins were brought before Marlae, it took only a gentle nudge from Rhain's well-practiced mental abilities to ignite lust within Marlae's mind. Of course, looking back, Rhain wondered if such manipulation was even necessary. Rhain found herself in Marlae's bed that very night, and for many nights after. She became Marlae's shadow, and while at the beginning Marlae saw Rhain as nothing more than another plaything, their relationship grew and changed. Other playthings came and went, but Rhain was the constant, until a confluence of events put them on a collision course with destiny.

Marlae shifted slightly, draping her arm over Rhain's waist and pulling her body close to Rhain. Rhain smoothed her hair back away from her face and gently stroked her cheek. A soft smile curled Marlae's lips for just a moment, and then she faded back into a contented sleep. A small pang of guilt fluttered through Rhain's heart as she watched Marlae sleep. The young woman had already absorbed so much in a short time. Even now looking down at Marlae, Rhain found it hard to remember the spoiled and violent woman who had been a heartbeat from the throne of Cadaria. How many people had she had killed because they looked at her the wrong way? How many cooks were executed for bland food? How many serving girls beheaded because her bath water was too hot or too cold? Could that evil creature have been the same woman that now shared Rhain's bed? She had stood in rebellion of her father's will, first for her own selfish desires, and then as a pawn and puppet of the Creator. And now, mere hours ago, Marlae could have freed herself of all expectation, all responsibility, and thirst for power. She could have gracefully stepped aside and let Quyhn Ravenheart become the target of scorn and descent. Perhaps the old Marlae would have done that. Perhaps she would have calculated the chances of Quyhn's survival, and then plotted when she could appear and wrestle away everything that the younger woman had worked to accomplish. She had learned for so long to take the easy and bloody road whenever possible. However, now she was a different woman. She was willing to do the work to save the soul of the Empire that she had once coveted merely for its title. She had cared so little about the people not so long ago, and now she was willing to risk everything for them. Rhain smiled at the thought of the days when the war was over and the Cadarian Empire would wake to the rule of Marlae Tamerlane. She would be a good and just ruler.

But she would have to rule without Rhain. The thought turned Rhain's stomach and made her heart hurt in a way that could not be put into words. It was a sorrow and an emptiness that weighed upon her, but those emotions were not the most disconcerting. No, it was the inevitability. Perhaps at one time she could have theorized a way out of what was about to happen, but now, there was only death that awaited her. Perhaps she would die in her sleep, devoured by the powers of the Blaze and the soul of Halicon that corroded her veins. Perhaps her heart would simply stop when another member of the phasia met their end through the malicious powers of Raenera. Or perhaps, she would find her end in battle. What was unavoidable now was the fact that she would die. She tried to think of when she knew that fact had crystallized. It took only a moment to find. It was the look in Logan's eyes. The same look he had in his eyes when Sabrina came to the end of her life. The profound look of sorrow mixed with futility. He had wanted so much to save her from her fate, and then to find out that nothing he did would have prevented what was coming, it broke something in him, something that remained broken when he looked into Rhain's eyes and saw what was coming.

Logan. She could not keep her thoughts from going to him and the path that he now walked. She was careful not to let any specifics leak out beyond her own heart for fear that one of the other Children or even the Creator would see what Logan had planned. She hoped that he was strong enough for the trial ahead, and that he had prepared himself for everything that he would have to sacrifice to make his plan a success. But even if he succeeded, even if he was able to win the war in one fell swoop, would it be enough to save Rhain and all the others who were touched by the Children of the Creator? As soon as Rhain felt Logan make up his mind about his course of action, she knew what was behind it, and why he was the only one who had the chance to stand against Tess and make his plan come to fruition. Logan was fond of saying that he never wanted power. But that wasn't entirely true. He wanted power, but not to become powerful. He wanted power out of the want for love. He didn't want power to win that love, it was already his. He needed the power to protect that love and ensure that it would never be stolen from him. How wrong he proved to be. No matter the power that he accumulated, the people that he loved were taken from him over and over again. He was used, manipulated, and was made to sacrifice over and over again, brought back from oblivion to be made to lose more. Friends that he lost were resurrected by the Creator and used to taunt him over and over again. The woman that he loved was taken from him, only for her soul to be bound into the body of a woman who didn't deserve to breathe the same air as Elwyne Tamerlane, let alone share her name. His son was used as a pawn by Talisia, his daughter hidden from him in an effort to protect them both from those who would use Isabella against him. Sabrina lost to the power of the Blaze. Pike dead at Logan's own hands. Rael, Trece, and Kamen sacrificed so that he could live long enough to make a difference and perhaps turn the tide once again. And now, now he was willing to make another sacrifice. Willing to deliver a death sentence. But could he really do it? Could he really be thinking of doing the unthinkable?

Rhain knew instantly how Logan would rationalize it. If the war ended tomorrow, if the Creator was defeated and the souls of the Children were banished back to the emptiness of the Living Cosmos, all those touched by that evil would be saved. Gideon, Wolf, Rhain, Cedric, Anabel, Mirana and Liara; they would all be able to have lives away from the war. Gideon would have to pay for the evils that he did in Raenera's name, and perhaps he would not be able to. Maybe that was the part of the equation that Logan could not see. He wanted so much for the people that he was trying to save to be the way that he remembered them. But none of them were that innocent any more. Gideon was no longer the belligerent thief who was as quick with a curse as he was with a knife. No, now he was a mass murderer, who had the blood of his own daughter on his hands. And Wolf? He would have to live in a world without his wife; a world in which he was willing to use Darrien Annis as bait in a trap meant for a Child of the Creator, knowing that it would likely lead to her death. Cedric was a man out of time, from a world in which he knew only pain and sadness. And now that he had enacted his vengeance upon his tormenter, was there anything left for him? Could he live in a world with his sister who he barely knew any longer? Would he find happiness with the woman who loved him more than life itself, but had lived without him for so many years? Would Logan's actions rob him of the daughter that he never knew? Anabel had never wanted to be part of this war and never wanted to be this immortal landmark to loss and futility. If the war were over tomorrow, what would become of a woman whose exhaustion hung around her like a cloud? Would it be enough to be reunited with her children and her grandchildren? Would she try to have a relationship with the father that she denied for so long? Could there be a happy ending for someone such as her? Perhaps Mirana and Liara were young enough to not bear the scars of their experience for too long. Perhaps they could adjust to life without their mother and lean on their extended family to craft something normal out of their new lives.

And as Rhain's thoughts drifted back to herself, she ran her fingers through Marlae's soft hair once again. Rhain knew without question that she could be happy here for as many days as she had left. She didn't need power, didn't need to be immortal. All she wanted was to go to sleep every night and wake up every morning with Marlae at her side. The thought of it was so powerful and so intense and so impossible that it broke her heart. Tears rolled down her face, and her breathing became ragged. The thought of not being with Marlae was too much to take, and then the thought of Marlae having to go on without Rhain compounded the sorrow. How could she explain to Marlae that one day she would simply not be there? They had gone through so much to be here in this moment of time, and to have it ripped away from them was too cruel. Rhain had found herself because of Marlae, and Marlae had found herself because of Rhain. For them to be pulled apart…

Rhain tried to steady her breathing, but it was no use. Then brilliant eyes were staring up at her. Marlae smiled softly and pulled herself up, draping herself across Rhain's chest. With one hand she wiped the tears from the right side of Rhain's face while kissing away the tears on her left cheek. No words were needed, and Marlae snaked her arms around Rhain and pulled them tight together. Marlae just held her for what seemed like hours until she leaned back, kissed Rhain gently on the lips and then slid back down the bed. Marlae took hold of Rhain's hand and pulled her down as well. When Rhain's head hit the pillow, the exhaustion of the past days hit her all at once, but once Marlae laid her head on Rhain's shoulder and snuggled close, peace descended upon her mind. Even if this moment would not last, even if there were fewer days ahead than behind, Rhain would not lose sight of this moment. The woman that she loved was lying beside her, and she would spend the rest of her life reveling in that love, no matter how long that life lasted.

Just before she closed her eyes, Rhain sent a thought out into the cosmos. She was unsure if it would reach its intended destination. Perhaps Logan could still hear her thoughts, or perhaps it no longer mattered. Either way, in the last moments, whether Logan succeeded in his plan, or if he found that he could not go through with it, Rhain needed him to know. Needed him to hear.

The Flickering Flame is more than an idea. It is more than the sacrifices of one to another. You have lifted up so many. You have made so many lives, loves, and futures possible. But you no longer see a future for yourself. You see only obligation and responsibility. For so long you have worked to overthrow tyrants and fiends, while trying not to become one of them. My father has always been fond of saying that he became a monster long ago which is why he is destined to fight and die battling other monsters. I think part of you believes that you have become a monster too. Do not let your light be diminished chasing responsibilities that are not yours to bear alone. Perhaps if you look for light where you think it could not possibly shine you will see that there is another path waiting for you, one that you could not see while you were blinded by the brilliance of responsibility and destiny. Your fate is your own now, Logan, and you must find a way to not be swallowed by it. If you can hear me, hear your own words and heart echoed in mine. Use my flame, use my love to lift yourself up when you can no longer rise by yourself. The path you travel is a long and lonely one, but you will never be alone. My love goes with you, as does the love of all those you have fought beside. May this light protect you in all the dark places that you must travel, and know that when your days and your travels are at an end, all those who love you will be waiting for you. That much my dearest friend, you have earned. Good night, Logan, wherever you are. And thank you for bringing my love back to me. I wish I could have given yours back to you.

Rhain's eyes fluttered closed, and no thoughts invaded her mind except for the sound of Marlae's slow and gentle breathing, and the feeling of her warm silky skin.

Wolf

There's no shame in admitting that you're a failure.

Wolf Ranthall sat quietly by the side of the fire and watched as the wind blew gently through the tall grass. Cedric had long since left their little conclave and gone on to his next stop, wherever that was going to be. Of course, Wolf had an idea where the man would end up and the task that the Creator would inevitably have for him. But there was a secret in Cedric's heart, one that could not be denied, and perhaps that was their best chance to prevent the catastrophe that was coming. And there was no doubt it was a catastrophe, one whose scale had not been felt in the cosmos for thousands of years. That was the truly terrifying reality. The staggering truth of just what the Creator was capable of, just what the Creator and the Children were willing to do to triumph. It was triumph at all costs in the worst sense of the phrase, and there would either be utter victory or utter defeat, there could be no middle ground, for either side. Now, the pieces were simply falling into place. The Creator planned for each and every one of those pieces and where they would fall. Perhaps it would only take one being out of place for the whole of the Creator's plans to be undone. Free will had created a crack in the grand plan, now it was time to see if the essence of the human spirit was strong enough to make good on the promise that its heroes created.

Heroes. Really?

Feeling the hairs on the back of his neck stand up and the bile rise up in his throat, Wolf felt the voice like a punch in the gut. It was impossible not to feel the menace rolling from the words crawling across his brain. Of all of the integrated personalities that tried to share Wolf Ranthall's body, Draven Batoe stood out like a shard of glass in a bed of feathers. For all of his posturing and all of his scheming, there was one thing that Draven was not, and it was subtle.

All that time on Onea, and I was the dangerous one with dangerous ideas. I was the one who needed to be kept from gaining control, the one who always went too far. I was the one who did the unexpected. I was the one who pushed past the norms that your so-called heroes had to keep to. I broke the rules that they were too afraid to get close to. Gwydeon Sandar...pawn. Logan Ranthall...fool. Pike Rhuiden...villain. The list goes on and on and on. The weakness and the stupidity of your champions was expressed time and time again. Manipulated by Emries. Manipulated by Halicon. Manipulated by the Creator. Manipulated by each other. All because you thought you knew the rules and how the game was supposed to be played. Raised on too many bedtime stories about the gallant heroes who took up arms against impossible odds and triumphed for the sake of good. The light would always extinguish the shadow, the princess would always be rescued by the handsome prince, and the villain would find redemption once he admitted his transgressions to the friend who was always willing to forgive him. What rubbish. No wonder the human race is populated with miserable sheep who can do nothing but die with any kind of proficiency.

Wolf's blood burned at the characterization, but he could also not help but admit that there was some truth to Draven's words. The power that the Children and the Creator continued to hold over the human race was their ability to manipulate perception and perspective to constantly keep patterns moving in the desired direction. But the brilliance of the manipulation was the scope of it. Throw a rock into a still pond, and at the point of impact the waves are massive and unmistakable. However, the farther out the waves travel, the less intense they become, but they are no less influenced by the impact of the rock. The human race in this metaphor is the pond, but the majority of those beings exist at the very edge of the pond. The rock of course is the manipulation perpetrated by either the

Creator, the Children, or one of their many agents. So, though these manipulations were constantly taking place, because of their distance from the epicenter of the manipulation, most humans would not be able to tell the difference between the hand of the Creator on a situation and the normal winds and tides. However, there were some who were closer to the manipulations, and they could feel something different. But they were not so close that they could actually see the rock hitting the water. However, the changes were too big to be ignored. Even though they could not discern the cause of what they were feeling, they were compelled to make an effort to change it.

Not all, just the stupid ones.

Draven's implication was not a new one. He felt nothing but disdain for the heroes of humanity who had stood against him, none more than Gwydeon Sandar.

Sandar. The original do-gooder.

There were many facets of each of the personalities that Wolf had tried but was unable to suppress despite all of the power and control that he had gained in his short time as a combined being. Whether it was Pyrrus' unbridled optimism, Basille's mistrust of everything, or Draven's complete and utter lack of empathy, some feelings were so powerful that they would not be denied. Perhaps the most powerful of all was Draven's utter hatred for Gwydeon Sandar and everything that the man stood for. But the hatred was more than just for the man whom Draven tangled with on several occasions, it was for what Gwydeon stood for. Gwydeon was a human who took up arms against Shau-ling and the phasia and not only survived but conquered.

He did no such thing. Gwydeon Sandar was a pretender, a charlatan, a con man with feathers. There was nothing ever special about him. He was the best swordsman in a farm town? So what? There is a best swordsman in every farm town on every world that has ever existed in every reality. The woman that he loved died? So what? So many people have lost loved ones, family members, friends, spouses, children. It does not make anyone special. Death is a part of life, and you can't on one hand say that death makes you stronger while on the other hand say that death makes you suffer. More human hypocrisy. Sandar hitches his wagon to the so-called hero Logan and it was through that association that Sandar rose to his reputation. And what made that reputation? He killed Rael in personal combat. Rael was a young member of the phasia who barely could control his powers, and to be fair was only half a phase. In the process of killing Rael he took a wound that proved to be mortal. And then he fought Jeroch to a standstill, and ended up dying because of his hubris. And for that he gets rewarded? He gets elevated to the position of Brother of Angels and is chosen to be the father of the third generation's Coromor? Yet more hypocrisy by the Creator and Emries. Rewarding mediocrity when it suits them.

Of course, it was an over-simplification yet again. Draven's hostility was without bounds and the venom leaked through with every word.

Even in his time as the Brother of Angels, Gwydeon was a coward. He hid behind his wife. He hid behind the walls of his castle. He hid behind the so-called rules of the Creator. And in the end he hid behind Aerith Seth and Logan Ranthall. Gwydeon never took responsibility, never took leadership, and never took ownership of the role that he was given. What's more is that he could never accept the fact that he was a pawn in a game that he could never understand. But in the end, that's all that martyrs are good for, fighting and dying, and all in someone else's name. How pathetic. You know all about that, don't you?

The jab was pointed and precise and landed with all the subtlety of a brick to the head. And as much as Wolf wanted to argue the point, it was very difficult to do. For all of the wonderful things that Gwydeon Sandar was able to accomplish as a hero of the light, everything worked to advance the agenda of the Creator and the Children. Whether it was allowing Emries to use his guilt against him in the resurrection of Gabrielle Crill and her son Gwillim. Or it was the subtle manipulations that allowed him to stand against members of the phasia thinking that it was his skill and his skill alone that sealed his triumphs. The training of his son Nathaniel to be Emries' greatest pawn in his war against Shau-ling. The easy sacrifice of his own life, not once but twice.

I wonder if Gwydeon knows just how instrumental he has been in the destruction of everything. The Creator allowed him to live time and time again during his time with the People of the Dragon because he was the only one who could battle Jeroch in the Hall of Terrors. His fate was determined from the moment he was born, and he never could see beyond his petulant desire to be a hero. Then in the Dark Mirror, he had but one responsibility, and that was to defeat me. Were it not for Gwydeon Sandar, I would have gotten what I wanted from Sabrina Binosear, empowered my Dark Riders with every bit of Aerith Seth's warped abilities, and torn down every last vestige of the so-called forces of the Light before I ripped Emries' heart out. How was it that you humans were so blind? Even your father was smart enough to see the light. Of course it was far too late. Sandar and Rhuiden ruined it for everyone, and by the time the blind among you were forced to see, it was too late. Our world was destroyed. All hope of defeating Emries was lost. The Creator gained more power. And now we may lose everything because you idealists chose the wrong ideal.

While the voice was clearly Draven's, there was more of Basille's edge to the words. Now that Wolf had access to not only Basille and Draven's memories, but also those of Pyrrus, all of the historically meaningful events took on a completely different hue. Whether it was the expulsion of Aryx from the forces of the Shadow which in turn lead to the birth of Aerith Seth. Or how Aerith Seth was allowed to grow into adulthood subverting every trial. Was this the Creator's doing, or were these the actions of some unknown force that moved outside of the view of the Creator? How was it that Ellis was allowed to possess the body of Victoria Rhuiden thus giving birth to Korrd Ranthall, the inheritor of Emries' mantle in the second generation of the prophecies? Was it in order to make the phasia feel more confident in their role against not only Emries but against Shau-ling? Or was it to leave enough residual power in Victoria's body to allow for the creation of Logan Ranthall?

Ranthall.

The name hammered through Wolf's brain like the most heinous curse ever uttered. Wolf's family had a reputation to be sure, on both sides of the war. The longer Wolf lived, the more he saw his family cast into similar roles to the Seth family, and it was not a comforting thought. Aryx Terian was the patriarch of what became the Seth family, a solider who fought with a conscience, much like the patriarch of the Ranthall family, Arin Ranthall.

After Aryx came the miscast and misunderstood anti-hero Aerith Seth. He was a man who would not die, but a man who continued to have an impact long after he should have been irrelevant. The phasia tried to make Aerith into a villain. The Hand of the Light tried to make him into a hero, but he could never be either. All Aerith could ever be was an agent of unbridled change and chaos, taking direction from no one, and altering the very fabric of reality with every breath that he took. The same could be said of Logan Ranthall. Miscast as the Lord Dragon of the second generation of the prophecies, Logan tried to lead the fight against Shau-ling. But for all his desire to do what was right, he was under the thumb of Emries every step. It was only after the pyrrhic success against Shau-ling in the second generation that Logan began to have his eyes opened to the true nature of the war between the Light and the Shadow, and who truly deserved the title of villain. They had been so wrong about everything, and so Logan set about making it right. In the Light reality, he was never given the chance. Emries foresaw the danger that an unrestrained Logan Ranthall with Elwyne Tamerlane at his side represented, and so Emries took great pleasure in snuffing the life out of his would-be champion. Of course, this was after the next generation of Ranthalls had already been born in the person of Wolf.

And like your father, you had a foot in both worlds.

It was Draven's voice again, but without the edge. It had more of the feel of Pyrrus' subtle but optimistic tone. Pyrrus did not speak much in Wolf's head, at least not directly in the same way that Draven and Basille did, but when the voice did join the chorus, it spoke with authority and unparalleled knowledge. As usual, Pyrrus was correct in his assessment. Wolf, like his father, had a foot in two worlds, except in Wolf's case he was aware of it. Logan never knew about the interference of Ellis in his family's bloodline, but Basille made sure that Wolf knew what was happening every step of the way. Of course it had been Basille's actions that had facilitated the creation of the Dark Mirror reality, and through that action, through that intervention, Logan Ranthall had been given another life. That life, that reality was not a happy ending with the woman he loved and a baby boy to carry on his legacy. Instead, Logan was jaded and hardened by loss, locked away from the world in a prison of his own grief. Isolated and sullen, Logan was no threat to the plan that Emries had concocted in the

Dark Mirror, and would not stand in the way of the corruption of Nathan Sandar. However, like Gwydeon Sandar, Logan could not stand by and watch the carnage continue, not while he still had the strength to stand against the tide of darkness. In the beginning, all Logan wanted to do was fight and die on his own two feet with a sword in his hand. When Logan didn't die during the many engagements in Trelon, or at Draven's hand on the day that Trelon fell, he shook himself from the fatalistic pathway and rededicated himself to the mission of rescuing the world from the darkness that enveloped it. But Emries could not countenance Logan's interference, and so as he had done in the Light Reality, Emries set about removing his former champion from the equation. However, Emries did not find an old exhausted man in his bed that he could easily smother with his bare hands. The Logan of the Dark Mirror was ready to fight, and was ready to do the unthinkable. That unthinkable took the form of touching the Blaze and having the audacity to stand toe to toe with a Child of the Creator, without the protection of the prophecies.

I've always had a grudging respect for what Logan was able to accomplish, but his actions at times bordered on the reckless. Touching the Blaze so openly in defiance of Emries while at the same time potentially drawing the ire of Shau-ling was brazen. It would not of course be the last brazen or rash act, as evidenced by what came shortly after the ill-fated confrontation with Emries.

There was a kind of pride in Basille's words, even though they were slightly undermined by Draven's violent and dismissive tone. Basille was right of course, Logan through his instincts to touch the Blaze because of the gifts left to him through Ellis' manipulation of Victoria Ranthall had opened him to reprisal not only by Emries, but by Shau-ling. Emries likely would have been able to kill Logan had it not been for interference by Caris, Rael, and Trece. But even before that, the moment that Logan touched the Blaze he became subject to the whims and the notice of Shau-ling. Had he wanted, Sha-ling could have burned Logan alive with the fires of the Blaze with a thought. At that moment, however, Logan served a purpose. That purpose however was exacerbated by what happened next.

My brother Halicon was pragmatic. And while he was not above eliminating some of his most powerful soldiers in order to gain advantage either in the present or in the future, Halicon at times sabotaged himself by not allowing those who would benefit most from his machinations to see the greater picture. Though he sacrificed Kamen, not once but twice, those other members of the phasia were not allowed to see the benefit of such action and what was created by the sacrifice. The same could be said for Aryx's release from his servitude. While Shau-ling was focused on the destruction of those loyal to Emries, Halicon had begun to see the cracks in the Creator's grand vision. Once Aryx had been removed from the equation, Halicon began to see the changes within the powers both within and without the Blaze, as well as the manner in which Emries was manipulating events. There was a nexus forming around Aryx Terian, one that could not be ignored. And so when Aryx fell under the sway of Emries' lies and was repurposed as a member of the Erieal *Halicon began to make hard choices; choices that he wished he didn't have to make, but knew were necessary in order to protect all possible futures.*

Pyrrus' words were prescient and cutting. If Aryx Terian, with his conscience and his tenacity could fall under Emries' sway, it was possible that the other original members of the phasia with their nearly unlimited power could also have been coopted. In theory at least. However, while the powers of the phasia were nearly identical, their temperaments were not. Aryx was in some ways a moral killer. He saw the purpose of the war, but did not see the point in carrying on a meaningless one. The deaths were meaningless, and as such he could not rationalize them. Conversely, Grawn, Bryn, and Ellis were killers, and unrepentant ones at that. Even though Ellis liked to hide behind her intelligence and Bryn liked to hide behind her appetites, they were no less ruthless than their older brother. Jeroch was not a killer, but he was loyal; loyal perhaps to a fault. Jeroch would never fall to the machinations of Emries, no matter how many promises or threats were lobbed in his direction. That left Kamen. Kamen could have been a problem if left open to corruption.

Kamen was too thoughtful, too much like his father. Halicon stood in the middle of us, the attempt to balance all the furies that spun around him, the furies represented not only by his siblings but by the Creator. But while Halicon tried to understand why his siblings did what they did, he left himself open to being manipulated by their action and inaction. To that end, the Creator used Halicon's thoughtfulness against him, consistently using him as the broom to sweep away the mistakes of his siblings. The phasia believed that they were great destroyers, that they somehow had become the quintessential killers in Creation. If they only knew how much of a killer their progenitor was. If they only knew how many worlds Halicon had been dispatched to remove from Creation; how many millions of lives had been snuffed out at his hands. Halicon was the Reaper of Creation long before he became the Nightmare of Men. Once Halicon saw what Aryx had been turned into, he knew that he could not allow Kamen to become a tool in the war. In Emries' hands, Kamen could have been an even more terrifying killer than Halicon ever was. So Kamen was removed from the equation until Halicon could find a way to utilize his power the right way.

Wolf could feel the pain in Pyrrus, but at the same time some of the sorrow came from Basille. Basille had never had the opportunity to have a relationship with his eldest brother, but that did not stop him from idolizing and respecting the phase that Kamen had been. In fact, Basille liked to think that he patterned his time on Onea after the lessons that he learned from Kamen through the Blaze. But as with everything Shau-ling did, removing Kamen from the equation came with a cost. That cost was the loss of trust by his fellows in the original phasia. Yes, there was manipulation by Emries and the lure of the prophecies, but would Ellis and Bryn have been so eager to find methodologies to defeat Shau-ling if they did not feel that they were betrayed by him? In the end, it would not matter. The prophecies were as much of a trap for Emries as they were for Shau-ling. Through the memories of the Blaze, Wolf had begun to try to put pieces together with those available to Pyrrus. Was Halicon aware of the prophecies? Did he know what was coming before the formation of the Hand of the Light and the revelation of Aerith Seth and his uncanny abilities? Was that why he took Kamen off the board, in order to be ready for the time when those powers would be needed most?

This was where your father's recklessness was most on display, and Halicon's impatience nearly destroyed everything. Halicon should have let Logan die in his attempt to absorb the Living Flame's power. If he had, perhaps Onea could have been saved for another generation. But Logan's transgression, coupled with Aerith Seth's interference showed the Creator just how much he did not know about what Aerith Seth's mantle was capable of. What Halicon did not see, could not have seen, was what those two powers did once they touched one another. Echoes of the collision rippled through the whole of Creation. And while the phasia found themselves wondering how their bitter enemy had become their ally, and while Emries was pondering how he let the opportunity to snuff out Logan's resistance pass by, the Creator watched. The Creator saw something in the Blaze, felt something it is power, and so how together with Aerith Seth's mantle, reality shifted. The man who was, the Logan that had been the champion of the Light, ceased to exist. He was remade down to his very essence, the very essence of every fabric of his being. Logan died. Logan died and was reborn. But the new Logan was not the child of Emries as other humans were. He was not the child of Halicon as the other phasia were. He was a child of the Blaze, the very force that the Creator could not control nor understand. In that moment the Creator was faced with all of the fears and uncertainty that had been festering within him since the dawn of time. From that moment the Creator knew that this version of Creation could not remain.

So, Wolf's thoughts came back to Draven's first jibe. Where his father had succeeded, Wolf had failed. Wolf had sent his wife, his daughters, his friends who trusted him to their deaths all in the service of the Creator's whims. He had not had the strength or the courage to find a way to break the cycle that held him. And now, that cycle was on the verge of breaking whether Wolf wanted it to or not. Wolf had felt the moment that the Creator had pulled his Servants back from the brink and felt the change in the fabric of Creation. Everything was beginning to unravel, but it was not as linear as the Creator had expected. Doubt still radiated through every quiet space. To that end, Wolf knew what was coming, but did not know the resolution as he once thought he did.

Wolf had prepared Darrien to deliver Talisia's powers to Anabel, completing the cycle that began with Rhain Seth. Gideon Viruci had gained his powers from Raenera, unleashing her army upon the face of Espre. Now Cedric had gained Emries' abilities and he was on his way to bring death to all those who could stand against the final act of the Creator's machinations. And though Wolf knew that he had been just a temporary host for Pyrrus' powers and that Ayden would be coming soon to become the permanent vessel, there was something about it that did not feel as final as before. There was a part of Wolf that knew it was what would come to pass regardless of his doubts, and yet there was a growing tide within Wolf that saw a potentially different outcome. Perhaps that was why there were still so many Ranthalls. If Wolf did not relinquish his powers to Ayden, there were other options. With Mirana and Liara both in Albitonin, they were logical repositories for the powers of Raenera and Talisia. Cedric could easily fall prey to his old ally Arin Ranthall, and the newly discovered Isabella Ranthall could be a logical host for the powers that Rhain Seth had done her best to keep under control. What would happen in the next few hours would shape everything that would come after, and perhaps mean the difference between victory and defeat. Victory for the Creator would mean the death of everything, and defeat would mean the end of Creation as it was currently constituted. Without the Creator, there would perhaps be no life and no light. There would perhaps be no hope or salvation. There might be only darkness. But those mortals who understood the oppression and danger of the Creator's continued rule were willing to take that chance.

Wolf felt the divine portal form not far away, and he prepared himself to draw perhaps his last breaths.

Cedric

I was dead once.

Cedric's gruff and aged voice bounced off the walls and echoed in his turbulent and confused mind. It felt as though everything inside of him was broken and where there had been clear and defined memories there was only darkness and dancing shadows that mocked any attempt to find answers. The dour and distracted nature of his mind did nothing but create darkness in his mood, and no matter how hard he tried, there was nothing that Cedric could think or consider that would brighten that mood. He sat at the edge of the sea, his boots just above the level of the water, skimming it as the winds caused gentle waves to rush toward the shore. The only other sound was a low wail in the wind that spoke of something terrible on the verge of coming into being. Despite his power, both that existed before the murder of his once-patron, and the power that he had inherited by that act, Cedric could not shake the cold that flooded through his body. It creeped into every part of his body and felt as though it would make his joints freeze. His heart felt impossibly heavy as though it was working so hard to pull the chilled blood through his body that it was on the edge of exploding from the effort.

I was dead once. I don't remember a lot about it except that it wasn't what I thought it would be. In the days after I defeated Shau-ling and was touched by the power of the Blaze, I remember always thinking about what it would be like to be dead. I heard the stories about the bright white light. I heard the stories about the darkness and the cold. I heard the stories about seeing all of my family members that had died before me. And of course, I had heard the stories about the fire and the demons with pitchforks. Every avenue was open to me. I was a hero, so I should have gone to the light of the Creator's domain and rested in that warmth and love. But I was also a villain, as I had touched the forbidden power of the Shadow, and so the Great Dark One was waiting for me as well. In my mind I had tried to envision what it would be like to simply not be any longer. Would there be any thought at all? What would it be like with no thought? Would I even be aware of it? Would it be just like snapping your fingers? Going from something to nothing before there is even time to process it. Maybe my consciousness would simply pass from this life into another life without any memory of anything coming before and with no break in between. I always tried to imagine how it would be when everything I was, everything I thought, simply was no longer there. Like an echo of a voice spoken long ago. How much of me would remain in the minds of others, in stories, in memories? How long before the mental image of my eyes, or my nose, or my smile would fade from the minds of my loved ones? How long before I would be reduced to nothing more than an anecdote? Or would my fame and my infamy last until there was no one left to remember?

The chill in the air was getting sharper as the night ground on. Daybreak would come in just under an hour, but there would be no warmth to be found even in the light of the twin suns. Not on this day. This day there was nothing but the cold of the grave coming. Death would be the order of the day, and before the suns set, hundreds, perhaps thousands, would lie dead. The Heart of Stone was about to be besieged by the most diverse group of forces ever assembled on one battlefield, and it was unlikely that any would survive the day. Certainly the Heart of Stone itself would be completely destroyed, and likely all of its defenders would be slaughtered. The gambit of course was to wipe out all of the arrayed attackers as well, but that was unlikely to change anything. Cedric had seen the darkness that was coming, had seen the true nature of the Creator's war in the mind of his former patron Emries. It would not matter how many angels or dragons or ghostly warriors were struck down. The Creator and his servants would persist. And they would be victorious.

I was dead once, and none of that happened. There was no fire, there was no light. There were no angels or demons or loved ones. No trumpets, no beating of wings. No feeling of cold or of peace. It was like time held its breath. Or maybe it was more like a hiccup; there was what came before, and what came after, and in between there was a blank space. It was like I skipped over those intervening minutes. But on the other side of that gap, things were different. I could see things. I could hear things. I knew things that I wasn't supposed to know.

Cedric looked up, his dark gray eyes filled with an otherworldly fire. His gaze pierced through the veil between worlds and stared into the formlessness that was the Heavens. His thoughts were chaotic, filled with pain, but also with such profound knowledge that he could not fully understand or explain. Some of the thoughts were like lightning bolts that struck his brain, while others tried to slide away like oil on water.

I'm not the only one who's been dead. I've seen things that no mortal should see, and that was before Emries' light was bonded to my soul. There are lots of people on this world; people who have drunk themselves to the point of death, survived terrible accidents, didn't quite commit suicide. All those people made it to the Other Side, but not everyone came back right. What I know now that I didn't know before was that there is more to this whole cosmic soup than just the Heavens and the mortal worlds below. There's this place between the different realms, the different realities; a place where countless souls roam without purpose and without hope of finding something more than the emptiness beyond the living world. Some of them are able to push through temporarily. Some call them ghosts. Some are broken souls unable to detach themselves from the pain of their former lives that could be referred to as demons. Some are angels who have been expelled from heaven, their warrior mentality lost and aimless, needing something to kill. And some are things that have no description from places that should have never existed, or don't exist anymore.

Cedric could feel pain rocketing through his body as the thoughts flowed through his mind. If he didn't know any better, he would have considered that the thoughts were the cause of the pain. Perhaps the Creator never intended for a mortal to know what he knew. Or perhaps this was not the doing of the Creator at all. Cedric had learned through Emries that the Creator did not know everything about the nature of the Cosmos, and perhaps the cracks and the voids in between were not the domain of the Creator at all.

The transition between this world and the next isn't fixed, it is uneven, unclear, and chaotic. It doesn't only stop in the Heavens. It's more like a river that flows in all directions at the same time. So those souls that don't get to their destination are vulnerable not only to the Creator, but to those who understand how the flow of souls works, like the Children and like Dorovar. But there are more dangers in those places of darkness, those souls that have been lost in the in-between have learned to watch for unguarded opportunities. Some are content to simply be a menace and pull souls out of the stream, devouring them to sustain themselves in the long dark. That's what happens to those people in a coma. They aren't quite dead, but they aren't quite alive either. Their soul is being tormented in the in-between place. Those aren't the ones I'm worried about. These souls in the in-between place aren't satisfied being in the in-between place. They want to come back here, to the land of the living. Well, of course they all have different reasons. Some are worried about their families, some have scores to settle, some just want to be alive again. And then there are some who have just been driven mad by the centuries of being in the void. When these greedy souls see someone coming back through to the land of the living, they hold on and hitch a ride. They can share that person's body, and depending on how strong the soul is, they may be able to take over.

Cedric took a deep breath and reached out his awareness to the world around him. Only the inheritors of the powers of the Children of the Creator could feel what Cedric could now feel, but he was the only one that could perceive the cracks that were beginning to form in the walls that held the dimensions apart. What the Creator was doing in his mad rush to force the hand of whatever other intelligence had been behind the creation of everything was having consequences that perhaps He did not even see. Perhaps were it not for the way that the Creator was destabilizing every reality, Tess would not have been able to pull Cedric through the veil into this reality. But then how could that have been possible? It was clear that for whatever plan the Creator had, it was important that Emries' power became trapped inside of Cedric's form. It was confusing and it made Cedric's head hurt. Instead, he continued to focus on the unintended consequences of the dissolution of Creation.

You would think the mad ones were the ones you had to worry about. But you'd be wrong. When any soul comes back from the in-between places, they all come back mad. They can hold the madness down for a while, pretend to be the person they are inhabiting, but eventually everything goes wrong. If they don't kill themselves, they'll kill other people, or worse. And there are more of them than you would think. Some, the lucky ones, follow the souls of babies back from the brink. The younger the soul is that they hitch on to, the longer it seems they can put off the madness. But it never lasts. Dictators, madmen, mass murderers, serial killers, and the worst of the worst that humanity has to offer, they all are connected. Now I'm not saying there aren't just plain bad apples in this world, but I bet you that more than a few are not alone in their bodies. Hate flows through every thought, but it is not the hate of the person that they were, or the person they inhabit, or for the Creator, or for the injustice, perceived or real, of their situation. The hatred is for life itself.

Cedric knew that if he shared what he knew with anyone else, he would seem delusional. He felt delusional. It was hard enough to go through life with one voice in your head, but now that Cedric had the thoughts of his former patron running through his fragmented and confused mind, he felt broken and on the edge of sanity. But there was even more than just his own thoughts and the thoughts of a Child of the Creator. Now that Cedric had been pulled into this reality, the memories of the Cedric from this reality were trying to meld themselves into his mind. It was clear however that the thoughts were not his own, the experiences and the pains not his own, but it did not stop them from having an impact, if that impact was just momentary distractions when they were not needed or wanted. For a warrior who had seen so much combat, any second of distraction was too much and could mean the difference between life and death. And there were still more thoughts. But these were not his, either from this reality or the other, and they did not belong to the powers that now inhabited his body. These thoughts came in spurts and in uneven measure, and they came from the other inheritors of the powers of the Children of the Creator.

Always, the Children shared thoughts, it was the nature of their beings, and while it could be suppressed, it could not be prevented completely. Even in the most guarded and ordered mind, there were thoughts that would slip through the defenses and leak into the minds of their siblings. More often than not, these unguarded thoughts would be ignored as they rarely contained pertinent information, but every now and then there would be a fragment of a plan or a scheme that could be tucked away for later use. The difference now was that the inheritors of the mantles of the Children were not as practiced with their mental defenses, and some more than others were unable to control the thoughts that leaked from their minds into the void. Of the new inheritors, Wolf Ranthall was by far was the one who let the least flow out of his control. Perhaps it was because Wolf had not been of one mind for most of his life. In life, Basille had been one of Cedric's closest friends and advisors, and Cedric had always admired the order and discipline of Basille's mind and the way he could reveal just enough to deflect inquiry while still keeping the majority of his thoughts and motives shrouded in mystery. Wolf had also learned to keep his own council from his mother, a woman of such character and strength that nothing could pierce her indominable will. Now though, infused with the abilities of Draven Batoe and Pyrrus, Wolf was a truly formidable force. It was a true shame that he would not be alive much longer. He was one that could have truly turned the tide for those who fought against the Creator, and perhaps that more than anything was the reason that he could not be allowed to live. What was truly fascinating was that Wolf understood this and had created a kind of peace with it. He had prepared himself for the coming of his end, and now focused on how his successor could be made to see the light of what was to come.

The newest inheritor did not make any attempt to hide the thoughts of the Child that dwelled within her, though how much of that was because of the inability of the inheritor or because of the sheer violence and ugliness of those thoughts. Talisia was a being comprised of hate, destruction, and devastation. She knew only one language, violence. The cosmology of her mind did not allow for the inclusion of things like love, kindness, and sentiment. Those who did not prey upon the weak were only making themselves targets to be preyed upon. And while this violence was often blinding and isolating, it created a kind of clarity if one were able to set aside the sickness that it inevitably manifested within the soul. Concepts like trust and symbiosis were alien in every regard. The only person that could be depended upon was the individual themselves, as everyone else would gladly slit your throat and take everything you own to gain just a moment of advantage in life. Now that violence and rage floated through the void with reckless abandon, leaking from the mind of Darrien Annis like a river. But like Wolf, Darrien knew that she was only a temporary vessel for the burning rage. However, Cedric knew that unlike Wolf, Darrien had not come to terms with her coming mortality. Wolf had lied to Darrien about the structure of the plan and her role in it. Wolf would not have lied were it not for Pyrrus' influence, and though he did not have a choice in it, he could not help but let some of the guilt and shame show. Unfortunately for Darrien, she was so corrupted by the blinding rage of Talisia's thoughts that she had not yet gleaned what was about to happen to her. She would pass her powers onto Cedric's sister Anabel, and the act would mean her death. For Darrien's sake, Cedric hoped that the process would be quick and painless. As it was, Cedric knew that Darrien's soul was in great pain and turmoil, and not simply because of the vicious and poisonous soul that shared her body. If there was any justice left to be found in the Creator's reality, Darrien would find it once her mortal life was robbed from her.

Rhain Seth was a cagy woman, which wouldn't have been a surprise to anyone who knew her parents. While Cedric had never had the kind of relationship with his father that perhaps he should have, there was a part of Cedric that never could consider Aerith as anything more than an ally in a war. They would never be father and son beyond their cosmic connection. How could they? During his time wandering the face of Espre, Cedric became well aware of an undeniable fact. With the exception of Rhain and Ayden, Aerith had a more fatherly connection with people like Evan Sinn, Logan Ranthall, and Sabrina Binosear than he would ever have with those individuals who were actually his flesh and blood. Cedric had become convinced that Aerith surrounded himself with surrogates in order to assuage some of the guilt that he felt for his failures as a parent. It was unfortunate because as he had proven with Rhain, Aerith could be a more than competent parent. In Rhain he had instilled a sense of self that could not be broken, even by the strong will of the being that Cedric had always known as Shau-ling. Within Rhain, Halicon and the young woman had formed a symbiotic relationship aided by Aerith's strong will and Bryn's incomparable stubbornness. Rhain had been a good choice to continue the fight against the Creator, even though that fight was destined to fail, no matter Rhain's intentions. But the longer it took the resistance forces to understand that Rhain was not their ally, the more likely the inevitability of their crushing defeat. Perhaps only Logan Ranthall had seen this truth and that was why his movements were shrouded from everyone, including the Creator. Cedric knew however that Logan's actions, though mysterious, were not a concern for the Creator. All eventualities had been seen and planned for. Victory was assured, and as the last pieces were put into place, there could be only total victory.

And the largest catalyst for that victory was in the form of the last of the inheritors, Gideon Viruci. Though Raenera's perfectly ordered mind kept some thoughts from leaking into the void, Gideon's thoughts were troubled. Unlike the rest of the inheritors, Gideon had very little agency in his actions. Raenera had planned for her assault on the world of the living, and she would not let something like the free will of her eventual vessel detract from the perfection of her plan. With the help of the insane craftsman Arturious Demascious, Raenera had created her phantom army that now was eliminating every living thing between Thorigald and Albitonin. Eventually the army would collide with the Heart of Stone and lay waste to the defense there. At least, that was the intention. Whether it would come to pass was still very much in doubt in Cedric's mind. And, if Darrien made it to Albitonin ahead of the phantom army and was able to infuse Talisia's powers into Anabel, not even Raenera's army would stand a chance. Unfortunately, once Talisia's hatred was unleashed, neither the phantom army, the defenders, or the Heart of Stone itself would survive the conflagration. No matter the outcome of the battle, the Heart of Stone was lost, and more than likely a great many of the so-called resistance to the Creator's will would be erased from existence as well.

But Darrien was not the only one who was deceived.

It was a thought that Cedric did not want, and one that he wished he did not have. Raenera had been so assured of the force that she was creating that it did not even enter into her mind that she was being betrayed. Perhaps it was because she could not conceive of a situation in which the Creator would deceive her. Cedric knew, knew beyond the shadow of a doubt, that the creatures that inhabited the impressive armor were not the reconstituted souls of the warrior angels that had fallen in battle doing the bidding of the Creator. From his time in the in-between, Cedric knew that there were no angelic souls there. The warrior angels did not have souls, did not have wills. They were only tools used by the Creator for tasks of the moment. But because the vision of the Children of the Creator could not extend into the in-between, they would not know this truth. Only the Creator could see into the in-between; it was an ability that he selfishly horded for himself. That was the reason that the Creator was able to resurrect souls for His own purposes at will, as many times as necessary. Emries had learned of this ability and had tried to find a way to peer into the in-between, but he had failed. Yes, he had managed to find a way to pull Draven's soul back from the beyond, but only because the Creator allowed a crack in the in-between to be visible to Emries for a short time. Everything that happened was a means to the Creator's ends, just like Raenera's phantom army. The souls that Raenera had pulled from the in-between were those lost souls that Cedric had seen waiting to prey upon those who were being called back to the mortal world. These were the worst of the worst. The insane, the violent, the unrepentant killers. They were perfect for the purpose that the Creator had devised for them, and they would stop at nothing until every living mortal that walked upon the face of Espre had been slaughtered. And while Raenera had though that she was saving those that were murdered at the hands of her army, the truth was far more sinister.

Dorovar's plans, for all of its faults, had just enough truth to it to be compelling. Souls were a source of power, if they were wielded the right way, but souls were not the domain of the living, even a being as powerful as Dorovar had become. Souls were the domain of the Creator, and as such only the Creator could allow them to be wielded. Dorovar had not created the Chorus of Souls, the Creator had. And, instead of Raenera's army saving the souls of their victims, those souls were simply being fed to the Chorus. Every person killed on Espre found their soul bound to the Chorus, and once enough souls were part of the eerie cacophony, the final act of the war would truly begin.

Dorovar believed that the Chorus of Souls would elevate him to the Heavens and allow him to tear down the Creator, but that was the worst kind of hubris and deluded fantasy. The Creator would never allow such a thing to come to pass. Dorovar was a tool, just like the warrior angels. He was imprisoned in the Vault of Terrors so that he would learn the skills to craft the Chorus of Souls, and then use the lessons to spread across Espre like a plague, collecting souls at every step for the Creator. Thanks to Raenera, even the souls of the dead were not immune to the pull of the Chorus. Halicon, Pyrrus, and Emries had kept the Dark Gods distracted long enough that they did not become aware of parts of the plan until it was too late, and the Creator himself was able to distract Aerith Seth through the misinformation fed to him by his closest ally, the late Sabrina Binosear. The so-called resistance had dawdled away their most important resource, time, and now the Creator believed it was too late for His plan to be subverted. The newest incarnation of the Servants had been dispatched on their final missions, and in a matter of days there would be no life left on Espre or on any world in Creation. It was likely there would not be a Creation left.

Dorovar was on a collision course with Aerith Seth and the spark of power that came from beyond the Creator's understanding. Dorovar, through Talisia, had been given all of the information he needed to rend that spark from Aerith's flesh and to unite it with the Chorus of Souls. Once done, the Spirit would eliminate Dorovar and assume control of the Chorus of Souls. That left but one last piece. The Dragon's Tear. Once the Tear was firmly in the control of the Creator's forces, it would be linked with the Chorus of Souls and that unlimited ability to reshape reality would give the Creator the one ability that He had been denied. He would be able to see into the places in the Cosmos that he only understood to exist but could not perceive. He would be able to wield the power that had created Aerith Seth and that had attempted to thwart his unlimited dominion over reality and creation. With the Chorus, Aerith's mantle, and the Dragon's Tear, there would be no need for the Children, or the Servants, or anything other than the Creator's own desire. He could remake the Cosmos in his image as many times as he wished. His understanding would be perfect and unlimited. Perhaps there would be no reason to create at all, and the formless void would be the prefect representation of the understanding that the Creator sought. Whatever the outcome, there was nothing that could stand in the Creator's way. His victory was assured.

So why is the Creator worried?

The thought itched at the back of Cedric's mind. He had seen too many things that he should never have seen. He had felt the endless void. Had seen the desolation of the in-between. Had felt the insatiable hunger of the formlessness and purposelessness. And if there was one truth, it was that the Creator was afraid. And what was maddening about that was the fact that the Creator did not know why he was afraid, or what he was afraid of. Like the part of the Cosmos that he could not perceive but knew, the fear was ever-present but formless. As much as the Creator did not want that fear to motivate His actions, it was impossible to prevent. And so, Cedric contemplated what was perhaps his last mission. He was going to kill a friend.

And then perhaps I shall be dead again, this time for good.

Darrien

*I*s this all that I am, is there nothing more?

Darrien Annis wandered through the wilderness, long since forgetting the pain in her body. Ever since the merging of her body with the powers of the Child of the Creator Talisia, Darrien's concept of the world had changed. Everything that she saw and felt had changed. All those feelings from her old life seemed like they were so far away, like memories from somebody else's life. As she trudged through the snow near the peaks of the barrier mountains that separated the Kingdom of Night, Galateria from the Kingdom of Stone, Albitonin, Darrien remembered what cold should have felt like. She was wearing little more than a thin shirt and a pair of light riding pants, and yet her skin did not burn as the freezing winds assaulted her. Her bones did not ache as the cold wet pierced through her clothes and inundated her with unrelenting raw and biting bleakness. She should have shivered from head to toe, and been forced to the ground trying to gather what warmth she could to her core. But the memory of the feeling would not evoke the feeling in her body. Nor would the pain that should have been coming from her blistered and broken feet. She had long since worn through the soles of her light boots, as they had been battered and torn by the rough terrain on her climb up the mountainside. But not her feet nor the cold had stopped her ascent. The ascent itself was beyond understanding. She had faced sheer cliffsides with no ropes, no anchors, and nothing close to the experience necessary for such a climb, and yet she had simply walked up the side of a mountain because she wanted to.

This is true power little girl. This is the power that your pathetic Dark Gods will never understand. So long as the little people with a little power think they are powerful, they will always be destroyed by those who understand the true nature of what is possible.

The voice had not relented in Darrien's mind since the moment of Talisia's defeat. Wolf had hoped that the shard of Pyrrus' power would work as a kind of muzzle for the evil and venomous desires of the hateful being that had once been the death of countless worlds, but his hopes had proven to be only that. Despite her desire for the voice to stop, it would not relent, and as the minutes became hours became days, the voice drone on, battering her defenses and casting an eerie haunted light on all the cracks in Darrien's soul.

How did you Dark Gods ever survive? Emries could have wiped you from the face of this world or any world with but a thought. So fragile. So human.

The word filled Darrien with a sense of revulsion. But was the revulsion hers or was it Talisia's? Unlike most of the Dark Gods, Darrien had never been human; not really. How could she have been considered human? She would never age, would never get sick, would never die of natural causes. She would only die violently, at the end of a sword or at the hand of another with power that defied the description of mortality. She had far more in common with her somewhat cousins in the Brotherhood of Phasia than she did with her own father or mother, born to power, born to the burden of it, and born to the misunderstanding of what limitations meant.

Limitations? What limitations? As a Dark God, you could have slaughtered every single member of the Knights of the Flashing Blade. You could have ripped the head from the neck of the Emperor of Cadaria. You could have lain waste to every single one of the Great Kingdoms, and there would have been nothing that any of the pathetic humans could have done to stop you. They are not the same humans that Emries had to contend with on Onea. These Cadarians are softer, weaker, more pliable. They are far more befitting the task that the Creator has in mind for them than the willful sheep that Emries designed.

When she was a child Darrien remembered hearing stories about the early days of the war on Onea, the time when the phasia killed with impunity. Aryx Terian did not like sharing those stories in front of Darrien, but Pike had always believed that it was important for the young woman to learn the truth of the war between the Light and the Shadow rather than be lied to as the heroes from Onea had been throughout their time in the war. Oftentimes however, Darrien found herself puzzled by the stories. Aryx spoke of a time when Bryn would walk through the center of a city, her hands extended to her sides, lighting every house on fire with a thought. She reduced whole armies to a cinder with a snap of her fingers. Grawn would walk from the coastline, a hundred-foot-tall tidal wave behind him, and watch as every person in the city before him drown and the buildings were smashed into rubble. From a perch high in the air, Ellis would rain down shards of ice, impaling anyone who was caught out in the open before she would freeze and shatter everything that was left standing. Then there was Kamen, who could stamp his foot into the ground and create a fissure so wide that it would swallow everything for miles around. Aryx Terian, the hero, once stood opposed by an army of thousands, and with the wave of one hand he murdered them all with volleys of lightning so bright that they could be seen for hundreds of miles in all directions. Only Jeroch was not credited with the wholesale slaughter of men and women in battle, but instead the tale of horror that was his Black Tower caused Darrien nightmares for years after hearing of its construction and use. And yet for all their power, for all their destructive force, the phasia fell to bickering, pettiness, and jealousy. Their power became their greatest weakness as they thirsted for more and would slaughter one another as their enemies were not the challenge that they needed. But it had not been common men that had defeated the phasia, it had been heroes. Those special men and women who had been touched by the divine.

Heroes? What heroes? They were sheep, like all the rest. Lied to, manipulated, utilized for a purpose. Every single one of them. Cedric, Diana, Aryx, Logan, Pike, Talon, Gideon, Korrd, Nathaniel, Sabrina, Wolf, Lissa, on and on and on. Nothing special about them except what Emries and Halicon gave them. So weak and frail and pathetic. They won the war against their enemy. That was the easy part. But when it came to saving their world, they failed. When it came to saving this world, they failed. Over and over again, every world that we have deposited so-called intelligent life upon, the end has been the same. These creatures are a disappointment, a failure, a mistake, and they must be purged from existence. The whole of their races reduced to the composite materials that they were forged from, and their worlds reduced to ash. Idle playthings quickly forgotten.

But those that had power were not the only ones who fought. Gwydeon and Midarin fought. Anabel Binosear fought. The Knights of the Flashing Blade were fighting. Could they all be so disposable?

And this is the true naivete of the Dark Gods and the rest of the misguided and self-important humanity. You believe that this is your story. It has never been. It has never been the story of the Children, or the dragons, or the phasia, or the Adhradair. There has only been one story. It is the story of the Creator. All is as He wills. If there is suffering it is because He wills it. If there is death, it is because He wills it. If there is war, or famine, or plague, or eternal peace, it is because He and He alone wills it. There is nothing that is outside of His vision. Not you, not your heroes, not your villains. Nothing moves without His hand moving it.

Darrien reflected upon the words and knew that she should have been angry. She should have felt the rage draw up within her, but there was nothing there. There was no resistance and no battle left within her. There was only the purpose. Her feet continued to move though there should have been no strength in her body. She knew not hunger, nor thirst, nor fatigue. Her body moved outside of her will, if there was any will left within her.

You poor thing. Here at the end, the truth will be revealed to you, and you will be powerless to do anything with the knowledge. You are no longer Darrien Annis. You ceased being that the moment you allowed yourself to be infused with the shard of Pyrrus' power. The moment you were betrayed.

The word resounded through her body, and for a moment Darrien's footfalls stopped. She sank into the thick coating of snow, her eyes blinking uncontrolled for several moments. The tears that started to stream from the corners of her eyes turned to ice before they fell from her cheeks, and for the briefest of moments, a shiver ran through her body.

Yes, that's right little Dark God. You were betrayed. The man you thought you knew, the so-called Wolf Ranthall ceased to exist the moment that his wife infused the powers of Pyrrus into his form. You all think that you know so much about the nature of things, and yet you are so deluded. How you can even be considered intelligent is beyond me. Did you think there would be no consequence to having the power of a Child of the Creature suffused into your being? Did you think that the power came without attachment to the Divine Plan? Why do you think that the Creator soured on the dragons so quickly after their creation? They were willful. They were secretive. They were their own beings. The Creator does not abide competition, and thus the dragons had to be reduced. Limited. They are a dying race. With every generation, their power is diminished, and more and more of their eggs fail to produce a viable creature. Only Tarot had begun to guess at their fate, and that was why he needed to be removed before this war escalated. Now the dragons like the rest of you mortals will be removed from Creation and the Creator's greatest miscalculation will finally be rectified.

And so the truth is revealed to your petty little mind. Though it was my hands around the throat of my dear brother Pyrrus during the so-called rebellion in the Heavens, it was the Creator who actually decreed his death. And in the same way that it was the Creator that put my hands around my dear brother's throat, it was the Creator who forced Pyrrus to allow his life to be taken. At no point has any of your so-called brightest heroes or villains even thought to ask the question as to how I so easily murdered my brother. Emries and Halicon fought for generations without scoring a single mortal wound on the other, and yet in a single hasty attack I was able to eliminate Pyrrus? Such a convenient contrivance. Just another move in a game that you were too stupid to see was being played at your expense. Dorovar's world, the creation of the monster that would unite all of your disparate factions, all at the Creator's behest. The fall of the Dark Gods, the "sacrifice" of Halicon's soul to save Sabrina Binosear, another contrivance to put the right pieces in the right places. Sabrina needed saving as much as Pyrrus had a choice in his own execution. They were both will-less pawns being moved by the Creator to get the pieces that needed to be moved into position. Aerith Seth, the children of Aerith Seth, and more importantly, the emerging Dragon's Tear. The final piece. The final blow.

Darrien suddenly felt the cold that she remembered. There was an ache in her knees and in the soles of her feet. The drive in her to move forward had ceased, and every breath of the cold air into her lungs pushed that drive further and further away. She turned toward the edge of the cliff and tried to will herself forward, but her legs would not respond to her command. Then the mocking voice of the Child of the Creator returned.

Are you beginning to see now the futility of it all, Darrien? I killed my brother Pyrrus because the Creator ordered that I do so, and Pyrrus let himself be killed for the same reason. Emries and I betrayed Dorovar and Raenera did nothing to prevent it because the Creator deemed it so. Then the souls of the Adhradair were trapped and passed to Lissa Terian along with the soul of my dear departed brother so that they could be infused into the body of Wolf Ranthall. The soulless husk of Sabrina Binosear tricked her former compatriots into allowing themselves to be cast down to this world, and then was put in place to receive Halicon's soul bringing the phasia back together for their part that was to come, and to create controls on the wildcards like Logan Ranthall and Aerith Seth. And what happened next little Dark God? Do you know? Are you intelligent enough to see? Even now after everything, are you still so blind as to not know the cosmic joke you have been a part of?

"Tess."

The word echoed in the wind for a moment and then died in the growing wail. Darrien remembered the moment when she knew that Tess was something beyond the sweet little girl that had grown up in her shadow. The moment she stood opposed to her own sister and saw the killer in her eyes. As she watched the power emerge from Tess's frail form and vaporize Alderin's arm.

Perhaps there is some hope for you after all, Darrien. Yes, you are correct in both your supposition and in your fear. Tess Annis was never anything more than an incubator. A test if you will of what the Creator had always been looking for. Which yet again shows your fundamental misunderstanding of the nature of the Cosmos and the players within it. The Creator only indulged the Children our bickering and our games in the event that we created that which He was unable to create.

For the first time in the mostly one-sided conversation, Darrien could feel her mind trying to make sense of the information. She was no longer simply absorbing the information as though it was already within her, but now it felt as though she was trying to make sense of it all and the pieces were not fitting into place.

And then my hope for you fades. You poor thing. That is one thing you missed growing up knowing part of the truth through the other Dark Gods. Those who grew up in the bosom of the Church of the Creator were fed their indoctrination cheerfully. But those who were more willful than their simple-minded cousins began to ask questions of the teachings. There were some who could see inconsistencies and holes in the teachings, and so they began to ponder issues so large that their minds could not even form concepts around them. And so they imagined platitudinal constructs that would sate their desire to understand while at the same time reminding them of their place in the greater order. And so, the question was breathed into existence, "could the Creator make a rock so large that He Himself could not lift it.' Though this was a new thought for the humans of this world, it was not a new thought for humans. Nor was it a new thought for the other beings of Creation. Moreover, this was not a new thought for the Creator. This was a thought so alien that humans did not have the capacity to understand the depths of its implications. But the Creator could. The Creator from His very beginning in the nothingness of the void wondered about the depth and breadth of His own abilities. Was there a limit to what He could make? Was there a finite capacity to His reach and grasp? How is that for a thought in the mind of a supposedly infinite being? Could a being truly be infinite if it pondered whether or not it was finite. And the Creator began to wonder if the very act of wondering about His own finite grasp made the limitation so. That was when the plan came into being. There at the very beginning of Creation, mired with the disappointment of the dragons. Perhaps it was the fact that the Creator found that He could be disappointed that helped to germinate the other thoughts. Or perhaps they were not connected at all. Either way, the end result was the same. The Creator began to ponder ways to expand that which only had a limit in His own mind, and so the thought of a being with the power of Creation burst forth.

Again, Darrien found herself lost in the thoughts of the moment. The implications were both staggering and absurd. If the Creator were all powerful, why could He not simply manifest the creature that we willed? Why was there a need for such machinations that stretched across worlds and millennia? If the Creator was truly all-powerful, what was the purpose of a being like the Dragon's Tear? Nothing made sense. And as her mind continued to pour over the impossible problem, her legs began to respond, pushing her closer to the precipice of the cliff, looking out over the vast nothingness obscured by the wind and snow below her.

And so you've struck at the very crux of the problem, my dear little Dark God. The Creator began to ponder a presence beyond Himself. A presence that either was His twin or was His superior. While the one was acceptable, the other was not. How could there be something superior to the Creator? It was a laughable supposition, but when Halicon returned from his sojourn into the dark spaces between the worlds carrying with him the thing you now call the Blaze, the Creator was faced with an undeniable fact. There were things that existed within the Cosmos that He Himself did not create. And if He did not create something, that meant that there was another force that did. And it was possible that that other force was in fact the very thing that created Him. That very thought, that very desperate realization was the death-knell of a thousand worlds; as the Creator's rage stretched out across Creation shattering everything in its path.

Darrien shivered at the thought of any being's power being so great that it could shatter worlds unintentionally. But it was Talisia's next words that nearly stopped Darrien's heart with fear.

The Creator's rage was so great and so boundless that half of the worlds that the Creator had made, as well as most of the life that inhabited Creation were destroyed. While the majority of the dragons were on the fringes of Creation and were spared from the wave of destruction, the first iteration of the Children and the Servants were not. The Creator's first children, whose names have been consigned to the mists of obscurity, were destroyed. Perhaps they were different than the ones that came after, or perhaps we were the same. What is disconcerting is the fact that both are possible, but there can never be an answer. The Creator was just as quick to cast off His own progeny as he was to cast off the worlds He created. When this world ends, the Creator will wipe the slate clean. He will destroy all of the Children, all of the dragons, all of his worlds, and simply start over with the new power that he has created.

Darrien's mind whirled. How could the Creator create something so powerful that it would change the very definition of the power of Creation? What was the connection to the Blaze and to Halicon? Why was the Creator so obsessed with something that could have existed without His intervention?

Have you not, my dear little mouse, begun to understand the truth of Creation? Have you not even guessed the awful lie that has been perpetrated? The Creator is as petty as He is powerful, and now that the last of the Children have fallen, the true depth of that pettiness can be fully expressed. All of the pieces are being put into place, and the whole of Creation will feel the repercussions of the Creator's need to understand and to control. By now, the shadow of Halicon is already on his way to the place in the void where he first discovered the Blaze. He coaxed the alien force from the nothingness once, and the Creator hopes that the destruction wrought upon Creation will be enough to coax it out once more. My shadow along with that of Pyrrus will be used to wipe out the last of the petty resistance to the Creator's plan. Raenera's shadow will unravel what is left of her own plans, and Emries will put an end to the troublesome Logan Ranthall and give the Creator all of the tools that He needs to make the Dragon's Tear complete. And this, my dear little mouse, is where the betrayal truly expresses itself. Are you ready my little mouse to know how your life will end?

Darrien's spirits fell. Somewhere inside of her she had known that this errand to capture the soul of a Child of the Creator would lead to her death, but she had only hoped that she would be able to see Alderin one last time.

You are the final piece of the puzzle that will trap Aerith Seth and his contemptable curs that he calls a family. First of course was the passing of Halicon's powers to Sabrina, which then made it possible to entrap Rhain Seth with an offer impossible to resist. The guilt of Sabrina's loss was enough to force Rhain's hand, but not only that, Rhain is her father's daughter and thus could not resist the opportunity to do more in a war she barely understood. Once Halicon's essence burned its way through what was left of Rhain Seth's soul, it was only a matter of time before Bryn felt tempted to rummage through Halicon's knowledge in an attempt to make sense of the Creator's plan. Predictable to the end. So Rhain allowed Bryn to find the information about Liette and the way to find her. Here Bryn was fed just enough information to make the assumptions that the Creator wanted her to make, and moreover it allowed the dragons to bring Aerith Seth to the Heavens where he could be goaded by the Creator down the right path.

Darrien's eyes went wide with shock.

Oh? Did you not guess, little mouse? The dragons are not all ignorant of the Creator's plans. How do you think I was able to so easily entice some of the dragons to back my little rebellion in the Heavens? The oldest of the race, the critical leaders were all aware; Shadowweaver, Tarot, and Serentis. They are enough to ensure that the dragons are where they are supposed to be when they are supposed to be there. It was Serentis' council that pushed Mariti Brightblade to align with Aerith Seth and create the civil war between Mariti's faction and Shadowweaver's. As with the Children, these dragons have no control over their actions, they are merely playing their part in the ongoing play. Once Aerith and Bryn were sufficiently distracted and Ayden Seth was brought into the fold as the Will, that left only Cedric, Anabel, and Gideon to deal with.

Gideon was the easiest. He had always been of weak character, eager to follow anyone who would give him a purpose. Raenera put that to perfect use, surrounding him with a band of lost children that were quickly slaughtered, giving the reformed thief a need for revenge and a need for the power to enact that revenge. Though he was wary of accepting that power, the need to fight Dorovar overwhelmed what little doubt he had about Raenera's motives. Also, he needed to protect a woman in distress. Humans are so predictable. And so Gideon took Raenera's powers and unleashed her endgame on the world, but not before fulfilling the purpose of drawing Dorovar in to the end of his purpose as well. Emries proved to have the most difficult test. He drew Tess Annis to him and gave her just enough knowledge to draw a version of Cedric Binosear across the veil into this world. Cedric was a balancing force for Tess, just enough to suppress the volatility and make her into the perfect weapon for Kaitain Lorien to unleash. Then Emries was no longer necessary, and his powers passed to Cedric Binosear, leaving his sister the last piece of the puzzle. That my little mouse is where you come into the picture. And thus, the betrayal. Pyrrus, through Wolf, utilized you to trap my powers, and then you will deliver me to Anabel Binosear just as soon as my powers burn through the last of your soul. Once you are my puppet, you will walk to her and allow yourself to be killed to transfer the powers into her body. And then, my little mouse, the trap is sprung and the three final pieces of the Creator's plan will be in place. Dorovar, Aerith, and the Tear. The Tear will absorb both Dorovar and Aerith's powers, ascend to the Heavens and be absorbed by the Creator. Then the Creator will rip the Cosmos apart until He removes every vestige of that which He did not create and start over. The thousands of years mean nothing, there is only the Creator's need for preeminence.

Darrien stood at the edge of the cliff rebelling against the voice in her head, not wanting to subject anyone else to the hell she had found herself in. But try as she might, she could not make her legs move any farther forward. She could not make her knees bend to jump. She could not bring an end to her own life to protect the rest of the worlds from the wrath of the Creator.

I'm sorry little mouse, your time is not done yet. You have an appointment to keep, and we wouldn't want to disappoint the Creator, now would we?

THE INHERITORS

Interlude 2

Those Who Hold Back the Night

Year Two of the Divine Empress and Child of the Creator Marlae Tamerlane, Creator's Calendar Year 1872

When he felt the portal forming deeper in the Heart of Stone, Jeroch cursed. Whoever created the portal was not trying to be subtle and the amount of power that fueled the conjuring of the portal would have been able to be felt for hundreds of miles in all directions. Jeroch wouldn't have been surprised if some of the people in the Heart of Stone that did not understand true power would have been able to feel the portal forming as well. But then, that was the point, wasn't it? Clearly Rhain knew much more about what was happening in regard to the movements of the enemy. If the portal was meant as a beacon to let the enemy know that forces were gathering to defend the Heart of Stone, that could only mean that the enemy was one perhaps two days from launching their assault. Unconsciously, Jeroch grimaced at the thought. Hopefully Rhain had sent an army. By the time Jeroch had made his way to the small canteen area that was reserved for the high-ranking members of the Church of the Creator near the kitchens, Hannah Ironheart had already arrived. As usual, wherever Hannah walked, Kiara Aren was not far behind. The supposed holy woman was like a little lost puppy. The portal was just opening to its fullest extent when Anabel Binosear arrived. For a woman unpracticed in the use of her abilities, she seemed to be adapting to the circumstances quite well. It was grudging admiration at best that Jeroch held for the sister of his old enemy, and while Anabel had proved her mettle once before in the throne room of Shau-ling, the test that was coming would be far worse. Two beings emerged through the portal, and no more followed. The portal closed, but not fully, a point of light hanging in the air like a stubborn mote of dust. Jeroch recognized the individuals immediately, and his annoyance grew.

"You are the reinforcements?" Jeroch spat onto the wind.

Orren Eldrath and Felicia Lorien certainly looked as though they had seen better days. Their clothes were ripped, and there were still faint lines of scars on their faces and hands that had not fully healed despite the powers at their disposal. They had clearly been in a fight. What irritated Jeroch the most was the fact that Saurn had not accompanied them. The coward was going to stay in the protective shell of his Shadow Guild and let others do the fighting as he always had. Jeroch shouldn't have been surprised of course. Saurn couldn't change what he was, even here at the end of days. Whatever abilities that Orren Eldrath and Felicia Lorien possessed, they could not match a full member of the Brotherhood of Phasia. More than that, Jeroch could tell that Felicia's powers had been diminished. No longer was Nightwing a part of her, and with that great power lost, what good would she truly be in the fight ahead? Very few of the humans had proven to Jeroch that they had what was necessary within them to face the kind of foe that was about to bear down upon them, and unfortunately most of them were either dead or relegated to lesser roles within the war. As much as he hated to admit it, there was part of Jeroch that wished Ranthall was there with them.

"There are more coming," Orren said quickly, "which is why the portal will remain open. The beacon should draw the rest here soon enough."

Hannah regarded the new arrivals.

"It looks like you have seen better days."

Felicia nodded.

"Two of Dorovar's Adhradair. They ambushed us in Zevarit as we were chasing Storm and Taya Mystic from Celidar. If it wasn't for Arin

Ranthall, Saurn, and Aerith Seth, we might not have survived. They were after Orren's Sacred Weapon. Fortunately, they weren't able to acquire it."

Jeroch folded his arms.

"And the Adhradair?"

Orren shook his head.

"Dead, thankfully."

Jeroch nodded absently, his mind elsewhere.

"Then that is two less assets that Dorovar can send against us," Anabel said finally. "Which I assume improves our chances here."

Jeroch looked first at Hannah and then at Anabel.

"Dorovar isn't coming here. We're fighting dragons."

Hannah shook her head.

"Plans have changed."

Jeroch's eyes narrowed as he regarded Aerith Seth's newest student. Clearly the woman had been gaining information from her patron. He marveled at the way that Aerith continued to be a thorn in the side of every side of the war. The secretive ancient man, if nothing else, continued to be an invaluable source of information and annoyance.

"What does that mean?" Anabel asked quickly.

What struck Jeroch immediately was the fact that neither Orren Eldrath nor Felicia Lorien seemed surprised by the news. Clearly when Rhain had dispatched them, she had been in touch with her father and had briefed their meager reinforcements on the state of things.

"That's what we were coming to tell you," Felicia said finally. "Aerith may have initially intended to draw in the dragons to this battle, but it became clear that with the dragons and the angels swarming the Heart, it would be unlikely that anyone here would survive. The sides needed to be more even, and since we can't draw more allies to our side for now, the next best thing…"

Jeroch interrupted.

"Would be to draw in more enemies and hope they waste time killing each other instead of killing us."

Anabel took the opportunity to sit down. She had not felt herself since they had come to the Heart of Stone, and the creeping doom was slowly squeezing her heart. Whatever was coming was close now, and it weighed on her greatly.

"It sounds like one of Aerith's plans," Anabel said as she perched uncomfortably on the edge of a simple wooden chair, her elbows resting on the table, "crazy enough to be plausible, and dangerous enough to be laughable."

Hannah took the opportunity to take up the narrative.

"There is more than the Adhradair coming. It may even be Dorovar himself. And beyond that something else. Gideon Viruci has accepted the powers of Raenera as his own, and he leads an army of phantoms who even now destroys all life between Thorigald and Albitonin. There is no hate and no malice in that army, only destruction. That is the army that Aerith hopes will distract the angels and the dragons from us. But should they not, should they band together to sweep us from this world, there will be nothing of the light left to stand against the tide."

Jeroch immediately suppressed the shiver that wanted to run through him. It was a dim picture that Hannah had painted, and yet at the same time, Jeroch knew that it was not a complete one. As long as there was the smallest flicker of light, there would be resistance to the Creator's dark vision. In the end they would be victorious. There was no other option. Should they fail, should they falter, there would be no light and no life left to take up the struggle.

"There is more," Orren said after a moment, letting the gravity of the task ahead fully sink in to the minds of the small group. "Raenera has somehow found a way to use the connection between the phasia and

Halicon to wound Rhain directly. Gideon murdered Taya, and in doing so, inflicted serious damage. Rhain's fortitude has begun to fail, and it is only a matter of time before Halicon's power consumes her. Because of this, she has requested that you return to Bellnoc, Jeroch, and help to devise a defense should we fall here."

Jeroch bristled at the suggestion, even though he understood the wisdom of it. If Raenera and her coming army could indeed inflict damage on Rhain through the phasia, then Jeroch could find himself turned into a weapon against his own. More than that, now that he understood the damage that his mere presence in the battle could cause, it was possible that he would fight too cautiously and thus be a hindrance to the defense of the Heart of Stone. But how could he possibly leave the battle? How could he possibly now let others fight in his stead when the stakes were so high? While Saurn clearly was quick to use the excuse to stay out of the fighting, Jeroch would not run. His place was here, in the fight, with the enemy in front and his allies at his side. That is what Cedric Binosear would have done, and the damnable Logan Ranthall. How could Jeroch accept any less of himself?

"With all due respect to Rhain," Jeroch said finally, "I'm staying."

From the shadows in the corner of the room a woman's voice flowed upon the air.

"Valor and honor finally find the heart of the Shadow."

All heads turned in the direction of the voice, but no one took aggressive action. No one even considered letting weapons form in their hands. The voice was too familiar. Bryn Aplee-Seth stepped from the shadows, her uncommonly conservative dress surprising many. She did not approach beyond the edge of the light in the room, and while her eyes quickly drifted across the faces of the assembled heroes, it did not pass over Anabel's. The tension there was palpable, but there was not time for the uncomfortable family dramas to play out now. Jeroch scoffed at the jibe.

"I see you are not concerned about your daughter's safety," Jeroch taunted.

Bryn regarded Jeroch as a frown twisted her features.

"Rhain is more than capable of looking after herself. And if I know Halicon half as well as I think I do, whatever trick Raenera has concocted, my daughter or Saurn will find a way to counteract it. I just hope that they have time to find a solution before Gideon and his army arrive."

Jeroch nodded. He thought of course that Bryn's faith was misplaced, but faith had never been a characteristic attributed to the Brotherhood of Phasia.

"And what ill-tidings do you bring us, Bryn? Some other hair-brained scheme concocted by your husband perhaps?"

Bryn shook her head.

"This time, the ill-tidings are not of our doing, but yet again of the Creator's. In his haste to bring about the end, he is consolidating power in places that he believes he can manipulate. Raenera's abilities in Gideon, Halicon's in Rhain. Now we've learned that Cedric has been brought back to this world and that he has murdered Emries and taken his powers."

Jeroch and Anabel had the same reaction, but for different reasons. Anabel's disheartened eyes sank at the mention of her brother's name and at the revelation that he was once again a pawn being manipulated by the cruel machinations of the Creator. For Jeroch, he found himself disappointed in the return of Cedric to this world. Cedric had known what was coming in the beginning of the war, which is why he had allowed himself to be destroyed before he could be turned into a weapon. But even that gesture was half-hollow. He had imparted knowledge to Leonora Wastri, dangerous knowledge that could be used by either side. That was why Jeroch had taken her memory away and hidden her in plain sight as a member of the Knights of the Flashing Blade so he could keep an eye on her. It was then that Jeroch's mind sparked and he turned to Orren and Felicia.

"Who else is Rhain sending? Is he sending Leonora Wastri?"

Hannah and Anabel's ears perked up at the woman's name. In response, Orren nodded.

"Rhain sent Leonora to meet with Chelsea Zarova. Camille Sandar was going to join them and bring them here."

Jeroch's eyes narrowed, and his voice became deadly serious.

"Under no circumstances is anyone in this room to speak about Cedric to Leonora. It could cause complications."

Hannah was about to speak when the speck of power hanging in the air began to spark back to life. In a matter of moments, the portal had reopened to its full size and the assembled heroes waited for more of their number to emerge. While Jeroch had seen this trick used in the first days of the war with Emries on the young lands of Onea, its use had been lost since that time. It had actually been Aryx that had come up with the idea of using portals that did not completely close. The idea was to portal into an area that the phasia were going to invade, leave a mostly closed portal in a secluded area, and then when the time was right move troops in quickly. The tactic could be used for ambush or for rapid reinforcement. The problem with the tactic was that it required immense concentration and a massive amount of power to open the initial portal. Once Emries taught his *Erieal* to feel the powers used by the phasia, the element of surprise for such a tactic was lost.

Once the portal opened completely, five more forms emerged into the suddenly crowded room. Yet again the portal did not close completely, and Jeroch wondered how many more of the remaining heroes would be committed to the coming battle. All of the new arrivals were known immediately to Jeroch as he had had dealings with each and every one. Chelsea Zarova and Leonora Wastri were allies of Jeroch's in another life when they were all members of the Knights of the Flashing Blade. In those days, Jeroch believed that the small and powerful group of men and women could change the world through their desire to uplift the race of human. But despite the desire of the Knights to do good works in the name of their emperor, they were still limited by the desires and frailties of the species. Though some amongst the humans could be counted upon to transcend that frailty, most would never be more than they were. Only for so long could the tide be resisted before it would consume all the good works that the Knights attempted to accomplish. It would only take the right push in the wrong direction for the worst of humanity to overwhelm the best. That push of course came in the form of Kaitain Lorien. His selfishness and greed infected all around him, spreading through the populace just as quickly as the Crawling Plague. Kaitain made sure that his wickedness would spread into the Knights of the Flashing Blade as well, appointing those that would advance his vision of the world, while destroying the reputations of those who came before. There would be no martyrs, only criminals and traitors that wore familiar and pleasing faces.

Alderin Terian was known to Jeroch, less for his association with his family and more for the corruption inflicted upon him by Pike Rhuiden. Alderin had the look of his father, with the same stormy eyes and firm chin, but there was a pall that held the man in a constant state of disdain and despair. It was as though the hatred of life had manifested into a being, and that being inhabited Alderin. Despite this, Jeroch knew that Alderin would fight with every breath in his body. That was the defining trait of all Terians. Something similar could be said for Camille Sandar. Like her mother and her father, Camille was possessed with the will to fight no matter the odds. She and Alderin would be able to hold their own in battle far better than the likes of Orren and Felicia, and Jeroch was glad to have them as part of the defense. While he had great respect for the abilities of Chelsea and Leonora, Chelsea was just a human and Leonora was unstable at best. Yes, Jeroch knew that simple humans had stood against unspeakable odds on Onea. But this was not Onea, and they were not dealing with an overconfident enemy who could not conceive of being defeated. The coming enemy was fierce, crafty, and were coming in force.

The last of the newest arrivals was one that Jeroch did not expect, and she was most assuredly not welcome on a field of battle such as what the Heart would become. Dominique Lorien may have been a formidable woman, but she was not a fighter. Like the High Priestess, the mortals who remained in the Heart of Stone would be quickly counted among the dead. It was an unfortunate truth, but a truth that needed to be understood.

"Welcome to Albitonin," Hannah said after a moment, sparing a glance in the direction of her old allies. "Though I should wish to be welcoming you under different circumstances."

Chelsea, ever the woman of action took the lead.

"And what are the circumstances?"

Hannah's reply was gruff and tinged with a hint of despair.

"We've made preparations the best we can under the circumstances. With Jeroch's help, we've evacuated all of the citizens of Albitonin. Though the Peaks of Patience and a large portion of the Order of the Flickering Flame were destroyed, part of the complex still exists and is safe. The remaining Masters of the Academy of Arcane Arts are there and have vowed to protect any refugees that are sent through to the Order. All that remain are those willing to fight from the ranks of the paladins and the other defenders of the Heart, as well as a few of the healers who are brave enough to protect those who fight. The humans who will fight number perhaps a thousand. Beyond that, Mariti Brightblade leads a contingent of dragons. It is unclear the number, but more and more arrive nearly every hour. Mariti has promised enough the darken the skies. More than that, there will be those that swim in the seas and crawl through the mountains in order to ensure we are protected on all fronts. However, of those with power, there are frighteningly few of us. Those in this room are all we have."

Camille added her voice a moment later.

"Mirana and Liara Ranthall should be added to our strength soon enough. They may not be talented warriors, but they have talent in shields, and healing. They are also incredibly insightful and intuitive. They may be able to discern patters that we miss."

"I suppose it would not be a battle without a Ranthall or two," Jeroch grumbled under his breath.

Chelsea took a long look around the room.

"And who is in charge of this defensive force?"

Jeroch resisted the urge to smile. He had always admired Chelsea's capacity to cut through the niceties of the situation to strike right at the heart of the matter. She did not earn the name the Wolf of Saldarine only for her prowess on the battlefield. Subtlety was certainly not a trait that she had in abundance. The room was filled with strong personalities that were used to working on their own. Yes, the four former members of the Knights of the Flashing Blade had worked together when it was necessary, but at home in their own kingdoms, they were the highest ranking military officers with responsibility for planning and implementing far-reaching military campaigns comprising tens of thousands of soldiers on multiple fronts. Chelsea, in her own way, was trying to clear up which of their strong personalities would have the last word, and who would report to whom in the heat of the moment.

"I would expect, Chelsea, that you would take command of the ground forces inside the keep. It is unclear what kind of forces that our enemy intends to loose upon us, but whatever it is, the casualties are likely to be highest there," Jeroch answered.

Cheslea nodded. It was what she wanted to hear. She longed to be in the thick of the fight, the bloodiest ground. Hannah was the next to add her voice.

"There will be more surprises on the ground and in the air," she said firmly. "Aerith and Rhain have seen to that. They will be here when the battle is joined. We need not worry about commanding them though, they merely need to be pointed at the enemy."

"I'll be organizing the healers and the internal defenses," Anabel added. "I know my limitations, but for those of us with the ability to shield the fighters from the weapons of the dragons, we will need to be strategically placed to get the most out of the few opportunities we'll have to use those abilities. I expect that the dragons will try to overwhelm us at the beginning, raining fire and lightning down upon our ground forces. If we can deflect the first few barrages, they may change tactics and it would give us and opportunity to strike back."

Camille nodded.

"We should keep our most powerful weapons in reserve. I don't expect that Dorovar will commit himself or his Adhradair until he believes he has the advantage. The longer we can hold out without Jeroch or Bryn using the full extent of their abilities, the more likely we are to be victorious. We will have to depend upon the dragons for the beginning of the battle."

Jeroch turned his attention to the young winged woman.

"You should be up there with them."

Camille blinked.

"You are the only one of us with the ability to fly," Jeroch continued. "Depending upon how the battle progresses, you'll be able to inform us if we need to make alterations to our strategy. I know its risky, but I think it's the best option."

"It sounds far too dangerous," Bryn countered. "With all of the dragons and warrior angels mixed together, there could be attacks coming from all directions. Surely, we can find better places to utilize Camille and her abilities."

Camille shook her head.

"I think Jeroch is right. We have to use all of what we have to the best of our ability. There are far too few of us that can fight on that level, and so any information we can gather could prove to be invaluable. Besides, if I can keep at least some of the warrior angels engaged in the air, that will be less you have to deal with on the ground."

Felicia closed her hands so hard her knuckles cracked.

"I wish I could join you up there. But Nightwing has been shattered."

Bryn looked at Felicia and then to Jeroch.

"We may be able to do something about that."

Jeroch thought for a moment and then knew where Bryn's mind had gone. Nightwing was a creation of Shau-ling that had been crafted from the same metal used to create the *Debuisa* used by the *Erieal*. The metal itself had properties that allowed for the more effective channeling of power. It was necessary for Nightwing because of the limitations that Shau-ling had put on the phasia regarding use of the Blaze. The real truth of the matter was that the metal was required in order to help Aryx Terian remember how to channel the Blaze. He had been separated from the roaring green fires for too long, and had lost the ability to touch it with any skill. But all that Nightwing truly was was an augmentation of the powers of a member of the phasia mixed with the form of a Shadowwalker. Because Felicia already had the ability to touch the Blaze, the essence of Nightwing could be bonded to any metal. The more special the metal, the more effective the bonding of course. If Bryn was right, perhaps Nightwing could be restored, and another weapon could be added back to their arsenal.

"You should all get some rest," Jeroch said finally. "The enemy will attack soon."

Hannah motioned towards the door.

"I'll make arrangements for rooms for everyone. They probably won't be up to your standards, but we do the best we can."

Bryn looked across the room for a moment before speaking.

"I'm not sure that this lot has much in the way of standards."

There were a few smiles at the jibe, but not many. As each filed out of the room, they seemed to grasp the weight of what was ahead of them. Finally, all that was left in the room was Camille, Bryn, and Anabel.

"I'm going to wait for the twins," Camille said after a moment. "I'm not sure how they are going to react to all of this. They've never been in a battle like this before, not with these kinds of stakes. They don't know death the way we have."

Anabel sighed and shook her head.

"Our family knows death too well," she said in a quiet voice. "Perhaps no one should be comfortable with it. My brother never wanted any of this for me."

She paused for a moment and then looked up at Bryn.

"And I know my father didn't either. There is no time left for old grudges, or for lost opportunities. If we are going to survive this, we must trust one another."

Byrn nodded.

"Perhaps in the darkness that is coming, trust will be the only light left."

The Five Queens

Marlae

Marlae awoke with a start, unsure for a moment exactly where she was. However, the next moment she felt Rhain's soft skin against hers and the soft sheets against her slightly sweat-soaked frame, and she knew she was exactly where she wanted to be. This was where she wanted to start and end every day, and it didn't matter whether or not the bed was in a palace or in a small cabin in the middle of nowhere, on the coast or in the mountains. None of that mattered so long as Rhain was with her. It was a comfort that Marlae had not truly known in her life, despite the relative luxury that she had grown up in. Her whole life, Marlae had wanted for nothing, but she had never been content. Part of that of course could be blamed upon her father and the environment of wanting and excess that he constructed around himself. But there was more to Kaitain Lorien than his thirst for power, and that desire that he taught to his daughter both through direct lessons as well as neglect. Kaitain was a man that was never satisfied, and he hated the need in him that constantly needed to be filled. He was the first-born son, the heir-apparent, and yet his brother was more loved and more respected. He was the Emperor of Cadaria, but he was in the shadow of his father and his grandfather. What's more, Kaitain fretted about the influence and love that would be siphoned off by his charismatic daughter and his wholesome second wife. He was a jealous man, a violent man, and a man who believed that his reach could never exceed his grasp. This was the model that Marlae had to learn from, the model that shaped the woman that she would become, at least for the first phase of her life.

Though she dreaded doing it, Marlae gently pulled herself free of Rhain's embrace and slipped as gently as she could out of the bed. There was a cool draft in the room and it felt good on her bare skin. In another life she would not have cared about her nakedness, but her new modesty caused her to immediately reach for the dressing gown that hung at the foot of the bed and wrap it around her shoulders. She considered for a moment tying the gown at her waist, but feeling a bit decadent in her comfort, she left the gown open as she moved across the room to the overly-opulent dressing table on the far side of the room. This bedroom had been utilized by the Grand Master of the Shadow Guild before Rhain had chosen to make the room her personal quarters, and the man clearly had gaudy tastes. The large mirror was in a jewel-encrusted golden frame mounted to the finely-polished wooden table. Marlae picked up the brush sitting on the table and regarded it for a few moments. It was made of finely polished bone with bristles made most likely of horsehair. There were a few stray strands of brilliant red hair caught in the bristles, and pulling one of them free brought a smile to Marlae's face. After a moment she ran the brush through her own hair and was immediately caught by the absurdity of the act. Throughout the beginning of her life, Marlae never was responsible for her own grooming. Attendants bathed her, brushed her hair, cleaned and trimmed her nails, and made sure that all of her hygienic needs were met. It wasn't until Elwyne Tamerlane came into her life that she began to appreciate the small and menial things that she had never even given thought to before. In her private quarters in Hedorah was the first time that Marlae could remember that she brushed her own hair. It was an alien feeling, and yet at the same time it served as a reminder of the new woman she had become and the entitled brat that she had left behind.

It wasn't until the brush hit the first tangle in her hair that Marlae became aware of the diametrically opposed lives. The act first filled her with anger and then filled her with shame. The anger was the reflex that dragged her back to the part of her that was the spoiled princess. That anger had struck fear into every chambermaid and servant who dared attempt to pamper the princess, because the slightest pull of the woman's hair might result in sudden painful death. Marlae's reactions to the failures of her servants was a direct response to the lessons taught by her father. While it became evident much later in his rule, especially with his treatment of the faithful of the Church of the Creator, even in his younger years,

Kaitain Lorien had no respect for those not of noble blood. To be fair, Kaitain had little respect for others of noble blood as well, as evidenced by the way he treated his brother and his niece. The difference however between Kaitain and Marlae was that Kaitain cared so little about the lives and indiscretions of those he viewed as beneath him that he rarely wasted his time to act upon them. Marlae on the other hand took each of these slights personally and sought retribution. While at times this retribution took the form of punishments, more often than not, those that failed her ended up paying with their lives.

As Marlae ran the brush through her hair once more, she reflected upon the woman that she had been and the words that Elwyne Tamerlane's spirit had spoken to her that sparked her conversion in the better version of herself. Why had she been so cruel? Why had she had no regard for the lives of others? Surely it was more than just the poor example that she had from her father. One of the largest regrets that Marlae had was that she had not had more of a relationship with her mother. Maybe if she had been able to have that relationship, there would have been a moderating factor to Kaitain's extremes. But such a thing was not to be, her father had seen to that. Kaitian was sure to keep Marlae busy with tutors and pretty baubles until such time as he was able to engineer the death of her mother. What's more, Kaitain did not hide the fact from Marlae. Of course, when he sat Marlae down to explain to her the circumstances behind her mother's death, she was neither shocked nor angered. She had already begun her path to self-interest and cruelty in the image of her father, and so when he used words like "political expediency" and "seizing opportunity" she sat and nodded dutifully. Of course, what Kaitain didn't realize was that he was creating the blueprint by which Marlae would remove her father from the throne, even if she had to hold the blade herself, all in the name of "political expediency."

However, the essence of Marlae's cruelty was only partly Kaitain's responsibility. Marlae herself had to take the blame for the larger portion. The truth of it all, the truth exposed to her by Elwyne, was that Marlae was searching for love. As soon as the thought entered her mind, Marlae felt that it was pedestrian and pedantic, but it was the truth. Marlae never believed that her father loved her. She was another "political expediency," an expectation that he had to deliver upon. In a way Marlae believed that

Kaitain was relieved that his only child was a daughter. Along with having a disinterest in the plight of those he viewed as beneath him, Kaitain also had a complete lack of respect for women. In fact, looking back on many of the decisions that he made during his tenure as Emperor of Cadaria, it was easy to see the misogyny in effect. Would Kaitain have felt that the Academy of Arcane Arts and the Masters of the Academy could be so easily dismissed and manipulated had they been men instead of women? Would he have married Dominique if he did not feel that it would cause pain to Chelsea Zarova and to his own daughter? Would Kaitain have taken such a powerful stance against the worship of the Creator if the Church had been under the purview of a High Priest rather than a High Priestess? So it was the height of poetic irony when Kaitain found himself manipulated by Irene Drage. But Kaitain could never bring himself to believe that a woman was a true threat to him, and thus having a daughter as his heir made him feel more secure in his rule. He underestimated Marlae, he underestimated Dominique, and he underestimated Quyhn. And he had done so at his detriment. Dominique, Chelsea, and Quyhn had proven to be a formidable trio more than capable of running the empire during Kaitain's illness. And what they had done since their flight from the ruined Imperial Palace was even more impressive. Then of course there was Marlae and what she had accomplished. She was the chosen of the Creator, the rightful Empress of Cadaria, and a better person than she had ever been in her life. More than that, she was happy.

But how had that come to pass? The answer was stunningly simply and yet mind-numbingly complex. For the first time in her life Marlae felt loved, and she knew what it meant to be loved. As the spoiled and self-centered Celestial Princess of the Cadarian Empire, Marlae never knew love, at least not really. She understood the concept of what it meant to be loved, but she didn't understand how it felt or the concept of how it was to be achieved. To that Marlae, love was demonstrated through supplication, subservience, and obedience. Those who were in her orbit were to ensure that they were utterly and completely devoted to her needs, her desires, and her every want. If they could not abide by that simple rule, then they were totally and completely expendable. Love was transactional and nothing more, and yet at the same time it was something that she wanted so much that it preoccupied her thoughts. The Marlae of that time, not so long ago in the grand scheme of things, could not even find value in the spark that she felt with Rhain, or with Gabriel Shadowfall for that matter. In another place, or in another time, perhaps she could have been happy with either of them, even the spoiled woman that she was. But that Marlae was ambitious, with but only one goal. She desired nothing more than to rule the whole of Cadaria and have thousands of people willing to live and die at her every command. Then Elwyne Tamerlane came into her life. From a certain point of view, the lessons that Elwyne taught about self-respect, poise, and dignity were the most prescient lessons at the time of her conversion to the Divine Empress. However, the lesson that mattered the most to Marlae was the thing that she learned simply through her contact with Elwyne's soul. While it was only a phantom in her mind in the beginning, it all crystalized when Marlae first set her eyes on Logan Ranthall.

In that moment, Marlae's heart beat so fast that she thought it was going to burst from her chest. Sweat beaded on her skin but it felt cold and clammy. Her breath caught in her throat and her lungs were on fire. The worst of it was the fact that her mind was numb and yet racing at the same time. It took little time to connect those feelings to Elwyne Tamerlane, and it was the startling revelation that unlocked something deep within Marlae, and a torrent of unfamiliar emotions bled through. This was her awakening to a world where love existed, love that required nothing more than to be felt. It was what brought her into the greater world and allowed her to find the happiness that now flooded her body whenever she was with Rhain.

After Marlae finished brushing her hair, she moved as silently as she could to the door that led to the private sitting room. She fully expected that Rhain would wake and call out for her, but the call never came. Marlae was relieved. Rhain had been through so much in the recent hours, so much so that those hours seemed like weeks. As she moved through the doorway, Marlae reflected on just how much she did not know about this new Rhain Seth and the trails that she had become subject to. Some of the pieces she was able to put together from the tutoring sessions that Anabel Binosear had put her through. Part of her wished that Anabel was there now to give her more instruction. She could ask Rhain of course, but Marlae did not want to distract her from the work that she was trying to do. It was clear that Rhain was very weak; she was far paler than Marlae had ever seen her. Marlae knew about the phasia and the war between the Dark

Gods and the Children of the Creator. She knew about the many layers and complexity of the conflict with the Creator and how it related to Rhain and her father and the rest of her extended family. However, for all that she knew, Marlae also knew that she didn't know nearly enough to help Rhain in what she was trying to accomplish. And so, her best course of action was to focus on the things that she could control and to be there and be supportive as much as possible. In this case, the thing that Marlae knew was the Cadarian Empire, and making sure there was something left should Rhain and the rest of those fighting against the Creator succeeded. That was going to be challenge enough even in the best of circumstances.

As Marlae softly and gently closed the door behind her, she tied the dressing gown around her waist and settled down into a plush chair by the fireplace. The fire had sparked to life the moment she entered the sitting room, a convenience afforded to those with the kind of power that the old Marlae had wished she had at her disposal. Perhaps that was the greatest lesson that she learned from her father. Power, in and of itself, was not enough. The beings that had the most power on the face of Espre were not the ones who were charting the course of its people. That responsibility had fallen to the people themselves, at least in theory. If the people who really had power were running Cadaria, Gwydeon Sandar would have taken the head of Terrik Lorien rather than the other way around. Perhaps the world would have been a better place if the Dark Gods had been in charge. Of course, it was a totally ridiculous thought. The people of Cadaria would have never accepted the rule of the Dark Gods, and there would likely have been bloody wars that would have resulted in many unnecessary deaths. Perhaps that was why Gwydeon had decided to sacrifice himself in the first place. It seemed that the Dark Gods understood humanity far better than the leaders of the humans of Cadaria did. And that would have to change if there was going to be any future beyond war and death.

The first step in the creation of a new Cadaria was the destruction of the old. Despite all appearances to the contrary, Marlae did pay attention to some of the lessons that she was taught when she was under the watchful eye of her tutors. Those lessons were crystallized even further by her conversations with Anabel Binosear about the political landscape of her world. How fascinating it had become to think about other worlds and realize that it was a normal and real thought. But what seemed to be a failing purely of the people of Espre proved also to be a failure on the world of Onea as well. At the end of the Founding Wars on Espre, there was barely a consensus on how to end the bloodshed. Yes, Terrik Lorien had won the war, but it was not a convincing win, nor was it enough to ensure that there would be no challenges to his rule. Though the Lord Grawn had been defeated which destroyed the collation behind the Kingdom of Thorigald, there were many of his partisans who were committed to making his dream of domination into a reality. And they weren't the only ones. Terrik had to make a lot of promises to keep his coalition together, and there were real questions as to whether or not he would be able to keep those promises. The first and biggest of the promises was to guarantee the sovereignty of every one of the kingdoms that supported him during the Founding Wars. This made the formation of a central government difficult.

Similar to the situation that Anabel described about Onean politics, what would become the Cadarian Empire was constituted of individual kingdoms with their own leadership. What differed between Cadaria and Onea was that Onea did not have a central government that oversaw all of the constituent kingdoms. The goal of the role of the Emperor of Cadaria was to focus all of the individual kingdoms to the collective good of the empire. And while that may have started out to be the purpose of Terrik Lorien's empire, what it became in the generations that followed was anything but. Terrik Lorien ruled through a combination of bargaining, pressure, and mysticism. Terrik was a master negotiator, and more than anything, he knew when he did not have a strong position to bargain from. His critics often said that Terrik was too quick to negotiate when he should have applied the strength of his armies. The problem with that, of course, was that Terrik did not have the greatest military when push came to shove. Thorigald and Iltorp, which were both loyal to Grawn's partisans had perhaps the most impressive military. Saldarine, whose loyalties were unclear at best were formidable enough to repel any assault. Albitonin, who had stayed largely to themselves during the war spouting something about adherence to the tenants of the Book of the Creator, had amassed around them an impressive military to defend their sovereignty and their faith. On the east coast, Pellatori had the most impressive military, and they also controlled most of the weapon foundries on the continent. Pellatori kept themselves relevant during the Founding Wars by selling weapons to any faction that was willing to pay, and then investing that money in mercenaries to jump-start their own military faction. Terrik's collation, which consisted of the kingdoms of Zevarit, Rashaleb, Celidar, and Bellnoc had some military presence, mostly consolidated in Zevarit, but it was not comparable to the other major militaries. Terrik had only been able to prevail when Grawn failed and Albitonin and Saldarine threw their support behind Lorien. Hedorah had kept to itself during the war, preferring like Pellatori to utilize its ports to ensure profit for the pirates and rogues who ran the kingdom. Then, to the south, were Oradrim and Menoris. Menoris put forth its own vision for Espre under a shadowy figure who called themselves the Flickering Flame. Now, of course, Marlae knew that this Flickering Flame was Logan Ranthall in disguise. Oradrim had put its forces behind Lord Grawn under the command of one of his lieutenants named Erdric. Despite calls for peace and calm by the Flickering Flame, Oradrim's forces continued to attempt to invade Menoris which created an unending state of war like what would come to exist between Thorigald and Saldarine. And so, once the Founding Wars ended, depending upon who Terrik found himself dealing with determined whether or not he was in a superior position militarily. That of course was where the first Empress of Cadaria, Liette Forer came into play.

When the Founding Wars began, Terrik Lorien had a wife and a family, one that he fiercely protected against outside influence. However, no amount of protection was enough against the forces intent on ensuring that Terrik's coalition failed. An assassin slaughtered all of Terrik's family, and would have killed him as well had it not been for the interference of a solider from Iltorp. That soldier would go on to become the first member of the Knights of the Flashing Blade. It was then that Liette Forer came into Terrik Lorien's life. She hadn't come exactly out of nowhere as the stories go, as she was an advisor to the Lorien partisans. Some said that she came from Menoris, while others said that she came from Albitonin. No one really knew for sure. What they did know, and what became very clear was that she was touched by the Creator with the gift of prophecy. Her abilities were not all-encompassing, but those things she did see did have an unerring habit of coming to pass. The death of Terrik's family caused him to rely on Liette's gifts more and more, and some said that the man became unnecessarily paranoid. When the Founding Wars began to turn in Terrik's direction after the fall of Grawn and the Thorigald alliance, Terrik married

Liette, cementing what would become the Lorien dynasty. The marriage was politically motivated of course, as it caused Albitonin to break with their isolated stance and throw their support behind Terrik Lorien as he was clearly chosen by the Creator to unite Cadaria under one banner. But however large a role that Liette had in Terrik's ascension to the throne of the Empire of Cadaria, it was her council and direction that helped to shape it in its infancy.

It was Liette who was the inspiration for the Knights of the Flashing Blade, and it was also her foresight that predicted the coming of the Dark Gods and the creation of the thirteenth kingdom of Cadaria, the Kingdom of Night, Galateria. It was her clan that presented the Sacred Weapons to Terrik Lorien as a gift for his protectors, and it was her clan the helped to formalize relations between the Throne and the Church of the Creator in Albitonin. Though she was Terrik's wife, she was not the mother of his son. That was a political alliance ending the confrontation between Terrik and Grawn's partisans. It was supposed to form an unbreakable bond between the Throne and Thorigald, but all it proved to do was put the Emperor in an awkward position in later years as he attempted to mediate the confrontation that quickly grew out of control between Thorigald and Saldarine. A great many political marriages were inspired by that conflict, on both sides. There were some in the other great kingdoms that wondered if Saldarine and Thorigald kept up their hostilities simply so that they could continue marrying into higher echelons of the Cadarian Empire.

That thought was something that brought Marlae back to the present, and the problem that she faced as the current recognized Empress of Cadaria. What was clear to Marlae was that the two-thousand-year experiment of letting the individual kingdoms rule themselves with the hope that in the darkest of times they would work together for the betterment of the whole was a miserable failure. It was too easy for the agendas of hidden hands to take the reins of power and attempt to steer the wills of the people. The conflicting agendas had only proven capable of steering the whole of Cadaria to the edge of a cliff and threaten to take it over into oblivion. The only way that Cadaria could move forward as a whole was if there was only one voice guiding it. That voice had to be Marlae's. Thankfully, the legitimate challenges to that eventually had been all but removed. Marlae quietly marveled at Quyhn Ravenheart's strength.

In exchange for her support in the government that would be responsible for picking up the pieces after the war, Quyhn's name would be restored and she would be given the role of Voice of the Empress. She would also have an ambassadorial role to the Academy of Arcane Arts to ensure that there would never again be a breakdown in communication between those two august bodies. Marlae did not see any weakness in Quyhn wanting to bargain. With Dominique and Chelsea behind her, as well as the contingent of Dark Gods that seemed to champion her cause, Quyhn would have been a legitimate challenger for the Throne. However, neither Marlae nor Quyhn wanted another war. Better to settle things quietly and then act in concert to create something that could outlive them both.

The problem now was determining what those pieces were going to be that would be left to pick up and attempt to reassemble. Cadaria had been shattered like a priceless vase on the ground, with many of its pieces ground into dust. Rashaleb was a desolate graveyard with but a fraction of its population still remaining. Hedorah had been broken in half; half under water, the other half deserted. Menoris had been shattered by the fall of the Peaks of Patience, and there was no telling how many were killed in that disaster. Oradrim had been largely untouched, but the Academy of Arcane Arts in Jelan was deserted, and there was no telling how long it would take to return it to a functioning school, if that were even possible at all. The wars between Saldarine, Thorigald, and Iltorp had taken their toll on the population, but not as much as the constant dragon attacks on the borders. The same could be said about Galateria, as the latest reports from that kingdom spoke of devastation at the hands of dozens of massive dragons who were massing for something sinister. Marlae now knew that that plan included an assault on Albitonin, which was quickly become the flashpoint that would ignite the final act of the war for Creation as a whole. Armies of all kinds were massing there, and whoever walked away, if anyone did, would likely be the one to determine whether or not there would be a future at all. Zevarit had been torn apart by Kaitain Lorien's advance and there were rumors of a peasant army that had marched from the borders of Celidar to resist the Imperial Army somewhere inside the borders of Pellatori. Bellnoc and Pellatori had been largely untouched by the ravages of war, with the exception of the attacks by the Grey Man Pestilence and the touch of the other Heralds of Dorovar throughout the countryside. The amount of death that had been inflicted on Cadaria exceeded anything ever seen before, including the Founding Wars. Some of the reports that Marlae had seen from the Grand Master of the Shadow Guild, the phase Saurn, estimated that no more than twenty percent of the population of Cadaria from the year before Kaitain Lorien took power still lived, and that number could have been as low as ten percent.

However, there was a beacon of light, and that beacon had been created for Quyhn by the Dark Gods, and it was the city of New Aradon. This city would be the new seat of power for the reformed Cadaria, and it promised to be a bulwark against the coming storm. Whatever good and pure was left in Cadaria would have to spread from that place, and it was in the steady hands of a woman who had proved time and time again that she was fit for the task. Quyhn would be a good ally and an even better voice for the fledgling new empire. Now that Marlae had found her new self and her new confidence, she hoped that she would be worthy of those that she would be called upon to lead. But there was a darkness in her thoughts, one that could not be ignored. There was a future, if the war came to its logical conclusion, where there were no Servants, no Dark Gods, and no people of power; just humans. That meant no Rhain, no Anabel, and no Isabella. Three of the most important people in Marlae's world and in her inner circle would no longer be there to advise and support her. But perhaps that was for the best. Despite the pain that losing Rhain would cause, as far as the government of Cadaria was concerned, perhaps it should have only been humans who plotted the course of the future. After all, wasn't what some of this fight was all about? The right to determine their own path forward? So, in the end, Marlae would have to rely on some familiar faces, some that she would have to prove herself to, to help guide Cadaria into its future.

The first person that came to mind of course was Chelsea Zarova. There were few people in the whole of Cadaria that were respected as much as the Wolf of Saldarine. So, when the disparate members of the militaries from each of the kingdoms as well as the fractured pieces of the Imperial Army needed to be pulled together into a cohesive force, there could be no one better than Chelsea Zarova to become the new General of the Imperial Legion. With Quyhn as the Voice of the Empress, perhaps Dominique Arais would consent to be the High Councilor, as Quyhn proposed. While Dominique and Marlae never had much use for one another, perhaps the softening of Marlae's character would allow Dominique to see her way through to helping build what she started during Kaitain's coma. Briefly Marlae considered whether or not there would be a Church of the Creator after everything was over. If there was, it was unclear if Baeata Catrinel would still be the High Priestess. Even if she was, the High Priestess would be required to stay at the Heart of Stone and whoever would be the liaison to the throne would be needed by Marlae's side as much as possible. Unfortunately, Marlae didn't have any candidates in mind for the post as her connections with the Church of the Creator were not what they should have been. Perhaps either Mother Amalia or Baeata's assistant Aelind would be able to serve in that capacity. Whether or not Quyhn would also serve in the capacity of Court Sorceress was a discussion for a later time, but with the bad taste left in the mouth by Irene Drage's tenure in that position, perhaps it was better the position remained unfilled. That left the trickiest position of all, Grand Master of the Shadow Guild. Was such an organization even still necessary after everything that had happened? Marlae would have to think long and hard on that question. But then another came into her mind.

What if I have to get married to cement my rule...

Quyhn

Quyhn sat in the small perch inset in the bay window down the hall from the room that had become her new home in the palace of New Aradon. Word had spread amazingly quickly thanks to the messengers that were sent to each of the kingdoms imploring all the refugees feeling the wars with the dragons, Dorovar, and the evils of Kaitain Lorien's crusade against the Church of the Creator and its faithful. The small bench had become her favorite place since taking residence in the palace, as it allowed her to see not only the city that was beginning to form around the palace but also the horizon that seemed to constantly be dotted with fires. The windows faced west where the future was on the cusp of being decided. There had been a great many comings and goings in the hours since the arrival of Sadrina Annis, Cairyn Binosear, and Jehna Faris. Though she hated to admit it, with both Gwydeon and Midarin out of the palace, the place felt empty and incomplete. This was supposed to be a place for the people of Cadaria, and yet at the same time it was built by power that Quyhn would never be able to understand. Yes, Quyhn was the daughter of one of the most powerful wielders of arcane power in the history of Espre, and her knowledge rivaled that of some of the current Masters of the Academy of the Arcane Arts. And yet, the power that she had watched the Dark Gods employ with such little effort was frightening and totally unlike anything she had ever seen in the Academy.

When Quyhn began her lessons in the Academy, her father and mother were both patient with her, yet demanding in the same breath. There was the assumption that Quyhn would have at least as much power as her mother Estelle had demonstrated, and there were also hopes that one day she would surpass her father Alistair. Each member of the Academy was rigorously tested to identify their individual talents. Of the five primal forces, each student at the academy typically had natural proficiency in one or two. With very few exceptions, no student had a proficiency in more than three of the forces with four notable exceptions in recent memory. The first of course was Alistair Ravenheart. When he was fostered to the Academy, he tested very strongly in four of the primal forces, with only Energy being beyond his grasp, which was not unusual. In fact, with the exception of Jastra Mythryn, no Master of Energy had ever demonstrated any proficiency in any of the other primal forces. It was thought that mastery over Energy required so much of the soul of the user that it allowed for nothing else. Some of the more advanced students had spent their whole lives researching that limitation, but as of yet no one had come up with a suitable theory. However, many of the advanced students who had tried to push the limits of what proficiency with Energy would allow had resulted in serious injury and even death. Eventually Grand Master Ravenheart outlawed those dangerous studies in order to ensure that no other students suffered undo consequences to their curiosity.

Two of the other exceptions to the primal forces rule were Irene Drage and Ayden Seth. However, since their time in the Academy, it was revealed that neither was who they proclaimed to be. Of course, while her father had known that Ayden was a member of the Dark Gods, he hid that fact from the other Masters and everyone else at the Academy. Ayden to his credit usually attempted to hide the depth and breadth of his abilities, but there were times that he could not help but show off to impress the girls. As for Irene Drage, her amazing abilities had come from her, for lack of a better word, relationship with the Child of the Creator Talisia. Unlike Ayden, Irene was much more disciplined in her application of power, progressing just fast enough to be impressive but not so fast that it was suspicious. That was why she was able to ascend to the highest levels of the Academy to enact her plans. That kind of cold and vicious intelligence was exactly what those who were detractors of the Academy always feared.

From the moment the Academy of Arcane Arts was established, there was a running battle over the nature of the lessons taught at the Academy and the disposition of the students who called the Academy home. Outside of the Academy, the mandate was clear; no student or former student of the Academy could use their abilities for any purpose that could bring harm. Though some had questioned that mandate in the upper echelons of the Cadarian Empire, none had done it openly. Of course, those in power always thought about the possibility of using students of the Academy as part of the military apparatus, but because of ancient mandates no one actively tried to make the theory into a reality. No one, that is, until Kaitain Lorien decided no matter the law, mandate, or tradition stood as impediment to his will. Even Kaitain however could not bend the will of the Masters to his cause. That was why he needed Irene Drage and Yaron Telsin to enact his will. The Dark Academy that Kaitain created was an affront to everything that Quyhn's father had dedicated his life to, and ran contrary to everything that Quyhn was ever taught. But even now, at the end of the world, Quyhn could not reconcile using what she was taught to harm anyone, even Kaitain Lorien. It was not who she was; it was not who she could ever bring herself to be. She had been raised by good people to be a thoughtful and peaceful individual who would only use her abilities to help the world around her. She had not touched those abilities since her father had died.

There were many parts to her reticence. First and foremost was the death of both her mother and her father. Neither had to die, in the grand scheme of things. They were both merely pawns sacrificed to the greater glory of Kaitain Lorien and the wars that he was waging both within himself and supposedly on behalf of the Cadarian Empire. Her mother, Estelle, was sacrificed so that Irene could get closer to Alistair and then ultimately be introduced into the circles of power in Aldere. Perhaps Estelle was beginning to see through to the core of what Irene really was. More likely however, Talisia counted on Alistair's mourning to interfere with his ability to see the wolf in sheep's clothing before its fangs were at his throat. But once Alistair had served his purpose, he too needed to be dealt with. Kaitain needed fuel for his war against the dragons, and the Grey Man Pestilence offered him the best opportunity. It was Irene that had suggested approaching the Demon Dragon Shadowweaver for the cure to the Crawling Plague. And it was Irene who suggested that someone as learned as Alistair Ravenheart would be the right person to make the approach. Because Alistair's reputation was above reproach, there were few that questioned the mandate from the emperor. However, there were whispers in the hallways of power that it was an ill-fitting solution. Some wondered why the head of the Knights of the Flashing Blade, Vallic Ultiv, who had constant dealings with the dragons of the Plains of Steam was not selected for the mission. Others thought that the best person for the job was the newly elevated Onyx Knight, Devlin Rannoch. He was half-dragon himself, and perhaps could have dealt with the winged lizards on their own terms. But while the deaths of either member of the Knights of the Flashing Blade would have been a loss to the Empire, neither would have generated the kind of outrage that the loss of Alistair Ravenheart would have. Vallic was well-known among the people, but his stand-offish attitude mixed with his gruff demeanor did not engender the same kind of good will that someone like Hannah Ironheart or Gregor Quicksilver did. As for Devlin, he was a half-dragon and he was new to the ranks of the Knights. Neither fact would have allowed the populace of Cadaria to grieve for him. Both would simply be replaced and forgotten. Alistair on the other hand would be raised up as a champion of the people and mourned like a hero. There would be parades, monuments, and cries for revenge. But Kaitain's plan did not work out the way it was supposed to.

Alistair Ravenheart didn't die when he was supposed to. Shadowweaver was supposed to be insulted by the temerity of the human begging for help in the face of the unknown. But Shadowweaver allowed the aged man to live and gave Alistair exactly what he was asking for, the cure to the Crawling Plague. Instead of a dead martyr, Kaitain was faced with a living hero. In the end, however, Kaitain got the war that he wanted, just not on his terms, and without the justification and support that he needed. Shadowweaver used the weakness that he saw in Alistair's visit to launch a crippling strike on the Kingdom of Night, Galateria, the part of Cadaria that the ancient beast claimed ownership of. More attacks followed in other kingdoms, and those attacks combined with the continued pressure from the Heralds of Dorovar brought grudging support for Kaitain's war-mongering. That left Kaitain to do his own dirty work, enlisting the assistance of his private assassin Geoffry Aramour to eliminate the hero. With Alistair out of the way, it emboldened Kaitain; elevating the student Irene to Court Sorceress, severing ties with the Academy, and putting forth his bid to usurp control over the Academy. While the attempt to wrest control over the Academy from the Masters ultimately failed, it was never his primary goal. Kaitain had invested too much time and too many resources into the creation of his Black Academy to let it go to waste. So, if that meant that the whole place had to be burnt to the ground with all the students and teachers inside, then so be it.

That brought Quyhn back to the second reason for her reticence to use her abilities. She was the child of murdered parents who was adopted by their murderer. And while Kaitain had not been the one who killed Quyhn's mother, he was the reason for her death. Quyhn had never thought of herself as someone who could be moved to violence for any reason. She had her mother's temper and her father's temperament and constantly tried to find ways to be in balance with all things. When she was a student, she mediated many disputes between students. At first, she was given respect because of who her parents were, but eventually she came to be respected for who she was. She never used her parentage for her own personal gain or to manipulate others. But she was not ignorant to the weight of her name. There were some that she had crossed paths with who were the relatives of royalty or nobility who wanted nothing more than to run from who they were. They changed their name or professed a lack of need for the attention of their rank and privilege. However, Quyhn always felt that making such grand declarations about the lack of need for privilege was perhaps the most privileged stance of all. The ability to deny the need to preferential treatment, to deny that such treatment even should exist ran counter to the tenants of the argument. Why deny what was clearly there? No one is bettered by such actions. Those that resent the privilege will only resent it more that it is being denied or that it is not being used for better purpose. Those that desire the privilege will become enraged at the frivolity of such a stance. The only true path was the true path for every human being; to use that which they have for the betterment of all. That was how Quyhn was taught, and that was how she tried to live. Which was why it came as such a shock to her that the violent impulses toward Kaitain Lorien became so all-encompassing. Had it not been for Dominique and Chelsea, it was likely that Quyhn would have done something rash.

Quyhn was the fourth person who had tested with proficiency with four of the primal elements. What made her unique however was that her proficiency was nearly equal across all four. Even her father had not achieved that. But it also meant that Quyhn was perhaps the second deadliest person in the whole of the Academy. Jastra Mythryn, with her mastery over Energy had the power to kill the entirety of the Academy with a thought, and with her martial training she theoretically could have utilized her abilities to deadly effect. Like all of the Masters thought, Jastra was committed to all of the tenants that governed the Academy and would not violate them. The difference between Jastra and Quyhn was the way they viewed power. Jastra understood her power and was committed to not let it control her. Quyhn on the other hand was afraid of her power and thus was unsure of the outcomes that could come to pass were she placed in a stressful situation and tried to use the power that she had. That was why she feared how she would react should Kaitain push her too far, and daily Kaitain had given her cause.

Quyhn remembered the first morning that she realized the monster that Kaitain truly was. There was a storm early in the morning, and Quyhn was awakened by the sound of thunder. Quyhn had never liked thunderstorms, ever since she was a young girl. When she was very small, she and her parents were making the journey from the Academy of Arcane Arts in Jelan to the Imperial Palace in Aldere. After taking a carriage to the port on the northern coastline of Oradrim, they took a boat that would bring them into the protected imperial port that sat on the border between Thorigald and Pellatori. From the dock there was a wide road that lay between the two kingdoms that lead directly into the Imperial Province of Aldere. On the road from the dock to the imperial palace, a great storm came seemingly out of nowhere. Lightning flashed from all sides and the thunder rolled so loudly that it shook the carriage that Quyhn and her parents rode in. One bolt struck mere feet from the carriage, spooking the horses and sending everyone and everything toppling over. Quyhn found herself trapped in the mud and wreckage of the carriage for almost an hour before her parents were able to get her free. Alistair wanted to use his abilities, but the ground was too unstable and the use of any kind of power could have jeopardized Quyhn's life. Quyhn was terrified, cold, and shuddered every time the lightning flashed. Since that moment, every time there was a thunderstorm, Quyhn couldn't sleep. When she was a child she would crawl into bed with her parents, but as she grew older, she would spend time sitting in a large chair in the Academy library reading a book.

Once she became a resident in the Imperial Palace of Aldere, she took to sitting in Dominique's private study. That morning when she slid open the door to sneak into the private study, she was not ready for what she saw.

On the mornings when Quyhn invaded Dominique's room at an indecent hour, the Empress would often rouse slightly, wave Quyhn away playfully and pull the covers up over her head in protest. Sometimes Quyhn would bypass her adoptive mother and wait in the private study until the servants came to rouse Dominique for her morning routine, while other times she would jump into bed with the fussy blond woman which usually resulted in them laughing uncontrollably. That morning however, Dominique was curled up in a ball on top of the covers, her dress from the night before clutched around her body, but the fabric was ripped and torn as though an animal had clawed through it. Her face was buried in a pillow and even as Quyhn softly and slowly approached, she would not look up. Finally when Quyhn put her hand under Dominque's chin and lifted it, Quyhn had to prevent herself from recoiling back in horror. Blood was caked in her nostrils and on her lower lip where it had been split. Dominque's left eye was black and swollen nearly closed and there was a jagged gash on her right cheek. Her eyes were red from crying and the tear streaks were still evident on her cheeks. Both of her wrists were bruised and there were what looked like finger marks on her arms and legs. Quyhn had heard whispers from some of the servants about Kaitain's violence in getting what he wanted from women, but she never thought she would see the results on Dominique. It was too much to bear. When Chelsea arrived, she shooed Quyhn from the room and dealt with the situation herself. For the rest of the day, Dominique was in seclusion, the rest of the court informed that she was ill. When Dominique emerged from her quarters a day later there was little evidence that anything had happened except for some slight swelling around her eye which was quickly explained away.

A rage built up inside of Quyhn unlike she had ever known and for the first time in her life she wished harm to befall another person. More than that, at her core she wanted to be the cause of that harm. It would have been so easy for Quyhn to suck all of the air out of Kaitain's lungs, or perhaps fill them with so much water that he drown with every attempted breath. Or she could have slowed the flow of blood in his body until his heart seized and exploded. Perhaps she could have filled his entire mind and body with fire until he burned from the inside out. There were so many ways that Quyhn could have murdered Kaitain. It could have been done a dozen ways that would have been completely undetectable to anyone, even Irene Drage. Or, it could have been done in loud ways that would have thrown all suspicion away from Quyhn. Either way, Kaitain would be dead, her parents would be avenged and Dominque would never have to endure the monster's touch ever again.

But that was something that Quyhn would never do. She could never. Not only would it have violated the teachings of the Academy and the oath that she had taken as a student there, but it would also have been an affront to everything that her parents stood for and everything that they had spent their lives trying to protect. Quyhn, despite her reticence understood the appeal of such power, understood the allure of using it for quick resolution to complex problems. But such uses of that power never solved anything. That was the lesson that her father had taught for years at the Academy. His constant refrain was "just because you can do a thing, doesn't mean you should do a thing." Responsibility was the watchword of every student who ever studied at the Academy, and it accompanied every lesson, was served with every meal. Every novice all the way to the Masters themselves were inundated with the responsibility that their abilities demanded and the vigilance needed to ensure the protection of the world, not with their power, but from their powers. And that brought Quyhn back to the third and most prescient reason that she had grown uncomfortable with the power that she had at her disposal.

Unlike the students at the Academy, the Dark Gods had no prohibitions on the use of their powers. Quyhn had seen them build castles out of solid barren ground, kill angels, and fly with wings of fire. But it was also the minute uses; floating a glass of water from the other side of the room, making a bed with the snap of a finger, snuffing candles with a glance. These uses of power might seem inconsequential, but it was not the use of the power, but the fact that it was nearly reflex that gave Quyhn pause. Such uses of power ran contrary to everything that her father had ever taught her. Power was to be respected and feared, not used frivolously. And yet, these Dark Gods were so noble, and they tried to do what was best for the people of Cadaria despite the hatred and scorn that they had been shown for generations. Did that nobility and that seeming purity of action help to alleviate some of the discomfort that their use of power stirred in Quyhn? She wasn't sure yet. But what she was sure about was that their cavalier attitude when it came to power made her own temptation from it wane. Perhaps that was why she had offered the truce with Marlae Tamerlane. Perhaps that was why the throne and the crown fit her so ill. She did not want the power, would have been hesitant in its use, and ultimately would have failed to protect those she would have been called upon to protect.

In many ways she envied Gwydeon and Midarin. She envied their love and devotion to one another. She envied their clarity of purpose once they had made their minds up. And she envied the strength and conviction in the use of their abilities. They saw a problem and they devised a way to solve it with every tool in their considerable arsenal. People are in danger? Summon lightning from the sky to strike down the threat. Refugees need a place to hide from the ravages of war? Create a castle out of thin air. People fear and hate you? That's fine, all you have to do is outlive them and perhaps the next generation, or a generation a thousand years in the future will see the error of their ways. There was a certain wonderful absurdity to it all. The thought of living for a thousand years, unchanged, patient, hoping that the world would eventually come to see you as not a threat but perhaps the only salvation. In abstract, the Dark Gods were terrifying and beyond reason. In person they were noble, flawed, and entirely human.

Quyhn took a deep breath and let it out slowly. This marked the first day of her new life. Not a child of the Academy any longer. Not a ward of the Empire. Not the would-be Empress of Cadaria, vying for her piece of a fracture whole. She was once again Quyhn Ravenheart, her name restored by the deal made with another child who had cast off the tarnished Lorien name. Now though, she had a purpose, a real purpose that she had had a hand in crafting. She was the Voice of the Empress, and her charge was to use her newly granted authority to give comfort and shelter to all of those who fled the war with Kaitain Lorien, the dragons, and any other forces that roamed the newly savage landscape. She was to be the beacon of light in the darkness, and with their allies in the ranks of the Dark Gods, they would protect that light and prevent it from being extinguished at all costs.

Quyhn heard rustling down the hall. The castle was starting to awaken for the upcoming day. There were many things to accomplish in the early hours, not the least of which would be saying goodbye to the twins, Mirana and Liara, perhaps for the last time. Quyhn could not understand all of the intricacies of the plan that was sending the two girls into danger, but she did not dispute the fact that it was necessary. Perhaps it wasn't that she couldn't understand, perhaps it was that she didn't want to understand. She had grown close to the girls in a short amount of time. Quyhn caught herself in that moment. Mirana and Liara were over two thousand years old, and she still thought of them as her contemporaries. Perhaps its was the utter absurdity of the Dark Gods that made them unable to be related to by the masses. But the days of constant exposure had made Quyhn forget, at least in part, that they were anything other than human. The three of them had so much in common. They were not warriors, they were not comfortable with causing harm, and they wanted nothing more than peace. They too had lost their mother, and now apparently their father had gone missing, and they feared the worst. Now they were being called upon to walk into a warzone. Quyhn felt for them but understood the duty that was required of them. She hoped they would come back safely. Moreover, she hoped that there would be a place for them in the new world that she would help Marlae build.

Though it had not been expressly discussed yet amongst the new leadership of the Cadarian Empire, there was a central problem that could not be ignored for long. What would be the disposition of the Dark Gods in the framework of Cadaria? Would they be able to be citizens? Would they even want to be citizens? Perhaps they would simply return to Mythryn and rebuild their palace there, consigning themselves to the distant mystery they had always been. Somehow Quyhn did not see Midarin returning to exile on Mythryn easily. Then there was the matter of the newly discovered Dark Gods like Rhionna. Would she be forced from Quyhn's side into exile simply because she discovered who her father really was? Quyhn certainly didn't see either Chelsea or Rhionna being content with that situation. It was a complicated matter to be sure, further complicated by the good works that the Dark Gods had been seen to do in the service of the Cadarian Empire. There would always be those that feared and resented the Dark Gods, and there would always be those that sought to do them harm. But unlike some, Quyhn could not see that the world would be a better place without them. The better world would have to begin with tolerance, and it would have to begin with understanding. Perhaps some of that could begin within the walls of New Aradon.

Out of the corner of her eye, Quyhn could see Rhionna coming down the hall. The time for quiet contemplation had once more come to an end, and her duties began to press down upon her. There would be a meal and then she would prepare for the speech she was to give to the people of New Aradon. The new order would need to be explained, and there would be some that would feel betrayed by the proclamation. Men and women had died so that Quyhn could sit on the throne and lead the people of Cadaria into a better tomorrow. Quyhn had to convince them that their sacrifices had not been in vain, and that the path forward still involved Quyhn, just not as Empress. She hoped that she had accumulated enough good will that the people would see through the disappointment and dedicate themselves to the new vision of the future. In her heart, she knew that they would, which is why she knew she had made the right choice.

Anabel

No matter how many times I find myself here, nothing ever changes.

Anabel Binosear stood at the window, looking down the steep drop that had claimed her would-be assassin only hours earlier. How many people had died because of her in the millennia that she had been involved in a war that she had no desire to be a part of? How many wanted her dead simply because of who she was, not because of anything she had ever done? How many assassins were emboldened by who her brother was, or who her father was? It seemed endless, it was exhausting, and yet, Anabel continued to persevere. And she continued for one reason and one reason alone. Because of every assassin, every unknown enemy, and every would-be oppressor, there were heroes that drew inspiration from her story. There were so many of strong character who wanted to make the world better who had listened to her words, or knew of her plight, and drew upon her as inspiration for the fight that lay ahead of them.

And yet, here I stand wondering how I can go on.

Anabel's eyes went from the harsh ravine below her to the view of the mountains. Neither Marcwell nor Trelon had had a view of the mountains from her window, but she did remember the smell of the trees when she would stand at her window when she was a girl in Marcwell. It was a time that she did not think of often, as it seemed so distant from where she was.

Even trying to imagine how she was as a girl was a difficult task. She had spoken to Logan once about how he saw himself, having lived for so long with the same face, never aging, never feeling the weight of mortality pressing down upon him. He had said that there was never a moment that he did not feel as though everything was a dream, that one day he would wake up back in his bed in Aradon beside Elwyne marveling at the ridiculous nightmare that had gripped his mind. But he knew that was the dream, and that every day that passed pulled him farther and farther away from that place and time. Everything was without time, but he did not let it be without meaning. Relationships were still important, even with those people that he would outlive by thousands of years. That was what he thought Aerith Seth's biggest mistake was. Aerith saw himself as apart, an outsider, a monster. But he made himself that. He lost part of what it meant to be human, probably because there was no one there to ever show him that attachment. The woman that Aerith loved cared little for humanity, and those that taught Aerith how to be the tool of fate that he would become didn't want him to know the value of mortal attachment. It was only thousands of years later that Aerith learned the value of those attachments, but by then, too much damage had been done.

Anabel didn't like thinking about Aerith Seth, and even in her mind she could barely stomach thinking of him as her father. He may have been the spark that had helped to give her life, but when she closed her eyes and thought of her parents, it was not his face that she saw. He was not at the core of so many wonderful memories, and she did not mourn him when she missed her father in the long and lonely nights that followed his death. Wolfric Binosear, by every definition, was a good man. He was such a good man, and such a pivotal character in fact, that Logan named his only son after Wolfric, a man that he never met. But Logan respected Anabel and Cedric so much, and had so much respect for the Binosear family, that he could think of no better tribute than naming his son Wolf. However, Wolf's namesake had no vision of what his future held when he was a boy, nor could he have imagined that his children would change the world so drastically. Wolfric Binosear was the only child of a slain father, raised by a sickly mother, and inheritor of a vast kingdom too early in his life. His father, Piotr had been slain by an assassin when Wolfric was just five. The assassin had also managed to kill his infant sister and gravely injure his mother Anastasia, but somehow Wolfric had escaped injury. Though after all these years, Anabel found it hard to believe that any of that was a coincidence. In fact, it stunk of Emries' handiwork. The injury to Wolfric's mother was in the form of a poison that slowly drained her vitality and gave her the visage of a ghost in her final years; pale, gaunt, and frail. So, for the majority of his young life, Wolfric's training was left to two men. The first was Wolfric's uncle, a miserly and cantankerous older man by the name of Cendric. Cendric was the oldest of Piotr's four brothers, and the last survivor of the venerable family, aside from Wolfric. Though Cendric was the oldest, his path to the throne of Marcwell was not assured. The bargain that was struck with the brothers by their father Aldric was that whichever of the sons had a male heir first would be the one to assume the throne. Cendric was never considered the most attractive or well-spoken of the brothers. He had a sour disposition and preferred books and scheming to human contact. What's more, Cendric was of the opinion that the true power of the throne was not the man who sat upon it, but rather the man who stood behind it, directing the action. But when Piotr and Cendric's other two brothers were killed in a supposed accident, another convenient occurrence that Anabel doubted, that left Piotr as the clear favorite for the throne.

Political marriages on Onea were much different than the ones on Espre. Yes, rival kings competed when they had only daughters for the hands of eligible and powerful princes. But the marriages themselves only created temporary alliances that could be broken at a moment's notice. The bonds on Espre seemed to be much longer-lived, though they too seemed to have a very convenient feel to them. And, just like on Espre, it was fairly common for non-lineage families to find themselves paired with quite regal ones in the blink of an eye. Again, Anabel felt Emries' hand at work in these situations, but she was starting to feel as though she was blaming him for every act or convenience that benefited his agenda. Of course, he was a Child of the Creator and one of the most powerful beings in Creation with the ability to wrangle the wills of men and women, so such interventions would not have been beyond his power. However, the more Anabel thought about it, the pettier those interventions seemed. Surely there was a level of mundanity that Emries would not wade into. Surely, there were grander methods for him to enact his master plan that did not require wholesale assassinations of families, children, would-be parents, or the arranged marriages of lords to commoners. From a purely human perspective, plans of such complexity were impossible to bring to fruition and often would collapse under their own weight. And yet, time after time, impediments to Emries' will would fall by the wayside, and the right people would end up in the right places at the right time.

In Piotr's case, that right person proved to be his wife Anastasia, who was of all things the daughter of Aldric's personal butler, Josef. The two men had grown up together, as Josef was the son of Aldric's father's butler, and thought of each other so fondly that they were like brothers. Of course, they were each respectful of the other's station, but were often found talking and drinking late in the evening to the early hours. In fact, Aldric thought so much of Josef's family that he honored them by naming his youngest son after Josef's father, Piotr. It became serendipitous then when Aldric's son Piotr fell in love with Josef's daughter Anastasia. When Anastasia became pregnant, Piotr's path to the throne was all but secured. Then Wolfric was born, Piotr ascended the throne, and there were nearly five quiet years before Piotr was assassinated and Anastasia was rendered effectively infirm. Though Wolfric was the heir to the throne, Anastasia was the recognized ruler of Marcwell. However, because of her delicate condition much of the day-to-day rulership responsibilities fell to the recognized regent, Cendric. As Wolfric grew and learned the position that he would eventually hold, Cendric took great pride and care in instructing his nephew. However, Cendric was not alone in that instruction, as a man by the name of Talinok also took an interest in Wolfric's lessons. Talinok was a member of the Moridon, and also happened to be the father of Mailock, who would become one of Cedric's advisors and member of the first generation of the *Erieal*.

What was that about Emries not being involved in every little thing?

Under the watchful eyes of the Moridon and a master manipulator, Wolfric should have turned out to be a much different kind of ruler. But as much as Anabel was willing to blame Emries for everything foul that walked through Creation, she also had to acknowledge that there was something inherently good in Creation that thwarted Emries' machinations at the last moment. If there was not that tide of goodness and mercy, how could Logan be explained, or Cedric, or Anabel, or so many of the other heroes that were willing to stand against Emries, and the Creator, and all of the other forces of darkness that were bent only on destruction? Perhaps that same tide is what prevented Wolfric Binosear from becoming the monster that all of the forces in his life were attempting to force him to become. If Cendric would have had his way, Wolfric would have grown up submissive to his uncle's perverse will, not willing to stand on his own and willing only to enact the policies that his uncle demanded. But then there was Talinok. The Moridon, as Anabel had learned later in life, were nothing more than extensions of Emries' will, the descendants of the most dedicated of Emries' followers from the time of the first wars on Onea. Some were even the descendants of the children of the first *Erieal*, and so they had the closest possible ties to the will of their patron. Through Talinok, Wolfric would have been molded into a tool for Emries' will, making sure that all of the disparate pieces of his agenda could come to fruition in the palace of Marcwell. And while it was true that Marcwell became the focal point of the first generation of the prophecies of the *Coromor*, it also proved to be the seat from which the resistance to the Child of the Creator's will began to manifest. Moreover, though the Moridon attempted to teach Wolfric about the war with the Shadow and the coming of a savior that would be known as the *Coromor*, Cendric dismissed these teachings and would not allow his nephew to become a fanatical puppet to a dying religion. The infighting between these two advisors proved to be all the space that Wolfric needed to establish his own identity and decide for himself what was truly important in the world. And that proved to be its people.

This was what Anabel loved the most about her father, and in the end, it was what made her love Logan more and more with every passing year. Wolfric was dedicated to the people who lived within the borders of his kingdom, and was also dedicated to the well-being of all of the people of the world whether or not the relations that he had with their rulers were on good terms or not. It had been Wolfric's grandfather Aldric that first envisioned a Marcwell without a standing army. Legends that had been passed down through the years typically ran through many variations of the process behind that decision, but there were two that Anabel believed. The first, and perhaps the more idealistic of those motivations was that Aldric wanted Marcwell to be a beacon and a bastion for what the world could be. When Anabel first took her position as the Queen of Trelon, she had discovered a journal hidden in one of the private libraries that had belonged to her mother. The journal supposedly was written by Aldric himself and contained what could have been considered heretical thoughts for his time. This was a time before the Hand of the Light, and when the phasia were nothing more than a ghost story told to scare children. There was no looming threat of the beasts that served the Shadow, and the most dangerous opponent was the one that lay across your borders. But Aldric dreamed of a world with no borders, with no kingdoms, no armies, no wars, and no suffering. It was a world where everyone worked together for the betterment of their neighbors, without worrying about the potentials for profit or for advancement. There would be no need for kings or lords, there would be no need for soldiers or fortifications. But as much as Aldric wished that such a world was possible, he knew that it was not. Human beings were not conditioned to accept a world without the self, and that was what such a giving and safe world would require.

Anabel had spent many hours pondering what those words meant, and she had never come to the same conclusion twice. Yes, there was something inherently wrong with any structure that saw one person as more important than another, but the ability to gain power and influence could not at its core be evil, could it? Surely it was how that power was applied that was the central issue. But this was where Aldric's philosophy haunted Anabel and where she saw echoes in Logan's motivations. Aldric's arguments did not say that power was evil, his arguments centered around the inability for the human race to utilize power in a responsible manner. Yes, there would be those that would wish to use that power for the betterment of their peers, but there were far too many that fell into the other two major categories. The first, and the broadest by far, were those who would use the power for their own advancement and enrichment. Now, this utilization of power would not necessarily be at the expense of others, but Aldric argued that utilization of power for you own gain always hurt another whether you saw the direct ramifications of your actions or not. Power on its face separates and isolates, it stratifies those who have from those who don't and the more power one amasses, the more one seeks those who also have power. Some seek these powered peers for a feeling of community, which all humans need, while others seek to ensure that they are the most powerful. Competition breeds conflict, conflict breeds loss, loss breeds suffering. These are the true lessons of power. But it was the other group of the powerful that worried Aldric.

For the altruistic of soul, power was a balm that could be used to salve the wounds of the world. Some did this out of true love for their fellow humans, some did this out of a need to fill the emptiness that the power had carved inside of them, and others did it to assuage the guilt that accumulating that power gave birth to. But those that craved power, needed power to define them, could only use that power for one purpose; to hurt others. Like Kaitain Lorien, there were thousands of petty rulers who wielded their power like a club to make their own inadequacies vanish. Some did this thoughtlessly, having come from generations of abusers and usurpers. Others did this viciously, with malice and malevolence. Aldric's supposition was that no one could truly know what they would do with power until they had it, and so he feared for what the world would be once his power passed to one of his children. Would they be thoughtful in their application of what they were given, or would they look at the world as theirs to control simply because they were born to a certain family in a certain time in a certain place?

Anabel's mind shifted from her great grandfather to her longtime friend and ally. She remembered once hearing Logan speak in his guise as Dane Rhuiden. This was when she was still in hiding in Hedorah, and she stayed as far away from where her friend was speaking as not to attract his attention. But she could not resist hearing his words, and feeling the connection that they gave her to the life that she thought she had left behind. Anabel had never considered Logan a practiced or polished speaker, and despite his best intentions, he was still from an insulated farm town. The millennia had not blunted that characteristic in his words, and he spoke plainly, often indelicately about delicate subjects. He did not have the politician's grace to temper his words, and he spoke from the heart about what he believed and what he knew. Often these speeches were designed to infuriate the Church of the Creator and force those blinded by the teachings to reevaluate their place in the greater world. But on this occasion, he singled out the leadership of the Cadarian Empire. The climate at the time was charged with conflict. Ender Lorien had just taken the throne after the death of his father, the universally beloved Kaldawyn Lorien. But the people of Cadaria were not ready to accept the newly minted Emperor. Something had changed in the climate of the empire, and there were rumblings that the time of the Loriens had passed. Perhaps it was the way that Kaldawyn died, assassinated in his own bed in the middle of the night. Perhaps it was because the perpetrator was so unbelievable; an agent from the Kingdom of Night who would have had no ability to infiltrate the palace. To Anabel it had all the hallmarks of another instance in which Emries had put his finger on the scale to ensure that his preferred outcome came to pass. This belief was furthered by the fact that the murmurs of who should take over control of Cadaria was the highest-ranking member of the Church of the Creator, Gregor Quicksilver. What a coup that would have been for Emries that the Church of the Creator would have taken over the whole of the Cadarian Empire. But now, all these years later, Anabel understood that Emries' and the Creator's agendas were better served through the chaos that would come at the hands of the Lorien family rather than through the auspices of fanatics and sycophants.

Logan's speech that day focused on the Lorien family and the benefits of having a separation between those that led the Empire and those that supposedly cared for the soul of the Empire. But at the same time Logan took both to task, not demanding for himself, but demanding for every citizen of the empire. He talked about the Order of the Flickering Flame and how people from every walk of life; masons, carpenters, soldiers, poets, and killers had found their way to a new life dedicated to the betterment of all people, regardless of their station. He was one of the few voices that castigated Kaldawyn Lorien for deepening the divide between the aristocracy of the Cadarian Empire and the people that they presided over. There were those who understood Logan's words, and those who could see nothing else than advancement for themselves. But like all of Logan's speeches, he was not trying to convert the people to his way of thinking, he was not even trying to tear down the establishment of the Church of the Creator. He was speaking to the one person who was hearing his words; the one person who felt down to their core the call to be better than they were. The one person that would walk away from the life that they were living, the unfulfilling and empty life and follow Logan and the Order into what was supposed to be a better world.

This was the kind of better world that Aldric Binosear dreamt of, but the better world that he knew he could not create on his own. Moreover, his fears that his better world would be torn apart by his own children was a very real possibility in his mind that he wanted to prevent at all costs. And so, the thought of abolishing the kingdom's standing army became the best method to ensure that. If there was no army, the children could not use the military to wage war against one another for the right to the throne, and thus could not hurt the people who called Marcwell home. Moreover, they could not attempt to establish a reputation as a leader through waging war on neighboring kingdoms and inflicting suffering on innocents for their own advancement. Many of Aldric's peers did not understand the gesture and saw it at best an idealistic failing that would be quickly reversed, while still others thought that it was a sign of weakness that would bring the downfall of the Kingdom of Marcwell. Neither came to pass. Even through the hands of those that would try to destroy it, even through the machinations of those whose hearts only knew want and greed, there was one constant. The Binosear family wanted what was best for the world and would do what it could to make the world a better place, no matter the cost. And so, it was fitting that Cedric Binosear became the first *Coromor* of the prophecies. When Lakestone fell, it was the Binosear family that came to the aid of the refugees. When there were droughts and famines, it was the Binosear family that sent supplies and support.

The thoughts burst forth in Anabel's mind accompanied by anger. Emries, Halicon, Aerith Seth, the Creator; all they had done was take from her family and use them. Time and again they were pulled to the forefront of a war they could never understand, just to be cast upon the pyre of heroism. Did it matter if they succeeded? Did it matter if they died? Did it matter if their souls were corrupted, and they were left broken and tormented by the horrors that they saw? There was always another Binosear to be sacrificed on the altar of someone else's agenda. Aerith Seth and his children in the center of the storm. Cedric, the champion and betrayer of Emries' will. Sabrina, a champion in her own right, but more willing than any of them to lay down her life in service of something greater than herself. All except for Anabel.

No matter how many times I find myself here, nothing ever changes.

The thought struck her like a knife in her temple. Where was the Binosear bravery when the sacrifice was asked of her? The great tale of bravery that was her claim to her fame was not even hers. There in the throne room of the evil Shau-ling, Anabel stood by mute and petrified with fear while her friends, her compatriots, and her own brother fought for their lives. So many fell, so many lives lost, and she stood silent. And then, when the time came, when her brother was about to be killed, she almost did not act. What she never admitted, what she never told Cedric, or Logan, or Sabrina, or any of those closest to her, was that she was going to do nothing. She would have done nothing, but then there was something there. Something beyond herself. She felt his hand on her shoulder, felt his heroism fill her, and so she dove forward and found a power she never knew she had. She shielded her brother long enough for Cedric to find his footing and put an end to Shau-ling, at least for a time. But even as she held the shield above them, even as she felt the strength of Shau-ling's fury threatening to shatter her resolve, she saw the shadowy figure where she had stood only moments before. Though she had never seen the man's face, she knew who it was who had spurred her into action, and it made her hate him even more. In the moment of her greatest humiliation, her greatest failure in the face of adversity, it had not been her own will that had summoned up the courage to act; it had been the absentee father, the paragon of everything vile in her mind. Aerith Seth had spurred her into action and had given her the power to turn the tide. And how did Anabel repay this boon? How did she thank the man who had saved the first generation of the prophecies from certain destruction? She denied that the act ever took place and let her hate fill the void between them so deeply that it could never be crossed.

And so, when that act of the war against Shau-ling was over, Anabel ran. She ran from her responsibilities as a hero of the battle. She ran from her responsibilities as the sister of the most influential man in the whole of the world. She even ran from her name. Anabel became someone else, and comforted herself by saying it was best for her brother and for the world that he stand on his own two feet without her interference. In truth, she was scared; as scared as she had been in Shau-ling's throne room. She could run a kingdom. She could look out for the people of the world, but she could not bear the responsibility of being a hero. Then when the second generation of the prophecies came, she shied away from doing what she could for the heroes of that generation. Fear and shame were her only motivations and after her death at the hands of the phasia, they would be the truest unspoken words of her epitaph. But like all of the heroes of Onea, she was given another opportunity to make the same mistakes over again on a new world. And Anabel did just that. She hid from her responsibilities as one of the most powerful people on the face of Espre during the Founding Wars. She refused to give her council when it would have made a difference to the fledgling Dark Gods. And when old friends finally learned of her existence, she shunned them and ignored their pleas for her involvement. It took her granddaughter and her old friend Logan to shame her into action, a decision that to that very moment she regretted and begrudged. And that was why no matter how many times she found herself in the position that she was in, nothing ever changed. Nothing ever changed because she refused to change.

Finally, she nodded to herself, turned to face the door and pulled her shoulders back hard. This time would be different. It had to be if there was going to be a future.

"I may not be a hero," she said to the empty room, "but I am a Binosear. I am a Seth. The world does not care what I think about those things, it only cares what I do with them."

Sadrina

New Aradon was bustling with activity, as there were two separate goals that were being worked toward at the same time. The first goal was to make the palace and newly established surrounding town of New Aradon ready for all of the refugees that would soon be pouring in from all corners of war-torn Cadaria. The second was to make sure that the palace and the city that would rise around it were strong enough to defend against the unimaginable assaults that would likely be visited upon its walls and its people. It was of course a miraculous accomplishment by the Dark Gods to raise a palace of stone from the barren ground in a matter of minutes, but the palace was only a shell. However, the shell was enough to inspire the people who had longed for the safety of a place to call home. One of the greatest tragedies of the beginning of Kaitain's march toward viciousness and malevolent tyranny was the fall of Aldere and many of its surrounding villages.

The people of Aldere were unique among the citizens of the Empire of Cadaria in that they did not owe their allegiance to any of the Great Kingdoms. But not just any family could find its way to living under the umbrella of Imperial protection in Aldere. Historically, the Emperor of Cadaria granted boons to certain members of the general populous who demonstrated devotion to the empire above and beyond that of ordinary citizens. These could be farmers that came to the aid of their fellow countrymen who fell on hard times due to natural disasters. Others were the family members of former Knights of the Flashing Blade who wanted new lives away from the politics of their patron kingdoms. Generations of the most devoted of Cadaria's citizens called Aldere home, but that was not always the boon that most expected it to be. As Imperial subjects and not subjects of a Great Kingdom, they found themselves at the temperate mercies of the Emperor of Cadaria, which varied dependent upon the character of the person who sat upon the throne. Fortunately for those who called Aldere home, the first Emperor of Cadaria Terrik Lorien decreed that anyone granted citizenship in Aldere could not have it revoked by any imperial action. It could be renounced, but never revoked.

One of the most interesting stories of granted citizenship came from the period in which Terrik Lorien toured the countryside gaining support for his new and fragile hold on the collective factions that would come to be known as the Great Kingdoms. One night, Terrik's caravan was traveling from one major city to another on the coast of what would become Thorigald when a freak storm blew in from the sea. A series of lightning strikes killed many of the newly crowned Emperor's guards and gravely injured his most trusted advisor and friend. Visibility was near zero in the driving rain, and Terrik wandered directionless through the storm with his friend's weight supported on his shoulder. Suddenly there was a light in the distance. It was faint, but it was enough to lead Terrik to a small fishing cottage in the middle of nowhere. When he knocked at the door, Terrik's eyes stung and his body felt as though it could give out at any moment. His friend and advisor had long since passed out and Terrik was dragging his dead weight through muddy ground and ferocious winds. When the door opened, the family of fishermen that lived in the cottage gave shelter to the beleaguered men. While the family didn't immediately know the identity of the men at the door, it did not take long for one of the four brothers who called the cottage home to recognize Terrik. Despite the desire of the members of the family to help the wounded man, such care was beyond their abilities, and the decision was made to take the man on through the storm to Thorigald. The two oldest of the four brothers volunteered to accompany Terrik and his advisor, acting as their protectors. The ailing mother who also lived in the house with her youngest daughter insisted that all four of the brothers accompany the emperor. They resisted, concerned for their mother's fragile health. The older woman would hear none of their protestations and insisted that they do their duty to the man who rescued them all from the horrors of the Founding Wars. Finally, the young men relented, and the six men made out into the storm. The path was treacherous, and many times the lightning stuck so close that the men could feel the shockwave of the impact. But despite the poor visibility, the lightning, the driving rain and hail, the six men made it safely to Thorigald and the advisor's life was saved. Terrik insisted on returning with the four brothers to the fishing cottage once the storm had abated, but when they arrived, the men learned that the ailing mother had met death quietly in her sleep. It was then that Terrik offered the boon of citizenship in Aldere to the remaining members of the family as well as postings to the Imperial Guard to any member of the family who wished it for as long as the Lorien family ruled Cadaria.

Sadrina Annis wasn't sure when she had first heard the story of the four brothers, but it was most likely during her time at the Heart of Stone. But as Sadrina looked out of the large windows of the palace onto the activity of the people below, she reflected on the rest of the story, the story lost to time, and the story that was never told. It wasn't until Sadrina had met Cairyn Binosear that Sadrina was told the rest of the story as she convalesced from her injuries at the hands of Kaitain Lorien. As Sadrina should have expected, while the building blocks of the myth and faded legend were true, there were important facts that had been lost to the fog of time and the deceit that tinged everything in Cadaria. While there had been a storm during Terrik's travels along the coast of Thorigald, it had neither been random nor natural. The storm had been caused by the Child of the Creator Talisia, and while it had not been intended to kill Terrik, it had been intended to wipe out his entire retinue. Though the fishing cottage that Terrik eventually found his way to was only a few hundred yards away from where the caravan was destroyed, Talisia had used the wind, the rain, and the lightning strikes to confuse Terrik's sense of direction and to force him to walk in circles for nearly an hour before she allowed the light from the cottage to be seen. The family living in the cottage as Sadrina had guessed, once more of the details of the story came to light, were not simple fishermen at all, but rather servants of Talisia, the first generation of the cruel individuals wearing the Melcab name. The staging of the death of the old mother, most likely Talisia herself, was simple to accomplish in order to ingratiate the brothers more fully into the mind of Terrik Lorien. With the boon of citizenship in Aldere and inclusion in the Imperial Legion, Talisia would always have agents close to the throne. The seed planted so long ago would eventually bear fruit in the form of Korin Melcab, who would become the terror that helped to enable Kaitain Lorien's descent into madness. The story however was not only about another of Talisia's schemes that proved to be effective, but also included a small barb that could not be ignored. The number of brothers struck Sadrina. Not three, not five, four. Four brothers. She remembered the story that Pike told her once about the old legend of the four brothers, a misremembered legend full of lies that foretold the coming of the *Erieal*. Was this an illustration that Emries had a hand in Talisia's scheme, or was it a taunt thrown between the two old allies?

The more Sadrina turned that fact over in her mind, the more it made her head hurt, and the more it illustrated the biggest problem in the war that raged throughout the countryside and throughout the Heavens. Sadrina was an intelligent woman, and while she would not have put herself perhaps in the same category as the wizened Masters of the Academy of Arcane Arts, she believed that she would be able to hold up her part of a conversation at that level. When Sadrina first moved to the Citadel of the Dark Gods, she felt like a moronic flea. It seemed as though the minds of the Dark Gods worked on a completely different level, and she was in awe of those great and ancient beings. However, it did not take long for that reverence to fade, and Sadrina to begin to see through the luster to the partially tarnished truth below. And the luster faded no quicker than with her seducer turned husband and tormentor, Pike Rhuiden.

Pike Rhuiden was a man of incredible charm and persuasion when the mood struck him. The first time the then Sadrina Ironheart set her eyes upon Pike, he was circulating through the room like a finely trained dancer gliding across the floor. There was no way to avoid noticing the broad-shouldered man with the square jaw and the stubble-coated cheeks. He wore finery befitting the station of a minor lord, but not so fine that he upstaged the host of the gala. Clearly someone had taught him the finer points of how to function in higher levels of society, which is what made it interesting that he was not clean shaven. It was acceptable in polite company to have a full beard, properly trimmed and shaped, but it was considered disrespectful to be anywhere in between. Though some may have bristled at his seeming disrespect, Pike was able to charm the room and remove any doubt of his status. Women and men alike seemed to hang upon his every word, and younger women hung on him as though they were drunk. Though as soon as Pike's eyes found Sadrina across the room, he excused himself for all of his entanglements and glided across to her. He was forward but not disrespectful, his thick baritone voice rolling over her like a fog. It took only a few words dripping from his silver tongue and Sadrina was under his spell. What she didn't know was that he had cast a literal spell upon her, and that she had been the target of his attendance at the gala.

While he may have been a great many things, Pike Rhuiden was not a subtle man. His intentions could be nuanced and well-thought but they could also be transparent. Pike knew who Sadrina Annis was before he even set eyes upon her. Through one of his spies, who Sadrina later came to know was Serrina Mystic, Pike had learned about the sister of the newly named Knight of the Flashing Blade, Hannah Ironheart. Serrina had been surveilling Sadrina for several weeks, reporting back on her movements, her demeanor, her likes and dislikes. Based upon the information that Serrina reported back, Pike devised the perfect opportunity. One of the minor lords in Rashaleb had a daughter who was coming of age, and he wanted to host a gala for her. The hope had been that all of the eligible young noblemen from the surrounding kingdoms would attend and by the end of the gala, the young woman would have a potential husband. Pike loved these types of gatherings, as there were so many people gathered in one place from so many disparate areas of Cadaria, it was nearly impossible for every face to be recognized. Pike had attended many of these functions over the centuries, finding conquests for a night and whatever other information about the inner workings of the Cadarian Empire he could gather. Though Pike was also aware that there were those within the Cadarian Empire that would recognize his face, so he made sure to confine his attendance to functions by minor nobility, as it would have been too risky to make an appearance in any major capital city.

Unlike most of his temporary conquests, Pike had targeted Sadrina to create potential leverage over one of the most powerful and influential members of the Cadarian Empire. Not only was Hannah Ironheart a member of the Knights of the Flashing Blade, but she was also the High Priestess of the Church of the Creator. If Hannah's sister became associated with the leader of the Dark Gods, such a revelation could shake the halls of power of Cadaria to their very foundation. Over the intervening years, Sadrina was never clear as to whether or not Pike had intended to make Sadrina his wife, but whatever the initial plan was, what came to pass was unexpected by both. Despite his constant infidelity, rages, secrecy, and lies, Sadrina had come to love and admire the harsh and intemperate man. However charming and engaging Pike was in those few hours at the gala, the Pike at the Citadel of the Dark Gods was a man who was constantly elsewhere. He obsessed about everything, spent most of his days in secret meetings with his closest advisors, and seemed to do everything in his power to avoid dealing with his children or the other members of the Dark Gods. Pike was well-spoken when Sadrina first met the ancient man, but the Dark God Pike was not someone who shared his thoughts quickly or completely, preferring to offer vague answers that rarely illuminated anything substantive.

Perhaps the most eye-opening revelation upon making the Citadel of the Dark Gods her new home was just how human the Dark Gods were. Of course, at the time, Sadrina did not understand the nature of the Dark Gods, or where they had come from. Once the great secret of the origin of the Dark Gods came to light in Sadrina's mind, she understood why the secret was kept. If the people of Cadaria understood that the Dark Gods were not these all-powerful creatures that were five-hundred feet tall and could level a city with a thought, it might embolden the leadership of the empire to launch an all-out invasion of Mythryn. However, where the people of Cadaria might have viewed the Dark Gods' humanity as a weakness, Sadrina instead saw it as a strength. While Sadrina sometimes had a hard time finding the humanity in the man that had become her husband, the other members of the Dark Gods soon seemed like old friends that she had not seen in years. The first person that welcomed Sadrina to the Citadel, and the woman that became her closest friend and confidant was Midarin Sandar. Midarin was a comforting force within the walls of the Citadel. She moved and spoke with the grace of a queen but did not have the air of one. Moreover, Midarin was willing to listen and also to admit when she did not know. In the beginning, Sadrina found it difficult to fathom that there was anything that the Dark Gods did not know. However, she would soon learn that while the Dark Gods may not have had access to some ancient repository of knowledge, what they did have was thousands of years of experience to draw upon that helped make it seem as though they were nearly omniscient. Their time on Espre had given them an intimate understanding of the nature of the people of Cadaria, and thus they had an uncanny ability to predict motivation and behavior. With the exception of the twins Mirana and Liara, Midarin may be been the best student of human nature.

But more than a student of human nature, Midarin was also an expert on the motivations and behaviors of her fellow Dark Gods. That was what made Midarin an incredible resource to Sadrina in the early days of her time in the Citadel. As Sadrina had expected, many of the Dark Gods were slow to take her into their confidence, and Midarin was invaluable in assisting the mortal woman in her navigation of those politics. The mistrust was not all because she was a Cadarian, or that she was the sister of a Knight of the Flashing Blade, or even that she was formerly a high-ranking member of the Church of the Creator. Most of the mistrust came from her association with Pike. There were many of the Dark Gods who had become disillusioned with Pike's leadership and his fixation on Cadaria. Contrary to Pike's vision of what the focus of attention should be, Midarin and many of the others believed that as long as the threat of the Creator and the Children existed, involving themselves in the petty politics of the Cadarian Empire was wasted time and effort. If Pike had believed that Sadrina's insights would have helped to shift the opinion of his old allies, he would find himself sorely disappointed.

Sadrina, in her time at the Heart of Stone, was not merely a student of the teachings of the Creator being groomed for a potential position as High Priestess of the Church, but she was also being groomed for a possible role as the Church's emissary to the Imperial Court. While not every Emperor showed equal deference to the Church of the Creator, all respected its power and influence with the population at large. As such, regardless of the emperor's personal beliefs, it was of benefit to have a representative of the Church close to weigh the potential impacts of decrees upon the minds and moods of the faithful. So, in addition to her studies that would lead her to qualification for the role of High Priestess along with her sister Hannah, Sadrina had additional studies concerning all of the diplomatic relationships and issues across the face of Cadaria. In the beginning, Sadrina had no desire to be a diplomat. The information did not function in her mind the same way that scripture did. However, it did not take long for her to understand why. Political information that filtered its way back to the Heart of Stone was sent by the Reverend Mothers of each of the Great Kingdoms. The heads of each of the smaller churches would send reports to the Reverend Mother who would then compile that information for the Heart. One of the greatest secrets held by the Church, and one of the reasons for the disillusionment that began to grow within Sadrina about the Church's influence in Cadaria, was the fact that all information that came to the priests and priestesses, no matter the source, could be fodder for these diplomatic reports. That included information that was supposedly protected by the sanctity of confession or private consultation. Sadrina barely believed her ears when she heard that the private confessions of lords and kings became information that the Church would use to press its diplomatic advantages. Of course, all of the priests were taught how to leverage the information without damaging the reputation of the Church. Many times, sermons were delivered with vague allusions to this privileged information in order to influence the tides of political discourse. While these efforts, in isolation, would have limited impact, as part of a coordinated effort spread across the entire tapestry of the Cadarian Empire, the Church of the Creator would have nearly unprecedented power; power that would rival that of the emperor.

The naïve Sadrina, the Sadrina that was raised in the Church, was of two minds about this revelation. The first mind, the mind of the devoted adherent to the teachings of the faith, believed the Church always had the best interest of the faithful in mind. The Church would never use the influence for ill-purpose, and would always utilize their diplomatic influence to better the lives and situations of those who were true to the faith. But the other mind, the critical mind, saw the temptation to use the advantage not for the faithful but for the Church itself. In disputes over land for a new church, or perhaps the need for donations for repairs or upgrades, would it not be advantageous to expose, through the subtlety of sermons or nudges in the confessional, patterns of graft, adultery, or other small treacheries? But where was the line, even for the pious? Pious men and women were still men and women after all, and the weakness of the flesh was not confined only to those outside the Church. Temptation could only be resisted for so long, and it took only one unscrupulous act to damage the good works of the Church. There were already enough among the populous that began to doubt the piety and righteousness of the Church, and the Church could ill-afford to throw more fuel on that growing fire. This was the fire that Kaitain Lorien would eventually ignite in his ultimate repudiation of the Faith. It would not take long for the lessons into what Sadrina would begin to see as the dark side of the Church of the Creator to damage her belief in the cause of the Faith, and lead to her eventual separation from that august body. What Sadrina didn't know, what she could not know given the tapestry of lies at the heart of the worship of the Creator, was that the dark side of the Church was the more accurate representation of the true nature of the faith of the Creator.

Sadrina's time in the Citadel of the Dark Gods made her question much of what she thought she believed and what she had been taught to believe. If she had been surprised by the true nature of the Dark Gods, she would be stunned speechless by the truth about the Creator. At first she could not believe the possibility that there was a Creator who cared so little about his Creations. How for so long the Church had demonized and sought to assassinate the character of the leadership of the Order of the Flickering Flame, despite the fact that they were apparently telling the truth. When Sadrina learned that the Order was founded by members of the Dark Gods, more of the pieces fell into place. However, what the Dark Gods made clear was the fact that they did not believe that any member of the Church of the Creator knew of the corruption that they were helping to spread. The Creator and his agents were adept at using the needs of a populace against them, making them dependent upon the teachings of the Creator, and the love of the divine light. Weaponized divinity created soldiers for the Children to fight their ideological wars, but that did not make the soldiers responsible for their actions. They were lied to. They were misled. But in the end, none of that would matter. The faithful would die, just like the faithless, as all tools are discarded once their usefulness was at its end. Sadrina could barely contemplate that the group so hated and vilified as the Dark Gods, could very well be the only hope for the people of Cadaria.

In the end, that was one of the reasons that Sadrina stayed with Pike, despite all of his failings. She truly admired the aims of the Dark Gods, as much as she admired the Dark Gods themselves. The other reason that she stayed, perhaps a misguided reason, was because of the children of the Dark Gods. As much experience through struggle and strife the Dark

Gods had gained before their time on Espre, their children did not have the worldliness or the breadth of understanding of their parents. Camille Sandar might have been the exception to this, but even she seemed to have blind spots in her understanding of human behavior. While Camille, Mirana, and Liara were willing to listen to Sadrina and take her advice, neither Alderin nor Serrina had time for the meddling mortal. Serrina made no secret of her disdain for Sadrina. Of course, that disdain was easy enough for Sadrina to understand. Serrina was in love with Pike. Anyone with eyes could have seen it. What Sadrina understood was that Pike had no true love for anyone but Pike. He would feign affection to get what he wanted, and then return to his deliberations and frustrations about the nature of things. If Serrina knew that she was being used, she clearly did not mind. Either way, the two women would never be allies or friends. Alderin on the other hand was far more polite about his rejection of Sadrina's friendship. He would give no reasons, but he kept his distance. It wasn't until much later, once Sadrina had broken down Darrien's walls and earned her trust, that Sadrina learned the truth. Alderin did not want a relationship with Sadrina because there might be a time in the future that he would be called upon to make her disappear.

That turned Sadrina's thoughts to her sometime children. She had wondered where they were, if they were safe, or if they were lost in the wilderness. But before they left for the Heart of Stone, Mirana and Liara had come to Sadrina to share with her news of her adopted children. As usual, they could not say how they knew what they knew, nor could they give specifics. What they would say was that Tess had died. They said that she had been in a great deal of pain before she met her end, but now that pain had been taken away. She was able to rest peacefully. Not even the Creator could touch her where she had gone. As for Darrien, all they would say was that her path was not yet at an end, but that there was a choice coming for her, one that she would have to make for herself. When Liara had said it, she put her hand on Sadrina's arm and smiled. She said that Darrien would not be alone, that Alderin would be by her side. No matter what, they would see Darrien's fate together. They had wanted her to know in case it was the last time they would see her.

It wasn't until the twins were gone that Sadrina let herself cry. She didn't know if she was crying for herself, for her adopted children, or for how much of her life she had sacrificed to be at this moment. For so long she had rationalized her choices. It was more important to know the truth than to live a comfortable life, she always told herself. However, now, as she sat with tears running down her face, she wondered if that too was just an excuse. Maybe there would be time enough for her to reconcile the choices that she made with all that she had suffered. But as much as she suffered she gained, and here she sat with an opportunity to still have a role in the war. She was no longer a queen, no longer an ally of the Dark Gods. She was what she started out to be. She was a healer. Whether that healing was of the body and of the soul, she would use the teachings of the misguided Church, to save the people of the misguided human race, from the arrogant war of the misguided Children of the Creator. Perhaps Sadrina had a greater understanding and peace than she thought.

Cairyn

There is the life in between, the life that is rarely seen, but the one that everyone understands. It's a place where the ordinary is the extraordinary and the extraordinary seems like the impossible. Expectation has a weight that is unbearable, and no matter the effort or the trial, the result always seems to be far below what is considered acceptable. Every activity is coated in an unmistakable malaise that can only be shaken through sleep or so much drink that the mind becomes numb to the sensation of constantly being crushed. It is always there, in the back of the mind, crawling over every thought and every feeling. While there are moments of respite that can be created or constructed, there is one place where the mind has dominion and where all of the demons can feel free to work their evils. Darkness. That's where it starts. That's where it always starts. Feeling safe, feeling like everything around is familiar. The safety is not even a conscious thought, it is a construct of the mind, a way to trick the body into a dormant state without the fear of death.

Cairyn Binosear knew where that constructed safety always began. It was in her home, the palace of Trelon, in her own room, a place that she didn't even have to think about. Each and every detail of the room were pressed into her memory and were reflexive to retrieve. The feel of the mattress beneath her body, the subtle slickness of the sheets, the way the light played on the walls and the ceiling, even the smell of the flowers that wafted in from the private garden. It was a place that when she shut her eyes, for the briefest moment she thought she could make everything around her that was wrong disappear. But now there were many times when the supposed safety of shut eyes weren't even safe. Now every time Cairyn shut her eyes, the demons of that moment and moments like it assaulted her along with the demons of the long years that ravaged her. Maybe they weren't different at all. She closed her eyes and she could no longer place herself properly in time, the years blurring together into one long smear of people, faces, and death. When she would close her eyes, whatever serenity should be there was flooded with images. Red images. Pain. Fear. Screaming. Horrible thoughts that Cairyn just knew were horrible without even having to have shapes put to them.

But back to those moments: The first of two instants that stayed with Cairyn the most may have been the most horrific while the second was more humiliating and soul-crushing. It was the first moment that something didn't feel right. Right before the explosion of wrong and fear and panic and powerlessness and confusion hit there was that moment. Like a blink in time. Cairyn could only remember glimmers of the moment, as though her mind was protecting her from the exact horror of it. She semi-remembered in that moment that she was looking down at the floor, or at least in that direction in the darkness. It was then that feeling hit, maybe a glimmer of paranoia, and she raised her head up just looking at the wall for a split second before everything went wrong. She couldn't even think. Couldn't even process and at the same time, time seemed to move at a painful crawl. It was all surreal, like it was when she tried to think about it. Blurs of motion in the darkness. Every bad childhood nightmare come to life. Cairyn could remember suddenly feeling impossibly cold, goosebumps covering her from head to toe. She still got that same feeling when anyone touched her on her bare skin. Perhaps that was why she had begun to wear long gloves all the time. After the cold there was a long endless shiver that caused her to shake uncontrollably. Her hands trembled and she was powerless, paralyzed. Her feet were rooted in place no matter how hard she tried to move them. Everything inside rebelled. Cairyn would still get nightmares like that all these centuries later. She couldn't move, her body wouldn't respond to anything and no matter how hard she tried to scream no sound would come out. Just like that moment. It was a moment that stretched on forever, a moment that would not end no matter how much terror or pain accompanied it.

There were realizations that hit eventually. Cairyn wasn't sure when, and she wasn't sure how, or if she even could understand everything. Cairyn knew there was a person there in the room with her. She knew that her daughter was there as well. She knew what was about to happen, and yet she was frozen. Part of Cairyn was screaming to run, part of her was screaming to fight, part of her was just screaming. There were words spoken, but Cairyn couldn't remember what they were, or even if she had heard them at all. The only thing Cairyn knew for sure was that they made her feel even smaller and more powerless. There was this feeling wrapping around her heart, like someone was reaching into her chest and squeezing. Every beat hurt. Cairyn felt as each second passed, and each second was filled with an gut-wrenching disgust. She felt like she was dirty. Like every inch of her skin was covered with this film of grime and shame and pain and she could almost feel blood coating her body from head to toe. Crawling like ants but still visceral and hot. Between the pain, the humiliation, and the horror, Cairyn wasn't sure which was the worst. She saw her death long before it happened. Felt his hands upon her neck. Felt the bile in her mouth even as she tried to spit in his face. Heard the raging of her heart as the fear and pain took over. The burning in her lungs as she tried to breathe but couldn't. He stood over her, looking down at her, the vile grin on his face. She could see the enjoyment in his eyes. Could see the pleasure that her fear was giving him. Cairyn tried to suppress that fear, tried to deny him that last victory. In the end, nothing that she did would save her life, save her daughter's life, or save her unborn child's life, but she would not go down letting him humiliate her further. She was stronger than that. She was a Binosear, and the last thing he saw on her face was defiance, no matter how she was feeling inside.

Confusion is the first thing that sets in after a tragedy, and the worst feeling is that feeling in the pit of your stomach that you can't seem to shake, no matter what happens. It just churns in the deepest parts of your soul, digging deeper like a knife through what once was clarity and calmness. The blanket of security ripped to shreds by what could be merely a second in time. But the trick that our memories play on us is that a mere second can be replayed time and time again, like it is still happening, and the body, mind, and soul can't tell the difference. It's like you're locked into the pain. Locked into the trap that hurt, anguish, and all those base heart-wrenching emotions drag a person through with every flash of memory and every waking dream. Some people call them demons or nightmares, but it goes deeper than that. Even the foulest demon from the pits of hell could not think up a more heinous or terrifying punishment than a person's own memory and the horrible questions that begin with "what if." What if I had gotten there sooner? What if I had tried to run? What if I would have said something different? What if? But there are no answers. There never are to those questions. All they bring is more pain, more heartache, and more long sleepless nights. And one night's suffering can seem to last for an eternity. Why can't it stop? When will it be enough to appease the demon in the mind, heart, and soul? When will the guilt let go? But the cruelest trick is that time has nothing to do with it. A day later, a week later, a year later, it doesn't matter when it happens, but that flash of memory will hit. It's inevitable. When Cairyn awoke on Espre, still pregnant with her daughter, or at least a version of her daughter, looking down at her, Cairyn cried. She cried for what seemed like hours. There were no words, there were no thoughts, there was just this sorrow that was so all-consuming that it broke every other emotion. When it was finally finished, when the waves of horror and humiliation and pain faded, her face burned, her chest ached, and there was an emptiness where her heart should have been. She should have been grateful to be alive, but she wasn't. She should have been grateful to see her daughter, but she wasn't. All she could feel was the emptiness of the life that was, and the life that should have been.

There are moments when everything becomes so clear. It is as though no problem is too difficult to solve. Puzzles that have plagued your mind for days suddenly seem like a child's game. The location of a lost item just pops in your head. Ideas flow like water, and there seems to be no stopping them. You feel like you can move mountains with your bare hands. But the feeling that those memories bring is different. It's like everything stops. Your mind becomes fixated on that one memory as it plays over and over in your mind. Nothing can stop it from droning on in your head. A fog descends over your brain, and you can't think clearly. Even adding two and two becomes difficult. Whatever mood you were in before is destroyed in that instant and depression falls down like a weight on your shoulders that is too heavy for any one person to bear. No matter how much you fight it, it is there. It's a scar on your heart and on your soul. How people respond to this pain depends on how strong they are emotionally. Some people break down and cry, letting their tortured soul vent all its frustration through tears of sorrow. Some let it come through rage; yelling, screaming, fighting, punching walls, etc. Some bottle it all up inside, letting the sorrow, pain, and anguish eat them from the inside out. It slowly kills all the things inside of them that makes life worth living, and then the hate starts. The "what ifs" mix with the hate, and then the questions turn angry. The finger of blame starts pointing back inward and the downward spiral into the darkest of depressions begins until it reaches the brink. Some people call it the point of no return, others call it the breaking point, while others call it the edge. No matter what you call it, it is that point when you look yourself in the mirror, and stare yourself straight in the eyes. What a person sees there and what conversation takes place is different from person to person. Sometimes it is angry, full of accusations, rage, hate, fear, and disgust. Other times it is merely questions with no answers that lead to more unanswerable questions. And still other times there is nothing at all except a grim and unbearable silence. At that moment, a person makes a choice. And that choice will affect the rest of their lives in ways they will almost never be able to measure.

The face in the mirror asks, "Right now, you can live or die. You can take the good memories, the good times, and pack away the pain living your life. Or you can tread on the pain, letting yourself slowly die."

There are only two answers to this question, the first is the one everyone would choose, and that is to live life. But it's not that easy. It's too obvious. There has to be a catch. At least, that is what the mind of a person going through this pain is saying. You can't just give up the pain. There has to be something more, something far more sinister beneath it all. But that's what's so difficult to understand for the people trapped in this spiral, there is no trick. It is as obvious as it seems, but the "what ifs" have poisoned their minds to the point where nothing is easy anymore, and every road is laced with pain and suffering. So, many take the second option, and that is to continue as they are. Some make it. Others see the light and go back to the face in the mirror asking for a second chance. Everyone knows about the ones who don't make it. Suicide victims. These poor people certainly are victims, but suicide is not what killed them. That is the term given to the act of ending one's own life of course, but what really killed them were the what ifs and the devious and destructive mind that created them. They are all victims of their own minds. But there is another point to be considered. Not everyone hears the voice and the pleading of the man in the mirror. Some people ignore its existence and just go on. These poor souls have it the worst. They suffer in their endless torment alone, without even the merest glimpse into the pain they are causing themselves and the options they have to escape their self-inflicted torture. Sometimes it takes years before they finally come around and listen to the voice that has been pleading with them. Sometimes it takes counseling, or a good friend, or a loved one. The most unfortunate of those are the ones who sleep-walk from tragedy to tragedy burying the pain of each further into the furrows of their soul, never realizing that unlike happiness which is a fleeting emotion, sorrow will last forever if given the opportunity. It only takes a moment in time, a fraction of a second. And yet even these poor souls have one advantage, a chance to snap away from the downward spiral and return to the land of the living and learn how to feel once again. However, there are those that do not have the ability to pull away from the pain and the degradation of their tragedies.

However, for those that were not bound by the normal cycles of life, like the Dark Gods, there was a third answer to the question. That was one of avoidance. Of course, the normal humans could try to avoid the question as well, however time usually forced one of the other answers to take over before too long. The Dark Gods were able to avoid the ramifications of the actions for hundreds if not thousands of years. Sometimes that avoidance was necessary. For all of their desire to do good with their presence and with their interpretation of the truths of the Cosmos, they were the cause of great misery and even greater death. Whether it was the loss of their home on Onea and all of the innocent people that were consumed by that fire, or it was the atrocities committed during the Founding Wars, or it was the hundreds of lives thrown away during the so-called Shadow Wars, the Dark Gods had a massive amount of blood on their hands. And while Cairyn Binosear did not share in the crimes and miscalculations of her fellow Dark Gods, she was as responsible. As the queen of one of the most influential and powerful kingdoms on Onea, it was her responsibility to protect the people who lived within her borders. It was a responsibility that Cairyn failed, and it had haunted her steps every moment of her second life on Espre, no matter how hard she ran from it, and she ran like she was being chased by the Great Dark One itself.

Many who had once called Onea home had a belief in the Great Dark One, even if they did not have a strong belief in the Creator, or the Onean version of the Creator which was the beast Emries. While Cairyn wasn't sure that she believed in the Great Dark One, she certainly believed in demons. She had seen one in the flesh, and the ugliness of his words and deeds would never leave Cairyn's thoughts no matter how she tried to suppress or escape them. Draven Batoe was not original, especially when it came to the phasia, but where he failed in originality, he more than made up for with persistence and guile. He made it his personal mission to subjugate everything that had one belonged to the Binosear family and make it his own. Of course, he wasn't able to settle upon Marcwell before Jeroch got his hands on it, and so he had to settle for the other jewel in the Binosear crown. At first, Draven followed the normal patterns for the phasia. He assaulted the walls with Jeresei and Kalbraks, and on occasion rained fire with Shadowwalkers. The military of Trelon was not as well-trained as the one in Marcwell or the one in Brea, but what they did not have in training, the had in numbers and equipment. And when Marcwell fell to Jeroch and his impossibly large army, a great many refugees and remnants of the Lion's Mane sought shelter in Trelon, bolstering the defenses and bringing an element of experience that had not been there before. Draven however was not deterred by these reinforcements, nor did his tactics change in the short term. He kept throwing wave after wave of monsters at the walls, never thinking for a moment that he would fail in overwhelming the pathetic human defenses. The creatures would make gains in every assault, killing as many of the brave defenders as they could, including Cairyn's own husband. He had been a good man, a man that wanted to be more than he really was, and he did not deserve to be cut down the way that he was. But it was just one of myriad losses suffered by the forces of the light during that one-sided war. However, Draven wasn't trying to conquer Trelon, not really. He wanted to draw one man out of hiding, one very special man.

The Logan Ranthall from that reality hated himself. Perhaps that was what drew Cairyn to him in the first place. Cairyn hated herself for her failures, and Logan hated himself for his. Cairyn's hatred of herself was based on nothing more than clear mathematics. The more people in Trelon died, the more Cairyn hated herself for her failures. Logan's hatred of himself was more esoteric. From the moment his quest ended in the debacle that cost him the life of the woman that he loved as well as too many of his friends, Logan began to spiral downward into a cycle of unrelenting depression and self-loathing. The battle against Shau-ling had been a victory, but perhaps a pyrrhic one at best. The forces of the Shadow came back stronger than they had ever been, and with a new and brutal efficiency that defied explanation. Gwydeon and Midarin had tried to enlist Logan's aid at the start of the new assaults by Shau-ling's forces, but he would not budge from his home in Aradon. Even when Jeroch slaughtered nearly everyone in Marcwell, Logan would not be moved to action. But when the assaults against Trelon became so fierce, and Draven's purpose was clear that he would make everyone possible suffer until Logan reemerged, the former misnamed Lord Dragon had no choice but to re-enter the fray that he wished he had no part in to begin with. However, what happened when Logan did choose to emerge was not what anyone expected.

Cairyn had heard the story many times, in fact, in the long nights when she was trying to reconcile her own path with the path that she had left behind, she told herself the story. One day, Logan had simply had enough. He took his sword from where he had buried it under piles of clothes and junk, cleaned the blade until it shined, and then fastened it to his hip. From there, he walked, just walked, through Aradon down the long road to Trelon. Despite the danger, despite the monsters that roamed the countryside, he simply walked. There were a few of the creatures that attempted to stop his advance, but they stood little chance against Logan. The most miraculous part of the story was that Logan arrived at Trelon during the middle of an assault. With little effort, he carved his way through the creatures at the gate, and then with a wave of his hand the fortified gate opened and he simply walked through. Not a single one of the creatures breached the open gates, and they closed before there was any threat to the soldiers in the main courtyard. The cheer that went up from the soldiers echoed through every home and every hallway in the whole of Trelon. The very force of it seemed to repel the creatures of the Shadow for a little while. But it didn't last. Once Logan appeared, Draven's assaults increased in frequency and intensity. However, Logan was not only undeterred by the challenge posed by the newest member of the phasia, but he seemed to thrive on the violence. The more creatures came, the more he waded into battle. He would come back to the palace after another engagement covered in blood and viscera and would simply sit, a blank stare on his face. In the beginning he kept to himself. He didn't sleep, he barely ate, he just moved from battle to battle like a zombie. Eventually, Cairyn would go to Logan and force him to clean himself from the remains of the battle over his half-hearted objections. Sometimes he would sit silently, other times he would talk. Many times the things he would talk about would make no sense. He talked about seeing through to another world, a world where none of the death had happened and where the forces of the light had won. Logan always had this blank look on his face during those times, almost as if he didn't even know what he was saying. Cairyn felt drawn to the broken man, her internal hatred resonating with his.

The episodes between battles grew between the two hurt people, and eventually something blossomed. Cairyn wasn't sure that she would have called it love, at least not then. They were both simply trying to find some kind of light in the darkness. The nights were nothing more than profound sadness and numbness colliding against one another desperately needing to feel something, anything other than pain. In time, Cairyn came to love the wounded man, and that was long before she realized that she was pregnant with his child, a child that would never see the world that she was sired upon. Logan however was a different story. From the moment they began their relationship, or affair, or pain-avoidance, whatever it could be honestly called, Cairyn knew that Logan would never love her. At least, not in any way that was recognizable to those who had not lost something so profound as the love of their life. Cairyn comforted herself in the fact that Logan cared for her, and that comfort was all that mattered during the hard times that would eventually fall upon them all.

It was only a matter of time before Draven's assaults became so continuous and so intense that there was nothing the defenders of Trelon could do to repel them. In the blink of an eye, Logan was gone, the defenders were obliterated, and there was nothing standing between Draven and the thing he wanted the most, to humiliate the Binosear family in the most personal and perverse way possible. While his aim had been to kidnap and terrorize Cairyn's daughter Sabrina, it did not stop Draven from enjoying the humiliations he inflicted on Cairyn before her ultimate demise.

She could still feel the shudder through her as his glowing yellow eyes stared down at her, his hands wrapped around her throat, the evil smile pasted on his lips. She was very nearly unconscious when he spat on her face that last time, not enough feeling left in her to spasm with revulsion. In fact, the last thing she remembered feeling was the warm liquid dripping down her cheek and her stomach heaving. So much humiliation and degradation had been visited upon her in those last minutes, so much that she didn't want to remember any of it.

However, remembering was a curse, and it was one she would never escape. The moment she arrived on Espre, still pregnant, she spent months nearly broken by the horrors that Draven had inflicted upon her. Sabrina had tried to be there for her, had tried to explain what had happened, but all that existed between the mother and daughter was shame. Isabella's birth saved Cairyn's life and her sanity. She poured every ounce of love and devotion into that little girl in an effort to crowd out the pain. And for a time, she was successful. In the end, however, she could not outrun the pain. Years became decades, and the decades became centuries. Cairyn lived through the Founding Wars, she saw the rise of the Lorien Empire, and she did her best to stay out of the way of progress while still ensuring the safety of her children and herself. When Sabrina finally came to Cairyn with the bold plan to place a spy in the ranks of the treacherous Talisia and her Hand of Chaos, Cairyn was eager to accept. She had become completely overwhelmed by the unresolved trauma and pain within her, as well as the memories of two disparate lifetimes that would not reconcile with each other.

Like all of the Dark Gods who began their life on Onea, Cairyn had the memories of both her incarnation in the Dark Mirror reality and the so-called Light Reality. She knew the person who had been Queen Cairyn Binosear of Trelon who had married the hero of the People of the Dragon, Pike Rhuiden. She knew of the misery and humiliation of that woman and the rages and infidelity of her drunken husband. It seemed that the one constant of her life had been her position and how it had been used for the gain of others. Whether it was Pike or Draven, she was only a means to an end. Logan never used her, never wanted her power, and never treated her as anything but his equal. However, that was betrayed by the inequity of their relationship and the impermanence of it all. It was that lack of agency in her life that generated the anger within Cairyn. It was an anger that raged hotter and hotter as the years passed, and it was that anger that she harnessed as the core of her adopted personality. Calindria was the avatar of anger, and the expression of rage for the Hand of Chaos. She began as an assassin in the service of Xavier Cormea. It took many years before Cairyn was able to prove herself to Xavier. While at first there was discomfort associated with being the cause of so much death, Cairyn eventually began to see hypocrisy in concern for the lives of the people of Espre. There were so many traits in the so-called humans of Espre that she did not recognize. They were passionless, almost disinterested in their lives. They left so much to the control of others, be it the leadership of the empire or those who spoke for the Church of the Creator. Coupled with what Sabrina had told her about the ideological war being waged by the Children of the Creator using the people of Espre as a proxy, Cairyn began to see them as nothing more than livestock. With that viewpoint, there was little to worry about in culling their population for the greater good. It was like removing diseased cattle from the herd, and Cairyn proved an excellent executioner. In the end, she was rewarded for her deeds, and placed at the side of Kaitain Lorien.

The goal had been to poison the relationship between Lorien and the Hand of Chaos, turning them on each other and destabilizing Talisia's forces, whom Sabrina had seen as the largest threat to the aims of the Dark Gods and those who opposed the Creator. Of course, Arin Ranthall's interference had cut short her timeline, and she made the best of a bad situation by rescuing Sadrina Annis from Kaitain's bloody hands. On many occasions Cairyn had wanted to execute Kaitain Lorien with her bare hands, but she had promised Sabrina that she would not act against the man. She had seen something during her time as the Spirit, and Kaitain was important to what needed to come to pass on Espre. He was going to be a lightning rod that would put the right people in the right place at the right time.

Now however, Cairyn was in a place that felt alien to her. Her life had once been the court, in finery, and working toward the betterment of those who lived within her kingdom. In the newly constructed palace of New Aradon, she was a piece that didn't properly fit. She could not be confined to courtly life any longer. She was not like her mother any more, she was more like her uncle. She had been reforged into a warrior, a killer, and there were still many members of the Hand of Chaos that were unaccounted for and needed to be removed if the Dark Gods and their allies were going to be successful. Even as she gathered her things and prepared herself for what was to come, she knew that there was perhaps little time left. Either she would be successful and Seraphina Masile would die, or she would fail and it would be her life that would come to an end. Either way, Cairyn believed that she would finally find peace. Her only regret now was that she might never have a chance to see Logan again.

The Lovers

Dominique

No matter how hard she tried, Dominique Arais could not get warm. When she was a little girl, her father had called the phenomenon the 'Touch of the Grave'. It seemed like forever since she had thought of her family, of her parents and her brothers. She felt a small pang of guilt that she had not inquired after them or worried about them during the troubles with the dragons and all of the other crises that they had faced. But Dominique rationalized that there were so many things to concern herself with that her parents would have forgiven her. She wondered what they thought of her being the Empress of the whole of Cadaria, even if it was a short-lived position. Would her mother have been proud or horrified that she would have to share her bed with that monster Kaitain? Would her father be impressed that she had had to shed so much of her shyness to address the whole of the Imperial Legions and the Knights of the Flashing Blade? Would her brothers be impressed that she was learning some swordplay and some archery from the great Wolf of Saldarine herself, Chelsea Zarova? That life seemed so far away, almost as if it wasn't her life. It had belonged to another Dominique, a Dominique that died the day she went to the Imperial Palace of Aldere and accepted the proposal from Kaitain Lorien to become his empress. Perhaps it was the quiet, the isolation, and the impending dread of what was about to happen in Albitonin that brought the Touch of the Grave, or perhaps she realized that she would never be warm away from Chelsea's touch.

In another time, perhaps if there was still an Espre after the war between the Dark Gods and the Creator was concluded, there would be bards to tell the unlikely story of Dominique Arais. A strange tale; one that no one would likely believe, but a tale worth telling. Dominique stood from where she had been sitting on the side of the martial palate deep in the Heart of Stone, and made her way to the simple mirror that stood in the corner of the room opposite the door. Despite her powerlessness in the battle that was ahead, Dominique was still at the heart of the new empire that would be built from the ashes of the old. She knew about the agreement that had been struck between Quyhn and Marlae, and knew about the plans that he been put in place for her. Those who felt that they would be left standing were planning for the after. And just as surely as forces were splitting Creation in a before and after, Dominique had been split into a before and after, so too had Marlae. She spoke differently, carried herself with a pride and a poise that was fitting of her station, and almost seemed meek and demure where before she had been bombastic and lewd. In some ways, Marlae had become more like Quyhn, and it looked good on her. The most clearly impactful catalyst for Marlae's transition to the new phase of her life was the connection that she had found with Rhain. Camille had been reluctant to discuss Marlae with Dominique, but the former empress would not take no for an answer, given the fact that she had a say in the newly formed conspiracy between the potential inheritors of the empire. But when Camille spoke about Marlae and Rhain, Dominique's own mind filled in many of the pieces. The love that held between the two of them was palpable through Camille's words, a spark that threatened to explode into a fire any moment. Each look, each touch, kindling added to the impending blaze. And in their eyes, something more than a hunger. It was an ache. An ache that would never go away. An ache of the mind, and of the heart, and of the soul. It was an ache that anyone who had ever been in love would know on sight. Dominique knew that ache all too well.

But as she looked at herself in the mirror, her mind did not go to the ache that ran through her, or even to the strange position she found herself in at the core of the end of everything. Her mind returned to a common room somewhere in the future, a room full of patrons, and a bard sitting near a fireplace tuning his lute. He promises to sing of the Common Empress, the tragic yet hopeful tale of Dominique Arais. She saw the smile come to her lips in the mirror, and laughed at herself for the unguarded vanity of the thoughts. How would the song begin she wondered? Would the bard tell of the small village in Thorigald where she was born, the only daughter to simple parents, the youngest of six children? Again, Dominique's thoughts went back to her parents. Her father had been a good man, but not a kind man. His father, Dominique's grandfather, had been a fisherman along with his three brothers. One day, when Dominique's father was only eight years old, a freak storm roared across the patch of sea where Dominique's grandfather was fishing. His boat capsized, and all three brothers drown. But instead of reducing the family to poverty, or somehow breaking the spirit of the young boy, it only forced him down a new path. The village was quick to find him an apprenticeship as a millworker, a place where his undiscovered gift for engineering emerged. By the time Dominique was born, her father was perhaps the most well-known of all the millwrights in Thorigald. But while his renown stretched the length and breadth of Thorigald, his desires did not extend beyond the small village where he had been born and where he and his wife had begun to raise their own family. He had received many offers to travel to other towns to assist in the creation of new mills or the repair of ancient ones, but Dominique's father politely declined all requests. He preferred to stay close to his family, as he saw traveling as a risk, and continue to tinker with the local mill, increasing its efficiency and making it as safe as possible. And while he did not prevent his children from striking out on their own to find their own path, he constantly cautioned about the untold dangers in the world, the ones that could appear with no warning and swallow you whole. Dominique's mother was the school teacher in the village, a role she shared with a priestess of the Church of the Creator who traveled from village to village spreading the words of the Book of the Creator. In fact, Dominique's mother had been on the path to entering the clergy, until as a young acolyte she met the man that she would marry and left the Church to find a quiet life as a millwright's wife.

Dominque's birth was not an accident per se, but after five children, the small house that Dominque would grow up in was not ready for a new occupant. Dominique's father had already planned to build another bed for the larger of the rooms, fully intending for the new child that was surely to be a boy to sleep with three of his siblings. However, when Dominique was born, plans had to be radically altered. Dominique wondered how the bard would tell that bit of the story, perhaps injecting some comedy, coming home from the mill to discover the baby daughter waiting for him. For the first few months, Dominique slept in her parents' room. During the day, her father worked at the mill and every night after dinner he would work on an addition to the house, a new room for his new daughter. Dominique's father could never be called a cold man, but he was certainly guarded. Something however changed when Dominique was born. He beamed with pride talking about his little girl, and he poured all that pride into the room that he designed for her. Dominique's room proved to be even larger than her parents' bedroom, and became a constant teasing point with her brothers.

As Dominique grew, she could not remember a time when she was not happy. Of course her brothers teased her mercilessly, but they also took great pride in beating up any of the boys that looked at her the wrong way. She had brilliant blond hair like her father that shimmered in the sun, while her brothers all had darker hair like their mother. She was neither shy nor sheltered, but while she was quick to roughhouse with her brothers or go tromping through the fields and forest without a care for rain or mud, she was not built for the exertion. An illness when she was a baby had weakened her body and slowed her physical development. As it was, she could still not exert herself for long periods of time. However, to her family, she was never frail. They never treated her differently, and her father always made her feel that she could accomplish anything. As the years rolled on, Dominique studied with her mother, flirting with the possibility of either becoming a teacher or entering the Church of the Creator. Part of her had wanted to study at the mill with her father, as she seemed to have his gift for understanding how things worked on a mechanical level, but he was concerned that her slighter stature might prove to be a hindrance in that profession. He didn't tell her she couldn't, but he wanted her to make smart decisions by weighing all the facts.

Perhaps that was her first introduction to what would become her second life. Now, after all the trials and tribulations, she could not look back on the incidents of her life and claim that she had always made the right decision, but she could confidently say that she had made the best decisions that she could based on the information she had at the time. And yet, she still made reckless choices. The one perhaps that defined her most was her decision to become involved with a married man. How the bards would characterize her relationship with Seraph Kore was perhaps the least mysterious of all of the parts of Dominique's story. It was the clearest because it was based on the least amount of facts, for a number of reasons. The first of course is because relationships between women and men are complicated, especially when one of those men is married. Never mind that it was a loveless marriage. Never mind that he was wounded from a loss that he could never speak of. And never mind that he was saddled with one of the most demanding positions in the whole of the empire. Seraph Kore was a soldier. He was a warrior. More than that, he was a god on the battlefield, Sacred Weapon in hand, and nothing before him but the enemy. In no way could Seraph be considered a subtle man. But that wasn't the Seraph that Dominique had met.

At first, she didn't know who he was. By this time, Dominique was the only child left in the house. Her two oldest brothers had already started families of their own, and Dominique's father had taken great pride in helping his sons build their own houses on plots of land adjacent to where they grew up. Dominique's oldest brother had joined their father working in the mill, while her second oldest brother had become a carpenter. All those years working to keep the house in proper shape had forged a good career for him. The middle child of the family had joined the Army of Water. While their father was not happy with the decision, he supported it. Her youngest brother was studying at the Church of the Creator, and would be leaving to begin his training at the Heart of Stone. During the day, Dominique helped her mother at the school, keeping the little boys' and girls' minds on their lessons and not the trouble they wished they were getting into. At night, Dominique worked in the tavern to earn a little money. At that time in her life, Dominique needed little. She knew everyone in the village, and everyone knew and respected her. It was a safe insular world, and Dominique saw the path of her future clearly. She would fall in love with one of the local boys that had been too scared to approach her so long as her brothers were around. She would settle down with him and raise a family just yards from where she herself was raised. Perhaps she would take over as the schoolteacher when her mother no longer was able. Or perhaps she would run the tavern one day. Either way, she would settle into a simple and safe life, with her husband, her children, and her quiet village. But then he came into her life. He upset everything from the first moment their eyes met.

It was late and it was raining, and Dominique should have left the tavern to go home at least an hour before but she didn't want to walk home in the rain. The tavern keeper's wife had been nice enough to fix her a bowl of simple stew and she sat in the corner looking out the window watching the rain when the door opened and a man in a cloak stumbled in soaking wet. Even though it was late, the tavern never turned away a patron, and so the tavern keeper offered the soaked man a seat by the fire and a pint of ale to help warm him up. The man said little, but Dominique could see him press a gold imperial coin into the tavern keeper's hand. That was a lot of money for a seat and a pint, but the cloaked man shooed away any protests. By this time, Dominique had finished her meal and was returning her bowl when the tavern keeper's wife emerged with another steaming hot bowl of the stew and half a loaf of freshly baked bread. The food had to have been from the tavern keeper's own dinner, but that was the kind of people that they were. They would always give to their patrons before worrying about themselves. The tavern keeper's wife pressed the meal into Dominique's hands and waved her in the direction of the man by the fire. How many little changes could have derailed that first chance meeting? What if it hadn't started raining until after Dominique had gotten home? What if the tavern keeper's wife had thought of potential profit and delivered the meal herself hoping for another gold coin? But instead, Dominique found herself oblivious to her supposedly secure future crumbling around her as she walked those few feet from the bar to the fireplace where the cloaked man sat. The memory of the meeting seemed to have been reduced to flashes in her mind. She set the stew and bread down on the table. He fumbled in his pocket for another coin that she refused. But then he looked up at her and she was lost in those stormy gray eyes. The room was gone, the rain was gone, there was nothing but his eyes. He motioned for her to join him, and she sat across the table from him as he ate. They spoke little, no more than a few words. He asked her name, and if she liked working in the tavern. She answered succinctly, and tried not to ramble though her heart was racing. She hadn't even realized that the rain had stopped until the tavern keeper tapped her on her shoulder and told her that she should be getting home before her father started to worry. The touch of his hand on her shoulder nearly made her jump out of her skin, and she could not help but think that her face had turned bright red. The man took her hand gently as she rose to her feet. He thanked for her company and suggested that she be careful walking home because of the mud and darkness. She was sure that she mumbled some kind of thanks for his concern and then excused herself. Neither the mud nor the darkness mattered because she practically floated home.

For the next week, all Dominique could think about was that man. She waited an extra hour every night at the tavern hoping that he would come in once more. He had to have felt the connection between them. He had to know that she was waiting for him. But the more she thought about him, the more small and silly she felt. The next time she saw him however, she didn't know whether to run or faint. Her brother had been accepted into the Army of Water and the local detachment was to be inspected by the general of the army, the famous Knight of the Flashing Blade, Seraph Kore. She remembered how nervous her brother was, fretting over their mother as she made sure his uniform was pressed perfectly and free of any wear or tear. Dominique stood with her proud parents, the entire village turned out to see the ceremonial inspection. Just before midday, Seraph Kore rode into the village, flanked on either side by two other generals from the Army of Water. His back was to Dominique when he dismounted his horse and began to look over the troops. Her heart was in her mouth when he stopped in front of her brother and looked him up and down quickly. The knight patted her brother on the shoulder, nodded quickly, and then moved to the next soldier. Relief flooded through Dominique and she was practically giddy with pride as the knight inspected the last soldier and turned to face the assembled family and friends. All she saw was his eyes, and Dominique felt like her heart stopped. The whole time he was talking, she couldn't breathe. Could this be the same man from the tavern? It couldn't be. She felt like nothing more than a silly girl who was daydreaming about something unattainable. She was half heartbroken and half angry at herself for letting her imagination get the better of her good senses. Finally Seraph finished his speech and went from family to family congratulating them on how well their children did in the presentation. When he came to Dominique's family, he shook her father's hand, said something nice that Dominique barely heard because her heart was beating so loud in her ears. Then Seraph looked at Dominique and smiled. Everything inside her melted in that moment. As they walked away,

Dominique's father was completely oblivious, and her mother gave her a knowing look followed by a quick shake of the head. The implication was clear, and Dominique understood it implicitly. How many other silly little girls had fallen in love with Seraph Kore just by looking in those stormy eyes? Besides that, he was a married man. He was so far beyond anything that she could ever hope to achieve that Dominique quickly laughed off the imaginary dalliance and returned to her normal life. That lasted for about half a day.

That evening in the tavern Dominique served all of the celebrating fathers and their sons, laughing and telling stories through the evening. Finally the room emptied and Dominque sat down by the fire to rest her feet and have a moment to herself. She barely noticed the person sit across from her at the little table by the fire, and when she looked over to smile and ask if there was anything she could get the person, her voice died in her throat when she saw those eyes. They talked until dawn when her father came looking for her with fire in his eyes. He had burst into the tavern, hammer in hand, and when he saw Dominique at the table talking to a man, she could only imagine what must have come to his mind. But when her father approached the table, Seraph calmly rose, shook her father's hand and apologized for keeping his daughter out so late. Dominique tried not to smile when she saw her normally stoic father stammer a bit. And that was the beginning of the whirlwind. Seraph made excuses to stay close to Dominique's village, and he would stop often to see her. Of course, in time the visits began to attract too much attention and so Dominique would sneak away to meet with him in a small cottage at the edge of the village. Before their relationship progressed past the point of no return, he had been honest with her about the nature of the relationship with his wife. There was no love there, at least for his part. He had a great deal of respect for Chelsea and for what the relationship with her represented for the empire, but as far as for himself, there was nothing there. He had spoken at length with her about his need to find something to heal his heart. And while he would never speak of the matter that had wounded him, Dominique now knew that it was the death of his child that had pulled him away from any chance for his marriage to Chelsea to be anything other than one of convenience and political gain. Armed with that information, and disarmed by the feelings that she could not control, Dominique became the worst kept secret in the whole of Thorigald. To their credit, her mother and father never looked at her differently, even when she gathered her things and moved into the cottage that Seraph had acquired for them. Granted, from that moment on the distance began, and the last time she saw her parents was the day that the imperial summons came for her. She had stopped by the house to say goodbye, but she didn't know what to say. All she could do was hug her mother and give her father a reassuring smile. What must they have thought when the heralds came announcing that she was getting married?

Hopefully the future bard would be kind when recounting the rumors about Dominque and Seraph. Perhaps they would not characterize her as an ambitious woman trying to advance her station by capturing the wandering eye of a vulnerable man. If anything, perhaps her tragic pairing with Kaitain would have cast her in a better light where Seraph was concerned. But there were more facts that Dominique hoped would never come to light. The abuse she suffered at the hands of Kaitain Lorien was not for anyone to speak of. There was no place in a common room to speak of her being beaten, raped, and humiliated by the man who was the leader of the whole of the Cadarian Empire and the supposed brightest light in the heart of the empire. If anything the stories should tell of a woman who resisted all attempts to diminish her light. They should tell of the strength that she showed in the face of adversity and tribulation. More than that, they should speak of the three women who emerged from the thankfully destroyed Imperial Palace of Aldere strong enough to shake the world with their words and deeds. Dominique Arais, Quyhn Ravenheart, and Chelsea Zarova. Dominique was grateful for her time in Aldere for those friendships. Quyhn was like a little sister and daughter rolled into one. She had a lightning wit for someone so quiet and reserved, and in private moments she had as sharp a tongue as anyone Dominique had ever met. When the three women were together, they would laugh and pretend to be anything but what they were. Reality was not daunting when they were together, and there seemed to be no danger that they could not face together. But the world got in the way of their partnerships, at least for a little while. Quyhn was parceled off to Lordhill, and Chelsea had to choose between her life and her role in the Knights of the Flashing Blade. In the end, Kaitain allowed Chelsea to live, thinking that protecting the woman who seduced her husband would have been the ultimate humiliation. But Kaitain was not adept at seeing anything other than what he wanted to see.

And so there was Dominique and Chelsea; two broken circles meeting and completing one another. Dominique couldn't have foreseen what would grow between them. Chelsea was formidable, strong, and impenetrable. She was a bulwark of strength, and she had to be. A female general at the center of one of the most volatile conflicts in the whole of the empire, facing doubts and detractors on all sides. But the Wolf of Saldarine brooked no defiance. She was tough, strong, but she did not leave being a woman behind. She wore it proudly. That was her strength. Every insult, every mumbled curse, everyone who looked down on her because of her husband's actions. It all emboldened her. Dominque was scared to death of Chelsea. The day they met, Dominique thought that Chelsea was going to kill her just by staring at her. But Chelsea's greatest gift was that in all things she was a pragmatist. There was no advantage in hating Dominique, much though she was hurt that the woman existed. But that would have been anyone who had gained Seraph's attention. Perhaps that was the reason that Chelsea was able to so quickly forgive Dominique. Seraph didn't leave his marriage to Chelsea behind because of Dominique. Seraph had left Chelsea behind the moment their child died. And when Chelsea learned that Seraph had taken a mistress, she had not been surprised. In one guarded moment late at night when they had both had too much to drink, Chelsea had confided in Dominique that she was glad that when Seraph found the woman that he wanted to be with that it had been someone as good and wholesome as Dominique. Despite her own personal feelings, Chelsea wanted Seraph to find peace, and if it was in Dominique's arms, so be it. Where Seraph made his mistake with Chelsea was that he was unrepentant in his actions, and often flaunted his infidelity in her face. He was wounded and didn't know how to hide his pain in front of the one other person who understood it. His pain was intertwined with his feelings for Chelsea and they could not be unraveled. And so he hurt her, because he could not stop hurting himself.

Here was where Dominique felt her heart flutter at the thought of how this part of the journey would be recounted by the bards of the future. Would they know of the small tent that they shared and the tearful admissions of the pains of the past? Would they know of the two friends, thrown together by fantastic circumstances and the tender moments where they found the broken parts of one another and tried to hold them together with all of the tenderness they could manage? Would they tell of the accidental brush of lips that fired into so much more? Could there be a place and time where the people of the future could understand what Chelsea meant to her? If her life had been the calm country that once had a path of simplicity that lead to her life, marriage, and death mere yards from where she was born, the path that led to Chelsea was a winding and broken path that Dominique was dragged kicking and screaming down. And yet through the storms and the uncertainty, the dangers and the drama, there had been Chelsea. In the same way that it had been Seraph's eyes that had inflamed her senses the first time she saw them, it was now Chelsea's eyes that haunted Dominique's dreams. Chelsea was the thunder that shook her sky and her eyes were the brightest and most perfect of all of the colors. At first, Dominique didn't want to admit what she felt, didn't want to give it the name that it deserved. It was not something that she ever had thought was possible. That was not the plan, that was not the way her life was supposed to unfold. The perfect sky shattered by a sharp rumble, an undeniable force.

Looking in the mirror, she thought of the bards again, thought how her story would be told. Perhaps it wasn't a tragedy or a farce; or even too fantastical to be believed. Her story was exactly what every tavern patron would want to hear. A story of redemption. A story of sacrifice and triumph. But most of all, Dominique's story was a love story. She had found the love that she wanted and needed in the arms of Chelsea Zarova, and she wanted nothing more than to spend the rest of her days with the woman that she loved.

Rhionna

There were many ways to view destiny, and one's view tended to be dictated by how that destiny was playing out at any given moment. From Rhionna Winter's point of view, destiny was nothing like all of the things she had heard during her life. As she stood looking out over the highest tower wall of the newly constructed palace of New Aradon she could not help but reflect on her own destiny and what destiny even meant in the upside down world that she awoke into every morning. The most consistent quality that was ascribed to destiny was the capacity for emotional motivation. Destiny was kind, destiny was cruel, destiny was aloof, and destiny hated. Moreover, destiny was fickle; it favored some, and it shunned others. Those who felt disenfranchised often viewed themselves as destiny's victims, their talents and abilities unable to break from the unfair grip of something beyond their control and understanding. The common refrain of "why not me, why them" burst from the heart of everyone who thought that they were slighted by destiny's touch. In the end, it was easier to blame forces beyond the mortal world than it was to seek reason in the common unfairness of a society based on inequality and ancient power dynamics that translated poorly to the circumstances of modernity.

Though perhaps it was no different to blame destiny than it was to blame the structures and strictures of the Cadarian Empire. Both were impenetrable monolithic constructs that determined how the lives of countless human beings would unfold. Whether it be war, support in times of famine and natural disaster, or the allowance of brutality and graft by those in power, it seemed that destiny and so-called nobility had much in common when it came to the plight of the disadvantaged. Those that found themselves favored by the powers that be, even if they came from common stock, found advantage far beyond their station. That advantage brought resentment by their neighbors and supposed betters, and perhaps the advantageous attention could be turned to ruin should the slight find recompense in the future. So power, like destiny, was fickle in its application, both consciously and unconsciously. But like destiny, power could exact an impossibly high price should its back be turned upon an individual. The applications of power itself sometimes exacted payment in blood and ruination from those who sought to gain advantage. How many petty kings and would be dictators found their end because their reach exceeded their grasp and they suddenly found their base of power was more unstable than they initially believed? It took only one shift, one wrong step, and the ground a power-mad tyrant stood upon shifted from stone to sand in a heartbeat. The lesson of power was that it was like water. One moment, as hard and cold as ice, the next as malleable and unpredictable as water, the next as ephemeral as mist. Those who wielded it ran the risk of it disappearing from their hands when they needed it the most.

Rhionna Winter was a woman who did not curse destiny. There was no real point. Whether you felt cursed or blessed by the winds of destiny, it was your perception of a conscious destiny that fueled the feeling of hopelessness and lack of agency. Rhionna did not believe in a conscious destiny, any more than she believed in a benevolent Creator that loved all of his children and watched them from the skies above. Yes, it was a rare belief for someone raised in the halls of power of Cadaria, but Rhionna always was a puzzle piece that didn't always quite fit. Even before she was old enough to understand the complexities of her parentage and her station, the attempt to make a silk purse out of a sow's ear was not progressing well. As a young girl she was rambunctious, brimming with energy that annoyed and tested the patience of her nannies and tutors. Of course, court nannies and tutors were used to dealing with spoiled and entitled brats who didn't know the meaning of the word no. But Rhionna was a different animal altogether. She wasn't as much disrespectful as she was distracted. Instead of focusing her eyes on a book, her gaze drifted out her window to the clear skies outside. Why should she practice penmanship with a quill when she could be practicing swordsmanship with an imaginary blade? What was the good of learning laws and treatises when the real power of the world was made on the battlefield?

Rhionna was her mother's daughter, without question, and she longed to find her place in the world with a sword in her hand, rather than with words in an audience hall. Again, though she resisted these teachings, she did not ignore them completely. What Rhionna took from these lessons was a mental discipline that she would weave into the life that she would build for herself upon her return to Saldarine. It was in part that discipline and self-assurance that would lead to her expulsion from the Army of Fire and her posting with the rag-tags and rejects in Lordhill. In her time with the Winters, Rhionna was given lessons in all manner of political and diplomatic skills, most notably the control and proper use of her voice. She was taught that like on a battlefield there were times to strike, times to feint, and times to parry. In political discourse the same was true. There were times to speak, times to remain silent, and times to wield your voice like a weapon. The more even the voice was kept in polite discourse, the more striking and effective the voice became when it was raised. Someone who argued, complained, and bloviated on every topic without exception would find themselves ignored more often than not. The same could be said for someone who never spoke and avoided attaching their voices to anything substantive. The person who was measured in all things gained advantage both through their raised voice but also through their silence. Control was at the heart of everything, and the person in control would be harder to manipulate into uncomfortable and unflattering situations.

Perhaps that was why Rhionna had a difficult time accepting the idea of the Creator that the Church of the Creator popularized through its teachings. A Creator that only loved, that only valued, and only required supplication and praise did not fit with the history of Cadaria, nor with the current political climate thereof. It was not only unbelievers that were afflicted with disease and crippled with infirmity. It was not only the skeptics that found their lives snuffed out early by accident or the malevolence of others. And it was not the impious who were cut to pieces on the battlefield. The faithful killed one another. The non-believers killed others who saw no light in the beyond. If there was a pattern to the horrors that the so-called loving and benevolent Creator allowed to come to pass, it was a pattern that only He understood and it was not one of compassion, but instead one of cruelty. When she was old enough, Rhionna began to wander the city by herself, and it was then that she first encountered a brother of the Order of the Flickering Flame.

It was early one evening shortly after Rhionna had reached her fourteenth birthday. She had already made her intentions clear to her adoptive parents that she was going to tender her enlistment to the Army of Fire and follow in her mother's footsteps. Her adoptive parents accepted this decision grudgingly, as in some ways they knew that the day would come eventually. Rhionna had always been an independent thinker, and that trait had always been encouraged as she grew from a girl to a young woman. So that evening in the common room of her favorite inn where she had listened to the stories of warriors and bards late into the night on many occasions, she met a man in a simple robe who was glad to speak to anyone who would listen about the Order of the Flickering Flame. What the man delivered was not a sermon, but was instead a conversation. He was not above answering and question or any challenge to his beliefs. He spoke calmly and evenly at all times, both about the teachings of the Order and of his own experiences in the world before and after joining.

The man who identified himself only as Duncan spoke at length of the privileged life that he grew in. His father was an important man, and his mother was from an influential family. He characterized in sometimes harsh and pointed words the way that such a privileged upbringing warped his mind and his sense of self. Because his parents were so important, of course he should have been held in high esteem even if he had never accomplished anything on his own. He was owed. And that was the word he continued to stress as he talked about his past. He felt, and truly believed down to the very depths of his soul that he was owed. He was owed love, he was owed allegiance, he was owed attention, and he was owed unconditional belief. Now Duncan, by his own admission, was not a good man. He resented and hated his parents, he lorded his position over those who were unable to challenge his cruelty. He took what he wanted at every opportunity because he knew there would never be true consequences. Duncan characterized himself as a brute in finery. Many in the common room that night understood exactly the type of person that Duncan was describing because they had felt a similar brutish behavior exerted upon their lives.

The foundation established, Duncan began to speak of a turning point. Unlike his description of his life before this turning point, Duncan was very light on specifics and spoke more in abstracts. He spoke about a reckoning that came between who he wanted to be and the man that he was. That everywhere he looked, there were impediments and obstacles to achieving his rightful place in the world. And all of those obstacles, all of those impediments, and the path of thwarted destiny could be undone once his parents were no longer alive. This admission brought gasps from the growing audience as they quickly contemplated the meaning of his words. Had this man really murdered his parents in an attempt to seize the destiny that was owed to him? Surely that was not a new story. People had killed for less, and nobility despite their elevated status, seemed to be much more willing to violate what would be considered societal norms to hold on to or to gain more power and prestige. But after letting the audience's imaginations whip through the myriad possibilities, Duncan put their worst fears to rest. No, he had not murdered his parents in some vainglorious attempt to rewrite his destiny. In fact, Duncan stressed the fact that the moment he even contemplated harming his parents, was the moment that he ceased being their child. In a way, those thoughts ended his life, and destroyed whatever future was to be found on that path. But despite the loss, a new path did not suddenly present itself. Opportunity did not come so easily just because he wanted it to, no matter his heritage, no matter what advantage could be found in his birth, or his education, or his training.

Duncan then spoke of wandering through the wilderness sure only of the fact that he was unsure. He had lost everything. He had no family. He had no home. His own failings of trust and loyalty had robbed him of his ability to trust others and he felt that he deserved no loyalty. In his wanderings he even began to question the Creator. These questions brought a new understanding of the world, a world in which suffering was the salve that cleansed the blemishes of the soul. Pain was the only truth of life, and that truth made it possible for all sins to be forgiven, eventually. But the other truth of pain was that if not properly applied and respected, that pain could consume the soul that it was designed to heal. It was a dangerous balance to attempt to strike, and Duncan had never been taught the lessons necessary to find his way through. That was where the Order of the Flickering Flame came in. The Order found Duncan at his lowest point, the point between life and death, and taught him the way to harness the holes in his soul for the good of not only himself but his community. One of the tenants of the Order was that the pain of the soul could not be healed through introspection alone. Only through service, could true redemption be found.

This was where Duncan veered into the more controversial part of his story. He began to talk about the differences between the Order and the Church of the Creator. How the Order was dedicated to protection and advancement of the community, while the Church was only dedicated to the advancement of the Creator through obedience and supplication. The Order did not believe in subservience of any kind, but instead was predicated on the idea that all of humanity, from the beggar in the street to the emperor on the throne, was equal. Not even the leadership of the Order of the Flickering Flame was elevated above the lowest of its members. The leadership was just as willing to give their lives for the good of the innocent, as sacrifice only existed when one was willing to make a sacrifice, not demand sacrifice of others. The Church of the Creator believed in sacrifice as well. The supplicants within the Church sacrificed so that the monolithic Church would continue. All was done for the glory of the Creator, but the understanding of the Creator was flawed at best.

Some in the common room were ready to walk out when this part of the conversation began, but Duncan was quick to make clear his points. The Order did not hold any ill will toward the Church of the Creator; if anything the Order believed in part of the Church's mission. The Church had the capacity and the resources to heal so many ills of the world, but there were too many conditions upon which that aid was contingent. The divisions within the world of Espre ran deeper than ideological squabbles. If anything, the Church and the Order should have been allies. There was darkness coming, darkness that could not be combatted by faith alone. And when the time came, it would not be the paladins and the priests of the Church of the Creator in the streets fighting against the darkness, it would be the members of the Order of the Flickering Flame. They would be the ones to uplift humanity and protect it, no matter who or what they had to protect it against.

That night, Duncan spent many hours talking and debating the finer points of his story, and finally as the night drew to its end, Duncan paid for the meals and drinks of every one in the common room and walked out into the dead of the night never to be seen in that city again. It would not be until years later that Rhionna would see Duncan again. Rhionna had not recognized him right away, and even when Duncan told his story about how he had joined the Order of the Flickering Flame, it had not jogged her memory. Perhaps it was because she was still wrestling with the revelations about her parentage, or perhaps it was because she was trying to make sense of the choices she had made in her life. But whatever the reason, when she watched Duncan lift himself into the sky and take the fight to one of the Servants of the Creator, the man's identity became clear. She wished she had gotten the chance to tell him how much that one night in a common room had meant to her. How it had opened her eyes and allowed her to question everything about her life and the path that she was on, and moreover, how it had allowed her to do what needed to be done when the time was right. While she had never been formally inducted into the Order of the Flickering Flame, in her heart she was always counted among their number.

Not long after the conversation with Duncan, Rhionna made good on her promise to follow in her mother's footsteps and enlisted in the Army of Fire. Despite the secrecy related to her birth, Rhionna was never denied knowledge about her parentage. This did not mean however, that Rhionna was allowed to have any kind of relationship with her mother that could be considered affectionate. Perhaps that was how Chelsea was built. There were quiet moments when Rhionna was a child, alone with her mother when it was clear that Chelsea was trying. She would hold her young daughter, rocking her gently in her arms. But even in those times there was distance. Chelsea could have just as easily been on the other side of the palace as she was in that room. What Chelsea lacked in parental skill however, she more than made up for in her attentiveness to Rhionna's development. It would be many years later before Rhionna truly understood all of the actions that Chelsea took on her behalf and the reasons for those actions. Chelsea Zarova never had a chance to be anything other than what she was. She was raised to be a solider, lived her life trying to prove just how strong and unrelenting she was. Chelsea had to be stronger, had to be braver, had to be more ruthless than anyone else just to be noticed. Sometimes she was noticed for the wrong reasons, but that didn't matter. Eventually people stopped seeing the woman in the armor. All they saw was the Wolf of Saldarine, the killer whose eyes were the last thing hundreds of soldiers saw before their deaths.

No matter the respect Cheslea gained for herself, it did not however reflect further down the ranks to the other women who served in the Army of Fire, nor did it begin some great revelation about the fitness of women to serve in the military of the other Great Kingdoms. Chelsea, like Leonora and Hannah were aberrations in the grand scheme of things. Men were the fighters. Men were the warriors. Men were the killers. They were the only ones with the drive and the strength to do what needed to be done in the worst circumstances. Hannah Ironheart was never seen as a warrior first. She was the High Priestess of the Church of the Creator, and whatever necessity of war existed, she fought for the faithful, to protect not to kill. The killing was left to the paladins in the service of the great Gregor Quicksilver. On the battlefield he dwarfed his wife. Perhaps that was why the emperor paired the unlikely couple. Was it a measure of control on Gregor so that people would no longer see him as a competitor for the throne? Was it protection for Hannah so that the faithful would not see their High Priestess as a killer? Or was it so that never again would a woman need to be at the head of the Army of Stone? Perhaps all were true, or perhaps none were. The truth was that it didn't matter what the emperor's motivations were, as he would never give them voice. The perception is what mattered. The perception was that women were not fit to lead and needed to be protected at all cost.

Like Chelsea, Leonora Wastri was an exception to this male-dominated view of military life. She did not have the reputation that Chelsea did for her prowess on the battlefield. Her reputation had been made on the mysterious nature of her history and her abilities. No one knew for certain how old she was or how it was that she could go for days without food and rest. How she could seemingly glide across the most treacherous of terrain without ever putting a foot wrong or leaving a trace. For many, Leonora was barely human at all, no matter her gender. She was apart, an other.

She was lichened and linked to Vallic Ultiv and the manner in which he floated through life on the edge of the understanding of people. In a world where the Dark Gods and the beasts that served them existed, there were those loyal to the throne that were outside as well. Alien threats needed to be met by inhuman champions, such was the role of the Knights of the Flashing Blade. This was another way that Leonora, Hannah, and Chelsea were separated from the rest. As members of the Knights of the Flashing Blade, they were held apart, given roles that could not be questioned due to imperial decree.

Life as the other was not a life that Chelsea wanted for her daughter. It was not a life that she wanted for herself, but those choices had been made long ago and were unlikely to ever be altered. Chelsea's political machinations ended at the water's edge. She knew enough to not embarrass Saldarine while representing the Kingdom of Fire in the Imperial Court or in other negotiations befitting her station as a member of the Knights of the Flashing Blade. But Chelsea was not arrogant enough to fancy herself a diplomat or a politician. She was a tool of the empire, a tool of the Kingdom of Fire, and a tool of the Army of Fire. In her daughter she saw the possibility to be much more. Perhaps she could be a member of the imperial court, or maybe even more. Chelsea Zarova was a warrior, a killer, and one of the most intimidating women in the whole of the empire, but she did not want that to be the fate of her daughter. Though like Chelsea, in the end Rhionna could not deny what she was. She was a soldier; she would always be a soldier.

But her path would not be that easy. What some would call another of destiny's twists, Rhionna saw as yet another opportunity to demonstrate her beliefs and how far she was willing to go in the defense of those beliefs. There was an uncomfortable practice in place in the Army of Fire that despite all of Chelsea's best efforts to snuff out, persisted. Some of the old guard of the Army, the ones who resented both Chelsea specifically and military women generally, did everything in their power to denigrate, humiliate, and intimidate female recruits with the goal of forcing them to resign their commissions. While most of the time this intimidation did not expand into physical altercation, there were more than enough rumors of sexual assaults being used as a weapon to accomplish this heinous goal. Though Rhionna herself was not the target of one of these assaults, one of the other young female recruits was. When Rhionna heard the assault taking place, she didn't think, she just reacted. A bloodied nose and a broken arm later, and Rhionna was brought up on charges for assaulting a superior officer. However, instead of drumming her out of the military, she was quietly transferred to Lordhill. Out of respect for what she did, and what she was trying to be, Chelsea did not intervene on behalf of her daughter, but she did take the opportunity to purge all of those corrupt military personnel who utilized fear and intimidation to rob anyone of their ability to serve their kingdom. Rhionna had made her sacrifice, and both Chelsea and Rhionna would be sure that that sacrifice was not in vain.

Though the official report of Rhionna's conduct was what was entered into the record, it did not take long for the true reason for Rhionna's transfer to find its way to Lordhill. When Rhionna arrived, she was not treated as a pariah, but instead was welcomed as a hero. There was bright light within her that could not be denied, and it was because this bright light and her unimpeachable sense of right and wrong that gained her the position that would change her life forever. She was assigned to the protection detail for Quyhn Ravenheart, another lost soul cast adrift on the whims of destiny. What Rhionna found with Quyhn was another woman who was willing to fight, to stand against the tide, and to make her own destiny. Whether it was Kaitain Lorien, the Dark Gods, the forces of the Heavens, or the common political wranglings of a world gone insane, Quyhn did not falter. She was often unsure, and doubted her own abilities, but that did not diminish her strength. It was that strength that drew Rhionna to Quyhn. She was the moth to Quyhn's flame, but strangely, Quyhn felt as though she was the moth trapped in Rhionna's irresistible light. They circled around each other, danced around each other, either unwilling or unable to see beyond their stations. But then, at some point, none of that mattered. All that mattered was being together.

And now, it seemed that whatever the force was that the people of Cadaria called destiny was about to exact its final cost. She felt the doom growing in the west. She felt the creeping hand of darkness as though it were wrapping around her own throat. Whatever was about to happen was going to change everything forever, and Rhionna hoped that when the shadow finally lifted, that whatever world was left would have a place for her and the woman that she loved.

Alderin

Alderin paced back and forth in the small room that had been made available to him in the Heart of Stone. To be fair, he did more than pace, he stalked. He was like a wild animal in a cage, and the longer he was confined in that small room, the more irritated he became. Of course, he could have left the room and wandered the Heart of Stone to get an idea of the fortifications of the structure and how they possibly could have defended it against the coming onslaught, but he had been cautioned against roaming the Heart at night by Jeroch. There had already been an attempt on the life of Anabel Binosear, and there was no telling if there were other agents with Talisia's power-stealing blades hidden within the most-holy city in the Cadarian Empire. In a matter of days, perhaps in a matter of hours, none of that would matter.

When Alderin was young, before he became jaded by the politics of the Dark Gods and the darkness that lay between them and the Cadarian Empire, he loved to sit at the foot of his father and listen to the stories about the world of Onea and the war between the Light and the Darkness. At first the stories were sedate, just the bedtime stories to quiet a child's mind. Once Alderin was older, the same tales took on darker and more visceral character. It was through these stories that Aryx first began to teach his son basic tactics and awareness of the realities of warfare. On Onea, Aryx Terian was an adept tactician with hundreds of years of warfare behind him. As a member of the phasia he took on whole armies single-handedly, and as a member of the *Erieal* behind the Lord Lion Cedric Binosear, Aryx waged a guerilla war against relentless foes that he was constantly outnumbered by. In the use of a sword, Aryx Terian was nearly unmatched, and with the use of his powers he was perhaps one of the deadliest people to ever walk the face of Onea. But Aryx Terian was also a man who was trapped between two worlds. He was a fulcrum, a tool, and what's more, he knew it. Aryx was the child of Halicon, and he was bred for one purpose, and that was to kill as many of Emries' creations as possible. However, the first generation of the phasia were not exactly what the histories of Onea remembered them as. Even the heroes of Onea had an unclear view of those phasia, simply because of the creatures that came after and the methods that they employed to fight the vague war against not only Emries, but each other.

On the surface, the phasia were unrepentant killers who were very efficient at their task. Armies, cities, whole generations of human beings met their ends at the hands of the phasia. But their resolve was tested every step of the way by an enemy who was every bit as ruthless as the phasia themselves. For many years, hearing the tales from the other members of the Dark Gods, Alderin asked his father a question about the incongruency between the powers of the phasia and the humans they seemed to slaughter by the thousands. How was it that the whole population of the planet wasn't wiped out several times over? The truth was perhaps the most terrifying thing that Alderin had ever heard. Aryx told a story about a plan that the six original phasia concocted. It was the last time that they ever combined all their powers, and the last time that the phasia were ever allowed to work as one. In one series of coordinated strikes, the original six phasia attacked all of the human settlements across the face of Onea, reducing them to ash and leveling every single city. By the time the day had ended, not a single human being walked or crawled on the face of the planet. Aryx believed that there was no way that Emries could have recovered from such losses, and that would have forced their ultimate enemy to finally admit that there was no victory to be found. However, when the new day dawned, there were new human cities and new humans populating those cities. It was if the assault of the phasia never happened.

Though the assault could have been considered a success, it would have ramifications that would trickle down through the following generations of the phasia. The first and most immediate ramification was the broken will of Aryx Terian. While many believed that it was the advent of Jeroch's Black Tower and the wholesale slaughter of innocents in that demonic edifice, it was actually the process of wiping out the entire population that began Aryx's questions about their true purpose. This began Aryx's long conversations with Halicon and Kamen about the nature of the war and the phasia's role in it. Aryx came to the conclusion that no matter what path the phasia took in fighting the war, they would never be able to defeat Emries. If he could watch as all of the humans were destroyed and simply create new out of thin air without batting an eye, then what damage could the phasia realistically cause? If the prohibition on acting directly against Emries continued to stand, then there could be no victory. Kamen and Aryx began to believe that a directed strike, all of the phasia working together, would be enough to topple Emries. But regardless of the reasoned arguments that both Aryx and Kamen made, Halicon rebuffed any advance. Though Aryx would discover the reasons for Halicon's reticence upon his becoming a member of the Dark Gods, at the time he could not fathom fighting a war that no one could win. The Black Tower was the last straw for Aryx, a continuation of a cycle of death that led nowhere. But what was a disillusioned, immortal, non-human mass murderer to do in a world of mortals who did not understand why they were being killed?

Many nights Aryx and Kamen sat discussing not only the nature of the war, but also the nature of humanity and Emries' hold over it. These people were content to die over and over again, sacrificed to beings whose power they could never hope to match. No matter how many times Aryx and Kamen sought to understand humanity, they could not. Then Kamen put forth the theory that changed the course of Aryx's life. Perhaps the phasia were not supposed to understand the humans. Perhaps Halicon believed that if the phasia understood the humans it would make it more difficult to kill them by the thousands. So Aryx devised a plan to learn as much as he could about humanity. He would become one of them, would live like them, and would try to make sense of their sacrifices. Which was the next ripple, the removal of Aryx Terian from the ranks of the phasia. Though it was an uneasy equilibrium, the phasia did exist in a balance. The six primal forces connected through the Blaze, embodied by each of the six members of the phasia. When Aryx requested that he be removed from the Brotherhood, even Halicon did not understand the ramifications of the act. The phasia were not like humans. The humans were creations of the Children and thus were creations of the Creator. The phasia were something else entirely. The phasia were made from the Blaze as wielded by Halicon. It set them apart somehow, in ways that even Halicon had never been able to explain, at least so far as Aryx had been able to discover in thousands of years of trying. No member of the phasia, even the most learned members like Saurn and Ellis, had been able to discern the nature of the Blaze or the nature of the phasia's attachment to it. The phasia were not the Blaze, but they were part of the Blaze. Perhaps the part of them that was Halicon prevented the phasia from knowing the true nature of the Blaze. Whatever the reason, there was a complicated relationship between the phasia, Halicon, and the Blaze, and far too much of it was shrouded in mystery.

Most of the information that Aryx had about what came after his departure from the phasia had come from Kamen and Ellis; Jeroch was loath to talk about those days, even once all the phasia had been returned to life on Espre. Halicon tried to form a new member of the phasia from the remnants of power that he had reclaimed from Aryx. However, the creature never clung to the life that was breathed into it. Halicon's attempt was a miserable failure. When he tried again, the result was the same. According to Kamen, Halicon became increasingly distraught at his failures and thought perhaps that by letting Aryx go, he had cost himself any opportunity to defeat Emries. So great was his consternation that Halicon began to contemplate extreme measures in order to keep the war against Emries alive. The most dire of these drastic measures was the destruction of all of the original phasia. Halicon's thinking was that the imbalance could not be corrected so long as any of the original six phasia remained alive. If Halicon returned all of the phasia to the Blaze, perhaps it would allow him to recreate them. However, even Halicon would not make such a decision in a vacuum. Halicon trusted Kamen with nearly every secret, and thus he was the one that Halicon approached with his plan. Kamen was understandably distraught at the suggestion, or at least as distraught as Kamen would allow himself to be. In the end, and true to Kamen's form, he volunteered to renounce his position within the phasia and allow himself to be merged with the Blaze. It was an experiment of sorts, the nature of which was hidden from everyone except Kamen and Halicon. Thus, the Flame was born, and the energies of Aryx and Kamen were utilized to create the next group of phasia. Warron and Saurn were first. But there was still an imbalance within the phasia. Despite his attempts to sever the ties of Aryx and Kamen from the Brotherhood, Halicon found that the process was either incomplete or impossible. In order to correct the imbalance, Halicon created Caris, Aldridge, Erdric, and Farax. The new phasia were different from the original six. They were diminished, but they were still phasia.

But there was yet another consequence of the failed attempt to defeat Emries by wiping out all human life on Onea. Halicon for the first time recognized the potential threat of the phasia, and also through his conversations with Kamen and Aryx recognized their growing desire to use their power against Emries despite Halicon's instructions to the contrary. The phasia were growing beyond Halicon's control, a consequence of the bits of humanity that were infused into them during their formation. There would be a time when the phasia would begin to think for themselves, and Halicon could not trust that they would always follow his commandments. Therefore, Halicon introduced a kind of virus into the phasia's connections to their powers. The more they used their abilities, the more it isolated them from one another, making it virtually impossible that they could ever link their powers again as they had when they devastated the face of Onea. The only reason that Kamen was given this information was that Halicon could not accomplish his goal alone, he needed the cooperation of one of his own. As he had time and time before, Halicon knew that he could trust Kamen's council. Like Aryx, Kamen had begun to question the methodologies of the phasia, and he had begun to grow concerned about the temperament of Grawn and the constant thirst for knowledge that Ellis possessed. In time, Grawn would be unable to be restrained from a direct assault against Emries, and Ellis would continue to concoct strategies that would take the fight to Emries without directly violating Halicon's commandment. In time, she would find a way to strike while still retaining her adherence to the letter if not the spirit of the law. If such an avenue were open to the phasia, Bryn and Jeroch would certainly add their power to the cause, and perhaps the four would be enough to overwhelm even a Child of the Creator, if he were not prepared for the eventuality.

It was early in his return to life that Aryx was able to discover the fact that Kamen was reborn and working with Logan. It was a secret that Aryx shared with only three others; his wife Diana, and his two children Alderin and Lissa. Kamen and Aryx always had a special relationship, and they viewed the universe in the same way. So it was for this reason that Kamen trusted Aryx with all that he had learned during his time with the phasia, his conversations with Halicon, and his time as the Living Flame. Kamen also had a measure of knowledge from Logan Ranthall, as well as Rael and Trece Starlin, including whatever Logan had shared during their time together founding the Order of the Flickering Flame. Kamen's knowledge was not endless, but he shared it freely with those he trusted and respected. Kamen always said that to share knowledge was to gain perspective on what is known. And so, by sharing what he knew, Kamen grew in understanding of what he already knew. What Aryx took from these conversations with Kamen was that there was something special about the original six phasia and the nature of their powers. Like Aerith Seth, the first six phasia were apart from the rest of beings on any world because of their connection to the Blaze. But unlike Aerith Seth, who found a way to extend his mantle and strengthen it, the original six phasia had diminished to near extinction. Jeroch had not been thorough in the information he chose to reveal to Aldridge and the other newly arrived defenders of the Heart of Stone, but only Jeroch and Bryn still remained from the original six, and they were both in Albitonin. Alderin took several moments to review the information that he had about the people who had been assembled to defend the Heart of Stone and the tactical defensibility of the structure.

Jeroch and Bryn were full members of the Brotherhood of Phasia, and through their many thousands of years of life they had honed the use of their powers to a deadly edge. But those abilities made deployment of those assets perhaps the trickiest of all. One thought would be to have them defending the walls, ensuring that nothing could approach the fortification without feeling their wrath. Another thought had them far from the Heart of Stone itself, taking the fight to the invaders. If the two experienced killers were able to thin the ranks enough, then it would give those with less control of their powers the ability to have a positive impact on the battle. There was one tactical issue with sending Jeroch and Bryn out to fight the enemy. Neither had ever fought a dragon. Only Hannah Ironheart had done that. Dragons, angels, and whatever Dorovar would send against the Heart of Stone; each complicated matters. The first and largest principal problem was the fact that this battle would be fought like no other in the history of Espre. Because dragons would be involved in the assault, the battlefield would not be confined to the grounds in and around the Heart of Stone. Because the Heart of Stone was nestled into a valley at the foot of a mountain range that separated it from the coastline, the battlefield had numerous facets that would prove difficult for the defenders. Dragons, because of their flexibility and maneuverability would be able to attack the Heart from the ocean beyond the mountains, through the mountains themselves, from the sky above, and perhaps even from the ground below. In traditional warfare, the Heart of Stone was a desirable defensive position, but with the addition of angels and dragons, the logistics were nightmarish at best. But, at least there were dragons that would be fighting alongside the defenders of the Heart. From a tactical perspective it helped to address some of the issues in defending the Heart. While Alderin was not aware of all of the abilities of the dragons that would be assisting in the defense of the Heart, he did know a few from the short briefing given by Jeroch after his arrival in Albitonin.

Mariti Brightblade was the leader of the allied dragons, and was coordinating defenses on the highest levels with Hannah Ironheart and Jeroch Yetre. Mariti had already apparently proven her combat acumen fighting alongside Hannah Ironheart in Iltorp defending the Masters of the Academy of Arcane Arts. Several enemy dragons were killed in that assault and it helped to cement the alliance between one faction of the dragons and those that allegedly aligned with Aerith Seth. Mariti Brightblade apparently had earned her reputation during the war in the Heavens, fighting alongside the forces that attempted to repel Talisia's assault on the Throne. So, Mariti had fought against her own kind as well as angels, giving her insight that would be invaluable in the fight to come. Mariti and Hannah would be responsible for coordinating the defenses within the grounds of the Heart itself. As for the defenses in the air above the Heart, that responsibility had been given to two of Mariti's closest allies. The first was Serentis, who had been the liaison between the Heart and the allied dragons since their arrival on the scene. Serentis was supposedly one of the oldest dragons in existence, but according to Jeroch, she had refused to fight against her own kind in the Heavens. To that end, her responsibilities for air defense of the Heart were split with Brightfang the Advisor, who fought side by side with

Mariti in the Heavens during the war. Brightfang was the principal advisor to the leadership of the dragons for thousands of years and according to Mariti was an accomplished tactician. Between Serentis and Brightfang, the aerial defense of the Heart of Stone would be in the best hands, even though it was highly likely that the dragons defending the Heart would be vastly outnumbered. The dragons would be solely responsible for defense of the skies with two notable exceptions. The first and most obvious was Camille Sandar. Her wings along with her fighting prowess would make her invaluable in the fight ahead. She also had full control over all of her abilities which put her ahead of most of the other defenders of the Heart. The other potential addition to the aerial defenses was Felicia Lorien. Though Felicia believed that the creature known as Nightwing had been destroyed during the confrontation with the Adhradair, according to Jeroch, that was not possible. The only being other than the Creator who could destroy Nightwing was Halicon, or in this case his proxy Rhain Seth. In time, Nightwing would regenerate within Felicia and its abilities would be restored. Hopefully, it would be in time for the oncoming assault.

The complicated portions of the defense came in the theatres beneath the mountain ranges and in the waters off the coast. The coastal defense would rely completely on the dragons as none of the human defenders had any level of expertise fighting in the water. That group would be led by Pazunia of the Deep. Mariti believed that the forces that would be assaulting by sea would be roughly equivalent to those of the defenders, giving no advantage to either side. The smart tactical decision would be to fight not to win the engagement but rather to fight a holding action that would prevent the sea-bound dragons from joining their fellows on the grounds of the Heart. While the ocean campaign was potentially a balanced affair, the mountain campaign was not. The leader of the mountain defenses was named Jovar the Unbreakable, a grim and humorless dragon who apparently had spent most of his life on Espre in the darkened caves beneath the mountain ranges around the Heart of Stone. He knew every tunnel as though he had dug them himself, a great many of which he did. However, according to Jeroch, there were only four of the allied dragons who were comfortable in the tunnels under the mountains, and they would likely be seriously outnumbered by the forces loyal to Shadowweaver. It would be the ultimate in close-quarters fighting and would likely see the most casualties. Many of the soldiers that remained of the paladin corps of the Heart of Stone would likely be deployed to the defense of the caves, but whoever went into that hell would likely not come out. Alderin was the most likely choice to lead the incursion into the caves, and he didn't mind.

Alderin's life changed forever the last time that he was in Albitonin, and there had been no doubt in his mind that he would see the place once more before he died. In Alderin's mind, he should have died that day in Albitonin, the day that Tess Annis showed who she truly was. He still remembered the feeling of the bubble of force that radiated from the girl's body. The feeling of his flesh being ripped apart, his bones being ground into nothing, his nerves burning and freezing at the same time. If it wasn't for Darrien, Alderin would have likely lost much more than just his arm. But that moment changed something in Alderin. His powers were taken; his very nature as a member of the Dark Gods altered. He was no longer a Dark God, but neither was he mortal. Even the new infusion of power that made him a member of the Brotherhood of Phasia did not change that feeling inside of him. It was as though he could see the moment of his death approaching. That death was here, in Albitonin, and it was most likely in the battle that was coming. What better end for a killer like Alderin than to die in perhaps the greatest battle ever fought.

But if Alderin had any regrets, it was that he would likely never see Darrien again. Their relationship had spanned most of their lives and had been both tumultuous and invigorating. Darrien was everything that Alderin was not. She was brash and outspoken, she never backed down from anyone regardless of who they were. Her heart raged constantly, both with passion and with need. Darrien had a great desire to love and to be loved, mostly because she never felt that her father loved her. In the beginning of their relationship, there was a part of Alderin that wondered if Darrien really loved him at all or if her need was so great that she was just using him to fill that empty part of herself. But the part of Darrien that was mercurial was balanced by the part of Alderin that was measured and calculating. The part of Darrien that was passionate and hot-blooded was balanced by the part of Alderin that was controlled and almost cold. They complimented each other in ways that didn't make sense, and yet it made perfect sense to them. They spent so much time together that they had established almost a language of their own and at times could communicate with just a look or a gesture. Since they had been separated, Alderin felt as though a part of him was missing, and it was very similar to the sensation of losing his arm. Deep in his heart though, Alderin knew that their time together had ended, even if he lived to see the other side of the battle for the Heart of Stone.

The suns were just beginning to crest over the hills to the east, and Alderin could hear a commotion from down the hall. There were shouts of alarm and other indiscriminate sounds that Alderin interpreted as fear and shock. That could mean only one thing, the enemy had arrived and it was time to muster the defenses of the Heart of Stone. Jeroch would come to fetch him in a matter of minutes, and they would have the hasty conversation about the deployment of fighting assets and how best to organize the overall defenses. Alderin knew that Hannah was working through the night with the High Priestess Baeata Catrinel to ensure that the innocents and faithful within the Heart of Stone were evacuated. Alderin hoped that they had enough time to get everyone out. He knew that the initial plan had been to send all of the refugees to the Order of the Flickering Flame, a plan that the High Priestess was not in favor of. However, with the information about the establishment of New Aradon, a better solution to the disposition of the faithful of the Church of the Creator was clear. The only objection had come from Anabel Binosear and Hannah Ironheart. The advantage of sending the faithful to the Order was the fact that they could use one of the stones that Aerith Seth had coded to that location. Aerith had never been to New Aradon, and there was no one that Aerith had coded a stone to that was in New Aradon. That meant using portals, and using portals brought attention. But it was Bryn who put an end to the objection. The enemy was coming, and it didn't matter if they knew that power was being used or not.

After a moment, Alderin turned to his bed, recovered his sword belt and strapped it on. The ancient sword had belonged to his father, and though Alderin had been trained to conjure weapons out of thin air, it felt good to have the steel at his side. He retrieved one last item from his pack, one of the last artifacts that survived the destruction of Onea. Pike Rhuiden had made a point of salvaging what he could in the last days of Onea, and he had somehow been able to bring them with him upon his ascension to the heavens and his eventual expulsion. The item was the Debuisa gauntlet once wielded by Pike Rhuiden during his days as a member of the *Erieal.* Alderin had used the Debuisa in the past when he was first learning to focus his mind and use his powers. In the battle that was coming, he needed every advantage that he could get. Gauntlet and sword at the ready, Alderin turned to the door and waited for the knock of destiny to come.

THE LOVERS

The Lost Children

Jerah

Retribution was a concept that was difficult to quantify in a life that lasted thousands of years. Human beings had their own ideas about what retribution was, but their view was rarely one that had any anchor in reality. Humans saw retribution as revenge against wrongs committed in their short lives. But that was not the retribution that the Creator spoke of in the Book of the Creator, nor was it the retribution practiced by the Children of the Creator on His behalf. The human concept was closer to reprisal than retribution. Concepts like perceptions mattered. Retribution in the Creator's mind was not limited to one lifetime, nor was it only for evil deeds. This furtherance that stretched across lifetimes allowed the Creator as well as the Children to reward or punish those that fit into their agenda. And now, this concept of Retribution had transcended the Creator and his Children and had come to be utilized by the dragons and Dorovar. Dorovar suffered unimaginable retribution at the hands of the dragons, and now Jerah suffered her own retributions. She was a child of Shau-ling, a traitor to everything she had ever been forged to believe in, and now she was a harbinger of death wearing another name and another face. Now, however, it seemed that role was coming to an end, and the next retribution was in fact a reprisal.

For the majority of her time on Espre, Jerah operated in the shadows, gathering allies and identifying those who would be susceptible to Dorovar's call. Jerah became a minion of Dorovar long before his imprisonment in the Vault of Terrors. When Emries prepared for the war that was to be fought on Espre, he reached into space between life and death and slaved those of his former followers that he felt would be most beneficial to his will. There were unintended consequences to this action, as the other members of the Children as well as the Creator Himself were able to duplicate the same efforts. What the Children didn't realize, but the Creator surely did, was that Dorovar through his amassing of knowledge and power had learned to see through the cracks between life and death, and touch the souls that resided there. This was the genesis of the Chorus of Souls. Communing there with the power of the lost, Dorovar found kindred spirits, those cast off by the Creator and His Children, abandoned to the nothingness beyond Creation. In his nearly immortal hands, Dorovar found a power unlike he could have ever imagined. More than the power of the Chorus, Dorovar found souls that were trapped by their own actions, by their own doubts, and by their own uncertainties. Caris was one of those souls.

When Onea fell, Caris was disillusioned. Learning the truth about the nature of the phasia and the true nature of the war between Shau-ling and Emries was perhaps the thing that burst the dam within Caris, but it was not the event that she would point to when she thought about what caused her to become the creature known as Jerah. When Dorovar's power flooded through the cracks between the living world and the place where the Creator let those who could still be of use to Him languish, Caris knew nothing but pain and anguish. Though she may not have been technically alive in that place, every moment lived in her memory no differently than her memories from her lives on Onea. The only difference was the red haze that seemed to tinge all of the memories. Every moment was filled with searing pain that echoed through every inch of her body, and her mind was filled with imagery that brought stress, panic, and confusion. Though she tried hard to reconcile where she was and what was happening to her, she could not keep her mind clear of the pain long enough to form anything that would be considered a coherent thought. The only thing that would ever leak through was the moment her life spun out of her control, and she was forced to acknowledge that everything she thought and knew was nothing more than a lie.

The Creator taunted her with the visions of Logan Ranthall suspended in the bowels of the creature known as the Flame. This version of the Flame was perhaps as far from the being that had once been known as Kamen as was possible. Caris had not known Kamen during her lives on Onea, but she had learned much about him from Bryn and Ellis. He had always been portrayed as a gentle giant who utilized his power only when needed and to such devastating degree that it left no doubt. Kamen was an undeniable force in the world when he was acting as the enforcer of Shau-ling's will as the first-born member of the Brotherhood of Phasia. However, the version of Kamen that Caris was very familiar with was the first version of the Flame. The Flame was the last line of defense for Shau-ling, and he guarded the entrance to Shau-ling's throne room, year after year. Even in the guise of the Flame, Kamen was still a gentle giant who had so much power that all of the intelligent members of the phasia feared what he was capable of. Caris on many occasions spent time talking to the Flame, learning all that she could about the nature of the war. The Flame was never very forthcoming with information, as it seemed he was forbidden to reveal too much, but the Flame found ways around those prohibitions by asking questions. The Flame would ask questions in response to questions posed to him, in an effort to change the direction of thinking, and to pose alternate theories to assumptions made by those who did not know all they could about the nature of the world. Caris in those days had always believed that the Flame saw well beyond the bounds of the world, and well beyond the bounds of the war between Shau-ling and Emries, and so she found his insights invaluable. But then the second generation of the prophecies ended, the Flame had been defeated for a second time by the forces of the *Coromor*, and the Creator had split everything in two. Shau-ling lost faith in the Flame's ability to do his duty, and thus freed Kamen from his eternal post, but did not return to him the form that he was born into. That left him susceptible to the machinations of perhaps the vilest member of the phasia to ever draw breath.

Draven Batoe was on one hand perhaps the most perfect example of what Shau-ling's phasia were designed to be. He had no scruples, no limits, and no conscience. Draven would go to any length to gain any advantage. But where that was a positive in taking the fight to Emries and the forces of the Light, it was a negative in all other ways. Draven proved to be completely uncontrollable, and he cared nothing for Shau-ling's rules. He cared nothing for his fellows in the Brotherhood of Phasia, and fancied himself as the next evolution of Shau-ling; a fitting replacement for his creator. Draven sought out the banished Flame and manipulated the disappointment and disillusion within the ancient man to learn some of the most well-guarded of Shau-ling's secrets. As the first of the phasia, Kamen had seen the creation of each of the phasia that followed, as well as the anomalies that led to the creation of Rael, Trece, and Draven himself. These secrets allowed Draven to craft his followers that he called his Dark Riders. The principal member of this group, when they emerged from the shadows, was a new version of the Flame that was devoid of all of the intelligence and restraint that had been personified by the previous version. What Caris didn't know then, but had learned since she became Jerah and gained unfettered access to the memories of the Blaze, was that Draven had cannibalized the remaining pieces of Kamen and used those pieces to forge each of the Dark Riders. However, because of the manner of their creation, the Dark Riders were incomplete entities. They didn't so much have personalities as they had abilities which forged what they were. The Dark Riders were the template that Dorovar used when crafting his Heralds, and in the same way that Draven cannibalized Kamen, Dorovar cannibalized Caris and used some of her spark and a great deal of the pain that she suffered in the place between in the creation of the Heralds.

While Dorovar may have been the creator of the Heralds of the Chorus of Souls, Caris was most certainly their mother. The Grey Man Pestilence, her first child, was the dark embodiment of what Caris was born to be, a plague on humanity. Dorovar took the piece of Caris that was imbued in her by Halicon that hated everything that humanity stood for. There was a part of her that hated their thirst for happiness, hated their love and compassion, and hated their subservience to everything that the Creator and Emries wished for them. Distilled from her, the hatred manifested into a potent plague which reduced any whom it touched to a shell of what they once were. The Crawling Plague was the first of the Caris' gifts to the world of Espre bonded into Pestilence's skin and blood. That hatred taken from her, Caris' skin and hair lost all of its color, reduced to the pale of the grave.

Caris's second gift, the Wasting Disease, came from her time in the in between. In that place of pain and torment, everything that Caris thought or once believed was weaponized against her. There was a part of her that thought she had found something other than hate and thought that perhaps she could understand love and devotion. That part of her had started with Cedric Binosear and had been crystallized by Logan Ranthall. However, in the in between those thoughts soured and burned. Anyone who was inflicted with love that could never be returned understood the pain and hurt that Caris felt in that place, but her torment was a thousand times more severe. Inside Caris, that pain became a disease that consumed every ounce of love, compassion, and warmth within her. The disease passed from Caris into Famine, set to devour anyone it touched from the inside out, making any nourishment into poison. It was said that love nourished the soul, and so the Wasting Disease would pervert any nourishment until none could ever remain. With all warmth purged from her, Caris radiated cold in all directions; a cold that transcended the mortal world and burned even the dead.

Caris, the Lady Wolf of the Brotherhood of Phasia was born and bred to be a killer. Nothing more, nothing less. She was born to hunt her prey, to stalk it, and to destroy it utterly. More than that, Caris, as a member of the Brotherhood of Phasia lived not one, but many lives. She was not immortal, but she would be reborn time and time again until her task was completed. These commandments from Halicon were the basis from which Death was formed. The very touch of the creature that would become known as Death would visit that unfettered destructive power upon any human, and if concentrated and channeled, Death would be able to lay waste to anything it could perceive in all directions. Death fed off of the death that it was responsible for, and the more it killed the stronger it became. Like the creature that would become Death, Jerah's very touch became lethal, and her fingers became coated with the blood of every being who met their end at Jerah's hands. Like Caris, all of the Heralds that were formed from her essence could be reborn time and time again until their task was complete and Dorovar had achieved his goals.

While Caris was a killer, that was not all that she was. Caris was a skilled manipulator who could wrangle the wills of even those with the strongest of characters and wrap them around her finger. Like her brother Saurn, Caris enjoyed making her presence felt from the shadows, starting wars and arranging for the humans to destroy themselves in varied ways. Though she did love the adoration of being the prime mover in her later days on Onea, attention was not always the best method for accomplishing her aims. It was this ability to influence the wills of humans that Dorovar took to infuse in the body of his Herald War. War, through Caris' essence, could influence any human within range of his voice and pull them to his service. This extended not only to the living but also to the dead, as Dorovar had learned to manipulate the body as well as the soul. There was no limit to Dorovar's hunger for success. This talent removed from her, Jerah lost the ability to speak beyond single words that would shake the world. Her voice would become so powerful that the human mind could nearly not process the sound, and in the early days of her time on Espre, she killed many humans before learning how to modulate the power of her voice.

The last piece of Caris, the one that finally made her into the creature called Jerah, was the part of her that was loyal to Shau-ling. For Dorovar's plan to ultimately come to fruition, Dorovar would one day need to turn one of the Dark Gods to his service. The part of Caris that was loyal to Shau-ling, the part of her that was tied to the primal string gifted to each member of the Brotherhood of Phasia, would become the leash by which a Dark God could be chained to Dorovar's will. Like all of those who would be shackled to Dorovar's will, they would need to accept his power willingly. Like his Adhradair brothers and sisters from Loinn, Dorovar would not force power upon his Heralds; they would be made to accept it on Dorovar's terms. But while the extraction of this loyalty would eventually be the catalyst for the creation of Conquest, it allowed Jerah to begin to question her service to Dorovar and also allowed her to act independently of his will.

These acts of defiance were small and limited at first, and usually consisted of delays in the execution of Dorovar's orders. Jerah's true willfulness didn't express itself until she came upon the idea of creating her own cadre of soldiers that she could eventually mold to her own purposes. These soldier who came to be known as the Blood Moon Inferi, were supposed to be extensions of Jerah; an effort to reclaim some of what she had lost during her fall from grace. The first member of the group was a woman that Jerah had watched for many years before making her approach. Kyrie Tensas was a woman of little note for the majority of her life. She was born into lowly circumstances, was consistently placed in situations that she should not have been able to survive, and yet she pushed through to adulthood. However, her trials did not end and she found herself practically a slave to an abusive husband who beat her mercilessly for any little mistake or perceived fault. One day, Jerah watched as Kyrie's husband took exception to his dinner not being hot enough. He took his belt and began to beat Kyrie over and over again. Blood flowed from the wounds inflicted by the belt on her back, arms, and legs. When his arm tired from whipping her, he moved on to punching and slapping her. Jerah could feel Kyrie's soul begin to leave her body and the cries of pain and anguish that called out to the Chorus of Souls. But there was another emotion that flowed with the pain and anguish. There was rage.

If Kyrie had simply given up and allowed the beating to finish what was left of her pathetic life, Jerah would have let her die. But the rage called out to Jerah. It called begging for the power not only to defend herself from the assault, but to revisit all of the pain that she had ever suffered at the hands of others onto her attacker. At the very last moment, just as the last threads of Kyrie's soul began to detach themselves from her mortal form, Jerah reached out and imbued a fraction of the power of the Chorus of Souls into Kyrie's dead form. When Kyrie rose again, she was not the meek woman that she had been. She had become infused with power unlike she could have ever imagined, and the woman that stood before the stunned blood-covered thug was changed inside and out. Kyrie possessed the beauty that she had always wished she had and the strength to prevent her power from being robbed from her under any circumstances. Kyrie reached out, and with a single touch she inflicted a lifetime's worth of pain upon her husband. His screams could be heard at the farthest end of the town and seemed to echo for hours in the ears of every man who had ever raised his hands to his wife. From that moment on, Kyrie Tensas became Jerah's most ardent supporter and servant.

*Lexa Silenti was the next to come to Caris' attention. She was sold into virtual slavery by her uncle after her parents died. It did not take long for her to move from cleaning the rooms of the brothel to working in her own room. Jerah watched from the moment this pain began, as she moved from one horrible circumstance to another, drifting from unconsciousness to unconsciousness using alcohol, drugs, and sleep to attempt to escape the waking nightmare that waited for her every time her eyes opened. In some ways, the unrelenting illness that found her was a blessing. The pain of the brothel was left behind, but she found herself without a place to live. Lexa wandered the streets, cold, in pain, and without hope. On the verge of starvation, her body failing due to the sickness that had creeped into every part of her being, Lexa found herself huddled in a corner in a dark alley. Like Kyrie, Lexa's soul cried out for release, cried out for solace. However, what Jerah saw was more powerful than anything that Lexa's soul was screaming. Even laying in her own filth, moments from death, she clutched at a wad of paper, rubbing it between her fingers. In her mind, Lexa wanted nothing more than to summon just enough strength to rub the paper long enough to create a spark. With that spark, she would light a fire, and with that fire and the last bit of life left within her, she would crawl to the brothel and set it ablaze. It wouldn't matter what happened after that. Jerah ignored the tormented soul's cries for release and peace, and instead at the last moment brushed her fingers across the cheek of the formerly broken woman, bringing her back to the world of the living. However, this version of Lexa Silenti was powerful, beautiful, and deadly. And when Lexa rose back to her feet, the flames danced across her fingers. There was little of the town still standing by the time Lexa was done punishing everyone who had ever set foot in the brothel, and once her revenge was complete, she joined Kyrie at Jerah's side ready to complete her dark work.

Macero Furiae lived a charmed life for so long that he nearly escaped Jerah's notice. He was the son of the mayor of his home town, and grew up in as affluent a manner as was possible for someone of his station. But the affluence did not place him above danger. There was a group of young men who resented the life that Macero had and devised a plan to make him pay for his privilege. It took little effort for the conspirators to arrange for a vile distillation to be introduced into Macero's food and drink, and only a little money to pay off the cooks, tasters, and other minor functionaries. There was a lot of jealousy to be found for those with power and money, and more than enough slights, real and imagined to find allies were necessary. It didn't take long for Macero to take a fever and to become bedridden. This was when Macero came to Jerah's notice. Through his soul she could feel the pain of the betrayal that he felt, but there was more. Macero worked tirelessly within the governmental structure to attempt make life better for those less fortunate. He gave as much of his time and of his means to ease the suffering of those effected by droughts and natural disasters. And yet, despite all these good deeds, it was his wealth and supposed status the marked him for death. Even as he lay dying, however, Macero did not have hate in his heart for those who brought his life to an end. However, there was hate in Macero's heart, and that echoed though his soul. Jerah could hear the call of that hate. It was hate for the systems that kept people oppressed. It was hate for the divisions that created strife and inequity. Jerah knew that hate all too well, as it was the hate for the systems that the Creator and Raenera had made that drove Dorovar. And so as his life ebbed, Jerah sent Lexa to bring Macero into the fold. Macero Furiae became Jerah's extinguisher of fury and pain, ready to help pull down everything that made Cadaria and Creation a place of pain, suffering, and death.

There were few people in the world who could have understood the desire within Lucian Vispilio and fewer still who saw the man as more than a common thief. Jerah had no interest in common, but what she did find interesting about Lucian was his complete lack of compunction regarding his methods, so long as his goal was accomplished. Lucian was orphaned on the day of his birth, as the process of bringing him to life had ended his mother's. The father had died some time before, the victim of a knife in a gambling den. From that moment forward, Lucian existed only on the charity of others and found himself growing up in a series of orphanages. By the time he was thirteen, the abuse that Lucian had suffered created a powerful resentment within him, and thus he became enamored with concept of freedom and self-reliance. His escape from the orphanage left several of the administrators as well as all of the guards dead and all of the prisoners free. Many went their own way, but some stayed with Lucian forming a kind of children's colony in the alleys and abandoned buildings of the city. Lucien felt a responsibility to those who followed him into the wilderness of the cruel city, and thus endeavored to ensure all those who were in his charge had food, water, and shelter at all times. This began Lucien's life of crime.

He would steal what the other orphans needed, and would often run afoul of the owners of what he stole as well as the law enforcement in the area. As Lucien grew older, he grew more hardened and quicker to use violence to ensure he succeeded in his task. Blood was a constant. Jerah watched Lucien with fascination, wondering when his luck would run out, and what his soul would cry out when his life finally was at an end. Violent life could only have a quick and violent end. Jerah found Lucien laying in a gutter, his stomach ripped open and his blood and entrails leaking out into the rain-soaked street. Jerah watched the final sparks of life fade from Lucien's eyes and listened for the cries of his soul. Unlike others that she had watched die, there was no cry of pain, or surprise, or even anger. Lucien knew that he was going to die, he was at peace with his death. Jerah was also surprised that there was no fear for the fate of those he had cared for all of those years. But then she felt it. She felt his disgust. She felt his contempt. He hated those that he protected. They could have taken some of the burden of caring for themselves and those who could not find their own way in the world. Instead, they relied solely on Lucien's kindness and brutality; living on the death and destruction that he caused. Weakness filled him with anger and hate, and if given the chance he would have killed all those who were unwilling to fight to live. Jerah granted that wish, and Lucian Vispilio was reborn. The next night, all of the former orphans were slaughtered one by one, and the streets ran red with the blood of beggars, vagrants, and other homeless and displaced people. The killing would continue for years to come, as Lucien believed anyone who would not fight for their own lives did not deserve to have one, and that their souls would serve better purpose in the Chorus.

Like Lucian, Orchid Strages was also an orphan, but unlike Lucian she did not have the strength to defend herself or someone within the structure of her orphanage to protect her. In fact, most of the damage done to her was done by the other children in the orphanage. Orchid was not the brightest child, but she was compliant which made her a favorite of the corrupt old man who ran the orphanage where she was born. By the time she was ten years old, the owner of the orphanage began to see the profit that he could make from Orchid's body. The abuse Orchid suffered at the hands of the vile men who paid for her broke her mind, and kept her locked in a nearly infantile state. But it was the abuse back at the orphanage that broke her body. Because of the favoritism shown to Orchid, the other children would beat her, push her down the stairs, and do everything to make her life even more miserable. Jerah watched all of this with detachment, wondering how long the little girl would be able to survive the brutality that she suffered. The answer was two years. As Orchid lay at the bottom of the stairs, both of her legs broken and blood filling all of the soft spaces within her body, Jerah approached, her intention already set. However, Jerah found herself surprised by what came from Orchid's soul. All that would have made her human had been beaten out of her, and all that was left was pain. She was the embodiment of pain and torment. But more than that, she did not want to inflict that torment on others, she wanted them to understand what torment really was. Her soul believed that only through pain could life be properly experienced. Jerah understood the pain that Orchid felt and it was a privilege to bring Orchid into the ranks of the Blood Moon Inferi.

However, the Blood Moon Inferi were all gone. They had all been murdered in the attempt by Lissa Terian to kill Talisia. Jerah felt each of those loses, but was not saddened by them. For nearly two thousand years, the Blood Moon and Jerah prepared the way for Dorovar's eventual freedom. Each of the souls that they saved from their physical prison were collected by Jerah and added to the growing Chorus of Souls. By the time Dorovar was free, the Chorus had grown to hundreds of thousands of souls, including Jerah's own lost followers. Now, Dorovar had begun his endgame, and Jerah had been given the order that she knew would come one day. Forces were gathering at the Heart of Stone and Dorovar was going to be represented in significant force. All of his enemies would be gathered in one place, and it was an opportunity that he would not pass up. Aerith Seth had isolated himself foolishly, and so that left but one thorn to be removed. Logan Ranthall. He was Jerah's last assignment, but one that she had no intention of completing. In fact, Jerah intended to be in the very center of the battle at the Heart of Stone, but she would stand with her former family, and she would bring with her something unexpected. Jerah was no more, and by the time the battle at the Heart of Stone was ended, the Lady Wolf would be reborn, and Caris would reclaim her lost soul.

Ayden

The Dark Continent of Mythryn lived up to its name. As Ayden Seth stepped out of the portal from the Heavens into the forest of black trees and dark, cloud-laden skies, he could feel the oppression pressing down upon him. Dread crept into his heart almost immediately, and he felt as though he was being watched from all directions. Of course, Ayden knew for a fact that there was nothing left alive on Mythryn. Emries had made sure to utilize the flights of angels available to him as a Child of the Creator to exterminate all of the remaining beasts and humans loyal to the Dark Gods from the whole of the continent. Thousands of lives were extinguished in order to guarantee that Emries' work with the girl Tess Annis was not interrupted. The last thing that Emries wanted was a rogue individual stumbling across Tess and disrupting her training. The girl was delicate and volatile. Anything unexpected could have disastrous consequences. So, Emries decided to leave nothing to chance. Perhaps it was all of that death that Ayden was feeling. The angry spirits of the dead screaming at him from the beyond. Whatever the cause of the oppressive weight that pressed down upon him, Ayden knew he had a mission to accomplish, his last true mission as an emissary of the Creator. Nothing would prevent him from accomplishing his mission. There had already been too much failure, and that was perhaps why he had been stripped of his position as the Will. He would not disappoint the Creator; not again.

Perhaps the fact that Mythryn had become a tomb was a fitting fate for the land of darkness. For too long the land had been the home of the Dark Gods, and their very existence was an affront not only to the divine light represented by the Creator, but also to the rightful inhabitants of Espre, the human beings that roamed its landscape. Though Ayden himself was counted among the members of the Dark Gods, he had been redeemed by the Creator, chosen for something better, for something noble. Of course, Ayden knew that there was nothing noble about his life before he was touched by the hand of the Creator and given the gift of a position within the Servants. Before, Ayden was a selfish and petty creature. He was every bit his father's son. He was irreverent, disrespectful, and had a true lack of understanding of his true place in the fabric of Creation. Like his father, Ayden had a severe over-estimation of his importance. Aerith thought that everything revolved around him and his family. Those teachings made Ayden into an arrogant, self-important brute who would stop at nothing to get what he wanted, no matter the cost. Thanks to the lessons that Ayden's mother taught about manipulating the wills of others, there were few mortals that Ayden could not bend to his considerable will. Arrogance of that kind had its place of course, but it could not be the default position of any successful being, certainly not one who would be as long-lived as Ayden Seth.

Trading on his skill and his bravado, Ayden ingratiated himself to so many, from the Masters at the Academy of Arcane Arts, to Jaccob Aldora of the Knights of the Flashing Blade. There was truly nothing beyond Ayden's reach, and it was not until Ayden had his eyes opened by divine light that he understood the error of his ways. Yes, Ayden had the ability to charm and beguile, but in his haste to find the quickest and easiest way to gain the information that his parents required about the goings on within the Academy, he unnecessarily caused pain and suffering. A good man would have found a different way. And Ayden, like his father, was anything but a good man. Aerith Seth was an irredeemable monster, one whose continued existence could only bring more pain and suffering to the world. Ayden did not want to follow in those dark footsteps. He wanted to be a bringer of light and of hope. That was what he thought that the Creator was offering him. A chance for redemption. A chance to be something more than the child of a monster destined to become a monster himself. And so, when the divine light descended upon him, lifting him up and choosing him for something so much greater than the crooked path of his father's footsteps, Ayden knew he had to seize the opportunity and make himself into a better man and a greater force for good.

His first assignment as the Will was one that showed great promise. With Marlae Lorien chosen to be the Divine Empress of Cadaria, the Creator's chosen vessel and emissary on the mortal plane, it was the responsibility of the Will to be her protector. Yet, even though he was tasked with such a monumental responsibility, the Creator was not content to leave the Will in one place for long. As one of the Servants, the Will had the ability to instantly move from one place to another, enforcing the will of the Creator. Such abilities could not be limited to protecting one fragile little girl. So, the protection of the Divine Empress was seconded to several flights of angels under the command of two of the Old Gods. While Ayden did not trust either of the Old Gods, he would not and could not question the judgment of the Creator. In a way, Ayden found himself relieved. He knew that the Creator would require tasks of him that would take him away from Marlae's side. With the additional support of the flights of angels, Ayden felt that he would not have to worry about Marlae's safety. Unfortunately for Ayden, he was proven wrong time and time again.

The first time that Ayden was sent on an assignment for the Creator outside of Hedorah, there was an assassination attempt. One of the warrior angels had become corrupted and attempted to plunge his spear through Marlae's heart. Though the girl Isabella was able to dispatch the angel, she was not able to prevent the warrior from ending the life of Terrance Aldora, a friend and advisor of the Divine Empress. This was a direct blow against the Creator's chosen representative, and Ayden felt personally responsible for the breakdown in security. And as much as Ayden wanted to return to Hedorah to retake his post as protector of the Divine Empress, the Creator would not allow it. As such, when Ayden learned of the fall of Hedorah, the destruction of the warrior angels dispatched to protect the kingdom, the betrayal and subsequent death of the Old Gods, and the near murder of the Divine Empress, Ayden felt as though he had failed in his primary responsibility. But through the eyes of the Creator, that was not the case. In a way, the Creator viewed Marlae as a bauble, a distraction, something to placate the masses while the real business of divinity was carried out on levels that the simple humans would never be able to understand. Ayden was not destined to be a protector as he was led to believe, his path was much darker, and much more suited to the pathos of his upbringing.

Now that the mantel of the Will had been lifted from Ayden's shoulders, his mind had begun to dissect his time as a Servant. The Will of the Creator was not a being of peace, nor was it a being of protection. In the end, Ayden discovered that the Will was a bringer of death. Time and time again, Ayden was deployed by the Creator to visit death upon a being that the Creator viewed as an obstruction to the designs of the Creator. It did not matter if it was a defenseless woman calling herself a seer, or his own mother, Ayden was the bringer of death. This mission, this final mission on behalf of the Creator was no different. Ayden was to bring death once more, this time to a man who possessed the powers of one of the Children of the Creator.

Had this been what Ayden had wanted when the divine light descended upon him? What good had he truly done during his time as the Will? Of course, in his time wearing the mantel, there were no questions, no outside thoughts. There was only the mission, only the next target. Now though, the divine haze lifted from his mind and from his vision, allowing him to reflect. When Ayden was at the Academy of Arcane Arts, he was there not only to gain information, but also to help him learn discipline and fine control over his abilities. But there was more than that. There was another reason, one that was obscured by the brilliant light that was receding from the deepest parts of his memory very slowly. Aerith had been concerned about the students at the Academy. There were so many people with awesome power that could have overwhelmed the Masters of the Academy and then turned the students into terrible weapons that could be unleashed against unsuspecting populations. Ayden began to remember the conversation between his parents. They worried that either Emries or Talisia had the talent to usurp the wills of the students if not the Masters themselves and turn them into mindless and powerful puppets. Aerith's concern had fallen mostly on Talisia. His agent from the Heavens, Sabrina Binosear, the former host of the Spirit, had gone to great lengths to warn Aerith about Talisia's dispositions and her drives. Aerith's major concern was that the evil and vicious Child of the Creator would turn the innocent children of the Academy into walking bombs that she would set out into the world and explode in highly populated city centers. Bryn's concern was more for Emries and his tendency for manipulation. The whole of Cadaria accepted and therefore took for granted the fact that the students of the Academy of Arcane Arts were forbidden from using their abilities in any offensive capacity, and that included such things as persuasion and mind control or the manipulation of emotions. If Emries were to take control of the Academy and its students, he could remove the Masters, remove the prohibitions that they enforced through simple magical oaths, and deploy the most talented students to the various kingdoms of Cadaria where he could use them to manipulate and control the minds of every person of power across the world. There were other terrible possibilities, represented either by rogue members of the Brotherhood of Phasia, the Dark Gods, or even the divine host of the Creator. The fate of the Academy of Arcane Arts represented a potential existential threat to the entirety of Cadaria, the whole of Espre, and the war effort against the Creator and the Children.

Bryn, in her true fashion as a member of the Brotherhood of Phasia and an expert in architecting the genocide of whole species was the first to suggest the possibility of destroying the Academy for the good of the war. Her reasoning of course was that in the grand scheme of things, it was better to eliminate a potential threat before it could be turned against you. Aerith, though not above taking such unilateral action when he deemed it necessary had softened in his time on Espre. Though he was still an unrepentant killer, his exposure to Logan, Sabrina, and others had softened some of the edge and allowed for options other than bloodshed to be entertained for a longer amount of time. Though Aerith allowed the possibility that the Academy would need to be destroyed, he wanted to give the innocents every opportunity to live. In fact, it was Ayden who interjected in the conversation the possibility of sending a spy into the ranks of the Academy. Someone who could gain information, keep an eye out for beings of power attempting to insinuate themselves among the leadership, and also to potentially protect the students should someone attempt to take the Academy grounds by force. Though Bryn was initially resistant to the idea, she relented when Aerith insisted that such an agent must also have the ability to destroy the Academy rather than letting it fall into enemy hands.

Ayden had volunteered for the assignment. The memory staggered him as it spread through his mind. He had volunteered. Aerith hadn't sent him to the Academy as a punishment or over his objections. Ayden had suggested the spy in an effort to steer the conversation away from the total destruction of the Academy, and he had volunteered for the post to save lives. His family wanted to save lives. That's what Ayden thought he was doing by embracing the position of the Will. And yet, as the Will, Ayden was required to kill, in cold blood. There was no negotiation, no reprieve, no appeal. Once the Creator had dispatched a Servant to bring an end to a being's life, that was the only possible outcome. But surely Ayden had been wicked since his deployment to the Academy. He was reckless and vain and arrogant. He was a terror to his instructors and he used people mercilessly. He was his mother's son after all, a being of violence, a being of manipulation, and a being who was not above twisting or subjugating the wills of others to get what he wanted. Bryn viewed humans as playthings to be used and then discarded once they had outlived their usefulness. Surely that view of humanity had been passed on in the lessons that she taught her son. In his time at the Academy, he was abusive, decadent, disrespectful, disruptive, intolerant, and cruel. All of the worst features that he had learned from his mother. He was a burden, a burden so terrible that he was expelled from the Academy and sent into the wilderness a dismal failure.

But that wasn't what happened, was it? No. That wasn't the way that it was. Yes, Ayden had been a terror to instructors and to the Masters in general, but he was not disrespectful in every interaction, nor was he overtly disruptive to the point of depriving the other students of the opportunity to learn. In fact, Ayden took great pride in staying late in the canteen to assist the younger students in their studies. Yes, Ayden played pranks on some of the older students, but he only targeted those who were bullies and picked on students who were younger and weaker. In some ways, the Academy of Arcane Arts was no different than the Cadarian Empire. There were those students who came from affluent families and others who came from poor families. There were children of warriors, children of scholars, and children of prostitutes. There were many in Cadaria that would not be caught dead in the same room as a member of a different class, especially those that were considered of a lower social stratum. Alistair Ravenheart did not bear any of these prejudices, as he saw them as archaic and contrary to the public good. Those that had the talent for magical ability needed to be protected.

But that protection went both ways. People, especially young people with magical ability were prone to rages and unintentional outbursts. These outbursts could harm themselves and more likely, innocent people around them, including their own families. An additional danger to these uncontrolled bursts of power is that it could erode the public's trust in the Academy as well as engender fear in those who use magic. Such fear had led to the persecution of magic users in the past, and Alistair was dedicated to ensuring that such disasters never happened again.

There were none who were alive in Cadaria today that remembered the dark past, but the Academy had a very long memory and those who were Grand Masters of the Academy were very aware of even the darkest of those memories. Alistair Ravenheart, when he became Grand Master of the Academy of Arcane Arts, studied the dark moments of the past, finding several occurrences over the two thousand years that the Cadarian Empire had existed, where the public lost faith in the Academy and began to openly persecute those with the talent. No matter the cause of these upsets, the outcome was always the same, death. Fearful vigilantes roamed the countryside hanging, burning, and beating to death those they believed had the arcane talent. Unfortunately for the hateful and reactionary mob, arcane talent was not something that could be seen. It wasn't as though people had glowing eyes or a different color hair, or some scar or birthmark that indicated they were special. People with the talent were no different than any other person in Cadaria. That was what potentially made them dangerous, and why the Academy of Arcane Arts was a necessity. When Alistair became the Grand Master of the Academy, he vowed that he would never let fear override common sense ever again. That was the reason for Alistair's constant forays into the world looking for those with the talent. That was why he would constantly sit in taverns and common rooms talking with those who may not have had the education or the worldliness to know exactly what the Academy did and how they improved the Cadarian Empire. However, this more egalitarian view of the world was not popular in all corners of Cadaria, and as such were reflected what was referred to as the quiet politics of the Academy.

In the same way that eye and hair color can be passed from parent to child, so can a world view. This some-time infection of the mind created inequalities and prejudices that were contrary to the very essence of what the Academy stood for. While it didn't normally impact the younger students, the upsets were seen in those who had their talents identified later in life. And these upsets were not confined to only the more affluent students as one might think. Yes, there were more issues with those students; not being willing to share rooms with those of a lower social caste, or not wanting to associate with those from a rival family or a rival kingdom. However, these prohibitions could also be found among the working classes, as there were ancient rivalries among trades, ethnicities, and belief systems. The Academy of Arcane Arts was an island in a divided empire, one that acknowledged the existence of the separations outside the doors of the Academy, but would not let those divisions inside. This was one of the unexpected places where Ayden became an asset to the Academy.

Despite Alistair and the other Masters' best efforts, there were still conflicts among the students that were caused by these quiet politics. The arguments were normally small and resolved themselves, but there were also times when those conflicts threatened to spin out of control. And just like out in the real world, there were factions that would develop around strong personalities, and those factions would sometimes become embroiled in rivalries that would spin out of control. While the Masters involved themselves in these conflicts should they grow out of control, they preferred to leave the diffusion of such upsets to the students themselves. If they could not control themselves in the confines of the Academy, how could they be trusted to control themselves in the wider world? In the Academy, Ayden would soon come to be recognized as the great mediator within the Academy. Ayden had a great sense for the underlying cause of the conflicts that would break out and the fastest way to bring them to a conclusion that both sides were able to live with. In fact, during Ayden's time at the Academy, some Masters commented that it was the quietest and smoothest the Academy had operated in years.

So why was Ayden expelled? Surely he must have done something terrible to deserve such treatment. Yes, Ayden crossed the line. Yes, he had made an enemy in Jastra Mythryn. But that was not enough for his dismissal. The key factor was the death of Alistair Ravenheart, and the lack of understanding among the remaining Masters of exactly what Ayden Seth was. When the secret was finally revealed to the Masters, the fear that

Alistair had tried to minimize about how those with arcane talent could interact with those without manifested between the Masters and a relation of the Dark Gods.

When Aerith Seth first approached Alistair Ravenheart about the inclusion of Ayden in the Academy, Alistair was understandably confused and concerned. Alistair, much as everyone else in Cadaria had grown up in a world where the Dark Gods were evil corruptors that could not be trusted. They were dedicated to stealing the souls of the good and righteous Cadarian people, twisting them into demonic creatures that were slaves to the will of the Dark Gods. The difference between Alistair Ravenheart and the previous Grand Masters of the Academy was the fact that Alistair, for all of his adherence to rules and tradition, was also a wise man who kept an open mind and a wide perspective. Aerith believed, that if Alistair was presented with a reasonable alternate explanation as to the nature of the Dark Gods, as well as being presented with the opportunity to learn more about one of the most mysterious topics in the history of the Cadarian Empire, that the wizened older man would be willing to at least consider a proposal as radical as harboring a member of the Dark Gods, despite the jeopardy. Besides the potential internal strife that such an inclusion could cause within the Academy, there was also wider jeopardy, as the harboring of a member of the Dark Gods was against Imperial Law. As expected, Alistair was taken aback when Aerith revealed his true nature, but the trepidation was balanced by a lifetime of curiosity as well as a lifetime of trying to see people for who they were, not what they were. It was an opportunity that Alistair could not turn down. But once Alistair had fallen prey to the machinations of Kaitain Lorien, that wider view of a potentially balanced world died with him. The remaining Masters, for all of their power and wisdom, did not see the world with the same egalitarian eyes, or if they did, that equality was limited to their concept of humanity.

Ayden could not fault the other Masters for their fear or their trepidation. Part of their concern of course had been fueled by the fact that they believed they had been deceived by a man they trusted without question. It was a betrayal. Even if it was for the best reasons with the best intentions, it was still viewed as a betrayal. In the moment, and really that was all that it was, a moment, the fear overrode the wisdom of perhaps the wisest group of individuals in Cadaria. But that was the danger of generations of accepted fear. People had stopped questioning why they were afraid, they were simply afraid, and it prevented them from seeing anything beyond that fear. And while perhaps the remaining Masters would have found another way to deal with Ayden and his disrespectful tendencies, his nature as a member of the Dark Gods made it easier for them to separate him from the rest of the Academy. However, even that separation proved to have advantage to the Masters and the Academy.

Ayden had become aware through whispers in the dark corners of the Academy that there were members who had heard rumors of expelled students and undiscovered potentials that had found their way into a dark cabal who were not confined by the strictures of the Academy. While there had been rumors of these dark magicians for centuries, they were never anything more than ghost stories. Even when Ayden began to hear these rumors, he dismissed them. It wasn't until Ayden heard from a younger student about his own brother and his disappearance that Ayden began to take the rumors seriously. The boy's brother had been a student at the Academy but had not fit there. Once the Masters were sure that the young man would adhere to the laws of the Academy and would not pose a threat to the greater community, he was dismissed from the Academy. The two brothers corresponded often, and in one of his final correspondences, the older brother gave vague allusions to a new opportunity to use his abilities for the good of the empire. Shortly after, the letters stopped completely. Ayden brought this situation to the attention of the Masters, which would lead to Ayden's assignment to infiltrate this dark academy. Again, it was not through any fault or any malevolence within Ayden that this dismissal was manufactured.

Standing in the middle of the dark forest, Ayden's mind whirled. Ayden had been a man in the mold of his parents. Not the monsters that they were out of necessity, but the creatures of light who wanted a better world. Ayden too wanted to be a catalyst for a better world, and as such did what he could within the confines of his abilities and his situations to manifest that better world, even if it were only in small ways, or one person at a time. The Creator had taken that desire to make the world better and had twisted it to an unbelievable degree. He had turned Ayden into an assassin, an instrument of death, and a tool whose only purpose was to continue to the Creator's agenda; an agenda that only could end in one way, the destruction of all living beings within Creation. How was that a better world? How was that a more tolerant world? It was no world at all. It was the most arrogant of all world views. If Creation would not bend to the Creator's will, there would be no Creation. Now Ayden was faced with a choice that he was unsure how to make. The Creator had sent him on one last mission. One last assignment to end the life of another being. This time, he was to murder Wolf Ranthall and steal from him the powers of a member of the Children of the Creator. He had heard the great secret from the Creator Himself that those who were touched by divinity and raised to the position of Servant did so at the cost of their own souls. But the part of Ayden Seth that was his father, the part of Ayden Seth that saw the world through clear eyes, could never believe in a Creator who would rather destroy all life than accept life that grew beyond his control. That Ayden Seth was not a murderer. That Ayden Seth was not an assassin, and that Ayden Seth would never again take action to advance entropy's relentless aphotic call.

Jillian

Jillian sat on a cold stone floor, looking up at the stars through a broken ceiling. For two days, her routine had been the same. She had been roused time and time again from her restless sleep to move from one shattered house to another, each in a different village or town. The army of armored ghosts moved swiftly and subdued everything in its path with brilliant, if not terrifying efficiency. At the center of the army was a man and a woman, one Jillian knew by reputation, the other she had learned about through the short time she had been in his presence. Jerrica Maldovrin, one of the famous seers of the Maldovrin Triplets, was a student of the Dark Seer Jehna Feris, Jillian's mother. They were fated to carry on Jehna's cursed legacy, protecting the one secret left to the clan. What Jillian had not known until she had been abducted by Taya Viruci was the fact that it was Jillian herself who was the secret and the legacy to be protected. The soul of the missing High Priestess of the Adhradair had been fused with her own soul, and soon would be infused into the soul of her unborn child, passing on the burden and at the same time passing on the hope for a tomorrow beyond the horrors of war with the forces of the Heavens. Whether it was Dorovar, or Kaitain Lorien, or the Servants of the Creator, or the Creator Himself, they all wished to control that which had been made part of Jillian, control the destiny of all who called the current incarnation of Creation home. Jerrica seemed to be swept along in the madness the same way that Jillian had been. She was less an active participant and more a passenger in the great procession. Every time Jillian set her eyes upon the seer, she seemed paler and gaunter. The journey was inflicting a great strain upon the seer, and it seemed to Jillian that was only a matter of time before Jerrica would be just another ghost amongst the rest of the army.

The man who was most often at Jerrica's side and who seemed to be directing the whirlwind that was the ghost army, was clearly fighting a battle that no one outside of his own mind could see, and it was clear to Jillian that he was losing that battle to his invisible opponent. Sometimes the man seemed to be fully in control of his faculties, and he would spend much of his time tending to the fading Jerrica. Other times however, it seemed that his only want was the utter and complete destruction of everything in his path. But that destruction was dispassionate, cold, emotionless. It seemed that to him the deaths of all of those innocents was akin to sweeping the porch of stray leaves after a storm. The army at this man Gideon's command was brutal, efficient, and without any measure of mercy. Men, women, children, the old, the infirm; it did not matter who the soldiers came across. All that was left in their wake was death.

These episodes to Jillian seemed almost like a dream. Though in the back of her mind she knew that this part of her world was the grim reality that she should have been disturbed by, it was not what held her attention. The new voice in her head and in her soul held much more interest. Genovefa's restored voice mingled with the deepest parts of Jillian's soul teaching her all manner of lessons that she would need for the fight ahead. She could not pretend to understand all of the implications of the information that was being imparted into her. When Genovefa first told Jillian of their connection, the same connection that the former High Priestess had had with Jillian's mother Jehna, she underestimated how much knowledge one woman could have. In the end however, Jillian became aware quickly that it was not just the knowledge of one woman's life in a sheltered and cloistered existence that Genovefa had to offer, but in fact it was the knowledge of every High Priestess that had ever walked her world of Loinn. Not only that, but there was some of the knowledge of the Goddess Raenera herself; knowledge and wisdom that spanned back to the dawn of Creation. Awe and wonder filled Jillian in equal parts with revulsion and terror.

As she floated between the dream of reality and the lessons from the immortal soul of a woman who died on another world, Jillian reflected upon her life and the three distinct awakenings that had marked her transition from the world of the mortal and the mundane to the shocking emersion into the transcendent truths of the Cosmos. The first was the morning when her village was destroyed by the Demon Dragon Shadowweaver and her mother was kidnapped by that malicious beast. On that day, she had been shown the harsh reality of her world, and though she was still only a child, it set the path that would lead her stumbling forward toward her destiny. Standing in the smoldering rubble of her village, Jillian became possessed with hatred for all dragons, and wanted nothing more than to see every last one of them flayed open on the ground before her. The only thing that could quench the burning rage within her was to be bathed in the blood of her enemy. However, that would not come easily to the now-orphaned girl from a small farm town in an obscure part of the Kingdom of Iron, Pellatori. For several days after the attack, the survivors of the village were left to pick up the pieces of their lives on their own. Because the village was on the border between Bellnoc and Pellatori, the attack ignited long-simmering tensions between the two great kingdoms. Forces from Bellnoc moved to render humanitarian aid to the survivors of the attack as a show of good will, however, their passage across the border was halted by border guards from the Iron Legion. A detachment of the Iron Legion was dispatched to address the potential invaders, and for several days the two armies eyed each other nervously across an invisible line rather than helping the displaced citizenry. All too often, the old grudges took precedence over doing the right thing for the people, and places that should have been safe for the children of Cadaria were turned into warzones with little to no warning. A week had passed before the tensions finally dissolved, and the Iron Legion troops moved from their posturing on the border to much-needed relief efforts. However, by the time this help finally arrived, many had already died from their wounds, and many others had packed what meager belongings they were able to scrounge together and had moved on to another village.

Jillian had lived on the little charity she could find from those villagers that survived, and eventually she was carted off with a group of refugees to the capital city of Pellatori. Jillian was placed with a family who had lost their daughter in a raid by agents supposedly loyal to the Dark Gods, and while the situation was not ideal, she took advantage of the small opportunity that her new living conditions had afforded her. The woman of the house was a severe and exacting woman with little humor who vacillated between periods of intense mourning for the loss of her daughter and unchecked irritation with the usurper who was filling the void. On the other hand, the husband and oldest son were both members of the Iron Legion, and they were far more welcoming and understanding of their new lodger's situation. The son took special interest in Jillian and was willing to teach her how to use a sword and properly wear light armor. Unfortunately, his interest in her was not limited to simply teaching. However, even more unfortunately, he proved to be too good of a teacher. When he would not take no for an answer, Jillian was forced to use the young man's lessons against him. While Jillian was content to simply fend off his advances; instead of retreating and rethinking his aggressiveness, he redoubled his efforts in a far more violent way. Jillian was forced to turn the knife meant to influence her back upon her attacker. The only bright spot of the whole situation was that it was the husband and not the wife who discovered Jillian curled up in a corner soaked with the young man's blood. Of course, her time in the house was at its end, and Jillian began her long lonely journey toward her uncertain future.

As a young teenage girl, Jillian was on her own, wandering the countryside with a clear goal and no clear way to fulfill it. She had enough rudimentary fighting skill to protect herself from common criminals and those that would seek to take advantage of her. But there was a moment when things could have turned much darker for Jillian. She was always careful to travel on highly trafficked roads during the day in order to lower the risk to her survival. But even in those circumstances there was plenty of danger to be found. On one of her travels, Jillian happened quite coincidentally on a group of bandits dividing the spoils from a carriage they had burned and the occupants of which they had murdered. Still young and inexperienced, Jillian decided that she would try to sneak around the bandits rather than to find a hiding spot and wait for the bandits to depart. Unfortunately, the ungainly and slightly awkward girl was not up to the task of stealthily avoiding the robbers. One of the more astute of the group detected Jillian early in her attempt to circumvent the killers, and was able to flush her out of her hiding place into the arms of one of his fellows. Before the brutes could contemplate the evil deeds they could perpetrate on Jillian, a young blond man appeared seemingly out of nowhere. He didn't rush to Jillian's aid, but instead stood outside at the edge of the small clearing and made his presence known through a long low whistle. The bandits tried to shoo away the interloper, but the man would not be deterred. Jillian was thrown to the ground, hitting her head hard on a rock immediately robbing her of consciousness. By the time she regained her senses, the bandits were all dead and the young man was helping Jillian back to her feet. It took a long time for Jillian to find her feet, her vision was blurry, and her head felt like it weighed a hundred pounds. No matter how much she tried to gain her balance, she could not. The world was spinning around her and the ground felt as though it was shifting underneath her feet in random directions every second. Though she tried, she could not hold onto the threads of consciousness. Though she expected the last feeling she had in the waking world was crashing back to the ground, that sensation never came. At the last moment, she felt as though she were floating on a cloud.

The next thing Jillian knew, she was waking up on a small bed. The fog was clear from her head and the small cut that was on the side of her head was completely healed. Her blond-haired savior was nowhere to be found. The inn that her savior had left her in was on the edge of a town over a hundred miles from where she had been, while only a few hours had passed. None of it made sense. No matter how she tried to reconcile the incongruencies, she was not able to, and so Jillian simply tried to make the best of her new circumstances. Jillian was able to secure both a job and lodgings at the inn despite her young age, and she settled into a steady routine while she was attempting to make plans for the next part of her journey. The need to track down the overgrown lizard that had destroyed her home was still foremost on her mind, but she was old enough to realize that it would take money and resources that Jillian did not have access to in order to make her revenge a reality.

The inn that Jillian began to call home was in the Flying Kingdom, Hedorah. Hedorah proved to be the best place for someone like Jillian, as the information that flowed through the city of Hedorah was easy to procure for the right price and covered matters in all of the Great

Kingdoms of Cadaria. While Hedorah was mostly regarded as a den of corruption and self-interest, it was also perhaps the center of secrets for the empire. Because the merchants, traders, and sailors who made Hedorah their hub of operations traveled to all of the Great Kingdoms of Cadaria as well as the few islands in the Pritan Island chain that were populated, they were able to acquire massive amounts of information. This opportunity gave rise to one of the most unique occupations, Information Broker. The issue however was that most of the Information Brokers of Hedorah were some of the most corrupt and disreputable individuals in the whole of the empire. They cared only for profit, and they alone determined the value of the information that they had acquired. Information could not truly be managed by other commodities like gold, grain, or precious metals. Those commodities had calculable values dependent on availability, quantity, and quality. Information's intrinsic value diminished purely because of how many people knew that information. Additionally, information's value increased dependent upon how difficult it was to acquire and how dangerous possession of that information was. These factors created issues for Jillian in regards to the information she wanted to acquire. It wasn't just enough for her to acquire information about the creature who destroyed her life, but she also needed to learn how to kill it. Dragons were a difficult subject because of the potential danger that they represented. There was an uneasy truce between the Cadarian Empire and the dragons of Espre that had been negotiated by the first emperor of Cadaria, Terrik Lorien. Because of that truce, dragon hunting was a taboo that most would not risk pursuing.

During the Founding Wars, dragons were a critical impediment to all of the factions that were vying for control of the continent of Cadaria. While the dragons did not often act directly against the forces of the individual factions, there were several flashpoints that could have raged out of control. One of the would-be warlords who was attempting to consolidate power in the area that would become the Kingdom of Night, Galateria, came to the conclusion that the surest way to victory was to form an alliance with one of the dragons that called the region home. However, the warlord either misunderstood the danger or did not care for the potential consequences. While the dragon was willing to hear the petition of the human, it was not willing to endure any level of insult or condescension. Whatever the warlord said to the dragon was apparently not said with enough deference, because the dragon killed him on the spot. But that wasn't enough for the dragon. The dragon took it upon itself to eliminate the entirety of the warlord's army as well as burn his stronghold to the ground. This became a cautionary tale for all of the other aspiring leaders of Cadaria, and no one ever approached the dragons for aid again. That did not mean however that the dragons did not have further impact on the Founding Wars. On many occasions, battles took place too close to the lair of one of the temperamental beasts, and the infringing armies found themselves under assault from above or below. More than one warlord watched helplessly as their forces were reduced to nothing in a single engagement. Though it seemed that Terrik Lorien's forces never ran afoul of any dragon despite operating nearly constantly near their lairs.

Once the Founding Wars came to an end, there was a great concern amongst the people as to whether or not the new fledgling government would be able to prevent what was considered to be an imminent invasion by either the Dark Gods or a group of dragons. In the days following the establishment of the capital of the new Cadarian Empire in the newly-built Imperial Palace of Aldere, the empress, Liette Lorien disappeared for several days. When the Empress returned, she brought with her a representative of the dragons. This representative, Serentis, spent five days in negotiation with Terrik Lorien hammering out the guidelines of how the Cadarian Empire and the dragons of Espre would co-exist. The terms of the deal were never disclosed, and according to Imperial Record were never codified in any form within the records of the government, but the accepted gist was that the Cadarians would not encroach on lands controlled by the dragons, and the dragons would not act openly against the Cadarians unless provoked. With few exceptions, that peace had held for almost two thousand years.

When the Demon Dragon Shadowweaver struck Jillian's village, she was too young to understand the politics around the truce between the dragons and the Cadarian Empire. What Jillian learned later in life was that one of the overzealous men of her village had injured a young dragon that had supposedly been feeding on his flock. Shadowweaver had visited the village on several occasions in an attempt to convince Jehna Feris to use her powers of prophecy for him. Jehna had rebuffed each and every one of those advances, and so Shadowweaver needed another angle. Once the young dragon had been wounded, it created all of the pretense that Shadowweaver needed to destroy the city and abduct Jehna. While politically within the letter of the agreement between the dragons and the Cadarian Empire, there were many like Jillian who saw the response as an overreaction and began to question whether or not the arrangement should have ben revisited. The strongest proponent of this was the Shadow Guild. Apparently, the Grand Master of the Shadow Guild, through his intermediary Natalia Pressen, the Sunstone Knight of the Flashing Blade, had been railing for several years about the danger that the dragons posed as the population and industrial diversity of the Cadarian Empire grew. It was inevitable that more conflicts between the dragons and the Cadarians would happen as the empire expanded, and it was only a matter of time before those minor incidents produced a flashpoint that ignited all-out war. The Grand Master's warnings proved to be prophetic, but not perhaps in the manner in which he foresaw.

The assault on Jillian's village gave rise to a new generation of those who disagreed with the very existence of the beasts, the dragon hunters. There had always been those who defied the accepted norms and had hunted dragons both for sport and to acquire dragon parts for brokers in exotic materials. It was a very lucrative and risky profession, and more people were willing to subsidize the death of dragons every day. This brought Jillian to her second awakening. It was the day that crystalized her path and enabled her to be exactly what she wanted to be. Jillian had heard rumblings for some time of a reputable information broker, one who could be trusted to deliver on his promises. It took Jillian several months to track down this enigmatic broker, but eventually she found her way to the shop of the man known as Blade. Jillian and Blade took a liking to each other very quickly. Blade understood that the brash young girl would not be deterred in her quest, and Jillian understood the gruff old man who was less interested in profit than he was in acquiring what he needed for his own agenda. Though it took some convincing, Blade taught Jillian what she needed to know to survive against a dragon and the materials that she needed in order to be successful in a hunt. He also showed her the pieces of a dragon that would fetch the highest price and sustain Jillian until she was able track down Shadowweaver and make the creature pay for its crimes. In addition, Blade acted as a matchmaker of sorts, helping Jillian create her team of fledgling dragon hunters. It was through Blade that

Jillian first met Kiara Aren, the unfairly exiled former priestess, the first member of Jillian's hunters and the healer of the group. Next was Jacqueline Escandi, the former member of the Iron Legion whose specialty was as an engineer and with all manner of siege weapons. Finally, there was Angelina Lynn Sydor, a former member of the Shadow Guild who was also the dragon anatomy specialist of the group. Because of her training, Angelina was able to ensure that every dragon part that they recovered was in the best condition and would fetch the maximum amount when sold. Jillian was not prepared for how expensive dragon hunting was in terms of supplies, armaments, logistics and necessary information procurement, and Angelina's contribution was perhaps the most critical in terms of their continued viability and survival.

It was just after meeting Blade for the first time that Jillian's blond savior reappeared. At the time, Jillian did not recognize him. Reflecting back upon that time, Jillian understood now that her blond savior was one of the Dark Gods, and he had used his abilities to remove knowledge of him from her mind. The blond man, posing as a traveling bard who was spreading the truth about the evils of the Dark Gods and their corrupt human allies in the Order of the Flickering Flame, had heard about the fledgling band of dragon hunters and their young charismatic leader. He brought what he called a gift from an interested patron. The gift was the sword Scaleripper which was supposedly made from the bones of a slaughtered member of the Council of Winds. The moment the weapon was put into Jillian's hand, she knew that her path was the right one, and any doubts that existed in her mind were immediately erased. Now of course Jillian knew that the doubts she was hearing came from the shared soul of the High Priestess of Loinn that inhabited her body and Scaleripper's primary purpose was to suppress Genovefa's voice. At that point in time however, all Scaleripper represented was another piece of the puzzle that would lead to Shadowweaver's demise. There was no doubt in her mind that the Demon Dragon would die at her hands, and Scaleripper would deliver the mortal blow.

For years it was so simple. They hunted, they killed, they benefited from the spoils of their kills, repeat. The only frustration was that no matter how many of the creatures they killed, no matter how many nests they burned out, Jillian was still no closer to Shadowweaver. Then the third awakening, another brush with death at the hands of supernatural beings intent on capturing Jillian for unknown purposes. Of course, the purpose was clear now that Jillian and Genovefa had been reunited, but at the time it made no sense. The most impactful outcome was the man who came into her life and saved her from an uncertain fate. That man was Dane Rhuiden or as he was better known, Logan Ranthall. Logan was a force of nature that turned her life upside down and introduced her to a reality she had trouble believing even after seeing it with her own eyes. The Dark Gods, the Children of the Creator, the politics of the Heavens, the Heralds of Dorovar and the secret war that would determine the future of humanity. It was all ridiculous, laughable, and impossible. Jillian was introduced to a Dark God passing himself off as a member of the Knights of the Flashing Blade, a Lord and Lady of a Cadarian Kingdom who were also Dark Gods, and the immortal leadership of the Order of the Flickering Flame. The scope of it made Jillian's head spin, but being with Logan made it all seem so normal. She even stood mere feet from a dragon and did not feel the urgency to see it dead at her feet. Jillian stood in front of the new Empress of Cadaria and was offered a place in the reformed Knights of the Flashing Blade because of her association with Logan, and she had also learned the truth about her parentage. Everything that she had known about herself for the majority of her life had been a lie. She was so much more than she had been allowed to be, and now that the veil had been lifted from her eyes and her soul, the possibilities were just beginning to become real in her mind.

And now, Jillian was a prisoner on a path of destruction that was leading only one place, the Heart of Stone, and a conflict the likes of which the world had never seen. Jilian was on the verge of a fourth awakening, an awakening to the woman that she was always supposed to be. Perhaps Gideon did not realize what he was getting when he had Taya bring Jillian to him. Perhaps he did not know the impact that the removal of Scaleripper would have. However, now that Genovefa had begun to tutor Jillian in the darkness of her mind on the history of the Adhradair, the powers of the High Priestess, and all of the powers that the Dragon's Tear was supposed to have, Jillian could feel herself changing every moment of every darkened day. There was something growing inside of her, along with her unborn child, a power that defied any level of description blossoming slowly. It was still too far away and too ethereal to be wielded in any real capacity, but that would soon change. Genovefa was very insistent with her teachings, and it would only be a matter of time before Jillian would be a force to be reckoned with. She knew that she would not be a match for Gideon, at least not at first, but in time she would be able to free herself from her bondage and find her way to her new path. Shadowweaver no longer mattered. Revenge no longer mattered. All that mattered was getting back to Logan and giving the Dark Gods the weapon they needed to unseat the Creator and tear down the Golden Throne forever.

Korrd

The rain fell hard in the small border town of Araghast, and the thick-packed dirt road that ran down the center of the town was already reduced to a muddy mess. The small tavern that doubled as the only inn in the town was a welcome change from sleeping out in the open, not that Korrd and his two companions had found much time for sleep since their flight from Thorigald. By Korrd's estimation they were at best two days ahead of the ghostly white army being led by their former friend Gideon Viruci, or at least what was left of him. The armored horde was brutal in their precision, eliminating every vestige of life in their path before advancing to the next city. But, despite their inhuman powers and origins, they still moved like men. They marched over ground, and advanced at the speed of a large force of soldiers on a forced march. While they did not seem to suffer from fatigue, or be as impacted by changes in terrain, they still had to cross the distance on foot. Korrd was slightly grateful for the fact that the ghostly warriors did not move as the Creator's Host of Angels did. The thought of the speed at which Gideon's army could inflict their grim business if they moved like locusts on the wind sent a chill through Korrd's blood. As it was, most cities barely resisted for half a day before blood filled the streets and the warriors were on to their next target.

Korrd sat at a small table by the window looking out into the darkness. He could see the water streaming down the thin glass and could feel the draft of cool damp air. While in theory he had drawn the short straw and chose to keep watch for the advancing horror that was following in their wake, in truth, Korrd wasn't sure that he could sleep even if he wanted to. Better to let Talon and Gwillim regain their strength for the trails ahead then to force another few hours of travel in the inhospitable conditions. After their brush with death at the hands of their former friend, the three men had discussed where they should go. Gwillim had suggested returning to Saldarine to gather an army to take the fight to the horde. There was part of Korrd that sympathized with Gwillim's position. He was a man who at his core wanted to do the right thing where it was possible. They had done so much evil for so long, and Korrd knew that Gideon's accusations about their culpability in their crimes had struck at Gwillim's core, probably more than it had for Korrd and Talon. Gwillim's motivations were simple. He saw a force of arms that was threatening the innocent. The only thing to do was raise an army to resist them and to fight as best they could, regardless of the fact that they would be hopelessly overmatched. Better to die trying to make right all of the terrible things they had done than to sit by and do nothing. Korrd's heart hurt when he rebuffed the idea. It wasn't that Korrd didn't want to fight, far from it. And while his blood burned at Gideon's words, he had to accept the reality of the situation. They could no longer shake the ground beneath their feet with just a thought. They were no longer gods among men who could strike down a thousand soldiers by calling down lightning from the skies. And despite their experience and their tenacity, on the battlefield they could be struck down like any other mortal devoid of their abilities to heal themselves or resist the effects of trauma. At the head of an army, they would be able to inspire, but perhaps the greatest strength they brought to an army was their ability to defend their soldiers by inflicting unbelievable damage upon the opponents. The more risk that Korrd and the others took, the less risk their soldiers would be subjected to. But with their abilities gone, their mortality restored, any army they led would face immense risk, and would certainly be slaughtered by Gideon's ghostly force.

Talon's idea had been more practical but no less fraught with potential danger. In his life before being touched by Emries the first time, Talon had been a troubled young man who only seemed to find joy in causing trouble for others. Though the trouble was good-natured more often than not, it still garnered him a reputation in the small town of Aradon where they had been raised. Yet, in the middle of a tavern with a lute or just his voice, Talon could capture the hearts and minds of even his most ardent detractors. Though Pike had fancied himself Talon's equal as a singer and a carouser, there was truly no comparison. That innate ability to wrangle the wills of men and women had been accentuated when Talon had been brought to Espre. At Emries' behest, Talon was dispatched during the Founding Wars to help bolster support for Terrik Lorien in his bid to unite what would become the Cadarian Empire. Then, once the Dark Gods were cast down, Talon's abilities were called on again to rail against the powerful newcomers, spreading lies and disinformation about the inherent evil nature of the Dark Gods, even coining the term. The clergy of the Church of the Creator were soon mimicking Talon's words in their sermons, whipping up fear and hatred for the former heroes. Over the years, Talon's abilities were called upon to advance whatever agenda Emries or Talisia wished. He whispered in the ears of impressionable rulers, started wars, broke marriages, and caused all manner of chaos from his safe position in the shadows. From time to time, Talon would assume direct control of one of the Great Kingdoms, but that was only until such time as someone more pliable was selected that would ensure that Emries' grand plan was not met with mortal resistance. However, it was Talon's centuries-long shadow battle with Logan Ranthall that had taken most of the former hero's time.

When the Order of the Flickering Flame first came into existence, Emries saw it as nothing more than a nuisance that would disappear in a matter of years with no true impact. That was of course before he learned who was at the heart of the Order. Logan Ranthall had been a thorn in Emries' side for a long time, and as much as Emries wanted nothing more than to crush the irritant under his boot, Emries saw an opportunity. Much in the same way that Emries had used the Church of the Creator to foment discord and disharmony in Cadaria by furthering the specter of the Dark Gods, he called upon Talon to begin to challenge the tenants of the Order of the Flickering Flame. In every court Talon would speak about the abhorrent affront to the worship of the Creator, the danger posed by rash heretical beliefs, and the misguided and perhaps criminal acquisition of men and wealth. But for every barb that Talon tossed in the direction of the Order, Logan was quick to counteract it with an act of charity or goodwill. Every word of dissent was met with a deed, every trap was deftly disarmed. In time, Emries felt that the expenditure of time and effort was not worth the results, and so the direct attacks and disinformation campaign were slowed, but never ceased. Talon continued over the years to jibe at his former friend, but with only mixed results. The Order would continue to do good work, but as long as the Church of the Creator continued to openly denounce their efforts the Order would only have minimal support. Of course, Logan didn't do himself any favors by provoking the Church at every opportunity, but even that did not seem to impact the goodwill generated by the deeds of the Order.

And so, it came as no surprise that Talon's suggestion was to use his, though diminished, ability to coerce and convince in order to save as many people as possible from the advancing army. Any life they were able to save was worth the effort. However, despite the looming danger all around them, many of the small towns and villages they passed through were unwilling to fly from danger. The more complicated part of course was the fact that even should they want to flee, there was nowhere for them to go. It wasn't until the third such village that the trio heard the rumors of a safe haven where those fleeing the darkness of the world could go. In a small common room that was almost too small to pass for a tavern, Korrd and the others came upon a man who had the smell of the road and too many days in the saddle upon him. He spoke with excitement, even through his exhaustion, of a place of refuge. It was supposedly built overnight near the site of the former Imperial Palace in Aldere. It was the new throne for the Cadarian Empire, and upon it sat the Imperial Heir, Quyhn Ravenheart Lorien. She had declared the new city a safe haven for all those fleeing the war, all those fleeing the persecution by Kaitain Lorien, all those fleeing the dragons and growing darkness of Dorovar and his Heralds. The place of course sounded too good to be true, but when Korrd heard the name of the city, his heart hurt. The place had been named New Aradon, and it was under the protection of the Dark Gods. Immediately Korrd's mind went to the stories of the Dark Mirror reality where Gwydeon and Midarin had turned Brea into haven of Light amidst the falling Shadow. Armed with this new information, Talon's attempts at salvation of the innocent gained more weight, and soon hopefully caravans of people would begin flooding east away from the coming conflict. However, Korrd could see the touchstone moment coming for the trio.

Korrd had taken great pains in plotting the course of Gideon's army, and there was only one possible destination. Soon the phantom army would descend upon the Kingdom of Stone, Albitonin and ultimately, the Heart of Stone. The last intelligence that Korrd had seen had that a host of angels was defending the Heart and the new High Priestess at the behest of the so-called Divine Empress Marlae Tamerlane. And though the name turned Korrd's stomach, he accepted that the Creator and by extension his Children had horrible senses of irony. But, it was clear, if the intelligence was to be believed that Gideon intended to strike a blow not only at the puppet monarch who wore a stolen name, but also declare war on the Creator in the most direct way possible. The problem was, that as Korrd and the others made their way south, they began to hear strange stories about the Heart of Stone. Some stories told that the High Priestess had been overthrown, that the Heart was in ruins, and that it had become a haven for dragons and Dark Gods. Of course, Korrd knew that rumors spread ten times faster than facts, and a hundred times faster than truth. But despite all the rumors, there was one consistent thread that seemed irrefutable. Dragons had taken up the guardianship of the Heart of Stone, and that could mean only one thing, Aerith Seth. It was no secret that Aerith and his new protégé Hannah Ironheart had struck a deal with a group of dragons in an effort to counteract the Demon Dragon Shadowweaver and its war against the Cadarians and the specifically Emperor Kaitain Lorien. However, Emries knew that there was more to Shadowweaver's advances. The ancient dragon had a pact with Talisia and would stop at nothing to possess the Dragon's Tear for her. Now that Talisia had fallen, the creature wanted nothing more than to possess that power for itself. To what end was anyone's best guess, but Emries believed that the ancient dragons wanted to return to a time before the Children, when the dragons were the paragons of power and they sat at the right hand of the Creator as his favored. There was a sinking feeling in the pit of Korrd's stomach, and it would not go away. That more than anything was why he sat alone watching the rain.

Korrd had fought on so many sides of the ideological war, that he no longer saw the lines. He had been young and stupid and idealistic for much of his young life, and that made him fodder for the creatures like Saurn and Emries. Much as he had with Aerith Seth before, Saurn saw the potential in Korrd, but had misunderstood the weapon that he had in his hands.

However, Emries had never lost track of his prize, using the shortsightedness of his enemies to put Korrd where he was most needed at the time. Whether it was fighting Caris, liberating Brea, or unknowingly assembling the *Erieal* of the second generation of the prophecies; Korrd was the perfect soldier. He just followed orders. Even at the end, when he stood face to face with Halicon and gave his life so that the game between the two Children could continue, he played his role. Unlike his son Gwillim, Korrd had had no role in the Dark Mirror. He was one of the few who stayed dead during that chapter of the war, a broken toy quickly forgotten. However, when the scale and the scope of the war changed on the new battlefield of Espre, Emries was quick to bring Korrd back from oblivion to become his agent. However this time, Korrd was not given the choice to blindly follow orders. When Emries snapped his fingers, Korrd jumped to attention like a marionette. Emries chose to leave nothing to chance this time around, and would not abide his servants developing a conscience or asking too many questions. Fortunately, most of the time Emries only required one job of Korrd, and that was to continue to destabilize relations between Thorigald and Saldarine.

Keeping the ancient enemies at each other's throats proved to be far too easy. Most of the time, all Korrd would have to do was select a small group of soldiers that he trusted, take them into the wilderness and stage an ambush on a detachment of soldiers from Thorigald who were on patrol. Korrd's people were talented enough to leave no trace, but when the bodies were found, the leadership of Thorigald would inevitably blame Saldarine. However, sometimes Korrd would turn the tables on his men and slaughter them on the edge of Thorigald's territory just to keep the tension stoked. These were the kinds of acts that Gideon was alluding to in his scathing review of Korrd's complicity in Emries' evil actions. But at the time, Korrd didn't see anything other than the justification. Talon had mused similarly during their travels together. Talon looked at the evil that they did with a much more detached air. He had changed much since his days as a young man in Aradon, and the lethal and hardened edge that he had developed under Emries' thumb was not going to disappear quickly. He was jaded, perhaps necessarily so, but it had given Talon a new perspective. Emries, though subtle in his manipulations, was not subtle when it came to directed action, and the Emries that had come to Espre was not the same one that had been on Onea in the later days of the war. This Emries had a much dimmer view of humanity, and had adopted a policy more like that of his sister Talisia. Why kill one when you can kill one hundred? Humans were expendable, so sometimes it was better to inspire fear with a slaughter rather than a surgical strike. In the end, the result would be the same, and perhaps there would be less resistance on the next portion of the plan. That however was what made being a blunt instrument for Emries so distasteful. The blood was not on his hands.

But it had not been all darkness. In the early years, perhaps that was all that Korrd could see. Or maybe that was all he wanted to see. There was just the work. He could not be bothered to think about anything else. Much like after the death of Korrd's mother or after the death of Gabrielle, Korrd was angry, and that was all he could see. He killed, he brooded, he killed. Such was the cycle for decades. There were many dalliances of course, but nothing that held his attention for long. How could it? He was immortal now. Nothing could really truly matter to him other than the work. And so he waited impatiently, sometimes for years, for Emries to return with a new mission, a new victim. Deep down though, Korrd could only see himself as the victim, and it filled him with more of the blinding all-consuming rage.

Was that the fatal flaw of the second generation of the prophecies? After being alive for hundreds of years, Korrd's mind began to work, whether he wanted it to or not. And so, over the millennia, Korrd began to think about everything that had come before. They had been so blind to Emries, to Halicon, and to the nature of the war that they were fighting. And for a time, Korrd became obsessed with figuring out what they had missed. The pieces of course never fit together quite the way that Korrd expected. But, with Emries' influence removed from his mind, Korrd had begun to see some of the pieces that he had been unable to see for so long. The first generation of the prophecies had been populated by some of the most renown heroes on the whole of Onea. Between the Binosear siblings, Cedric and Anabel, the Geoffry siblings, Arathorn and Diana, Aryx Terian, the Moridon Mailock, the Wind Sisters Alahanna and Corin, and on and on. They were the best and brightest drawn from all corners of the world, united under the banner of the Lord Lion. The first generation was one of idealism. It started simply enough. An enemy appeared who threatened the good people of Lakestone. The responsible and valiant hero gathers champions around him to vanquish the evil creature and save the world. There was even the love story and the happy ending. Korrd always found the first part of the story of Cedric's battle with Shau-ling to be trite and impossible to believe. But regardless of Korrd's opinion, that was the story that the bards loved to sing in the common rooms and taverns. It was a much easier story to tell than the second quest.

Of course it was a better story. The young respectable lord, flanked by the woman that he loved, travels to the kingdoms of the world, assembling a fighting force of mercenaries and heroes in an attempt to save the poor neglected citizens of a remote town from the monstrous host under the control of a hideous dragon. Add in the respected warrior who had become a farmer in Arathorn Geoffry, his tenacious kid-sister Diana, and the mysterious nomadic warrior Aryx Terian, and that is just enough to make any storyteller foam at the mouth thinking of the profits. But wait, there's more. There are the last of an ancient race of mystics who stood against the evils of the world as part of the Hand of the Light. An organization, by the way, that was so mysterious that the only proof of their existence was in stories and legends. Add in a swash-buckling pirate, a couple of mercenaries, and a priestess, and you have every element of a good epic tale. Top it off with the fact that they saved the innocent townspeople, eliminated the evil creatures, and returned triumphant without so much as a single casualty suffered amongst the heroes. Everyone comes home to a hero's welcome, a parade, and then the final nail in the coffin of absurdity, the fairy-tale wedding of our hero the Lord Lion and the love of his life. Stop the story right there; say no more. Send the people home with a smile on their face, a song in their heart, and the belief that their happy ending is out there waiting for them. No need to talk about the bride being assassinated during the wedding, or the fact that it wasn't really the hero's love in the first place. It was a pretender trying to manipulate him, only to be killed by the hero's best friend, who by the way also happens to be the pretender's brother and child of the great evil. No, no need to mention that. Then of course, there is the mysterious revelation that our hero is not just a hero, but the chosen hero, ordained by the Creator himself to face down an ancient evil and save the world. So, in the blink of an eye, we transition from a heroic tale of victory over evil to a revenge and religion motivated quest where suddenly the heroes are no longer invulnerable to the slings and arrows of their foes and begin succumbing to the impossible odds with staggering frequency. In the end however, our hero is victorious once more, though only a small number of his companions survive, and the great hero returns bewildered and broken, pondering a prophecy that he does not understand.

If Korrd wasn't jaded before, just thinking of the preposterous nature of Cedric Binosear's "quest" was enough to make his stomach turn. They were so oblivious and so trusting, that when they came back from the War of the Lion, all they had clinging to them was darkness and the stench of a pyrrhic victory. They had failed in saving Lakestone, as half the city ended up under water and the fraction of the population that survived had to be evacuated. So many of their number were lost that they was barely a third of their number at the height of the quest. Cedric Binosear was a broken man. His advisors spent most of their time hiding him from the responsibility of his actions, and the greatest secret was that it was all going to happen again. They did nothing to prepare the world for the next generation. They did nothing to bolster defenses or make sure that the phasia did not take over any of the kingdoms as they had done in the first generation. More than that, they waited until the last possible moment to identify the hero of the second generation, and even that they didn't get right. The hubris of their entitlement and their distractions. They were the more well-known heroes of the prophecies, but they paled in comparison to those who came after. Was it any wonder that only one member of that group still lived? The reborn Cedric didn't count. Only his sister, Anabel, the one who didn't want to be a hero at all was still having an impact.

But if the downfall of the first generation was their hubris and their entitlement, then the downfall of the second generation was their emotional instability and their naiveté. And those weaknesses not only impacted the second generation, but the third, and now the whole of the war on Espre. Korrd was angry and hated the world and just wanted to watch it burn. Pike was unstable and mercurial, and once Eldar was murdered he became a powerful but uncontrollable creature on a collision-course with his own self-destruction. Logan was strong but so filled with self-doubt and feelings of inadequacy that he made every mistake that he could. Gwydeon should have been the leader, should have been the hero, but he didn't want to lead. He wanted to support and hold the middle. He was too quick to sacrifice himself over and over again, a mistake he continued to repeat on Espre.

The cracks in their group were easy to find, and that was why the phasia were so successful at pulling them apart. Eldar hurt Pike, Elwyne hurt Logan, Korrd hurt Gwydeon, and so on and so on. Gideon was a spy, but was probably stronger than any of the other members of the group because he actually had a pretty good idea of who and what he was. They were a volatile mix, and honestly they got lucky. If the phasia had been truly united against them, if they truly had wanted to win, then they most likely would have. Jeroch's ambush in Marcwell was masterful and should have resulted in more casualties. As it was, they lost too many along the way. And when it was over, there was no parade, no hero's welcome, and no fairy-tale wedding. There was only the empty feeling of something half-done. Of course, Korrd wasn't around for any of that. Wasn't around for what came after.

And that led to the downfall of the third generation. The broken remnants of the first and second. It all flew apart. But perhaps that was why they were able to learn the truth about Emries and Halicon. Perhaps that was why there was a fighting chance on Espre. And yet, the more Korrd thought about it, the less he actually cared. His chance to be anything more than a footnote in his brother's rise to transcendence was long past. Now he was what he always was destined to be. He was a broken man, used, abused, and set aside. Powerless, pointless, and holding on to something that he could no longer be. In that moment, Korrd came to the realization that his companions were far better men than he would ever be. Talon for all his hardened edge was still a good man who wanted to do right, regardless of the situation. He accepted his place in the grey between light and shadow and knew how to use it to do the right thing. Gwillim was just a man who defied self-doubt. He was a bulwark against the tides of hopelessness and would stand between the on-rushing tide and save as many as he could. They were good men. Korrd was not. He had come to accept that. He was the pale shadow, the bitter older brother.

But even as he took another drink from his glass of the bitter liquid, his mind went to the last happy time that he could remember. It was in Chelsea's arms. In the beginning he wasn't sure if he was with her because he loved her, or because Emries demanded it of him. But regardless of how it started, Korrd knew that he had loved Chelsea. Knew that he missed her more than he could put into words and hurt because he knew that he would never see her again. But that was the way it should have been. Chelsea deserved the chance at happiness after being manipulated by everyone in her life. She had been manipulated by her family into joining the military. Manipulated by Emries to put her in the arms of a man who would give her a child but never make her whole. Manipulated by the Emperor into the bed of a man who could never love her the way that she deserved. Of all the terrible things that Korrd had done, Chelsea was the one thing that he regretted. She had been his true chance for redemption, but he just couldn't see it. And now it was too late. Too late to be anything other than the villain he had always seen himself as.

After swallowing the last gulp from the mug, he could feel the liquid burn his throat, and the haze fall over his senses. Fumbling in his pocket, he pulled out the small empty glass bottle and let his eyes focus upon it. His hand shook and his vision blurred, but he would recognize the accursed bottle anywhere. Emries had placed it in his hand years ago with a simple instruction. There could be no peace between Saldarine and Thorigald. There could be no hope for love and light between those bitter enemies in what was to come. Korrd couldn't remember if his hands shook when he crept into the secret retreat that was to be the respite for Seraph Kore and Chelsea Zarova, light and shadow wrapped around him to prevent being seen. Couldn't remember if his eyes even focused on the face of the tiny baby that was cradled in its father's arms as he lowered the clear dropper to the infant's mouth. Didn't remember if he held his breath as he made his retreat. All Korrd remembered is that he left whatever humanity that remained within him in that room. The site of his greatest act of betrayal. The moment he knew he could never look Chelsea in the eye ever again. The moment that he knew he didn't deserve to live.

All sound was gone except for the soft rain against the window. There would be darkness, and there would be silence, but there would be no peace for the man who was once known as the Lord Dragon, Korrd Ranthall.

Alise

Alise Modrall woke with a start, not sure for several moments where she was. As she opened her eyes, she forced them shut once more, the light from the twin suns too bright to stand. Her head ached, her body felt impossibly heavy, and her brain felt as though it had been scrambled. Finally, blinking away tears, Alise was able to open her eyes against the midday light and force her way to a sitting position. The long metal claws that had been her signature weapons were too heavy, and she carefully unstrapped them from the backs of her hands and let them fall to the muddy ground. It was then that she noticed the stench. All she could smell was death. The air reeked of it. The ground was soaked in it. She tried to force her way to her feet, but the moment she put weight on her legs, her knees threatened to buckle and collapse. After one more aborted attempt, Alise was able to make her way back to her feet and take in the scene. All around her were the broken armor and weapons of the Imperial Army. There were no bodies however, but the weapons and armor were laying in massive pools of blood that were slowly being absorbed by the marshy ground. It was then that she saw the singular body lying in the middle of the carnage. The identity of the fallen woman clicked into her scrambled mind quickly, but the fact that it was her was impossible. Staggering more than walking, the normally graceful Alise made her way over to the body and practically fell to her knees beside the fallen form. Alise pulled the girl out of the mire and cradled Tess's head in her lap, smoothing her mud-caked hair away from her placid face. There was no look of horror, no look of betrayal, no madness in her golden eyes. There was only peace. Whatever horrible forces had driven her right up until the moment of her death, there was no trace of it in her eyes. There was only peace. It was then that the fragments of memory began to click into place in Alise's mind. She had followed her father, Kaitain Lorien as he madly ran after Tess across the dew-soaked field. He was laughing like a mad-man and swearing to the heavens. And then he was simply gone. Reduced to a pillar of blood as though he was nothing. But it wasn't just him; his entire army, the supposedly fiercest fighting force in Cadaria had been erased from existence right along with their master. All that was left was Alise. But why? Why was she the one left standing amid the carnage? Why had Tess allowed Alise to be the last living witness to the depredation of the Cadarian Empire? Perhaps she had only been an oversight to the god-like girl's destructive rampage. Or perhaps Alise had been so far beneath Tess's notice that the girl didn't even feel that she was worth killing. Alise wasn't sure which thought she liked less.

Letting Tess's body rest back on the ground, Alise dragged herself through the mud to the spot where her father had been obliterated by Tess's power. Looking at the rapidly disappearing spot of blood on the ground, Alise was bombarded with the ignominy of the situation. Here was the great Kaitain Lorien, the man who shook his fist at Dark Gods, dragons, the Academy of Arcane Arts, and the Creator himself. This was the man who had designs on using Tess's power to ascend to the Golden Throne and reshape the whole of Creation in his image. And all that was left of him was a bloody smear on the ground. No monuments. No feasts. No weeping well-wishers. No funeral processions. No days of lying in state on the steps of the capitol. No tour through the kingdoms so that the faithful could pay their respects. There was only this. No great battle that saw him thrown down in his hubris. No crafty assassin that defeated the best of defenses to rob the great leader of his life. There was only a smear of blood, and no one left to know what had happened. As far as the rest of the world knew, Kaitain Lorien was still alive. Perhaps he had gone into hiding, overwhelmed by the sheer number of forces arrayed against him. Perhaps he had been tracked down by one of the many dragons that he had declared war against and had met his end between gnashing teeth. It didn't really matter, did it? No one would know for sure.

But Alise was not the only witness to the fall of Kaitain Lorien. There was another man, a man that Tess had called Logan. Had he been the one who had killed Tess? What had become of him? It took only a few moments to find the tracks that led away from the carnage, heading west toward Aldere. Alise's first instinct was to take up her weapons and follow after the man, but as she started in that direction, her breath caught in her throat, and she dropped to the ground once again. The realization of everything that had happened slammed into her mind and heart full force, knocking the wind out of her and causing her vision to blur. Before she knew what was happening, she was doubled over, sweat pouring down her face as she vomited bile and stomach acid onto the ground. The heaving would not stop, and her body shook violently. Finally, the dry heaving abated, blood trickling from the corners of her mouth and tears streaming from her eyes. Now the sickness rushed through her body and she was on her hands and knees openly weeping. The sorrow and confusion crashed through her like breakers, and while she was uncertain as to their source, she could not resist them. After what seemed like an hour of alternating between sickness and sorrow, she regained the hold on her emotional equilibrium and sank down to her knees. For the entirety of her life, she had never experienced an emotional outburst like that. And then her eyes shifted back to the blood smear that had been her father. A thought ran through her that was equal parts terror and exhilaration. She was free.

From the moment of her creation, Alise Modrall knew only one constant. She was a tool. Of that there could be no confusion. As much as Kaitain Lorien made use of the Shadow Guild, he never truly trusted them and he knew that at any moment, the Grand Master of the Shadow Guild had the power and connections to attempt to remove Kaitain from his vaunted perch as the Emperor of Cadaria. Alise had listened to her father's ravings many nights. When he was in a particularly foul mood, he would muse that the Grand Master fancied himself as the true Emperor of Cadaria, pulling the strings from the darkness no matter who sat on the throne. Kaitain did not like the thought of being anyone's puppet and always fancied himself as the one who pulled everyone's strings. One thing was certain, and it was something that Alise could never deny. Kaitain was a vile and evil man. And it was through those characteristics that Alise came into being.

Kaitain Lorien was like a spoiled toddler much of his life. If there was something that someone else had, he wanted it. And if he could not have it, he would break it. Of course, the most detestable example of this trait came in the form of his brother's wife. Kaitain wanted her only because she wanted Feyd. Only wanted her because she had Feyd's child when she had the opportunity to be the mother to the Imperial Heir. But she had the audacity to chase love rather than power. And for that transgression, for that crime, Kaitain took great pleasure in having her killed by the Shadow Guild. It was not enough to simply kill the woman, she had to be defiled in as many ways as possible. Using the forbidden magic practiced by Yaron Telsin, Kaitain had material retrieved from the woman that enabled the creation of a child. Alise was formed from the blood of a dead woman and the living tissue of her demonic father. She never had a childhood, her growth accelerated from fetus to teenager in a matter of hours, and she was taught by the darkest of teachers how to maim, murder, and destroy anything in her path. She had but one allegiance, and that was to her father. She had but one responsibility, to follow all of his orders without question. There could be no failure. Failure was death. And that was the only absolute.

Alise was a good student. She learned the arcane forces of the world from Yaron Telsin, the martial practices from Korin Melcab, and the ways of the assassin from Geoffry Aramour. Her mind and body were honed into the perfect weapon. Her first kill was a simple one. A dignitary from Bellnoc was overheard saying disparaging things about Kaitain while he was still heir to the throne, and before the death of Ender Lorien. Kaitain had no intention of letting the slight stand, and so he dispatched Alise to deal with the man. The mission was simple, to make an example of the man so that no one else would dear to speak ill of the crown prince. Alise caught up with the dignitary's caravan just as it left the imperial province of Aldere. She perched on a limb above the road and waited for the carriage to pass by before she fell upon the carriage's driver, severing his head from his body with a single slash. He pulled up so hard on the reins that the carriage nearly flipped on its side. As it was, the doors were thrown open and the dignitary, his wife, and his two children were thrown from the carriage. One of the children was killed when her head hit a rock, and the other was run over by the back wheel of the carriage. Before the dignitary knew what was happening, Alise was upon him, her claws ripping into his stomach and spilling his entrails upon the ground. It was a horrific death, but did not last nearly as long as it could have. Alise turned her attention to the man's wife. Alise pinned the woman to the side of the carriage with a dagger through her shoulder, and then smeared her husband's blood all over her face. Just before the guards from the front of the caravan arrived to investigate, Alise had disappeared, but not before whispering in the woman's ear that slights against the good name of Kaitain Lorien would never go unpunished.

Over the next few years, the missions and the bloodshed blurred together. So many faceless victims, so much pointless vengeance. However, once Kaitain ascended to the throne, Alise believed that she would be used for more important purposes than whispered insults and imagined slights. It was her first mission in her new position however that would change Kaitain's opinion of her. She was dispatched to murder Feyd and Felicia Lorien, and had she succeeded, it would have changed the very nature of Cadaria forever. However, she was unable to complete her mission due to the interference of a man named Wynne. The man's name still caused her blood to burn, and the need to revenge herself upon him ached in her bones. But following that failure, Alise was pushed into the background. There was the attempt on Kaitain's life, and Alise's failure to eliminate Vallic Ultiv. Alise found herself lost, listless. When Kaitain recovered, their relationship was not the same. They were both broken in some way, and though Kaitain still counted her among his closest and most trusted allies, the madness had taken nearly everything from him. He could no longer distinguish between friend and foe, and he raged at everyone and everything and was indecisive. Many nights Alise would be called to his room for an assignment. He would detail who he wanted killed, their transgressions against him, and then by the end of the conversation he would change his mind and dismiss Alise without giving her the order.

The center of those plots always involved the same people, the ones that Kaitain blamed for his waning power in the eyes of the people. Alise knew that Kaitain did not care about the opinion of the people, which was why the rambling justifications for his plans never made sense. Kaitain's nature was to rule through fear and blood. He had no desire to be loved; no desire to be popular in the hearts of his people. That was a critical difference between Kaitain and his demonic daughter Marlae. Kaitain would have crushed any resistance to his rule and bullied the remainder into supplication and submission. Marlae on the other hand wanted the adoration, needed it. She wanted everyone to love and desire her no matter how poorly she treated them. Both of those lessons came from Kaitain of course, one purposeful, one accidental. The need for love came from Kaitain's complete indifference to those in his life who should have been the recipients of his love, and the other came from Kaitain's callous nature when it came to human life.

Alise also felt these lessons, though she was bred to be a killer, not a ruler. Alise did not need love to survive, but she did need to kill. That was all she was for. That was what she was bred to be. And so, there was no concern or guilt within her when Kaitain began to plot to loose Alise upon his other daughter. Marlae was the one who drew the most of Kaitain's ire. However, Alise believed that Kaitain never gave the order to assassinate his daughter because somewhere deep inside of himself he admired what she was attempting to do. It certainly wasn't out of love, or guilt, or remorse. Alise recognized that those emotions were not in the makeup of Kaitain Lorien. Even in his rage, there was a recognition of the gall that Marlae showed, and her willingness to attempt to take what Kaitain had. But no matter how many times Alise was angrily summoned to Kaitain's chambers and she listened to him rage on, sometimes for hours about the audacity and disloyalty of his own daughter, he would never send Alise on the mission to murder Marlae. In her own way, Alise was relieved that she was not required to kill Marlae. While Alise did not believe that there would be a moment that Kaitain would outwardly show regret for his decision, that was a weight that Alise did not want to carry. Perhaps in the future Kaitain would blame Alise and not himself for the situation involving his daughter and heir, and would use that against Alise should she fail in one of her assignments. Regret never tends to come out in the best of times.

Targets that Kaitain would not regret murdering however were Dominique Arais and Chelsea Zarova. They were often discussed in the same breath and with the same level of vitriol. The same audacity that Kaitain had a grudging respect for in the willfulness of his daughter was reviled in his wife. He would often call Dominique the brainless broodmare, as he believed her only use was as a receptacle for his carnal passions. What made her believe that she had either the intellect or the fortitude to attempt to lead his empire? Late in the evenings when Kaitain had had too much to drink he would often muse that the gutless would-be assassin had never intended to kill Kaitain, that the poison was only designed to give his bumbling worthless bride the opportunity to destroy his empire while he slept. For a time, he believed that Marlae had been the architect of the seemingly failed plot to assassinate him, and when the knowledge came to light that the bolt from the assassin's crossbow had only been intended to maim and incapacitate the emperor, his suspicion of his daughter's involvement grew even deeper. It was the kind of assault that Marlae certainly would find fitting. She would relish the opportunity to disfigure and humiliate her father and then swoop in to take over the Throne. Instead, however, while Kaitain slept, Dominique had the audacity to believe that she could manage the empire on her own.

There had never been an Empress of Cadaria, and as far as Kaitain was concerned, there never should be. Women were not fit to lead in Kaitain's opinion. That was one of the reasons he had no respect for the Masters of the Academy of Arcane Arts, and why he had little in the way of respect for the female members of the Knights of the Flashing Blade. It certainly wasn't a coincidence that none of the new members of the Knights were women. The only major post that was given to a woman was that of Court Sorceress, and that was purely meant as a way to irritate the Masters of the Academy. Despite the annoyance that Dominique's hubris caused Kaitain, he also would not fully commit to any order that would terminate her life. Alise believed that this was for two reasons. The first was that if he had her killed, it would be an admission that he perceived her as a threat to his rule. The second, and perhaps the more troubling of the two was that Dominique was universally loved by the people, and her death would create nothing more than another martyr that could be claimed as motivation against Kaitain, especially as Kaitain countermanded the policies that Dominique arrogantly put into place.

Chelsea Zarova was the other half of the Dominique problem, and the greater part of it as far as Kaitain was concerned. In Kaitain's mind, while Dominique was too weak to find the will to enact policies for the empire without Kaitain's council or approval, Chelsea Zarova was not. She was hostile, callous, and hated men. As far as Kaitain was concerned she wasn't even a woman, as she actually believed that she was a man's equal. In

Kaitain's mind, such a thing was preposterous. One night when he was very drunk, Kaitain mused that Chelsea probably felt that she was a more appropriate and compatible sexual partner for Dominique. He considered loudly having Alise subdue Chelsa and make her watch as Kaitain used his empress for the only thing she was good for before dispatching them both. But he never got further than idle rage on that subject. Where Kaitin's rage was fully ignited by Chelsea Zarova, was the fact that she was an accomplished warrior, had the respect of her peers, and if there was a singular person who could lead an armed insurrection against Kaitain, it would have been the Wolf of Saldarine. But again, Chelsea was not an easy obstacle to remove without consequence. With tensions at an all-time-high between Thorigald and Saldarine, thanks to manipulation by Kaitain and his allies, the death of Chelsea Zarova could have sparked Saldarine renouncing membership in the Cadarian Empire and becoming a rogue state. Such a turn of events was unacceptable. Though Kaitain had no fear that the Imperial Army could crush any attempted coup, he was already fighting a war on several other fronts, and it was not worth his time or attention. And so Kaitain chose to keep his enemies close rather than to eliminate them, though he reserved the right to change his mind.

But then all of the petty things disappeared. Kaitain became fixated on the Dragon's Tear and all of the miraculous things that it could do. He cared less about being the Emperor of Cadaria and began to fixate on the possibility of being a god. That was what brought Tess Annis into Kaitain's life, and that was ultimately what resulted in his death and the place that Alise found herself. Kneeling in the middle of a body-less graveyard, a startling revelation came to Alise's mind. Though she was not free of the influence of her somewhat father, she still defined herself by the successes and failures of his whims and the petty rages that drove his agenda. For perhaps the first time in her life, Alise realized that she had no definition without Kaitain. It was a very sobering and disconcerting feeling. She had never been forced to define herself. She lived from assignment to assignment, always dependent upon the orders of others. If Kaitain was not giving her assignments, she would receive orders from Geoffry Aramour. But outside of those two people, no one but her targets knew that she existed, and they were all dead. For all intents and purposes, she was a non-entity. She had no title, no home, no money of her own, and no real skills beyond killing. The truth, however, was that she would always be able to get by on killing if she wanted to. There would always be someone willing to pay her for her skill, and if they tried to take advantage of her, she had no compunction against killing them as well. But that would make for a lonely existence, however long her existence lasted.

That was another question that Alise never gave herself time to ask. Due to the nature of her own existence, it was unclear how long she would live. In all reality, she was barely six years old, but her maturity and her power was of a woman five times that age. The unstable arcane forces that forged her could not be trusted to sustain her life, nor had anyone been forthright with how long she could survive. Would she live another year? Another five? Now that Yaron Telsin and Kaitain Lorien were dead, was there anyone left who knew the secrets to her existence and what remained of it? Would she age? Would she simply cease to go on one day? Did she even deserve to go on?

The one thing that Alise knew for sure was that she needed to find answers. But where could she go? With Kaitain and Yaron Telsin gone, the Black Academy or at least what was left of them would go underground and be nearly impossible to find. The same could likely be said for the rest of the Hand of Chaos and the other creatures that Telsin claimed as his allies. As far as legitimate sources of information, the Academy of Arcane Arts and the Masters of the Academy were gone. The Peaks of Patience had been destroyed, which meant that the Order of the Flickering Flame was likely gone as well. There was no one in the Heart of Stone that would be able to help her, as the study of arcane forces were taboo for the students in the Heart. The few members of the Knights of the Flashing Blade who had any arcane knowledge were either missing or dead. That left only one option. Alise would have to seek out the Dark Gods and hope that they would be willing to listen to her rather than simply ending her existence. There had been sightings of the Dark Gods in the recent days, but Alise had one particular member in mind; one that would bring her full circle and perhaps help her find the meaning that she was looking for.

Ever since her confrontation with the man who called himself Wynne, Alise had had her suspicions about the nature of the man. The way that he fought and the manner in which he repelled her attacks made it clear that he was not a normal man. At first, Alise thought that it was her own arrogance and confidence in her abilities that made her believe that anyone who could best her in combat was more than human. But the more she replayed that confrontation in her mind, the way that he held himself and the way that he was able to allude all of her methods of tracking him could not be denied. If he wasn't a member of the Dark Gods, perhaps he would know the best way to locate them. He would have no reason to help her of course, considering the fact that she had vowed to be the end of his life, but perhaps his good nature would be enough to overcome his need for self-preservation.

Alise forced her way to her feet and centered herself. She still had the taste of Wynne's blood on her lips and the smell of him in her nose. Given enough time she would be able to feel her way to him using just a modicum of the power that she had at her disposal. Reaching out with her enhance senses, she caught the faint smell of him on the wind. It was coming from the west, in the direction of Aldere. The other man's tracks, the ones that Logan had made following his apparent victory over Tess Annis led in that direction. Was that where he was headed? Was he perhaps an ally of Wynne's? Perhaps Logan would have information that would help her understand what she was to do next. Then a startling thought came to Alise's mind. A power like Tess's could not simply cease to be. What if this Logan had somehow stolen Tess's powers for himself? Did this make him the same kind of threat that Tess became? No single person should have had that kind of power, especially Alise conceded, someone like Kaitain Lorien. In hindsight, perhaps it was better that Tess had put an end to him. The world largely would be a better place, even Alise had to grudgingly admit. But there was one inescapable truth.

Cadaria was a land of villains, it had always been and it would always be. From the time of the Founding Wars all the way to the birth of Kaitain Lorien, there had always been someone who believed that the world existed to serve them. There had always been wars, assassinations, and palace intrigue that fueled each and every iteration of the Cadarian Empire. Some of the villains were benign, causing problems only on the small scale. Others like Kaitain Lorien and the Lord Grawn were malignant and sought to bend the very nature of everything to their will. And though Kaitain Lorien was gone, soon enough, after all of the wars and ideological nonsense passed, things would settle back to the truth of humanity. Greed would infest the heart of someone with a little power and make them thirst for more. And as Kaitain often said, there was little that separated heroes from villains. Both heroes and villains killed. Both heroes and villains were willing to ignore law and subvert authority to advance their agendas. The principle difference between a hero and a villain was that while each had power, a villain was willing to do anything to get more, and in the end, the reason that one was called a hero and the other was called a villain depended upon who won the conflict.

Alise Modrall knew that she was a villain. What she was unsure about was whether or not she wanted to stay a villain. Even more than that, she wondered if she even had a choice.

The Knights

Orren

As a member of the Knights of the Flashing Blade, Orren Eldrath was supposed to be able to handle diplomatic situations in any of the Great Kingdoms of Cadaria. Of course, he hadn't gotten much of a chance before the world went mad. Now, he would have given anything to be in Albitonin representing either the Emperor or Rashaleb for some high-minded purpose, but instead he sat alone in a room waiting to fight a battle he barely understood. Orren considered himself an intelligent person, and yet in a short period of time he was faced with far too many things that made him question that assessment. At the Academy of Arcane Arts in Jelan, Orren was a good student. Some might have even said that he was a little too good. Orren liked solving puzzles, and the more complicated the puzzle, the more Orren loved trying to solve it. For the most part, Orren stayed in his books, in his puzzles, trying to do exactly what all of the other students in the Academy did. Then Ayden came to the Academy. Most of the other students at the Academy had one of three opinions about Ayden. The first and most common was that Ayden was perhaps the most irritating human being on the face of Espre. Ayden was a prodigy, even to other prodigies. But for every bit of talent that he had, he had twice as much ego. There was never a moment when he wasn't talking, bragging, or telling stories about his exploits, real and imagined. The more he talked, the more he irritated people, largely because for all of his bluster he had the capacity to back it up with ability. There were others that admired Ayden because of his skill and wanted to be like him. The idolatry only seemed to bring out the worst in Ayden. He constantly looked for new ways to impress those who looked up to him. It made his stunts more fantastical, which irritated more people, and increased the adoration of others. Whether he was changing the gravity in the hallways, changing all the water in the cisterns and bathtubs into wine, or making clothing shift one person to the left in the middle of class; the more daring the stunt the more Ayden got exactly what he wanted, attention.

Ayden inspired people. That inspiration came in many forms, but the inspiration that struck Orren was suspicion. Ayden should not have been as powerful as he was, moreover, Orren had his suspicions that Ayden was holding back. Students at the Academy of Arcane Arts did not come into their new abilities fully aware of their capabilities and limitations. At times the learning curve could be steep, while at other times it could be dangerous and disjointed. When Orren began his studies at the Academy, it took a long time for him to understand the relationship between what he could feel in the world around him and how to bend it to his will. Of course at the time, Orren Eldrath did not have any idea of what he was capable of, nor did he have any frame of reference beyond stories and the imagination of youth. Orren fondly remembered the first time that he consciously was able to do anything with his abilities. He had been studying for almost a month in the Academy, and most of the other students who had entered the Academy at the same time were already able to light candles with consistency. It was the first lesson that the teachers at the Academy taught, and it required not only concentration but control. For hours on end, Orren would sit at his table, the candle in front of him. In the back of his mind, he could feel the flows of fire and he fumbled with them in the same way that one would fumble trying to find their clothing in a dark room. When he would find a way to take hold of the flows, it was never quite with any dexterity, and it took quite a bit of effort to get things aligned the way they should be. After time, Orren was able to take hold of the flows of fire with regularity, but then connecting those flows to the wick of the candle was the challenge. It wasn't like aiming an arrow at a target and watching it launch from the bow. It was more like trying to flick the end of a string and make it stick on a small spot on the other side of the room. At least, that was what it was like in the beginning. There was a part of manipulating the arcane forces that Orren would not understand until later. Instinct and intention played much more of a role in the manipulation than any kind of tangible physical skill. And so, when he continued to fail time and time again with lighting the candle, his frustration boiled over.

While the students were constantly admonished against berating and belittling each other based on their progress in their studies, there was a great deal of competition between the younger students to master skills before the others. There was a fair bit of teasing and snide comments aimed at those who were not as advanced as the other students, and a pseudo caste system rose up around who accomplished what and how quickly. There was one student, roughly six months older than Orren, who took a great deal of pleasure in reminding Orren how his progress was significantly slower than those his age. This student, whose name was Vineram, was the only son of a fairly prominent family in Zevarit, and believed that his superior lineage was the reason for his quick mastery of his lessons. He had openly boasted that he was going to be one of the next Masters of the Academy, and that all of the other students needed to get used to the fact that he was clearly superior. After one too many comments about Orren's lack of progress, Orren resolved that he needed to prove Vineram wrong, and needed to show that he belonged at the Academy.

Sitting in the classroom, staring at his candle, Orren focused all of his intention on lighting the candle, but again failed. Vineram, as was the routine, was the first to light his candle and sat back with his arms folded, a smug expression on his face. After several moments, Vineram started looking around the room to see the status of the other students. When he finally looked back in Orren's direction, the smirk on the boy's face was enough to cause something to snap within Orren. At that moment Orren completely forgot about the candle and the flows of fire. All he wanted to do was blow out the candle sitting on Vineram's desk. The next thing Orren knew, a small cloud had appeared over Vineram's head and rain began to fall onto him in steady torrents. The candle went out immediately, but the rain did not stop falling. The teacher, Fiona Ebonsight, could have dispelled the cloud immediately, but she let the rain go on for several moments before finally waving it away with a subtle motion of her hand. What Orren had done was far more advanced than anything the students at that level had been taught, and it marked Orren as a student to watch.

As Orren advanced and learned, each lesson opened his mind to new possibilities. In the same way that the irritation over the failures of the candle test had made Orren aware of the importance of intention, the very nature of the lessons being taught made Orren realize something very important about the Academy. The Academy did not teach students in a way that lessons translated directly to skills. The instructors at the Academy taught concepts and constructs, but it was up to the students to make the connections for themselves between the theory and the practice. It was continually said that the mastery over the arcane was not rote recitation of incantations from moldy old books. The power over the arcane was a very personal connection, and it was as much a philosophical pursuit as it was an intellectual one. The Academy was not interested in creating drones. The Academy was not a military organization that wanted mindless soldiers who only knew how to follow orders and kill. Perhaps it went back to the old prohibitions against using the powers of the arcane to kill; students of the Academy of Arcane Arts were required to learn a personal connection to their abilities, and therefore always knew the cost. Armies did not want their soldiers to think about the cost of their actions. They only wanted the most efficient killers possible. Use of the arcane was not efficient by any stretch of the imagination. It was messy, emotional, and personal in a way that made it ill-suited for martial use. Better to spend time contemplating the nature of the Cosmos rather than learning how to immolate the soldiers of an opposing army. Better to learn how to encourage the soil to create more plentiful crops than to force the ground beneath a castle to open and swallow it whole. These were the fundamental philosophies that the Masters guided their students toward, and it was the process of growing into that power that engrained those philosophies in the hearts of every student.

This brought Orren back to Ayden. While all of the other students grew slowly into their powers, Ayden simply seemed to know what to do once he was presented with a lesson. Once he saw something he simply could do it. There was no curve, no self-reflection and identification, there was simply power. What's more, Orren constantly felt that Ayden was holding back. This was further proven in Orren's mind by the continual stunts that Ayden perpetrated on both other students and the Masters of the Academy. Ayden unconsciously connected lessons that students twice his age had never even considered connecting, and some of his displays seemed to baffle even the Masters. But there was an unintended consequence of Ayden's easy power. The more Ayden excelled, the more jealousy he inspired in those who believed that they were every bit as talents as the laid-back and disaffected Ayden. That of course was part of the problem; the more casual that Ayden was with every trial that he passed, the more it infuriated the would-be superior students like Vineram. To that end, Vineram pushed himself further and further down dangerous paths, exposing himself to teachings far beyond what he was ready for. It could only end one way, in disaster. It should have been much worse. Vineram had gotten his hands on a text from a former Grand Master of the Academy, something not just years ahead of his level of knowledge, but perhaps so far out of his intellectual grasp that he would never be capable of fully understanding it. But that did not stop him from trying. Spurred by his desire to close the gap between himself and Ayden, Vineram pushed himself further and further, ignoring the first rules taught at the Academy. The study of the arcane was not for the accumulation of power or for the advancement of one over others. The arcane could only be used for the advancement of society at large. Despite how he tried to control the new power he had accessed, the enterprise was ultimately doomed to failure, and Vineram lost control. No one at the Academy was ever certain of what Vineram was trying to accomplish, but when it went bad, the outcome was explosive. The entirety of the room where he was studying was consumed by an inferno of such intensity that it melted the stone of the walls and floor. A dozen other study rooms were similarly destroyed, and it took quite some time to determine the number of missing and dead. By the time all was said and done, twenty students were dead, thirty more were injured, and two full floors in the east wing of the Academy were unusable. Unfortunately, this was not the first time such accidents had occurred, and it certainly would not be the last. This was where Orren and the Academy began to be at cross purposes.

When he was young, Orren understood that trust in the instruction of the Masters and the other instructors at the Academy was a must for progression. Young minds were not ready to grasp the complexities of the arcane without guidance, and that guidance, in the manner in which the Academy chose to teach, came with a price. That price, unfortunately was a dependance that Orren found grating. The Masters and instructors of the Academy were rigid in their adherence to a method of teaching and a schedule for that teaching. It did not preclude the students from seeking their own knowledge in the same way that Vineram had. Orren felt that there were too many similarities between the Academy of Arcane Arts and the Church of the Creator. The Masters, like the priests of the Church, preached about the necessity of personal responsibility and following the path laid out by the teachings. Every quest for knowledge was a test, and those who put knowledge above responsibility would always find poor results to their quests. Orren began to resent the Masters and the lies that seemed to form the basis of the Academy. How could someone like Ayden Seth be allowed to masquerade as a student, encouraging dangerous and subversive behavior by other students? Surely the Masters knew what had driven Vineram to the acts that had ended his life and the lives of so many others. And yet they did nothing to stop him. They did nothing to dissuade others from taking the same path. How many others would die or be permanently crippled because of the disinterest of the Masters?

Orren made it his personal mission to understand the manner in which the Academy was founded and the reason for the rules that formed the foundation of its teachings. He gathered all of the writings that he could find, spending hours pouring over hand-written notes that were both in ancient dialects that were no longer in use and also those that were in codes that were nearly impossible to break. Impossible for some, but certainly not for Orren. In time he began to piece together some of the most closely guarded secrets of the Academy, including the fact that it had been the first Grand Master of the Shadow Guild who had created the foundation for the Academy of Arcane Arts with the first Emperor of Cadaria. The intention of the Academy was to prevent those who could natively touch the powers of the arcane from being used to destabilize the fledgling empire or start another Founding War. It was a method of control, and one that had endured for almost two thousand years. The fact that the Masters of the Academy were undoubtedly aware of this made their continued adherence to the code nothing less than a betrayal to every single student who had ever set foot on the grounds of the Academy. Orren made it his personal mission to create a new charter for the Academy, and to define a new destiny for all of those that were born with the talent to feel and manipulate the arcane forces of the Cosmos.

Unlike Kaitain Lorien's attempt to pervert those who could touch the arcane in the form of his Black Academy, Orren did not lust for power or for control. He simply wanted to create a place where those who were special could determine their own path forward. Orren thought it unfair that the Academy of Arcane Arts, despite its power and influence in the Cadarian Empire were still considered subjects of the Kingdom of Oradrim. But despite their inclusion in the Kingdom, no member of the Academy had ever been eligible to be a member of the Knights of the Flashing Blade or had been considered for leadership in the kingdom. So, despite how special those who could touch the arcane were, they were forbidden from ever attaining anything other than being controlled by those people who could never understand the responsibility they faced. For two thousand years the rules that had been created to control the students of the Academy had created generations of second-class citizens. The Academy represented a prison of fear. The Grand Master of the Shadow Guild had feared that the wielders of the arcane could be used. The first Emperor of Cadaria feared that the wielders of the arcane could unmake everything. The first group of Masters of the Academy feared that if their students knew the truth that they would lose control. The royalty of Oradrim feared that their power would be undermined by those they could never truly match. The superior were being held down by the inferior, and only by earning their freedom from the oppressive systems that had held them in bondage could the students of the Academy truly be considered citizens of Cadaria.

For so long every system that made Cadaria the place it was had ignored the gifted. The only way that the students of the Academy would be on even footing with the rest of the Cadarians was if they were granted their own kingdom. Orren began by drafting an outline by which the city of Jelan, which was the home of the Academy of Arcane Arts would become its own sovereign kingdom within Cadaria. It was not without precedent, and the laws of the Cadarian Empire had guidelines within it which detailed the circumstances by which a new Great Kingdom could be formed. The first and most important of these guidelines was the fact that the region that was to become its own kingdom had to have stable leadership that would be recognized as such by the Emperor of Cadaria. That would not be an issue when it came to the Academy of Arcane Arts. The Masters of the Academy of Arcane Arts had well-defined roles and rules for the assumption of their posts. Additionally, the Masters of the Academy had been recognized by the Emperor of Cadaria and had served as advisors with distinction, at least until Kaitain Lorien came into power. The second of the guidelines had to do with the economic impact on both the region that would become a new kingdom and whether or not an existing kingdom would be negatively impacted by the restructuring. This was a trickier situation to quantify, and one that Orren was working on outlining when the world went mad.

Estelle Ravenheart died, and there was never a clear reason given as to how it occurred. The shock had barely begun to wear off when word of the Grey Man Pestilence made its way to the Academy, and Alistair Ravenheart was called to the Imperial Palace of Jelan to give council to the emperor over how to deal with the plague that was ravaging the countryside in the creature's wake. When Alistair picked Irene Drage to accompany him to Aldere, it raised the ire of many within the Academy, none more than Ayden Seth. Everyone knew that Irene was an excellent student, but Ayden was merciless on the girl. He continually pointed out her shortcomings and the fact that she should not have been favored over the clearly more talented students in the Academy. He stopped short of accusing Alistair of having an affair with the young pretty girl, but only just. Orren remembered a shouting match that occurred between Ayden and Quyhn Ravenheart. She had finally had enough of his bullying ways and confronted him in the courtyard one day. Ayden smirked and laughed as Quyhn aired her grievances, and when she finally grew tired of his smug attitude, she slapped him. While Ayden showed no outward effect of the situation, Orren remembered seeing an impossible fire in the young man's eyes. Orren feared for Quyhn's safety for just a moment and had started in their direction to place himself between the two. However, before Orren could take a single step, the danger had passed and the murderous look in Ayden's eyes had faded. He laughed and turned away, laughing to himself. A day later, Alistair, Quyhn, and Irene left for Aldere, and the Academy was placed into the hands of the other four Masters. Then Alistair was gone.

Nothing made sense at that point, and Orren's suspicions could no longer be denied. He grew reckless and broke into Alistair's private study and rifled through his notes looking for something, anything that would make sense. He stumbled onto a small notebook in a locked drawer that detailed Alistair's observations about Ayden Seth. Though there was little in the realm of specifics, it was clear from the notes that there was something more about Ayden than anyone knew. Alistair carefully charted each of the powers that Ayden manifested and the manner in which those powers manifested. He was very interested in how the powers that Ayden manifested paralleled with those that he as well the other Masters were able to produce through their mastery of the arcane. It struck Orren that the manner in which Alistair made his notes recognized that Ayden was not like the other students at the Academy. There was a creeping doubt that crawled into Orren's heart, and at that point he guessed at the truth. Ayden was a Dark God, and somehow Alistair had allowed a Dark God to join the Academy of Arcane Arts. Orren's intrusion did not go unnoticed. When Orren looked up from the notes he was pouring over, he saw Fiona Ebonsight standing in the doorway. Rather than making some kind of excuse or trying to talk his way out of the obvious transgression, Orren confronted Fiona with the information that he found. When the acting Grand Master did nothing to deny Orren's suspicions, he wasn't sure how he was supposed to feel. He was confined to his quarters while Fiona determined his fate.

Orren's expulsion was assured, and the story that was spun about his studying of forbidden topics was a convenient cover. It had just enough truth within it and would prevent uncomfortable questions. Yes, it would make Orren into a pariah, but he didn't care about that. What Orren cared about was the fact that the institution that he had dedicated his life to was far more hypocritical and corrupt than he had first feared. Even though Alistair had known what Ayden was, he still allowed the man to cause the amount of damage that he caused. The knowledge and curiosity at all costs was a fallacy. The realization of it changed Orren Eldrath irrevocably. But what Orren had to admit, as he stood looking out the window of his small quarters in the Heart of Stone, that shocking dose of reality was what prepared him for what would come after.

It was easy to see what Kaitain Lorien was trying to accomplish when he named a clearly unqualified Orren Eldrath to the ranks of the Knights of the Flashing Blade. Kaitain Lorien had nothing but disdain for the Academy and he was doing everything in his power to alienate them. Whether it was expelling the Masters from the Imperial Court, or naming

Irene Drage as the Court Sorceress, Kaitain's disrespect could be felt with every act. Orren Eldrath, while he understood the purpose of his appointment was not one of Kaitain's puppets. Kaitain thought that he was getting someone whom he could use to hone the lethality of his Black Academy, someone who bristled at the strictures of the Academy. But the truth was that Orren understood why the students of the Academy were prevented from killing. The arcane was to be respected. It was not a tool of destruction, though it could be used to destroy. It was the very essence of everything, and the more it was manipulated for destructive purposes, the more it could destabilize reality. Even though Orren had been expelled from the institution, he was still bound by its laws, and even if he hadn't been, he would still adhere to them. Of course, in time, none of that would matter, and Aryx Terian would shatter everything Orren thought he knew about the world around him.

Now Orren understood what the Dark Gods really were. He knew why Irene Drage had gained her position within the Imperial Court, and he saw the machinations around him in a way that scared him to the core. No human should have had the knowledge that Orren now had access too, not even the vaunted Masters of the Academy of Arcane Arts. Humans were not made for such things. At least, not the humans of Espre. The people of the world known as Onea were human, but they were clearly different than those of Espre. Their minds worked differently, their imaginations, their ambitions. They seemed far more rebellious and unwilling to accept what was placed in front of them. Heroes like Logan Ranthall and Gwydeon Sandar fought and questioned because it was the right thing to do, and they were curious in a way that would not allow them to be shackled to the lies that forged the life around them. Was there a member of the Knights of the Flashing Blade that Orren could have seen doing what any of the heroes of Onea had done? Was there any single person within Espre who would have stood for humanity had the fog not been cleansed from their eyes by someone who had already seen the horrors waiting beyond the veil? There was a time in his life that Orren was arrogant enough to think that he could change things, but now that he had seen the truth through the eyes of someone who had lived a life of war and heroism, Orren knew that he was not that caliber of man. What could not be denied however was that Aryx Terian had seen something in Orren

Eldrath, and whatever that quality was, Orren was determined to prove Aryx right.

What Orren had not expected however, was the bond that would come with the powers and the responsibility. Orren could feel Felicia Lorien, and knew exactly where she was in the Heart. In some ways he could feel her uncertainty and her fear in the battle that was coming. What he could also feel was her anxiety. Orren felt it too. Even as the suns were starting to lighten the sky to the east, there was the feeling of something coming. Malice was on the wind, and it would only be a matter of hours, if not minutes before the war for the very soul of Cadaria would begin. After fighting one of the Adhradair briefly, as well as seeing the power of those who were in the service of the Children of the Creator, Orren was unsure if he was going to be up to the task. Even as doubt began to gnaw at his soul, Orren felt the confidence and resolve flow from Felicia. She too had been humbled by the battle with the Adhradair, but she was not going to let it beat her. She was stronger than Orren by far, and he in some ways could not relate to her strength. But that strength was what he needed. He was not going to let her down, no matter what.

Chelsea

The Heart of Stone was quiet, but Chelsea Zarova knew that it would not be that way for much longer. She knew that she should have been trying to get some sleep, but even if she tried, Chelsea knew that there would be no sleep to be found. So, Chelsea did the only thing she knew how to do in her situation, and that was to walk the grounds of the Heart and familiarize herself with the battlefield. It was a habit that she developed early in her time with the Army of Fire when she was just a rank-and-file soldier. In her earliest days as a soldier, Chelsea felt like an outsider among the other soldiers. There was a period of time when women serving in the military was forbidden across the whole of Cadaria. It was an archaic law born out of the Founding Wars when elements of the Army of Thorigald under the control of the Lord Shark targeted women and children indiscriminately. Once the wars were ended and Cadaria was united under the banner of the Lorien family, the law forbidding women to fight was instituted along with laws forbidding the targeting of non-combatants. The first exemptions to the law were enacted in Thorigald and Saldarine because of the losses that the war between those two Kingdoms incurred. It caused a great deal of consternation in the other Great Kingdoms which led to an eventual repeal of the law prohibiting the service of women in the military with two exceptions. The first and most important exception was the fact that women were barred from serving in the Imperial Legion. The other exception was in Albitonin where women were forbidden from joining the paladin core that protected the Heart of Stone. But despite the change in law, women were still considered by the long-standing military establishment to be undesirable.

Women who chose to attempt the military route found their lives and dignities under assault at nearly every turn. They were given challenges that even their male counterparts would have found difficult and were humiliated into admitting that they were not capable of the rigors of the military. Those that refused to quit and somehow made it through the terrible and painful initiation rituals often found themselves serving under violent and abusive superiors whose only goal seemed to be to make their lives a living hell. Some of those women bore scars deeper than any they would find in combat. But it did not deter others for fighting for a place of acceptance, and as the years dragged on, the unwritten prohibitions lessened but were never truly erased. That was still true when Chelsea entered the military. She was one of three women who entered the Army of Fire at the same time, and all three of the women suffered the same abuse. They were run longer, they were worked harder, and they found their rations cut and their sleep disturbed. That was when Chelsea's constant battle against sleep began. One night, after she had been roused by a pan being banged too close to her head, she wandered through the camp trying to quiet her mind and the anger that threatened to boil over. She heard muffled screams and rustling coming from behind one of the tents. Every instinct in her was telling her to keep walking. She had been warned by the few female soldiers that had survived before her to keep her head down and not to put herself in danger. But something was different about that night. Something within Chelsea snapped. A red haze fell over her vision and she didn't remember exactly what transpired after that. All she had were flashes. She crossed the distance between where she stood and where the rustling was coming from in a flash. She didn't see the man's face at first, nor the woman's, but she could hear the muffled cries, the sound of tearing fabric, and the smell of tears, sweat, and fear. Chelsea was on top of the man the next moment, ripping at his flesh with her fingernails and snarling like a wild animal. The taste of flesh and blood was in her mouth the next moment, as she had unconsciously ripped at his throat with her teeth. But the time the red haze had disappeared, the other woman was long gone, and Chelsea was sitting on the ground covered in the man's blood, his gurgling gasps sickening and filled with fear.

CHELSEA

She was arrested and thrown in a cell, never allowed to even clean the blood off her face and out from under her fingernails. Formal charges were prepared against her but were never brought. The soldier recovered from his injuries, but barely. He would never speak without an impediment ever again, and the damage that Chelsea had done to him would have prevented him from ever assaulting anyone ever again. For three days Chelsea sat in the cell, living on bread and water. Finally, one day a man came and opened her cell and told her that she was free to return to her duties. One of her superiors had all charges against her expunged and had even recommended her for a commendation for protecting her fellow soldiers from a surprise attack by an assassin from Thorigald. When she returned to the barracks the other soldiers looked at her with different eyes. Behind her back as she made her way back to her bunk, she heard one of the soldiers call her a wolf. The name stuck, and from that moment forward Chelsea was the Wolf of Saldarine. Over the years the tale behind the birth of the name changed to something more palatable, and Chelsea never bothered to try to correct the misconceptions. A legend usually worked better without the inconvenience of truth. Those acts, the acts that gave birth to the Wolf of Saldarine had brought her to the attention of very dangerous and powerful people in the hierarchy of the Army of Fire. It had been the man calling himself Arin Chandara, the man that Chelsea now knew was the villain Korrd Ranthall, who had arranged for her release and exoneration. The then General Chandara took great interest in Chelsea's career, and it was then that her meteoric rise through the ranks began.

Chelsea wanted to believe that everything she gained in the Army of Fire was done on her own merits. Every task that was asked of her, she excelled at. She was fearless and fierce, and she intimidated the other solders in her own detachment as much as she intimidated the enemy on the field of battle. There was always a nagging feeling in the back of her mind however that someone kept a finger on the scales for her. Eventually, everyone in the Army of Fire began to respect Chelsea more than they feared her, and the Wolf of Saldarine became comfortable in her own skin. It was then that she allowed herself the relationship with Arin Chandara and everything that followed. He never distracted from her duty. He never tried to shield her from danger, and if anything, he seemed to give her sensitive and dangerous assignments, at least until she was forced to take her sabbatical from the army to address her secret pregnancy. By the time

Chelsea returned, Arin Chandara's role in the Army of Fire had changed, and Chelsea had been elevated to the position of general. In a short amount of time, Chelsea was the tactical commander of all of the forces of the Army of Fire, and was on the short list for elevation to the Knights of the Flashing Blade.

Chelsea's role in the Knights of the Flashing Blade did not take her away from her role as the general of the Army of Fire very often, except for rare diplomatic missions or relief operations in other kingdoms. Most often she found herself in the neighboring kingdoms of Iltorp or Albitonin to mediate disputes or deal with incursions from the Army of Water, dragons, or rogue creatures from the Kingdom of Night. Chelsea had actually had many opportunities to spend time in Albitonin, and many opportunities to spend time with Hannah Ironheart and her husband Gregor Quicksilver. Chelsea didn't exactly consider Hannah her friend, but they were somewhat closer than acquaintances. To that end, Hannah had given Chelsea several tours of the fortifications of the Heart of Stone, allowing Chelsea an opportunity to assess one of the most heavily fortified structures in the whole of Cadaria.

Chelsea was not a stranger to fighting, as she had spent most of her life doing it. She had fought in swamps, on plains, in forests, and in cities. Chelsea had been trained to make the best of any tactical situation, whether fighting on the offense or in defense, undermanned or with superior numbers. Nothing in her years of warfare had forced her to prepare herself for anything like the siege that was coming. However, over the last few weeks, Chelsea had been introduced to a whole new level of warfare, and did not consider herself ready for what was coming. For years, Chelsea had heard horror stories and fables about the power of the Dark Gods, but Chelsea considered herself a skeptic. How was it that the Dark Gods were so dangerous and so without bounds if the first Emperor of Cadaria, Terrik Lorien was able to defeat one in single combat? Of course, these doubts existed even before Chelsea met the very Dark God that Terrik had supposedly killed. Cheslea's first taste of the power of the Dark Gods was during the fall of Aldere and the power of the truly terrifying Midarin Sandar. Chelsea completely understood why Dominique was impressed with Midarin. She was not a woman who brooked defiance, regardless of whether she was a Dark God or not. Chelsea had a great deal of respect for

Midarin the same way she had a great deal of respect for all killers. She did not for example have the same level of respect for Mirana and Liara that she had for Midarin. Of course Chelsea respected the power that the girls had, and respected the damage that it could do, but the girls were not killers. They were not trained and practiced in the taking of life. Midarin was. But even Midarin was different. She had been an archer, that was clear from her bearing and the choice of weapon that she always conjured for herself. Yes, Chelsea respected the lethality of a bow, and saw its uses on the battlefield, but it was hard for a visceral warrior like Chelsea to compare what Midarin did with a bow to what Chelsea did with martial weapons. The member of the Dark Gods that Chelsea found terrifying was Gwydeon Sandar, Midarin's husband. He had the bearings of a fighter about him, even when he stood still; especially when he stood still. Nothing about his body or his posture spoke of ease or relaxation. He could spring into battle in a moment's notice with a poise and purpose that would be difficult to match. Gwydeon reminded Chelsea of the Arin Chandara that she had known, even down to the way he wore his sword.

Chelsea shook herself away from the unpleasant thoughts and tried to focus her mind on the matter at hand. The power that the Dark Gods could bring to bear was impressive and would be a great asset in the battle ahead. All told there would be seven of the Dark Gods fighting on their side during the battle. Added to that were her fellow members of the Knights of the Flashing Blade, Orren Eldrath and Leonora Wastri, who had apparently inherited or developed power akin to those of the Dark Gods. Then there was Felicia Lorien, who also could be counted among those with power. There was no time to understand the ins and outs of how a person that Chelsea had known nearly all of her life could suddenly have powers that could shake the world. It was hard enough to understand how a man who she had always known as Vallic Ultiv, a close ally, was really Jeroch Yetre, a member of the Dark Gods. What did humanity really mean anymore? Then there was Hannah Ironheart. There was no telling really what she was any more either. Had she died? Was her death merely a convenient lie? Then again, were these really things that Chelsea really needed to concern herself with? In a fight would it really matter where the person got their powers? It only mattered that they had the power and that they were going to use it to do the right thing in the battle to come.

Chelsea knew immediately that the thought was naïve. Of course it mattered how people got their powers and who they were. Wasn't that what this entire war was about? Unlike many of the other members of the Knights of the Flashing Blade, Chelsea never considered herself much of a politician. She got her position because of her reputation as a warrior, much like Seraph Kore. There was a push within the hierarchy of the Cadarian Empire to appoint less warriors to the ranks of the Knights of the Flashing Blade, and more cultural leaders who could help to advance the causes of peace and harmony in the empire. There were many within the empire, at least during Ender Lorien's time on the Throne, that felt that the Knights of the Flashing Blade were too militant and needed to be moderated with more enlightened voices. Until Hannah Ironheart, no priestess of the Church of the Creator had ever been named to the Knights of the Flashing Blade. Typically it had been the head of the paladins of the Heart of Stone that would be inline for the post. In the same way, there were those that believed that instead of a militant personality, one of the Masters of the Academy of Arcane Arts should have been a member of the Knights of the Flashing Blade. Of course, those that were advocating for a Master to become a Knight of the Flashing Blade rarely had an answer to the clear contradiction and limitations of such an appointment. If the Masters stayed to their prohibitions against using their abilities to cause harm, how could a Master who was a Knight of the Flashing Blade be depended upon to defend the Empire without killing? That was one of the clear discriminatory elements about the Knights that created discussions in the highest echelons of power. The Shadow Guild had seen inclusion in the Knights of the Flashing Blade since its inception. The same could be said of the odd organization known as the Order of the Flickering Flame. Even though it wasn't a recognized organization for the empire, they somehow had always found a way to be represented. But august institutions like the Church of the Creator and the Academy of Arcane Arts had been denied time and time again. The closest that the Academy came to having a member in the ranks of the Knights was Orren Eldrath, and he was only included so that Kaitain Lorien could continue to antagonize the Academy.

The Knights of the Flashing Blade were all about power. In theory, the Knights were supposed to be defenders of the empire first and foremost. That had never been put to the test until Kaitain Lorien proved to be an existential threat to the continued existence of the empire. However, by the time that Kaitain was identified as a threat, he had already done irrevocable damage to the institutions of the Academy of Arcane Arts as well as the Knights of the Flashing Blade and the Church of the Creator. He had declared wars, antagonized the dragons, and murdered his enemies with impunity. There were those in the Knights that wanted to act, but were caught up in the rebellion of Marlae Lorien and the budding civil war. But even before the insanity of Kaitain's reign, the Knights of the Flashing Blade were rife with the potential for corruption and power brokering. In theory, the Knights of the Flashing Blade was supposed to be a collection of the best and brightest of Cadaria, one representative from each of the Great Kingdoms. However, that theory was never proven to be possible in light of the diplomatic squabbles both within the Great Kingdoms themselves and in the empire at large. When a vacancy was created within the Knights of the Flashing Blade, either through death or through retirement, the custom was for the leadership of the kingdom whose representative needed to be replaced to present a list of potential candidates for the vacancy. Unfortunately, the custom was not codified in any way into law, and the number and quality of the candidates was left completely to the whim of kingdom's leadership. This allowed petty leaders in the Great Kingdoms to ensure loyalty and fealty of a member of the Knights of the Flashing Blade, as well as to create a source of information within the seat of imperial power. It was a situation that often created uncomfortable conflicts, or at least the potential for conflict.

While there was precedent for the emperor to override the wishes of the leadership of each kingdom when it came to appointments to the Knights of the Flashing Blade, it was not a contingency that was invoked with any regularity. However, previous emperors had found a way around such difficulties. One of the most effective ways to sidestep unqualified or underqualified candidates was for another member of the Knights of the Flashing Blade to recommend an ally who had distinguished themselves. That was how Leonora Wastri became a member of the Knights; Vallic Ultiv had recommended her for her position. It was a controversial choice at the time as Oradrim was again attempting to have a Master from the Academy of Arcane Arts named to the post. They had their strongest candidate in quite some time in Jastra Mythryn. She was from one of the oldest families in Cadaria, as her ancestor had been the first to set foot on the Dark Continent, thus its name. As the Master of Energy, Jastra had the most control of her abilities and should she be moved to violate the teachings of the Academy, she could have been one of the deadliest humans to ever live. Vallic as well as the Grand Master of the Shadow Guild strongly objected to Jastra's inclusion. Even Alistair Ravenheart had his reservations about elevating one of the Masters, but his objections were overruled by the leadership of Menoris. In the end, Vallic's recommendation was heeded and Leonora was added to the elite organization, though it did draw the ire of many.

Those conventions ceased to be of any use once Kaitain Lorien took the throne. Instead of waiting for the individual kingdoms to name successors to outstanding posts, he hand-picked those who he believed would be best suited to advance his agenda. Orren Eldrath, Tolon Morr, Jaccob Aldora, and Devlin Rannoch were unfit for the roles that they were given, and in the time of Ender Lorien never would have been considered for elevation to the Knights. Of the four men, only Orren came close to meeting the criteria, but his expulsion from the Academy of Arcane Arts made it highly unlikely that he would ever be put forward by the leadership of Oradrim, for fear that they would offend and irrevocably damage their relationship with the Academy. Tolon Morr was a thug, and the only reason that he was not considered a criminal was because of archaic traditions that ruled the killing that he did as a sport rather than as a crime. He was the antithesis of everything that the Knights were trying to become. There was no question that Tolon was a means to an end; a defender of the emperor who would kill upon command without question or compunction. In a similar fashion, Devlin Rannoch was a soldier who could have no other function than to defend the emperor should worst come to worst. As a half-dragon, he would be the target of distrust, bigotry, and outright hostility wherever he went. That alone disqualified him from being a member of the Knights of the Flashing Blade because of the diplomatic component required of the post. How could the leadership of any of the Great Kingdoms negotiate in good faith with someone that they fundamentally believed they could not trust? The newest member of the Knights that made the least sense was Jaccob Aldora. He was perfectly indicative of the Kingdom of Hedorah of course, as he was a drunk, a womanizer, and largely corrupt. But even all of those vices and corruptions did not guarantee fealty to the goals and aims that Kaitain Lorien held for the empire. The only potential that Chelsea could see was that Jaccob was an object lesson for the rest of the Knights. Stay in line, or you'll be replaced by someone much less qualified and much easier to control. Kaitain had taken so much from all of them, not just the people of Cadaria, not just the faithful to the Church of the Creator, but also the fundamental essence of every pillar of Cadarian life. Kaitain was actively tearing down the institutions that helped to give structure to the empire as it attempted to define itself following the Founding Wars.

Kaitain however proved to be merely a preview of things to come, and on a level so inconsequential now that it would likely be barely a footnote in history, if there were to be a history after the battle to come. On the order of magnitude, Kaitain barely rated consideration when compared to the dragons, Dorovar, and the creatures that owed their allegiance to the Creator. Cheslea had seen the Dark Gods in battle, both against each other and against one of Dorovar's Adhradair, and they would certainly be an asset in the battle to come. However, the more Chelsea dwelled upon the situation, her assessment was completely inaccurate. The Dark Gods were not an asset, they were the only hope for victory. As much as Chelsea considered herself an excellent fighter, she had to admit that she was no match for either the Dark Gods or the Adhradair. She even had to wonder if she would be a contest for one of the warrior angels that she had heard about. And so, in the battle to come, she might be more of a liability than she was an asset. That thought filled Cheslea with an immense sense of dread and disappointment. The fact that the vaunted Wolf of Saldarine was reduced to a helpless waif in the face of the greatest battle to be fought in the history of Cadaria was intolerable. That said, there was more to the battle to come than just fighting.

Despite all of Chelsea's protests, Dominique would not allow herself to be sent to either New Aradon or to the headquarters of the Shadow Guild in Bellnoc. However powerless Chelsea felt in the face of the dangers that were coming to destroy the Heart of Stone, Dominique was utterly and completely helpless. If she somehow found herself in the crossfire between the invaders and the defending forces, she would be burned to nothing in a second. Dominique was not the only so-called innocent that had elected to stay in the Heart of Stone against all protestation. Baeata Catrinel and Hannah's ally Kiara Aren also resisted calls to abandon the Heart of Stone in favor of their own safety. Baeata believed that the High Priestess should not abandon the Heart of Stone under any circumstances. As far as Kiara was concerned, she would not leave Hannah's side, but at least she was a practiced medic in combat situations from her years as a member of Jillian Corven's dragon hunters. Her skills would come in handy, even if it meant constantly putting herself in harm's way. When it came to Dominique and Baeata however, there was no place in the whole of the Heart of Stone that would be safe enough.

This put Chelsea in more than a little of a quandary. Since their flight from the Imperial Palace in Aldere, Chelsea had dedicated herself to ensuring Dominique was protected from all danger. So far that had been done with mixed results, and every potential failure had filled Chelsea with more and more dread about the possibilities of either Dominique or Chelsea surviving through the confrontation. So, Chelsea had a choice. She could try to put Baeata and Dominique somewhere that they would be safe from danger and hope that the whole of the Heart of Stone did not come crashing down upon them while Chelsea took part in the battle, or Chelsea could sequester herself away from the fighting ensuring that the two non-combatants remained safe. The real question was, would Dominique allow herself to be protected, or would she opt for allowing Chelsea to fight in a battle where she was hopelessly overmatched? Whatever their relationship had become, Dominque knew that Chelsea was a fighter, and she would not want to deny the Wolf of Saldarine her pound of flesh in defense of her world. But could Chelsea honestly fight as fiercely and carelessly as she wanted knowing that Dominque could be put in a life or death situation at any moment? That was a question that Chelsea did not know the answer to, and it bothered her immensely that she didn't have an answer.

In all of her years, she never fought with doubt before. Now, she was filled with nothing but doubt. Was she strong and resilient enough to take the fight to her enemies even though it would surely mean her death? Was she courageous enough to put someone who meant so much to her in danger just for the sake of her own pride? In the end though, wasn't that what the fight was all about? The Dark Gods were fighting to defend people who hated them, feared them, and wished they did not exist. They showed such compassion and such bravery, and yet they too had people that they loved and wanted to protect. They knew the cost of taking the stand that they were taking and they did not hesitate. Gwydeon and Midarin put their own daughter at risk. How could Chelsea have for even one moment not considered doing the same? If humanity were truly worth saving, the only thing left to do was risk, fight, and maybe even die for a chance at victory. And if the Wolf of Saldarine were going to go down, she was going to go down with a weapon in her hand and the taste of the enemy's blood on her lips.

Felicia

There were moments that defined a person's life and then there were moments that irrevocably redefined everything that came before. In a short period of time, Felicia Lorien had experienced several of both. It had all started with the trip to Aldere to pay her respects to her uncle on the occasion of his ascension to the throne of Cadaria, and on his marriage to his new bride, Dominique Arais. If she would have had her druthers of course, she would have skipped the occasion, if for no other reason than to spare her father the ignominy of having to deal with his mercurial and malicious brother. The two men hated each other more than words could ever express, though Feyd did a better job of disguising his disgust for the good of the empire. Even though Felicia's first concerns were for her father and his ability to control his temper around a brother who tried to provoke him at every opportunity, Felicia had her own emotions that she tried hard to keep from public view. While Felicia did not have the adversarial relationship with her uncle Kaitain that her father had, there was something uncomfortable about the kind of attention that Kaitain showed Felicia. He tried often as she grew into adulthood to create time when they would be alone together, opportunities that Feyd always found ways to foil. In the beginning Felicia bristled at the overprotectiveness of her father, but eventually she began to see the lecherous eyes of her uncle for what they were. Perhaps that was why Felicia had dedicated her time to learning to defend herself, or perhaps it was because Felicia very much did not want to become like the other member of her family that constantly drew her ire.

Felicia and Marlae had a complicated relationship to say the least. They were complete opposites in every way, and Marlae never let Felicia forget it. It was Marlae that first turned the phrase warrior princess into a kind of slur, using it to denigrate not only Felicia but to cast aspersions on the parenting skills of her father. Marlae, despite her rampant cruelty and self-obsessed preening and posturing was a practiced courtier. She knew how to walk the halls of power and carry herself as though she was supposed to be there. Even with the advantages of being the only child of the next emperor, Marlae's behavior could have been considered extreme and unacceptable. However, when she wanted, Marlae had a soft touch and a soft voice that could be used to ply the will of even her most ardent detractors. These were skills that Felicia never chose to develop, because they were never necessary in Lordhill. Marlae grew up with the casual lies and dissembling of career politicians while Felicia grew up in the rough and hard world of mining and the martial necessities to protect the fruit of that enterprise. Marlae mocked Felicia for growing up in the mud, and for her flamboyant red hair. Felicia tried to insult Marlae's loose morals and easy disregard for human life, but those insults never impacted the way they were intended. Marlae often would laugh off any attempts that Felicia made to verbally joust with her, once going so far as to pat her older and taller cousin on the head and calling her cute for her impudent attempts at barbs and jibes. Though Felicia and Marlae were intolerant of each other, it did not rise to the level of hatred that held between Feyd and Kaitain. Marlae held contempt for Felicia that much was clear, but Felicia never believed that Marlae held a high enough opinion of Felicia to hate her.

Kaitain and Marlae aside, there were other reasons that Felicia had not wanted to make the trip to Aldere, and they all centered around her grandfather, Ender. Felicia loved her grandfather and they had always had a great relationship. It was a relationship that annoyed Marlae because she felt that someone else was gaining the attention that was due to her. But, the way that Marlae looked at it, there was nothing that her grandfather could do for her to advance her station. She would already be the heir to the throne once her father took his place as the Emperor of Cadaria, so as far as she was concerned she was just biding her time until her father was on the throne and then she could make whatever moves were necessary to guarantee her ascension. The greatest insurance that existed was the fact that as long as Ender was alive, Marlae could not move against her father. If Kaitain would have died before his father, then it would have been Feyd and Felicia who would have been next in line for the throne of Cadaria. Hindsight being what it was, perhaps the world would have been better off if either Feyd or Felicia had arranged for Kaitain to suffer from one of the accidents that he was so famous for creating. But, with Feyd on the throne, Marlae might have become the existential threat that her father became but without the insanity. It was possible that the Dark Gods never would have come to the aid of those Cadarians that were willing to listen to reason, and there was no telling how much damage Dorovar would have done. If Kaitain had not taken the throne, there would have been no assassination attempt, and Felicia would not have met Gwydeon Sandar, his wife Midarin, or Diana Terian. And so, if it was the trip to Aldere that defined her future, it was what she found after the trip that created a new life.

Felicia didn't know what she was getting into when she accepted the gift that Diana gave her, and she didn't know the road that it would eventually lead her down. Diana Terian was everything that Felicia had wanted to be all of her life. She was poised, she was fierce, and she was confident. That was one thing that Felicia had not been in her life, confident. Perhaps it was the lack of her mother during the trying times in her life. Perhaps it was the fact that her father was constantly running from who he should have been. Perhaps it was even the fact that she knew there was really no clear future for her. Whatever the reason or combination thereof, Felicia was uncomfortable in her own skin. Felicia had never lived for herself, and so she never developed the skills that were required to do that. When Felicia's mother died, there was a part of her that never accepted that she was really gone. During the day she would be strong for her father, and then at night she would sit and talk to her mother as though she were still there, letting her know about all the things that happened during the day. It was a way to feel close to her. But it also never allowed Felicia to truly grieve. Feyd never truly grieved either, but his avoidance was channeled into duty and doting on his daughter. The two were so good for one another most of the time, but they were also what held each other back. Feyd never allowed himself the opportunity to move on and perhaps find another love in his life, and Felicia was stunted in her development in that regard, never knowing what that emotion could mean outside of the needs of her father. There had been many suitors for her hand over the years of course, but she bristled at every one. They were never good enough in her father's eyes, but she was never good enough in her own. That was perhaps the thing that Felicia resented the most about Marlae. Yes, she was a terrible human being, but she knew who she was and she liked who she was. Even the spoiled rotten bitch knew more about living than Felicia did.

What Felicia could do however was fight. That was the place where she felt comfortable. With a sword in her hand and an opponent in front of her, she didn't have time to worry about her shortcomings and couldn't think about all the ways that her life was deficient. Felicia idolized warriors like Chelsea Zarova and Leonora Wastri who had ascended to levels that made them cultural icons and completely unimpeachable regardless of whatever deficits may have existed in their personal lives. Even without understanding everything that her choices had cost her, Felicia wanted so badly to be Chelsea Zarova. But that opportunity could never come. Felicia was both a beneficiary and a victim of her name. As a Lorien, she needed to be protected. Should something have happened to Kaitain, Marlae, Quyhn, and Feyd, suddenly the weight of the empire would come crashing down fully on Felicia's shoulders. What she wouldn't have given for the opportunity to be someone else, to rise through the ranks of the military and live a life on her own terms. But Felicia was a child of the empire, and her life would never be her own so long as her last name was Lorien and the Lorien family was the one shaping the destiny of the human race. Once Felicia met the Dark Gods however, she realized that was a lie.

For all the talk and the bluster and the overblown history, the idea that the Lorien family was somehow behind the prosperity of the Cadarian Empire now seemed so foolish. Of course, most of the population of Cadaria would never see the things that Felicia had seen or would have the knowledge that Felicia had inherited, but even most had begun to see the cracks in the veneer of the Lorien legacy. The steady human hand guiding the fate of the Cadarian Empire had been exposed for the fraud that he had always been, and not because of the petulant greed and violence of a child who thought himself a god. But like a child throwing a tantrum, Kaitain lashed out at anything and everything he could, and because of the indiscriminate nature of his aggression, more and more of the carefully balanced mechanisms and lies that held the kingdom together began to break down. The Emperor of Cadaria, while important, was not alone in his responsibilities to the well-being of the empire. There were many layers of administrators and functionaries whose job it was to ensure that the empire continued to run smoothly and that there were not disruptions in the great machine. And there was no mistaking the fact that the Cadarian Empire was a machine with many moving parts that all depended upon the other for the empire to be successful.

Everything started with Aldere of course. Aldere by its very nature was not one of the Great Kingdoms. It was the Imperial Province whose major function was to secure trade between the thirteen Great Kingdoms and also to act as an independent zone where disputes could be settled. The only caveat to that of course were the mines at Lordhill. The mines were once in a disputed section of the border between Zevarit and Pellatori. In the days of antiquity, workers from both the Kingdom of Blood and the Kingdom of Iron worked the mines at Lordhill, and each kingdom reaped the benefits of the arrangement. However, in time the workers became too competitive, as they believed that the more their side mined, the more their kingdom got. The belief was a fallacy of course, but there was no way to convince the miners of that. So, in time, the emperor decreed that the workers of Zevarit would retain the rights to work the mine, and that the people of Pellatori would be responsible for providing security for the mines. All profits would be split equally between the kingdoms. This solution was clearly doomed from the start. Resentment was immediate between the miners and the soldiers, as the former believed that their blood was being spilled to benefit people who were unwilling to share the responsibility, and the latter believed that the former did the minimum possible in an effort to sabotage Pellatori's prosperity. There were a great many brawls that resulted from these arguments, until eventually a group of soldiers from Pellatori decided that they were going to teach the miners a lesson. That lesson resulted in a massive amount of bloodshed, and over two dozen dead miners. That was the last straw for the emperor. In order to avert all-out war between Zevarit and Pellatori, Lordhill was absorbed into the Imperial Province of Aldere, and responsibility for the mining and distribution of the natural resources was assumed by the Imperial Family itself. There was a great deal of dissent regarding this course of action, and several protests filed by both Pellatori and Zevarit. However, the emperor would not relent in his decision. Lordhill was the property of the empire, and many years later, Felicia would call the ugly pit home.

Though Zevarit and Pellatori had their issues going back to the Founding Wars, the two kingdoms had a kind of symbiotic relationship that caused both to thrive, even though it often tended to ignite resentment. Both the people of Pellatori and of Zevarit were miners by trade. Pellatori, as the name indicated, had the richest veins of iron beneath its surface, and the people were quite adept at removing it from the ground with speed and efficiency. The people of Zevarit also had rich mines, though these were filled to the brim with precious stones, copper, coal, and other precious metals that were used throughout the empire. More than that, however, the northern half of Zevarit was filled with thick groves of trees whose timber was needed to reinforce the mines both in Pellatori and Zevarit. Pellatori had long since depleted their forests, and depended largely on trade with Zevarit and Rashaleb for their timber. While Zevarit had the raw materials to spare, their infrastructure was not designed to handle the processing of the material, which is where Rashaleb was invaluable. Rashaleb had the key lumber production facilities in the empire, and they were responsible for providing timber not only for the imperial shipyards in Aldere, but also the shipyards of Hedorah, and the mines of Pellatori. Additionally, the builders in Rashaleb were the preeminent carriage builders in the whole of the empire. Which, when Rashaleb was laid to waste by Dorovar's Heralds, had incredible impact on the ability for the empire to sustain its production of almost every resource. But that ripple effect was also felt in many of the other kingdoms, especially Celidar.

Celidar, the Kingdom of Steel, was as the name implied, the principle producer of steel and weaponry in the empire. Zevarit provided coal to stoke the furnaces of the great smelting vats and Pellatori provided the iron that made the smelting possible. Without those materials, the vats fell silent, and the production of all manner of weaponry and armor for the armies of the empire all but ceased. With the lumber production of Rashaleb crippled, Zevarit in a near civil war because of the actions of Kaitain Lorien in regards to Gregor Quicksilver and Gabriel Shadowfall, and all of the able-bodied men from Pellatori mobilized for the war against the dragons, much of the war economy of Cadaria had ceased. Add to that the rebellion in Lordhill, and the functional economy had suffered major blows as well. While Dorovar could be blamed for the attack on Rashaleb, the impacts felt in Zevarit, Pellatori, and Celidar were all because of the choices that Kaitain Lorien made. However, the impacts were more than just on the economy of Cadaria, but also to the very essence of what it meant to be Cadarian. Whether it was the discrediting of the Academy of Arcane Arts, the dismantling of the Knights of the Flashing Blade, or attempting to make the teachings of the Church of the Creator illegal, Kaitain's decrees struck at the very soul of what Cadaria was supposed to be.

Though she knew it was not possible because of her name and her status, Felicia had once dreamed of becoming a member of the Knights of the Flashing Blade. They were supposed to be the pinnacle of everything that it meant to be Cadarian. Not only were they defenders of the empire, but they were also the fiercest warriors and diplomats. They were exemplars, people whose lives were to be aspired to, and in most cases, Felicia had found that to be true. At least until Kaitain Lorien came along and decided to put his own imprint on the Knights. Felicia had always had a great deal of admiration for both Chelsea Zarova and Leonora Wastri. They showed a grace and elegance in their duties that few others in the history of the Knights had been able to match. The difference between the two women was as clear as the difference between night and day. Chelsea, the Wolf of Saldarine, was perhaps one of the fiercest warriors in the history of Cadaria, and she had the reputation for being as deadly at the bargaining table as she was on the field of battle. While she had the reputation of being impatient and quick to anger, it was not a reputation earned by unnecessary outbursts. Each of the diplomatic incidents that she was a party to, or were blamed upon her quick action, were later proven to be astute tactical aggression that resulted in achieving the goals of the negotiation quickly. Her reputation on the battlefield served her well, and thus any threats of military action had much greater weight when snarled from the lips of the Wolf of Saldarine. Leonora on the other hand was very careful and measured. Her style was to let both sides exhaustively plead their cases until they began to make mistakes under questioning. Leonora believed that the longer people were forced to argue their points, the more likely they were to let what they really believed to slip out beyond the practiced arguments. These exhaustive tactics were exacerbated by the fact that Leonora never showed emotion during negotiations and she simply wore down her opponents. The more her opponents tried to rattle her or trap her in logically fallacies, the more they practiced their own defeat.

Felicia did not feel that she could be either of those women. As much as Felicia liked to fancy herself a warrior of some repute, she knew that she could never be the kind of warrior that Chelsea Zarova was. No matter the practice that Felicia dedicated to the blade, she knew that she would never be Chelsea's equal. There was something transcendent about the woman, and she had a will that could not be denied. Of course, the younger Felicia, the one who did not understand the nature of things, believed that she could be that good one day. That was one of the many illusions shattered when Felicia gained Diana Terian's powers. Diana had grown up watching her brother practice and practice, dedicating himself to being the best there would ever be with the sword. When he entered into the People of the Lion, Arathorn quickly found himself bested by Aryx Terian. Of course, Aryx had the unnatural skill that generations of life had given him, as well as the fact that Aryx was not completely human. But it was when Diana saw Gwydeon Sandar that she realized the difference between her brother and the savant with a sword that Gwydeon was. Arathorn worked and sweated and perfected his craft to the best of his ability, but what Gwydeon had that Arathorn didn't was an element of artistry. There was something organic with the blade when it was in Gwydeon's hand that was not there when in Arathorn's. To a degree, Diana had that natural skill with the blade, though some of it may have come from her melding with the power of Nightwing. So, when Diana's powers and memories were melded into Felicia, she began to see her own deficiency with the blade. Like Diana and Gwydeon, Chelsea was a natural fighter, and no matter how much Felicia practiced, she would never acquire that; at least not by natural means.

As far as Leonora was concerned, the woman always seemed beyond human in the way that she held herself. Felicia remembered the first time that she met the ethereal woman. It was shortly after Feyd had accepted the leadership of the mines at Lordhill. There was a request by the Academy of Arcane Arts to discover some artifacts that had been recovered from deep in the mines. Some thought that the artifacts might have been from the time of the Founding Wars, while others believed that they came from a time before humans first set foot on the planet. These differing opinions created a conflict between the Church of the Creator and the Academy of Arcane Arts, not that the two bodies ever required such an incredible circumstance to find grounds for disagreement. The first of the delegations to arrive in Lordhill was the delegation from Oradrim. Felicia was so excited to meet one of her heroes that she spent the three days before trying to find exactly the right dress to wear. It was an unusual circumstance for Felicia, as she never cared about clothes or the manner in which her hair was done, but on this occasion, she felt more like Marlea than herself. Finally, her hair was done perfectly, and she was wearing a dress that she felt befitted her station. She stood beside her father beaming with pride as the doors opened and the delegation from Oradrim entered. The air seemed to stand still when Leonora Wastri came into view. Her gait was so smooth and effortless that her traveling clothes barely moved with each step. Despite her long trip, there was not a hair out of place, and not a smudge of dirt was on her clothes or her skin. Leonora was very pale, but not in an unhealthy way; she almost matched the descriptions of the angels from the Book of the Creator. When she reached the dais she bowed low enough to honor Feyd and Felicia's station, but not so low that it demonstrated any real subservience. When she spoke, her voice was filled to the brim with power and confidence, but there was no arrogance there. She was assured, but not overly so. To say that Felicia was impressed was an understatement, and there were several moments that she realized that she was holding her breath. However, now Felicia realized something that she didn't realize then. Leonora's poise and power were gifts from her training by Cedric Binosear and the fact that the woman had touched the Blaze.

Felicia returned to her thoughts about the nature of Cadaria. The Knights of the Flashing Blade were formed by a member of the phasia, Jeroch Yetre, as a measure to prevent the fledgling empire from falling to its own insecurities. The Shadow Guild was created by Saurn Macco, a darker version of the Knights of the Flashing Blade who could quietly remove impediments to the desired order of things. The Academy of Arcane Arts was an interesting bauble proposed by Saurn, and Felicia knew from Diana's memories that it was created in an attempt to prevent those with arcane power from having their abilities used to further the goals of someone like Emries or Talisia. On Onea, there had been a group who had the ability to touch arcane power called the Moridon. They were nothing more than a religious order whose only goal was to advance the false prophecy of the being called the *Coromor*. Saurn saw the potential for such a force coming into being on Cadaria. He had been unable to stem the creation of the Church of the Creator. It was a clearly a manipulation by Emries to ensure that there were those that would do his bidding regardless of what came to pass at the end of the Founding War. If those that had the ability to touch arcane power had been recruited by the Church of the Creator and leveraged for the advancement of either the Creator's or one of the Children's agendas, the war may have ended before it began. Without the Academy of Arcane Arts, those with arcane ability could have been taught to use that ability for aggressive purposes, and when the Dark Gods fell to the face of Espre, the students would have been quickly leveraged by the empire as a weapon of mass destruction. Saurn could not allow that to happen. He knew that the arcane and the devout could not be allowed to function on the same plane. They had to be separate. The fact that the first Masters of the Academy created the prohibition against using their abilities to inflict harm was a happy accident.

Diana had felt the end coming that day in Celidar, and she did not want to face that end without the man that she loved. But Diana and Aryx had seen the eventuality, and were unsure of how it would come to pass. Part of them wanted to be there for their friends at the end, but the other part could not see a way that they would not be a hindrance. Aryx was a man who owed an allegiance to too many sides during his life, and could potentially have been dragged to places that would have made him a threat to the very people that he wanted to protect. Diana would not turn her blade on her husband again, that much she knew, and so she could not allow herself to be placed in a position where that could come to pass. The best thing that could have happened to them was an opportunity to walk away, and to give their powers to those who could use them to benefit the world. Through Diana, Felicia was where she was supposed to be, a blade in her hand ready to fight the largest battle in the history of her world.

Felicia moved over to the window of her room and looked out. Inside of her she could feel the powers of Nightwing beginning to reform. In a matter of hours, she would have all of her abilities back under her control, and the fight against the Adhradair had taught her a lot about her limitations and her strengths. Nightwing had made her feel invincible, the shell of powerful armor too thick and daunting to be penetrated by any force. Now that Felicia had tasted that humiliating defeat, she would take the lessons and learn. She could not be overconfident, especially with all that was coming to destroy them. In the end, all they would have was guile, tenacity, and whatever experience they could rely on. But more than that, they would have to depend on each other. Felicia was about to fight side by side with her heroes and with people that Diana's memories told her were the worst of villains. Now, Felicia was fighting for her family, for her world, and for a future where she could possibly have all of the things that Diana had in her life, but Felicia had denied herself for too long. After this war was over, the Lorien name would no longer be the prison that held Felicia back from living a normal life. She would find that for herself and that was the most powerful thing to fight for.

Leonora

Leonora Wastri sat in the corner of the room, her back to the wall, her eyes fixed on the nothingness between herself and the door. Clutched in her hands was the last remnant of Cedric, an artifact from another world, the Lion Sword. Ever since Logan Ranthall put it into Leonora's hands in Hedorah, she could feel Cedric close to her heart. The longer she held the sword in her hands, the more she could feel the two Leonoras diverging from one another. One half of her mind was still Leonora Wastri, the revered and respected member of the Knights of the Flashing Blade, the woman with the impeccable reputation, a pillar of the spiritual community and the supposed soul of the Cadarian Empire. The other half of her, the half that was sleeping for so long, was the teenaged version of herself, Leah, who was so in love that she could see nothing else. Cedric had become her entire world, and more than that, he had opened her eyes to a whole world that she didn't even know existed. He taught her about the mystical force that he called the Blaze, taught her to touch the fickle green flame and to let it fill her to nearly bursting. He told her stories of heroes and devils, of forces beyond imagining and beyond reckoning. More than that, he taught her how to fight the monsters that would one day come to take her world as they had taken his.

Do you remember the first lesson I taught you?

Of course she remembered. She remembered every lesson that Cedric ever taught her, from the moment they met when she came upon his campsite to the day when she thought that he had died. The day that he died. It was all so confusing. He was dead, wasn't he? Then why could she feel him so clearly when she was holding the sword? How could she feel his thoughts and his love pulsing through the powers stored in the blade?

Focus, Leonora. You're drifting.

Her nose wrinkled at the voice in her head. She had hated when he said things like that. He never called her Leonora unless he was irritated with her, or if he was trying to irritate her. She never could stand her full name, and she never understood why her mother would give her such a formal and totally ill-fitting name. Leah fit her so much better, and she loved the way that Cedric said her name. For the life of her she could not understand how should could have spent so many years being called Leonora and not once realizing how much she hated it. But yes, the voice in her head was right, she was drifting. It was something that she had tended to do in the early days of Cedric's lessons. He imparted so much, and while she was trying to figure out all of the connotations of what he was saying, she would stop listening. Some of his earliest lessons had been attempts to focus her mind, to keep her on task. Aware and observant, but never distracted.

But that wasn't the first lesson.

No, that wasn't the first lesson. The first lesson had been about the mistake she had made when they first met. She made assumptions about Cedric based on what she saw. Cedric's first lesson had been simple. Do not act based on what you think, act based on what you know. It was the basis of all of the lessons that followed after, especially the lessons about fighting the monsters that would one day try to take over her world as they had tried to take over Cedric's. Too many demons wore innocent faces, and she could not let sentimentality impact her ability to do what needed to be done. Cedric taught her, sometimes painfully, that while she was standing there trying to figure things out, her opponent could be gathering all the power that he needed to strike her down where she stood. There would always be time to figure things out once the danger had passed, but there would be no answers if you were dead.

So who can you trust? Remember that lesson?

That was a hard lesson and just the thought of it sent a shiver through her. When she was just thirteen, Cedric told her mother that they were going away for a few days. He had said that he had business in a nearby village, and that Leah would be tagging along with him for lessons and for more exposure to the real world. Her mother had initially been resistant to the idea, but Cedric knew just the right things to say to make what he wanted come to pass. And so, the next morning, Leah and Cedric set off on his business trip. While they could have taken horses or a carriage, Cedric preferred to walk everywhere. He had always said that it kept the mind and the body sharp, and it removed many complications. You could travel lighter, and you never had to worry about the things you could not see or hear. Carriages and horses made sounds that could muffle the approach of an enemy. Riding made the mind wander or focus on the needs of the horses and not on the environment around you. Carriages had bad sight lines, and too many angles that hid potential threats. Not only that, camping could be difficult and required different levels of vigilance. You had to carry food for horses, spare parts for wagons or carriages, and those things made ripe targets for thieves and bandits. Cedric had what could generously be called a dim view of human nature. He often said that while we wish that people did the right thing all the time, we must prepare for them to do the wrong thing when it suits them. He also said that opportunity brought out the worst in people. A person who would never dream of picking another person's pocket would however fail to make an effort to return a dropped purse. Any action could be rationalized if one tried hard enough.

And what was the action that you rationalized?

Leonora's heart fell. They were in the village, about five days walk from her home. Cedric had gone into a tavern to gather some information, and Leah had been left to wander through the market. She had assured Cedric that she would not go far, and that she would stay within sight of the door of the tavern. Of course, being a precocious newly-minted teenager,

Leah believed that she was armed with enough knowledge from her bristly tutor to navigate a small village by herself. That's when she caught sight of the small stand with beautiful weapons. Leah knew enough from her time with Cedric to recognize excellent craftsmanship, and the woman who was selling the weapons had the posture of one who worked at a forge. Her blond hair was cut short, and the muscles of her shoulders and arms were clear through her tunic. The woman greeted Leah gruffly at first, but warmed as Leah demonstrated her knowledge. After a few moments of conversation, the woman stated, matter-of-factly, that she had a few swords that might suit someone of Leah's stature, but they were back in her shop. Leah did not even hesitate. The woman motioned to her assistant to mind the stand and Leah followed the woman back to her shop. She never felt the blow coming. The moment the door to the shop was open, the strong women slammed her fist down on the back of Leah's head, knocking her unconscious. Leah learned later that if the woman had hit her just a little harder, Leah likely never would have woken up. When Leah did return to the waking world, Cedric was standing over her. His expression had been blank, and even her waking did not bring any emotion to his eyes. All he said was that she had forgotten his first lesson.

When Leah had gotten back to her feet, she finally got a look around the shop. Weapons and shelves were strewn everywhere, and the forge itself had been cracked down the middle. On the forge was the broken body of the muscular blond woman, her blood flowing down the broken anvil in all directions. Cedric seized Leah by the collar and led her out of the shop and before he shut the door, she felt him channel as small stream of fire into the forge itself. The damage to the forge would cause the fire to rage out of control and eventually engulf the shop as well as the evidence of the murder that had taken place there. For the first two days of the trip back, Cedric did not say a word to Leah. Finally, on the morning of the third day, Cedric had explained that the woman was his errand. She was one of the monsters from his world, a member of the Brotherhood of Phasia known as Cash. She had no doubt seen Cedric enter the village with Leah at his side and had decided to use Leah's naiveté to set a trap for her pursuer. Fortunately, Cedric was more than a match for Cash's abilities, and the fight was over quickly. He had not wanted Leah to see the result of the conflict, but he had hoped that it would reinforce his lessons. The world was dangerous to those who could not see the bigger war at work, but it was even more dangerous to those who had been initiated to the truth of Creation and the ugly conflicts that made it work. It was a harsh lesson, but one Leah took to heart.

Did you?

Leonora immediately felt the condemnation. Cedric was supportive and understanding, but he did not suffer repeated mistakes. The first time Leah did something wrong in her lessons, he would gently correct her. The next time, he would correct her, but less gently. If the mistake was repeated, Cedric would press on the mistake, forcing her to learn though pain rather than through reinforcement and coddling. Cedric had always said that the world did not suffer fools, and did not forgive mistakes. Mistakes were the quickest path to death. While lessons would sometimes lead to condemnation, Leah felt her mistakes most in sparring. He was not opposed to letting his blade find her flesh when she was not concentrating. Cedric was not a cruel man by any stretch of the imagination, and he had great capacity for love and tenderness as Leah would find when their relationship evolved. Cedric needed Leah to be ready for what was coming, and he knew that if one of his enemies had a chance to make her pay for her mistakes, they would. The more Leonora sat with the blade, the more she felt Cedric's darkness and his worry. There were many nights after they had become lovers that Cedric would dip into the darkness and the regrets of his soul and let them show to his young protégé. These stolen moments allowed Leah to see the complex man that Cedric was, and the wounds that no longer showed on his body but were seared into his heart forever. He spoke of the loss of the first woman that he loved, how she was taken from him before he ever really got a chance to love her the way that he should. He spoke of the friends who were taken from him one by one by the ravages of war. And he spoke at length about the ideologies that had caused so many to fall away from the path. The work would not be done, and Creation would not be saved until every last one of those with the power to unsettle Creation were dealt with. Cedric had dealt with as many as he could, and there were others who had similar missions, but Cedric never believed that they were carrying out the executions for any reason other than to remove obstacles from their own paths.

Like your old friend. My old enemy. The one who has lied to you all these years and turned you into something you were never supposed to be.

Leonora's thoughts immediately went to the man who sat in a room mere yards from where she herself sat. The man who once she had thought of as one of her closest allies, but instead was one of the most wicked villains ever to draw breath. Cedric had told Leah many stories over the years of the man called Jeroch Yetre, the Lord Shadow of the Brotherhood of Phasia, the most favored child of the living nightmare Shau-ling. Jeroch and Cedric had been enemies for thousands of years, and no matter what changes were made to the nature of the war, Jeroch and Cedric would always be on opposite sides. Jeroch was a monster, beyond redemption, and if Cedric could not bury his blade in the man's heart before the end of his days, he would ensure that Leah had all the tools that she needed to end his life. Of course, all of that had been hidden from Leah by that very same villain. But now Leah knew the truth of it. Reawakening to the Blaze had freed her mind of Jeroch's control, and communing with Cedric's spirit in the Lion Sword had set her firmly back on the path she was always meant to walk.

So what is it you see?

The first lesson. What Leah saw around her should have been comforting. She was in the Heart of Stone, the center of the worship of the Creator on Espre, and she was surrounded by allies ready to take the fight to those who were coming to destroy them. Alongside her were three of her oldest allies. First was the woman who was perhaps her greatest friend in the whole world, Hannah Ironheart. She and Hannah had been through so much together and had bonded during their many relief missions into the heart of Galateria. They had fought against monsters, dragons, bandits, and rebels in their time as members of the Knights of the Flashing Blade. They had even stood side by side against the creature calling itself Death. Then there was Chelsea Zarova, the Wolf of Saldarine. One of the worst battles that Leonora had been witness to was at Chelsea's side. It was just after Chelsea had been named to the Knights of the Flashing Blade, and there was a faction of the Army of Fire that refused to follow her leadership. They broke away and declared themselves to be the true defenders of Saldarine, and they vowed to overthrow the government of

Thorigald and Saldarine and unite the ancient enemies under a single banner. Leonora was dispatched by the emperor to assist Chelsea in dispatching the rebels. Together Chelsea and Leonora led a small detachment of the Army of Fire against the rebels. Leonora had questioned whether or not it would have been wiser to take a large force, but Chelsea wanted only to take those men that she could absolutely trust until such time as the rest of the rebel faction could be purged from the ranks of the Army of Fire. When the battle was joined, they were outnumber four perhaps five to one, and yet, when the battle was over, the losses suffered by those loyal to Chelsea were minimal. On the battlefield, Chelsea was a force of nature, and with Leonora by her side, there were not ten men in the world who could have stood against them. If there was a battle coming to the Heart of Stone, there was no one better to have at her side than Chelsea.

Then there was Vallic Ultiv. Of course, Jeroch Yetre had shed that name after the fall of the Knights of the Flashing Blade. Once upon a time, Leonora would have looked at Vallic and felt the calm of being close to someone she trusted without reservation. Vallic had been her teacher, her friend, and her sponsor into the Knights of the Flashing Blade. Together they had tracked down assassins and arcane threats to the Emperor. Many nights while they traveled together they would fall into deep philosophical conversations and debates. Vallic had an amazing mind and an intricate and nuanced way of looking at every issue. The man did not see any issue in black or white. Everything was gray, and coming to the right conclusions demanded seeing the situation for what it was, not what everyone wanted it to be. Many times this way of looking at the world put Vallic at odds with Hannah and Gregor, but those debates were some of the most interesting conversations that Leonora ever found herself party to. And while Vallic / Jeroch offered complications, so too did Anabel Binosear. Cedric had told Leah many tales about his sister during their time together, and Leah had always wished that she had been able to have a relationship with the woman. Just knowing that she was there in the Heart of Stone made her feel closer to Cedric, just as it had the moment they met back in Hedorah in the basement of that shop with Logan Ranthall.

The rest of their allies in the fight read like a who's who of the Cadarian Empire. Orren Eldrath, one of the newest members of the

Knights of the Flashing Blade, and one that Leonora did not have much of a relationship with. He was named to his post by Kaitain Lorien in an effort to drive a wedge between Aldere and the Academy of Arcane Arts in Jelan. Then there was Felicia Lorien, the only daughter of Feyd Lorien, Kaitain's brother. Leonora knew the woman quite well, and her penchant for doing things that were far beneath her station. In another life she would have been a warrior the caliber of Chelsea Zarova, but in this life she was required to be the steward of her father, and to be a voice of reason for the imperial family. Many did not view Felicia with that level of esteem, but those who appreciated the sacrifices that Felicia had had to make for her father had nothing but respect for the young woman. And while she had not seen them, Leonora was aware that there was a contingent from the Dark Gods in the Heart of Stone, there to help in the defense, and there to usher in the last act in the great war that was coming to Espre. Dragons, gods, angels, and demons swirling around the fortress of stone. It felt as though everything hinged on what was about to happen next, the fulcrum upon which the future would be shifted.

And now tell me what you know.

What Leah knew was far more complicated. The Dark Gods could not be trusted. All of them were Cedric's enemies. Some of them were members of the Brotherhood of Phasia, like Jeroch, or were counted among their children. They could talk about wanting to save Espre and the whole of Creation from the darkness represented by the Creator or whatever it was that they were trying to sell as their motivation for their so-called magnanimous gestures. In a fight, Leah would have to keep one eye on them to make sure that some magical dagger didn't get buried in her back. They might have been fighting the same enemies, but they could not be considered allies. Once Leah had set eyes on Orren Eldrath and Felicia Lorien, Leah knew they had to be counted amongst the untrustworthy. They had been granted powers similar to those of the Brotherhood of Phasia, and so they were Cedric's enemies too. It was clear that the insidious corruption that the phasia and the Dark Gods represented ran far deeper than Leah could have imagined.

Leah thought she could still trust Chelsea, even if she was traveling with a member of the Dark Gods, the one who called himself Alderin.

Danger hung around the man like a fog, and Leah knew that he could not be trusted. He and Chelsea had the same bearing. They carried themselves like killers. Perhaps Chelsea had been corrupted herself. After all, how else could anyone explain the fact that somehow Chelsea had become so close to the woman who had stolen her husband from her? Chelsea clearly wasn't making sound decisions, and so when the time came, Leah couldn't trust her to be loyal to the true cause.

The thought that hurt Leah the most was the fact that Anabel Binosear had to be counted among the enemy. Yes, she was Cedric's sister, but the two had been estranged for so long. Even from Cedric's stories, he made it clear that Anabel always took her own path and was only interested in what was best for her. She only went on the quest to face down Shauling because Cedric forced her, and that was the last time she had direct interaction with the war. She didn't want to fight, but she didn't have a problem with consolidating power in her name. She ran her kingdom under an assumed name, reaping all the benefits of her duplicity without any threat to her own safety or legacy. And then she did the same thing when she came to Espre. She formed a shadow government with the help of her children and grandchildren, duping Marlae Tamerlane into trusting her with the formation of her new empire. Another Lorien puppet whose strings were controlled by a member of the Dark Gods. Anabel was not an ally of anyone but herself, and the thought made Leah's blood burn. And how could she be in league with her brother's greatest enemy? That was the final nail in the coffin. Anabel allied with Jeroch Yetre. Impossible. Absurd. She was an enemy; that much had become blindingly clear.

Then there was Jeroch Yetre, the villain, the liar, the horror that had haunted not only Cedric's steps but Leonora's as well. Forget for a moment all of the terrible things that Jeroch had done to Cedric during their time on Onea. Forget that they were mortal enemies who wanted nothing more than to kill one another. What Leah could never forget was that it was Jeroch Yetre who took Cedric from her. Jeroch had murdered the man that she loved, and murdered that love before it could become what Leah needed it to be. From the moment their affair began, Leah knew that its days were numbered, but every day was cherished and every day mattered. There could have been more of those days. There should have been more of those days, but Jeroch had taken them all. But then to add insult to injury, Jeroch had taken the memory of all of the days that came before. He stole from her the memory of the man that she loved, stole from her all of the lessons and all of the tenderness. All of the stolen moments, the kisses in the rain, the days on the road, and the sound of his laughter. Years of her life, taken, and replaced with a dream that Jeroch believed Leah should be living. He even took from her her sense of self. Leah was taken, replaced with the pretender Leonora. The loving, fiery, inquisitive girl who had known the strongest and most intense love one could imagine had been reduced to the cold aloof Leonora who would never know the touch of a man because of her dedication to a purity that no human could realistically touch. He had made her a stranger in her own body, in her own mind, and he had stolen every dream she had ever had. Jeroch Yetre was never her friend, never her mentor. He was her tormenter, her jailor. She was a prisoner in a jail of his design, but she had broken free. He would pay for every stolen memory, and he would suffer for every indignity that he had ever inflicted upon her.

Leah's mind floated to Hannah Ironheart, her closest friend. Her confidant, her compatriot. Her mind whirled with thoughts, a violence and bile rising up within her. But she could not face those thoughts, could not face that eventuality.

Leah, you're drifting.

The voice had changed. It still sounded like Cedric in her mind, but there was a malice there that she could not make Cedric's voice portray. But the voice was right. She was drifting. She was trying not to embrace the path the voice wanted her to go down. As she clutched the Lion Sword in her hands and felt the icy cold white power that was stored there, the thoughts were unavoidable. Hannah Ironheart was not her friend. Hannah was the friend of the person that Jeroch invented. Hannah was Leonora's friend, not Leah's. There was something else though, something different about Hannah Ironheart. No longer was she the High Priestess of the Church of the Creator. No longer was she the champion of the Cadarian Empire. She had been corrupted, touched by the hand of the heretic known as Aerith Seth. She had become his champion, his zealot, his instrument of chaos upon Espre. Hannah had been drawn into the madness that was consuming this world as it had consumed Cedric's. Cedric had spoken often of Aerith Seth, and the danger that the man posed.

Aerith is the real enemy. He is the one that is going to destroy us all. No matter what happens during the battle at the Heart of Stone, Aerith's agenda cannot be allowed to continue. He must be stopped at all costs, and you are the only one who can stop him. Let Hannah help defend the Heart of Stone, let her stand against the dragons and the minions of Dorovar. But once the danger has passed, if she still stands, you must use this sword and strike her down. No matter her defenses, and no matter the powers that Aerith Seth has given her, she will have no defense for the power I have stored in the blade. Perhaps there will be enough left for you to strike down Jeroch too, but Hannah Ironheart is the one who you must focus your rage upon. She is the true threat to everything that stands before us.

Leah clutched the sword to her chest and closed her eyes. The voice continued to speak to her, quieting her mind and reaffirming her mission. Cedric's voice had disappeared, but that no longer mattered. It wasn't Cedric that had loved her anyway. Cedric was just the shell for the love that had sought Leah out. The power stored in the blade, the power placed there for her had come from the creator of all humans, the true source of the love and acceptance that Leah needed. Cedric may have been taken from her, but she no longer needed that phantom. She had been reunited with Emries and his love, and they would never be separated again.

THE KNIGHTS

Epilogue

Redemption's Price

Year Two of the Divine Empress and Child of the Creator Marlae Tamerlane, Creator's Calendar Year 1872

Logan Ranthall walked slowly through countryside, his body aching in a way that it had not for thousands of years. For hours he had had nothing but his own thoughts to keep him warm against the brisk wind; his thoughts, his memories, and the ancient litany that had consigned him to a fate that he could have never imagined. He was a man out of time, and one that was running out of time. And yet at the same time, he was a story, a story that was passing from legend to myth to absurdity. Perhaps those were only the thoughts of a man who saw the end of his journey ahead of him; the weight of the days behind so heavy that they squeezed every bit of perspective out of the days remaining. Whatever the truer sentiment may have been, one thing was clear. Logan Ranthall had a finite amount of sunrises left that he would see, and the more steps he took to the west, to his destiny, the more he hastened the end of the story. And that filled Logan with a mixture of relief and sorrow.

As with all things, experience grants the wisdom of perspective, and a massive dose of it had been crammed into Logan's head in a short amount of time. The plan, if that was what it had ever been, had come from the exchange that he had with Pike Rhuiden, and then the infusion of power that Logan had received from his fellow phasia Rael, Trece, and Kamen.

Kamen had seen what was coming long before Logan had, and perhaps in a different time and in a different place, it would have been Kamen who would have been the hero of the story. Logan smiled as he corrected his own thoughts. Kamen was the hero of the story. As much as Kamen wanted to credit Logan for saving his life when he arrived on Espre, it had been the other way around. The Logan that arrived on Espre was not the well-thought, higher-minded individual that now had been placed upon the path to his end. That Logan was angry, vindictive, and full of pain. That Logan wanted nothing more than to find Emries and to rip the Child of the Creator to pieces with his bare hands. However, when Kamen arrived on Espre, Logan found that the broken giant needed something that Logan himself did not possess. Kamen had been a being of purpose for the thousands of years that he had drawn breath. Whether it had been as the first member of the Brotherhood of the Phasia, crushing the enemies of Shau-ling, or it had been as the fearsome Flame that guarded the life of the Master of the Shadows, Kamen had always known what he was supposed to be. That was a luxury that Logan had never known. As a son, a brother, a friend, a lover, a husband, a father, a hero, a villain, none of the names had ever fit, and there had never been a clear path for him to walk. Kamen saved him. Kamen helped him see the truth of his life, and the truth of a purpose not defined by labels. Logan was not a hero or a savior. He was not the creeping shadow of Aerith Seth inflicted upon the world. What he was meant to do was to spread the truth. The truth was not an easy thing to hear, nor was it an easy thing to tell. But those who carry the truth are faced with one awesome inescapable fact: Truth can only be carried by those who are willing to question everything, even those things they think they know about themselves. Prophets with no self-doubt can be nothing but false.

As the decades of philosophical discussion faded into centuries, Logan and Kamen found ways to heal each other's' souls through the excavation of the truth that lay buried beneath lies and misdirection. Kamen, through his time at the foot of Shau-ling had learned much about the nature of the war, and with the help of the memories of Aerith Seth and the clandestine activities of Sabrina Binosear, the two ancient men had more than enough information to begin their task in debating the dogma of the Creator and protecting Espre from the fate of so many other worlds. But very early in the deliberations that would form the basis of the teachings of the Order of the Flickering Flame, Logan and Kamen both came to the same realization at nearly the same time. It was not enough to save Espre from the Creator and the Children. The only way that all of the death and suffering would end was if the Creator was removed from the Golden Throne and the Children destroyed forever. It was a staggering thought. And when it was clear that both Logan and Kamen agreed on the course, they set about understanding the path they were about to walk. Of course, over the intervening years, others came to the same conclusion, but no one truly thought through the consequences of the act.

Destroy the Creator and the Children, end the suffering. Simple. Besides the enormity of the act, there were the additional concerns. What would become of Creation without the Creator? Would it simply go on as though nothing had happened, or would there be a ripple of death that would flow through everything that the Creator had manifested? As more information about the nature of Aerith Seth and his powers came to light, the more Kamen's suppositions began to ring true. Though the people of all of these worlds liked to view the Creator as just that, that fallacy was no different than the people of Onea believing that Emries was the Creator. Emries simply presented himself as such and utilized that adoration for his own purposes. Perhaps the Creator was the same. Perhaps he had simply stumbled upon something that already existed and exerted his influence for his own curiosities. The revelation of the Living Cosmos seemed to reinforce this possibility, but to Logan's mind it did not cross the barrier into Truth. It was a possibility, perhaps even a strong one, but still just a possibility. The supposition however that there was a possibility for Creation to continue without the presence of the Creator gave both Logan and Kamen enough hope that they could continue their deliberations. It was Kamen's next postulation that concerned Logan the most. There were many beings who had been brought back from the Other Side, and even from death, by the will of the Creator. What would become of those beings should the Creator cease to exist? Would there be enough of that power to keep those beings manifest, or would they simply fade away? What about those beings who owed their entire existence to the will of the Creator and the Children? Would they too be struck down when their patrons were gone? The postulation brought with it a moral quandary, one that neither Logan nor Kamen had good answers for. Did anyone have the right to end that many lives, no matter how many lives it would ultimately save?

That became the central question of the entire ideological war. Even before Kamen and Logan entered the conflict between Halicon and Emries, millions if not billions of lives had already been sacrificed on the alter of the Children of the Creator's hubris. Even if those deaths had not necessarily been humans, they were still sentient beings that deserved greater respect than they were shown. It had become clear, through countless millennia of poor stewardship, that the Creator and the Children were not fit to continue charting the course of Creation. And so, the answer to the question was clear that while no one should have the right to choose who is sacrificed and who is saved, there were levels of necessity that could not be ignored. However, at the time when Kamen and Logan collaborated on the creation of the Order of the Flickering Flame, neither man could have conceived the twists and the turns that would lead Logan to where he stood approaching the end of both his journey and most likely the Creator's as well.

Logan's body begged for rest. His legs burned and his joints ached. The cold wind whipped around and practically through him with every step. His head ached, and his stomach twisted. Logan had not known hunger, thirst, or exhaustion in thousands of years, and while Logan still did not require food or water in order to sustain his life, the removal of the powers of Aerith Seth and Halicon had stripped Logan's ability to ignore their lack. The exhaustion was another matter entirely. Logan would not need sleep of course during his long walk to Albitonin, but he would feel every step of those miles. However, this was the test of the powers of the Dragon's Tear. The Tear wanted to be used, needed to be used. And despite the mental discipline that Logan had always showed in the use of his powers, every bit of control that he had would be tested with every step. Logan knew in the deepest parts of himself that all of the pain and discomfort that he was feeling could be banished with a thought. All of the miles that lay ahead could disappear with but a blink of the eye. This was why Logan had given up the powers of Aerith Seth. This was why he had given up his connection to the Blaze and the Brotherhood of Phasia. If Logan slipped, for even a moment, the power of the imperfect Dragon's Tear would overwhelm him and complete the task that Tess began. The power would be unleashed in a single burst, destroying everything within Creation, sealing the Creator's ultimate victory. Logan could not and would not allow that to happen. No matter the trial, Logan would persevere. No matter the hardship, Logan would endure. He had to. There was no other option.

＊ ＊ ＊ ＊ ＊ ＊ ＊ ＊ ＊ ＊ ＊

Logan was unsure how long he walked. Though the Days of Star Fire had ended, the sky had been darkened by the growing gloom that spread from the west. It was impossible to see the light of the twin suns or the stars of the night sky. Espre was plunged into unnatural darkness sparked into existence by the entropy that the Creator clearly wanted to consume all of Creation. Despite the desolation that the countryside had seen at the hands of Kaitain and his perverted followers, Logan did not feel that traveling the main roads was the wisest course. Instead, Logan trudged slowly through the wilderness, through forests and over hills. As Logan broke through a dense patch of forest into a wide clearing, he saw a form sitting on a log beside a stream. For a moment, Logan considered returning to the forest and making his way around the clearing, but recognition sparked in Logan's mind. The young man sitting on the log was familiar. Making sure to keep his eyes on the young man the entire time, Logan approached the log and sat on the far end. For a long time neither man said anything, until finally it was Logan's voice that broke the silence.

"You were one of the last people I would expect to see out here, Storm."

Storm Mystic kept his head down. Even without his powers, Logan could feel the dread and despair rolling off of the young man. His cheeks were stained with the salt from his tears, and his nails were bloody from where he had bitten them down to nothing.

"How do you do it, Logan?"

Logan and Storm had had very little connection with one another over the years, but both men were familiar with each other through their association with Storm's father Jerrard. Like his sister Taya, Storm was well-educated in the nature of the war between the factions of the Heavens, and he had served well as a member of the People of the Ram. Storm was his father's son, that much was clear. Storm was patient and well-thought, though Logan always felt that Storm was not the man that his father was. It was not Storm's fault of course, as Jerrard cast a very long shadow.

"Do what, Storm?"

Storm kept his head down and his voice poured from his lips like a cold wind.

"How do you live every day with the ghosts of all of the people you've killed?"

Logan considered for a long moment, but before he could respond, Storm continued.

"You have killed so many people after all, some of which you know, and some of which you even called friends and allies. How do you continue with all that weight on your soul?"

At that moment, Logan began to entertain the thought that it was not really Storm Mystic that was sitting across from him, but instead an apparition conjured by the Dragon's Tear to test his resolve. Was it paranoia? Was it even possible for the Dragon's Tear in its confinement within the deepest part of Logan's soul to project such life-like apparitions? If the Dragon's Tear had the ability to reshape reality and exterminate all life in the entirety of Creation, surely conjuring an illusion of an old friend and ally was not beyond it even in captivity. The Dragon's Tear seemed intent on testing Logan in every way possible to ensure that he was worthy of the power that he would never use. After several moments of deliberation and internal reflection, Logan returned back to old lessons that he taught broken and disillusioned warriors that found their way to the Order of the Flickering Flame.

"Death is an inevitability of war."

A long sigh came from the young man.

"Platitudes are not an answer."

The thought could have come directly from Logan's own mind. There were so many times while he was counseling the war weary former soldiers that he felt like a fraud. As a member of the People of the Dragon, Logan had been the cause of death early in the quest. Starting with the innocents from his home of Aradon, people that he knew and loved from the day of his birth, all slaughtered by a flight of Shadowwalkers simply because he might be the *Coromor* of the prophecies. Even before his quest began, Logan was saddled with the guilt of all of those deaths. In those days, however, Logan was young and inexperienced, and he surrendered himself to the whirlwind. Because of the urgency of the quest, Logan never gave himself time to grieve, not even for his friend David. Then there was Rana and Rama, an ancient war that moved to a different level as soon as the People of the Dragon arrived. More death in Logan's name. It was not until the quest was at its end, after so many friends had died, that Logan truly gave himself time to reflect upon his responsibility. Perhaps that was why he withdrew from the world.

"No," Logan allowed, "platitudes are not an answer, but neither is withdrawing from the world in an attempt to avoid responsibility. Yes, I was the cause of death, both directly and indirectly. Though the first deaths of our quest were not because of anything that I did, it was simply because I existed. Shau-ling tried to eliminate me simply because he believed that I was the *Coromor*. Did it matter that I was not in fact the *Coromor*? Did it matter that the people of Aradon were not a threat to Shau-ling? Did it matter that the people of Rana and Rama would have killed each other even if I were not there? There is a difference between accepting responsibility and understanding that responsibility. Responsibility is not fault, but lack of fault does not abdicate responsibility. It is a difficult tightrope to attempt to walk. There must be balance, and that balance starts in the soul."

The shadow in the shape of Storm considered for a moment. He nodded wordlessly, and then turned halfway toward Logan, his head still down and his eyes hidden beneath heavy eyelids.

"So, the only time that the death matters is if it impacts the soul?"

That moment, Logan felt his heart sink. This phantasm was going to twist every word that Logan uttered. However, there was no duplicity in Storm's words. As Logan reviewed what he had said, there was a clear possibility that Storm's view of Logan's explanation was a viable one. Was

Logan rationalizing death that way? Was he truly differentiating the importance of death based upon how it impacted his soul? Shouldn't every death impact his soul if he was as good a man as he claimed to be?

"Have I not considered that I value the death of someone like David or Eldar more than I value the death of a soldier from Rana that I never knew the name of? They died for the same reason, so should not their losses be grieved with same measure? But what purpose would that serve? If every death had the same weight on the soul, would a leader be willing to make the hard choices? I sacrificed so much trying to save lives. Would I be willing to sacrifice my friends, my own life, to save millions of lives now and in the future if I allowed my soul to weigh those losses on those terms? Losses must have weight, but they must have appropriate weight. Soldiers are soldiers because they accept the risk of their station, and as such are willing to fly into the heart of danger no matter the risk. However, the merchant and the mother, while willing to defend those things that they value with their lives should necessity dictate, they would not be on the front lines defending the lives and freedoms of their fellow human beings unless all else had failed. That does not make their lives worth any less, but the sacrifice of the willing has to be valued for that sacrifice."

Storm nodded.

"Sacrifice," he rolled the world around in his mouth as though it were an ill-tasting bite of food. "Should you determine whether a sacrifice is worthy? Is your judgment any different than that of Emries, or the Creator, or a member of the Brotherhood of Phasia, or Dorovar. You demand death and honor simply because of your name. How is that any different than those you fight against? Why is your judgment of the value of death and sacrifice superior to anyone else's?"

Logan felt the words like a punch in the gut. Storm's words illustrated the very core argument of the war between the mortal world and the various forms of divinity. From the Creator's perspective, He had the right to demand the death of any of the creatures in his domain. Just because the beings within Creation did not understand the Creator's motivations, did that make Him wrong? Could the same be said for Dorovar? Could the same be said for Emries, Raenera, and Talisia? But Storm was not content to let Logan twist on that assertion.

"Your assertion that the Creator is wrong comes from what point of view? Is it because you are mortal therefore the judgment of mortals is superior? Should not the Creator be given the opportunity to justify His actions?"

The words lit a fire inside of Logan, and he wanted to lash out. But a moment before the hateful words flew from his lips, Logan could feel the surge of golden light at the corners of his vision. Logan bit back the words and was considering another tactic when Storm's words poured out once more.

"This isn't about you, Logan, or even about the Creator. I think in a way, you're right. We must take responsibility for our own actions and try our best to understand the motivations of those who attempt to make decisions for us. I suppose I'm trying to blame you for my own failings."

Logan found himself speechless. For the first time, Logan began to realize that the being sitting in front of him was not in fact a phantasm created by the powers of the Dragon's Tear but was in fact Storm Mystic. Logan could see the younger man's hands begin to tremble as he struggled with the turmoil that was consuming his soul.

"Was I really not in control of my own hands?"

Storm raised his hands to look at them. Logan could practically see the blood staining his fingers.

"Do you know what I did, Logan? Do you understand what I did?"

Logan waited, his heart and head aching from the exchange.

"I murdered my father."

Logan had felt the moment that Jerrard had died, but he could not discern the circumstances. Now that Storm sat in front of him, Logan was able to guess the truth. Storm was under the control of Emries, and perhaps it had been Emries that had been the catalyst behind Storm's actions. But as Logan looked and Storm and saw he reactions, it was clearly not that simple.

"I wanted you to tell me that it wasn't my fault," Storm continued. "I wanted you to tell me that Jerrard's life was no different than any other life that I ended. I wanted you to tell me that it wasn't my hands that wielded the blade that ended my father's life, that I could be totally absolved of my actions. I wanted to be told that I was a puppet who could not resist the pull on his strings. But that is not what you are telling me, is it?"

Logan sighed and shook his head.

"I wish I could say that you weren't responsible, Storm, but you and I both know that isn't true. I don't know the pressure that Emries was able to exert upon you, but surely if you feel the guilt of it weighing upon you, you believe that you could have resisted his orders to murder your father."

Storm raised his head slightly, and Logan could see the tears streaming from his eyes.

"Was I ordered to kill my father? I don't remember an order. I remember that I was to free Taya from her imprisonment. I was to hurt or kill Orren Eldrath and Felicia Lorien. Those things I remember clearly. I do not remember if I was ordered to murder my father. Did I do it simply because he was in the way of my other orders? Did I do it because deep down I resented my father? Did I do it because I hated myself for not living up to the example that he set for me? In the end, does it really matter? My father is dead by my hand."

Before he relinquished his powers, Logan would have been able to see what was going to happen next, and he would have had multiple avenues available to him to stop it. He could have sped across the distance and seized Storm's wrist, or he simply could have reached out with his abilities and arrested the movement of Storm's hand. However, with no powers, diminished reflexes, and slowed wits, there was nothing that Logan could do. In a smooth, steady motion, Storm's hand went to his belt, drew the dagger that hung on his hip and drew it effortlessly across his throat. There was no hesitation or a hint of trepidation, and even as the blood began to flow from the deep and fatal cut, he did not drop the dagger and fall back, instead he laid the knife in his lap and slid off the log to the ground. His back relaxed against the damp and rotting wood, blood flowing down his chest, soaking his shirt. Logan, despite the shock and dulled reflexes moved as quickly as he could to Storm's side. He knew that there was nothing that he could do to prevent Storm's death, in fact too much of his life had already drained by the time Logan made it to the younger man's side. Logan put his arm around the man as the last of his life drained from him, his head slumping into Logan's lap. Logan wasn't sure how long he sat there, but he knew it was probably not as long as he thought. Without his powers, Logan had lost some of his perception of time, and every moment seemed to last forever. Sitting there, Logan reviewed every tragedy that he had seen and felt throughout this entire war, every lost friend or lost loved one. Every senseless death. In a way, they were all senseless deaths.

"Yet again someone dies at your feet."

Logan didn't look up. He knew the voice. It was impossible that the voice was there, but then, nothing was impossible when it came to the Creator.

"That's funny coming from you, Emries."

Logan felt as much as saw the man approach. Instantly Logan's mind went back to the first time he laid eyes on Emries and all of the lies and sorrows that would follow that meeting. While that Emries seemed compassionate and wise, this Emries carried an aura of malice and malevolence. Logan finally looked up and met Emries' cold blue eyes.

"You know why I've come."

Logan nodded wordlessly.

"Do you intend to defend yourself, or will you sit there and die like the weakling I've always known you to be?"

Logan sighed and shook his head.

"Do you even know why you're here, Emries?"

Emries' eyes widened slightly.

"The Creator sent me to kill you. I thought that much would be clear to you."

Logan closed his eyes for the briefest moment before locking them back on Emries once more.

"A puppet to the end, Emries. How disappointing. I would have thought after all of the years trying to mislead us and drive us you would have learned a little something about true manipulation. You're not here to kill me. You're here to provoke me. The Creator knows what I've done, knows the threat I pose to his plans. He wants you to make me defend myself, make me use my powers to destroy you, because if I do that, he wins."

Emries searing blue eyes burned a hole through Logan.

"Then sit there, human, and let me destroy you."

Logan made no move to resist.

"He won't let you do it," Logan said finally. "The Creator is a lot of things, but he's not stupid. I don't think he knows what will happen if you kill me. I'm not sure I do. There's a part of me that thinks if you strike me down that the powers I have bottled up will all be released in one unfocused burst, destroying everything in Creation, perhaps even destroying the Creator. Then there is another part of me that thinks if I die the power dies with me. I don't think that the Creator is willing the gamble away his one sure-fire way to accomplish his endgame. Do you?"

Emries smiled a wicked smile.

"I think you are forgetting one possibility, Logan," Emries said finally. "Perhaps if I strike you down, the power you have stolen will flow into me, and thus into the Creator."

Logan's eyes narrowed. Emries was right, Logan hadn't considered that possibility. But Logan fixated on one word of Emries answer. Perhaps. Emries didn't know. The Creator hadn't told him the outcome of the attack. Emries was operating purely on orders. But there was something else. Something in Emries' voice. It was devoid of fire, devoid of life. This was not the Emries that had taken such pleasure in choking the life out of Logan millennia ago. This was nothing more than a shadow of what Emries had been. Whatever the outcome, Logan was dedicated to his course. He would not use his powers, even to defend himself from certain death.

"Then perhaps," Logan said stressing the word, "we shall find out which one of us is right, and which of us is dead."

Emries stalked forward, a blade of pure divine energy appearing in his hand. Before he was able to bring the weapon to bear however, a stream of fire erupted from somewhere behind Logan, claiming Emries full in the chest and forcing him backwards. As Emries pawed at the burn mark on his chest, the person who was the source of the attack leapt over the log and stood between Logan and his long-time nemesis. Logan recognized the young woman by her bearing immediately. With twin blades of fire in her hand, Isabella Ranthall spit her hatred onto the space between herself and the Child of the Creator.

"My father may not be willing to defend himself," she said, the venom dripping from her tongue, "so I'll have to do it for him."

Appendicies

Dramatis Personae

The Imperial Court

Terrik 'Godslayer' Lorien
Emperor Lorien I

Liette Lorien
Wife of Terrik Lorien
Empress of Cadaria
Seer

Kaldawyn Lorien
Emperor Lorien X
Father of Ender Lorien

Ender 'Justhand' Lorien
Emperor Lorien XI
Father of Feyd and Kaitain Lorien

Meara Lorien
Wife of Ender Lorien
Mother of Kaitain and Feyd Lorien

Kaitain Lorien
Emperor Lorien XII
Father of Marlae Lorien
Adoptive Father of Quyhn Lorien
Twin Brother of Feyd Lorien

Irene Drage
The Ethereal Sorceress
Court Sorceress
Protégé of Alistair Ravenheart

Galen White
Member of the Imperial Guard
Personal Guard of Felicia Lorien

Geoffry Aramour
Imperial Historian and Bard
Master of the Shadow Guild

Alise Modrall
Personal Assassin of Kaitain Lorien

The Lordhill Rebellion

Feyd Lorien
Prince of Cadaria
Brother of Kaitain Lorien
Overseer of Lordhill Province
Father of Felicia Lorien

Felicia Lorien
Princess of Cadaria
Daughter of Feyd Lorien
Host of Nightwing

Quyhn Ravenheart Lorien
Sorceress
Ward of the Empire
Voice of the Emperor
Daughter of Alistair and Estelle
Ravenheart

Dominique Arais Lorien
Wife of Kaitain Lorien
Former Mistress of Seraph Kore

Rhionna Winter
Personal Protector of Quyhn
Ravenheart
Archer from the Army of Fire

Connor Peregrim
Lord of Lordhill
Former General in the Imperial Guard

Gabrielle Peregrim
Lady of Lordhill
Cousin of Kaitain Lorien

Arent Fox
General in the Rebel Army of
Lordhill

Strum Anvilguard
General in the Rebel Army of
Lordhill

The Knights of the Flashing Blade
Bernhardt Yeoman
The Moonstone Knight
Kingdom of Iron, Pellatori
Wielder of the Hammer Gravity

Chelsea Zarova
The Garnet Knight
Kingdom of Fire, Saldarine
"The Wolf of Saldarine"
Wife of Seraph Kore
Wielder of the Katars Tenacity
Personal Protector of Dominique
Lorien

Devlin Rannoch
The Onyx Knight
Kingdom of Night, Galateria
Half-Dragon
Wielder of the Kopesh Discipline

Gregor Quicksilver
The Ruby Knight
Kingdom of Blood, Zevarit
Husband of Hannah Ironheart
Paladin of the Church of the Creator
Son of Ivan Quicksilver
Wielder of the Greatsword Valor

Hannah Ironheart
The Celestine Knight
Kingdom of Stone, Albitonin
High Priestess of the Church of the
Creator
Wife of Gregor Quicksilver
Wielder of the Mace Spirit
First *Chosen One* of Espre

Leonora Wastri
The Jade Knight
Kingdom of Soul, Oradrim
Wielder of the Naginata Wisdom
Trained by Cedric Binosear

Jaccob Aldora
The Topaz Knight
The Flying Kingdom, Hedorah
Former Member of the Academy of
Arcane Arts
Wielder of the Double Sword
Temperance

Natalia Pressen
The Sunstone Knight
Kingdom of Gold, Bellnoc
Master of the Shadow Guild
Wielder of the Rapier Perseverance

Orren Eldrath
The Sapphire Knight
Kingdom of Ice, Rashaleb
Former Member of the Academy of
Arcane Arts
Wielder of the Long Sword Courage

Seraph Kore
The Emerald Knight
Kingdom of Water, Thorigald
Husband of Chelsea Zarova
Wielder of Twin Sword Patience

Tolon Morr
The Amethyst Knight
Kingdom of Steel, Celidar
Former Gladiator
Wielder of Battle Axe Strength

Vallic Ultiv
The Serpentine Knight
Kingdom of Steam, Iltorp
Wielder of Scythe Harmony
Alias of Jeroch Yetre

Xaran Firesoul
The Tiger's Eye Knight
Kingdom of Knowledge, Menoris
Blind Since Birth
Wielder of Staff Faith

Gabriel Shadowfall
Member of the Imperial Guard
Personal Guard of Marlae Lorien
The Ruby Knight

Ivan Quicksilver
Former Ruby Knight
Father of Gregor Quicksilver
Advisor to the Dark Court

Tutio Illik
Former Onyx Knight

Heremon Tal
Former Amethyst Knight

The Academy of Arcane Arts
Alistair Ravenheart
Grandmaster of the Academy of
Arcane Arts
Master of Water
Imperial Sorcerer
Husband of Estelle Ravenheart
Father of Quyhn Ravenheart

Estelle Ravenheart
Sorceress
Wife of Alistair Ravenheart
Mother of Quyhn Ravenheart

Fiona Ebonsight
Master of Fire
Mother of Aris Ebonsight

Aris Ebonsight
Master of Air
Daughter of Fiona Ebonsight

Jastra Mythryn
Master of Energy

Ashinica Maupin
Master of Stone
Member of the Imperial Family

DRAMATIS PERSONAE

The Seers
Jehna Feris
The Dark Seer

Jania Maldovrin
Oldest of the Maldovrin Triplets

Jerrica Maldovrin
Youngest of the Maldovrin Triplets

Jordyne Maldovrin
Middle of the Maldovrin Triplets

The Dragon Hunters
Jillian Corven
Self-Titled Lady of Cadaria
Wielder of Scaleripper
Leader of the Dragon Hunters

Kiara Aren
Dragon Hunter
Former Priestess of the Creator

Angelina Lynn Sydor
Dragon Hunter

Jacqueline Escandi
Dragon Hunter
Former Member of the Iron Legion

The Chorus
Dorovar
The Destroyer of Worlds

Pestilence
The Grey Man
Carrier of the Crawling Plague

Famine
Formerly Isabel Relin
Carrier of the Wasting Disease

Death
Formerly Ardis Franel
The Collector of Souls

Jerah
Alias of Caris

Conquest
Alias of Pike Rhuiden

Haricos
Member of the Adhradair

Redissa
Member of the Adhradair

Coriden
Member of the Adhradair

Faelara
Member of the Adhradair

Zaraven
Member of the Adhradair

Drust
Member of the Adhradair

The Hand of Chaos
Dimitri Sulano
The Voice of the Lost

Syren Belloch
The Priestess of Blood

Torda Safrick
The Master of Secrets

Xavier Cormea
The Corruptor of Souls

Erik Relcan
Pursuer of Lost Love
Former Personal Assistant of Hannah
Ironheart

Seraphina Masile
Second in Command of the Hand of
Chaos

Korin Melcab
Captain of the Imperial Guard

The Children of the Creator
Emries
The First *Coromor*
Creator of the *Erieal*

Halicon
Formerly known as Shau-ling
Father of the Phasia
Powers imbued to Rhain Seth

Talisia Masile
The Dark Goddess

Pyrrus
God of Light
Powers imbued to Wolf Ranthall

Raenera
Goddess of Order
Powers imbued to Gideon Viruci

The Phasia
Rhain Seth
Mistress of the Blaze
Former Personal Guard of Marlae
Lorien
Daughter of Aerith Seth and Bryn
Aplee

Jeroch Yetre
The Lord Shadow
First Born of the Phasia
Father of Hawk Yetre

Bryn Aplee
The Lady Fox
Member of the Brotherhood of Phasia
Former Lover of Aerith Seth
Wife of Grawn Aplee
Mother of Gideon Viruci

Ellis Chandara
The Lady Leopard
Member of the Brotherhood of Phasia
Mother of Korrd Ranthall

Grawn Aplee
The Lord Shark
Member of the Brotherhood of Phasia
Husband of Bryn Aplee

Warron Ysamaran
AKA Blade
The Lord Boar
Member of the Brotherhood of Phasia

Basille Mystic
The Lord Raven
Member of the Brotherhood of Phasia
Father of Jerrard Mystic

Farax Soar
Creator of the Snags
The Lord Vulture
Member of the Brotherhood of Phasia

The Flame
Kamen
Personal Guardian of Shau-ling
Keeper of the Hall of Terrors
Originally known as Kamen, Member
of the Brotherhood of Phasia

Zarsi Aeron
The Lord Cobra
Member of the Brotherhood of Phasia

Aldridge Farran
The Lord Hawk
Member of the Brotherhood of Phasia

Saurn Macco
The Lord Viper
Member of the Brotherhood of Phasia

Caris Vale
The Lady Wolf
Member of the Brotherhood of Phasia

Erdric Yarrow
The Lord Scorpion
Member of the Brotherhood of Phasia

Taron Steen
The Lord Jackal
Member of the Brotherhood of Phasia

Draven Batoe
The Lord Crow
Member of the Brotherhood of Phasia

Rane Larion
The Lady Falcon
Member of the Brotherhood of Phasia

Stryfe Cadre
The Lord Python
Member of the Brotherhood of Phasia

Grimm Salde
The Lord Bear
Member of the Brotherhood of Phasia

Cash Griffon
The Lady Lynx
Member of the Brotherhood of Phasia

Nightwing
Member of the Dark Riders
Shau-ling's Assassin

Hawk Yetre
Son of Jeroch Yetre and Caris Vale

Natalie Yetre
Daughter of Jeroch Yetre and Ellis
Chandara

Jessica Chandara
Daughter of Ellis Chandara and
Grawn Aplee

The Court of the Dark Gods
Sadrina Annis
Queen of Mythryn
Wife of Pike Rhuiden

Darrien Annis
Half-Dark Goddess
Daughter of Pike Rhuiden

Tess Annis
Half-Dark Goddess
Daughter of Pike Rhuiden

Alderin Terian
Dark God
Son of Aryx and Diana Terian
Protector of Darrien Annis

Camille Sandar
Dark Goddess
Daughter of Gwydeon and Midarin
Sandar
Protector of Tess Annis

Serrina Mistic
Dark Goddess
Voice of the Dark Council
Daughter of Jerrard and Erika Mystic

Mirana Ranthall
Daughter of Wolf Ranthall and Lissa
Terian
Twin of Liara Ranthall

Liara Ranthall
Daughter of Wolf Ranthall and Lissa
Terian
Twin of Mirana Ranthall

The Celestial Court
Marlae Tamerlane
The Divine Empress
Chosen Representative of the Creator
Daughter of Kaitain Lorien

Ayden Seth
Son of Aerith Seth and Bryn Aplee
The Will

Anabel Binosear
Sister of Cedric Binosear
Mother of Cairyn Binosear
Daughter of Aerith Seth
High Council to the Divine Empress

Azure
God of the Heavens
Advisor to the Divine Empress

Krysis
God of the Heavens
Advisor to the Divine Empress

Terrance Aldora
Brother of Jaccob Aldora
Advisor to the Divine Empress

Isabella Ranthall
Advisor to the Divine Empress

The Dark Gods
Aryx Terian
White Lightning
Fire *Erieal* of the First Generation of
the Prophecies
Husband of Diana Geoffry Terian
Father of Lissa Terian
Father of Alderin Parran
Former Host of Nightwing

Diana Terian Geoffry
Wind *Erieal* of the First Generation of
the Prophecies
Sister of Arathorn Geoffry
Wife of Aryx Terian
Mother of Lissa Terian
Mother of Alderin Parran

Pike Rhuiden
Water *Erieal* of the Second
Generation of the Prophecies
Refugee from the Dark Mirror
First Cousin of Logan Ranthall
Eldar Merin's Former Husband
Husband of Sadrina Annis
Father of Darrien and Tess Annis

Gwydeon Sandar
Brother of Angels
Husband of Midarin Rice Sandar
Father of Nathaniel Sandar
Father of Camille Renar
Also Known as Wynne

Midarin Rice
Wife of Gwydeon Sandar
Mother of Nathaniel Sandar
Mother of Camille Renar

Lissa Terian
Fire *Erieal* of the Third Generation of
the Prophecies
Daughter of Aryx and Diana Terian
Wife of Wolf Ranthall

Sabrina Binosear
Third *Chosen One* of the Prophecies
Refugee from the Dark Mirror
Daughter of Cairyn Binosear

Wolf Ranthall
Son of Logan Ranthall and Elwyne
Tamerlane Ranthall

The Forgotten

Aerith Seth
The First *Chosen One*
Husband of Bryn Aplee
Father of Ayden Seth, Cedric
Binosear, Anabel Binosear, Gideon
Viruci

Taya Viruci
Daughter of Gideon Viruci and Erika
Belnosian
Refugee from the Dark Mirror

Logan Ranthall
AKA Dane Rhuiden
Second *Chosen One* of the Prophecies
Brother of Korrd Ranthall
First Cousin of Pike Rhuiden
Father of Wolf Ranthall
Leader of the Order of the Flickering
Flame
Refugee from the Dark Mirror

Jerrard Mystic
Son of Basille Mystic
Husband of Erika Belnosian
Father of Serrina Mistic

Erika Belnosian Mystic
Wife of Jerrard Mystic
Mother of Serrina Mystic

Other Cast

Cole Breon
Freelance Assassin
The Living Shadow

Liandra Nightshade
Freelance Assassin
Death Blossom

Dane Rhuiden
Monk
Leader of the Order of the Flickering
Flame

Blade
Merchant
Purveyor of Oddities
Alias of Warron Ysamaran

Isa Shar
Companion of Vallic Ultiv
Alias of Ellis Chandara

Evan Sinn
Inheritor of Aerith Seth's power
The Voice of the Creator
Husband of Meredith Heron

Taya Mystic
Daughter of Jerrard and Erika Mystic

Meredith Heron
Emissary of the Creator
Wife of Evan Sinn
Murdered by Dorovar

Tera Dawnrunner
Guardian of the Council of the Winds
Guardian of the East
Last of the Tigrelle

Jander Eveningstar
Guardian of the Council of the Winds

Eldar Merin
The Spirit
Best Friend of Elwyne Tamerlane
Wife of Pike Rhuiden

Leane Torne
General in the Army of Rama
Former Member of the Army of Brea

Nathaniel Sandar
The Lord Ram
Third *Coromor* of the Prophecies
Son of Gwydeon Sandar and Midarin
Rice
Brother of Liette Forer

Gwillim Sandar
Earth *Erieal* of the Third Generation
of the Prophecies
Son of Korrd Ranthall and Gabrielle
Crill
Adopted Son of Midarin Rice

Storm Mystic
Son of Jerrard and Erika Mystic
Water *Erieal* of the Third Generation
of the Prophecies

Jared Vale
Son of Caris Vale and Cedric
Binosear

Cairyn Binosear
Daughter of Anabel Binosear
Niece of Cedric Binosear
Queen of the Kingdoms of Kandor,
Trelon, and Marcwell
Wife of Pike Rhuiden
Mother of Duncan Rhuiden and
Sabrina Binosear

Sabrina Binosear
Former Host of the Spirit
Third *Chosen One* of the Prophecies
Sister of Duncan Rhuiden
Daughter of Pike Rhuiden and Cairyn
Binosear

Duncan Rhuiden
Heir to the Kingdom of Marcwell
Brother of Sabrina Binosear
Son of Pike Rhuiden and Cairyn
Binosear

Talon Aielin
Wind *Erieal* of the Second
Generation of the Prophecies
Best Friend of Pike Rhuiden

Arin Domae
Fire *Erieal* of the Second Generation
of the Prophecies
Former Soldier of the Army of Brea

Gideon Viruci
Earth *Erieal* of the Second Generation
of the Prophecies
Killed in Battle with Shau-ling

Baeta Catrinel
High Priestess of the Church of the
Creator

Aelind Torral
Assistant to the High Priestess

Reverend Mother Amalia
Priestess of Hedorah

Heralds of the Creator
The Voice
Formerly embodied by Evan Sinn
Currently embodies Gregor
Quicksilver

The Will
Currently embodies Ayden Seth

The Wrath
Destroyed by Aerith Seth

The Spirit
Formerly embodied by Sabrina
Binosear
Currently embodies Eldar Merin

The Council of Winds
The Elder Dragon Tarot
Leader of the Council

Mariti Brightblade
Second in Command of the Council
Companion of Tarot

Khalas Skydancer
Friend of Xaran Firesoul

The Demon Dragon Shadowweaver
Chief Opposition to Tarot

Krangoth Granitewill

The Arcane Dragon Serentis
Ally of Mariti Brightblade

Brux Mightytide

Charnada Ivorytooth
Ally of Shadowweaver

Stormbane the Traitor
Ally of Shadowweaver

Sheyruushk Bottomdweller
Ally of Khalas Skydancer

Aspertis the Just
Ally of Mariti Brightblade

Derelor the Manipulator
Ally of Shadowweaver

About the Author

Brian Kershner is a life-long dreamer, writer, and problem-solver. He grew up absorbing anything and everything he could get his hands on, and as a child of the Star Wars era he constantly wanted to see the worlds beyond the little Indiana town he grew up in. There was no adventure too far, and no problem too big.

Emboldened by parents who always supported his curiosity and his thoughtfulness, Brian found himself bounding from Space Camp to Laser Summer Camp to Athletic Training Camp to Piano Lessons to Football Practice to Basketball Practice to Choir Practice and back again. Despite all of the roaming and traveling, his family remained close-knit and supportive.

Though he flirted with the idea of becoming a doctor, Brian's attentions always fell back to the computer world. He got his first computer when he was six, and not long after found his way into a word processing program and began crafting his own fantastic worlds and even more fantastic characters.

As he has grown and changed and experienced life, so too have his characters. He continues to write, craft, and create; whether it is websites for his customers, or characters and worlds for his audience.

www.ingramcontent.com/pod-product-compliance
Lightning Source LLC
Chambersburg PA
CBHW051533020726
47506CB00010B/877